"Would you kiss me again?"

He almost smiled. Whenever she grew frightened, she trusted his kisses to ease her fear. So far they had, and this one appeared to be no different. He used his tongue with extra care, teasing the corners of her mouth, urging her to respond. She did so tentatively at first, then with more and more abandon. It severed the last thin thread of his control.

Heedless of the water he sloshed over the side of the tub, coming to his feet, soap bubbles sliding down his chest.

"Rayne!"

He chuckled softly, reached for her, dragged her against him and kissed her. Sliding an arm beneath her knees, he lifted her up and started walking. The white lace gown was drenched in an instant. So was the carpet as his big wet body strode across the floor toward the massive canopied bed. He came down with Jo in the middle of the soft feather mattress, careful not to hurt her, ravishing her mouth.

She stiffened only for a moment, then she was kissing him back, threading her fingers through his hair, arching her slender body against him.

Jocelyn started to tremble and it wasn't from the dampness or the cold. Rayne's hard-muscled frame pressed against her. *Sweet God in heaven.* She had never felt such fiery sensations, never been so swept up, never blazed so totally out of control. Rayne took her mouth, plundered it, possessed it, driving her to f

Other Books by Kat Martin

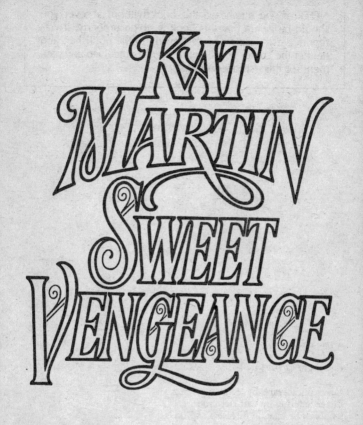

KAT MARTIN

SWEET VENGEANCE

St. Martin's Paperbacks

SWEET VENGEANCE

Copyright © 1993 by Kat Martin.

Cover photograph by Herman Estévez.
Cover lettering by Carl Delacroce.
Stepback illustration by Sharon Spiak.

ISBN: 0-312-95095-0

Printed in the United States of America

St. Martin's Paperbacks edition/September 1993

10 9 8 7 6 5 4 3

For my brother, Michael, who took the big plunge in more ways than one. Congrats on both. Luck and happiness to you and Sue. I love you!

A special warm greeting to a couple of old and dear friends, Carol Drury and Carol Van Horn. Thanks for being there when I needed you. I think of you often.

Chapter One

London, England
March 1807

*W*HAT A BLOODY FOOL.

Rayne Garrick, Fourth Viscount Stoneleigh, propped his broad shoulders against the tufted red velvet seat of his gleaming black barouche while one big hand clenched unconsciously into a fist. He'd known better than to get involved with the lady again, had done it out of nothing short of boredom.

Now he wondered if he'd be spending the night in the voluptuous woman's bed or facing her wrath—and her husband's pistols in the morning.

Rayne cursed roundly. What demon had driven him to accept the woman's passionate overtures yet again? He was well aware he was asking for trouble. From the day she had burst upon the London scene in a swirl of expensive silk skirts, Genevieve Morton, Lady Campden, had been nothing *but* trouble. Still, who would have guessed that trying to end their brief affair would result in the lady threatening to expose him to her husband?

And the old fool was just crazy enough to call him out.

Bloody hell. Cursing his own stupidity—and the ache in his breeches that had caused all this trouble in the first place—Rayne glanced out the window of the carriage. It was dark outside, no moon, no stars, and the streets were relatively empty. Just a few elegantly garbed ladies and gentlemen of the *ton* adjourning their fashionable West End town houses for an evening of entertainment somewhere in the City.

Rayne heard the shrill whistle of his coachman calling to the pair of perfectly matched bays that pulled the carriage. The man tugged on the ribbons, and the conveyance turned off Haymarket onto King Street, heading for Lord Dorring's town house on a small lane near St. James's Square.

Every Tuesday night for the past several years, Dorring had hosted the members of his box club, the Pugilist's Hand. The small group of men who sparred together at Jackson's Parlor gathered at Dorring's to drink, play cards, and gamble. Later in the evening, they paid visits to their mistresses, kept assignations, or sought the pleasures of a favorite brothel.

Having ended his relationship with his current mistress some weeks ago, then broken off his renewed affair with Lady Campden, Rayne had envisioned an evening of cards, then a pleasant diversion at Madame Du Mont's, the most elegant brothel in the City. Instead, if he submitted to Genevieve's blackmail, he would be forced to see the lady in question at least one more time.

Rayne frowned. Would one more night of seduction be enough to persuade the lusty countess not to endanger the life of her aged yet overzealous husband?

Maybe. If Rayne could bring his volatile temper under control—which he was far too often unable to do.

Rayne grumbled into the darkness inside the carriage. If it wasn't one thing, it seemed it was another. What he needed was a change of pace, something different, outside the rigid strictures of society—not that he paid them much heed. Something to add the spark that had been missing from his life ever since he'd left the army and returned to London.

It was obvious, now more than ever, what he didn't need was another damnable woman!

"Do ye see 'im, Jolie gel?"

"He'll be here. You can bet y' last quid on that. Night watch just called the hour. The bloody bastard will be here in less than fifteen minutes—just like he always is."

Brownie chuckled, a harsh rasping sound that came from deep in his chest. "Right ye are, gel. 'Is bleedin' lordship's as regular as a wise whore's monthly flux."

Jo felt the heat rush into her cheeks. She should be used to Brownie's ribald humor; she'd been hearing it every day for the past two miserable years. Truth was, she had picked up more than her own fair share of buckish slang, and she used it well and often, a means of passing unnoticed among the ragtag unfortunates she'd been forced to live with on the filthy London streets.

Funny thing was, if it hadn't been so sad, Jocelyn Asbury, once a model of genteel decorum, now a thief and pick-lock, a rum dubber among the lowest dregs of the City, might rather have relished being able to blister the ears of the vilest cant beggar, to stand up to the lowest doxy on St. Katherine's wharf.

"'Ere he comes!" That from Tucker, a thin blond boy of thirteen she and Brownie had adopted into their ragged little band. "Carriage is roundin' the corner. Ye can see it passin there 'neath the street lamp. 'E'll be turning down the lane any minute."

"Get down!" Jo whispered.

According to their carefully laid plan, they ducked behind the hedgerow that ran from the side of the narrow town house all the way to the street. It was just a few short feet away from where the viscount's carriage would roll to a stop. Just a pistol shot away from where the tall thick-chested man would be stepping to the ground on his way into the house, the man responsible for her terrible years of poverty and grief.

Jocelyn pulled the heavy weapon from the waistband of

her breeches. She wore a ragged pair of faded brown twill pants that hugged her slender curves, a full-sleeved home-spun shirt, and a tattered, cast-off, once-elegant brocade waistcoat spun with tarnished gold thread. She had stuffed the short black curls around her face beneath a woolen stocking cap pulled low across her forehead.

God in heaven, grant me the courage I need.

"Get ready." Her grip tightened fiercely on the pistol, and Jo held her breath. Any moment, the viscount's carriage would roll to a stop and he would descend the stairs. A few moments more, and Jocelyn Asbury would step from behind the hedge to fulfill her vow of revenge.

"We're here, your lordship." The footman pulled open the carriage door and stood aside so that Rayne could climb down.

He grabbed his narrow-brimmed beaver hat from the seat beside him, his mind still weighing the course he would take later this evening, stepped down from the carriage, and the footman closed the door.

Rayne had taken only two long strides when he felt cold steel shoved against his ribs, heard the unmistakable cocking of a hammer.

"That's far enough, gov'nor." An older man with a slight paunch, long graying hair, and a thick mustache, held the weapon that protruded from the hedge.

A younger man, slender, shorter than Rayne by nearly a foot, also stepped forward. "I'd suggest, y' lordship, nei-ther you nor y' servants make any too-sudden moves."

Rayne flashed a brief look toward his coachman, then motioned for his footmen to stand away. He noticed a thin blond boy behind and a little to his left, wearing an ex-pression of disdain.

"If it's my purse you're after, take it and be gone." Rayne reached carefully into the pocket of his white pique waistcoat, withdrew a small leather pouch laden with coins, and tossed it to the graying man.

"Give o'er the rest." The man stuffed the bag into the

waistband of his breeches and nudged Rayne painfully in the ribs with the pistol. "Rich swell the likes o' ye is bound to have a bleedin' fistful o' the king's pictures."

Cursing, Rayne started to reach inside his waistcoat pocket.

"This ain't about your quid," the second man said with a sharp warning glance at his partner.

Rayne's dark brow arched up. "Is that so?"

The youth had the bluest eyes, he noticed, taking in the boy's long black lashes and lush, almost sensuous lips. "If it isn't money you're after, then what is it?"

The lad's skin looked clear, his features so refined they seemed almost feminine. In fact . . . Rayne studied the young man closely, saw the subtle curves outlined by the worn brown breeches, the small but obvious peaks of a pair of feminine breasts. He reached for the low-slung stocking cap pulled nearly to the arch of a pair of black-winged brows and jerked the tattered woolen from her head.

"Keep your bleedin' 'ands off me!" Glossy jet-black hair tumbled forward into the woman's pretty face, which hardened into lines of rage. "Make another move like that, your bloody lordship, and I swear by God's breath I'll pull the trigger."

Rayne perused her slender figure, assessing her weight and slightly above average height. She couldn't have reached her twentieth year.

"You're the ones who tried to hold up my coach last week in the alley outside Boodles." He hadn't gotten a clear look at them then, but there was something familiar about the size and build of the woman who stood in front of him, and this time he was prepared.

"Too right, gov'nor," the graying man said. He chuckled, the sound a little harsh. "Black'earted cove the likes o' ye oughtn't to be such a man o' 'abit." Though he carried a bit of a belly, his shoulders were thick and solid and there was a hardness to his features that left no doubt the man could be a formidable foe. "Times a'wastin'. Go ahead, Jolie gel, say yer piece and get on with it."

"Yeah, Jo, shoot 'im," urged the skinny blond boy.

Rayne fixed his attention on the girl. The lines of her face were strained, her lips pressed firmly together. One look at the hatred in those ice-blue eyes and he knew all too clearly that murder was exactly her intent. Except that Rayne wasn't about to let it happen.

"Now, Finch!" he shouted to his coachman, erupting in a torrent of movement, heaving his muscular body into the graying man and lashing out at the girl. Atop the carriage, the coachman swung up the pistol he carried beneath his seat while Rayne grabbed the one in the graying man's hands. He jerked it free, spun, and knocked the girl's arm upward just as she discharged her weapon, the gunfire shattering the stillness in the air.

"Run!" she ordered her companions. "Get the bloody hell outta here!" For a moment the pair stood frozen, watching her struggle in his grip, eyeing the pistol Finch pointed in their direction.

"First one moves is a dead man," the coachman warned.

"Run!" the girl shouted again, afraid more for her friends, it seemed, than she was for herself. "Y'll wind up in Newgate for sure!"

Her words galvanized the two into action, the boy diving forward toward the hedge, the older man spinning away, his big feet pounding against the earth.

"Halt, I say!" Finch waved the gun unsteadily, aimed, then pulled the trigger, the pistol shot echoing loudly. The big man tripped as he rounded the corner, but both of them kept running till they disappeared into the darkness.

"Let them go." Rayne tightened his hold on the girl's narrow waist, making her gasp for breath, but still she continued to fight him.

"Bloody bastard!"

Even as he dragged her toward the carriage, she kicked

and scratched, pounded his chest and tried to bite him. Cursing, he wrenched one of her arms behind her back, jerked open the carriage door and shoved her in, blocking her exit with his tall frame as he followed her inside.

"Get us the hell out of here," he called up to his driver, and the man whipped the horses away. The girl named Jo studied the inside of the carriage, eyed his hard, determined features, and lunged once more for the door.

"Oh, no you don't." Rayne grabbed a handful of her shiny black hair and hauled her backward, tossing her onto the seat on the opposite side of the carriage. "I'd advise you to sit there and behave," he warned, his voice cold and rough.

She watched him a moment, weighing her chances, the peaks of her breasts beneath the waistcoat rising and falling with each ragged intake of air. "I'm not swingin' from no gallows, y' bleedin' sod!"

He eyed her with a cool regard that belied his raging temper. "Maybe you and your friends should have considered that sooner."

"Bugger off, y' bastard!" Shrieking like a fishmonger's wife, she launched herself at him, her hands balled into fists, her slim feet kicking his shins, all the while calling him a string of vile names Rayne hadn't heard since his days in the army.

"Bloody hell!" Dodging the nails she raked down his cheek, he gripped her wrists, dragged them above her head, then twisted and used his body to pin her beneath him on the seat. "Dammit, hold still! I'm not going to hurt you—not unless you force me to—and I don't intend to see you hang, at least not until I find out why the hell you want me dead."

She swallowed, her body still tense, her breathing even more ragged. "Then where . . . where are you taking me?"

He looked at her hard, saw the fear she worked to hide, felt her trembling, noticed that even though her clothes were old and shabby, her face and hands were clean, her breath sweet, and her hair shiny. She smelled of lye soap, but it was tempered with the soft scent of woman.

"What's your name?"

"Y'll know that just before I pull the trigger."

A muscle bunched in his cheek. "Is that so?"

Her look turned mutinous, but she said no more, just stared at him with those cold blue eyes and a look of bitter loathing. As tough as she tried to appear, she didn't fit the image of a typical gutter waif, nor that of a seasoned doxy. Even her speech seemed a little off the nod. At times she spoke with an accent straight from the London docks, but every now and then her words sounded almost refined.

He wondered what her past was, wondered *who* in the devil she was. And what any of it had to do with him.

She grunted at his heavy weight, and he shifted a little of it off her.

"I asked where y' were takin' me?" She flashed him a look of contempt, but he felt her trembling again. He watched her steel herself, saw the way her eyes had turned a deeper shade of blue, the way her thick black lashes swept down to hide her uncertainty, the way her breasts pushed softly against her dirt-smudged tattered jacket.

"Stoneleigh."

The single word echoed across the confines of the carriage, and the moment it fell from his lips, the girl's struggles ceased.

Stoneleigh. Jocelyn could scarcely believe it. For three long years the huge stone mansion on the edge of Hampstead Heath just north of London had haunted her nightmares and inflamed her temper. *Stoneleigh.* She had dreamed of going inside, been fascinated by its awesome beauty—and appalled by its vicious, cold-hearted master.

Stoneleigh. She looked at the man who carried that same name, and it occurred to her that the house and the man both exuded that same disturbing mix of beauty, strength, and cruelty. Though she had followed the viscount's movements off and on for the past two years, other than his habits, she still knew little about him.

She had seen he was handsome, but up close he was more than that. There was a power about him, a raw, sensual masculinity that made other men seem frail in comparison. There was a danger about him, too. A lethal quality that emanated from every muscle and sinew in his big hard body.

She wouldn't have guessed it from the ease with which he moved in his impeccably tailored velvet-trimmed coat and snug buff breeches, the casual way he wore his elegant white cravat. She hadn't guessed it, and now it was too late.

She twisted beneath him, then shuddered at the ease with which he held her.

"I'm twice your size; you might as well quit struggling."

She could feel his strength in the bands of muscle across his chest as he pressed her down on the tufted red velvet. The large, powerful hands that gripped her wrists held her immobile, yet oddly, she felt no pain. He hadn't hit her, though she had certainly given him cause. Still, his actions meant nothing. She knew the kind of man he was, the crimes he had committed, and nothing on the face of this earth could keep her from making him pay.

"I'll let go of your wrists," he said, "if you'll promise to stop fighting me."

Jo glared up at him coldly. "Go to bleedin' 'ell." She surged against his hold, then winced when he easily forced her back down.

"I warned you before, you had better behave."

"Why should I?"

"Because if you don't, I shall unleash the temper I'm trying so hard to control and give you the thrashing you deserve."

"I'd expect a beatin' from a man the likes of you."

One corner of his mouth curved up in a smile that really

wasn't. "Then you won't be surprised when I start by blistering your scheming little bottom."

Jocelyn's eyes went wide. He could certainly do it. And she would be powerless to stop him. In the years since she had left home, she had suffered all manner of indignation—fortunately, not that particular one. And the thought of the hated viscount being the man to deliver such a blow to her dignity made the idea all the more repugnant.

She nodded stiffly. "All right, you win." For now, she thought. Besides, why shouldn't she do as he asked? He wasn't taking her to Fleet Street or Newgate—at least that's what he'd said. Instead, as she had fantasized since childhood, Jocelyn Asbury was going to Stoneleigh.

She raised her eyes to his face and found him watching her, trying to see if she intended to keep her word.

"Don't think for a moment I won't do exactly as I promised—and I assure you, I shall relish every blow." He released his grip on her arms, and Jo eased away from him until her back pressed into the plush red velvet on the opposite side of the carriage. "The blond boy called you Jo. Is that your name?"

"None 'a your soddin' business."

His sensuous mouth thinned into a hard grim line. "You had better start watching your tongue, you little minx, or I'll make good my threat just for sport."

Jo felt the blood leave her face. "Just because you are bigger than someone doesn't give you the right to bully him."

The viscount's coffee-brown brows shot up. Realizing she had spoken without a trace of her gutter accent, Jo thrust out her chin. "Go to bleedin' 'ell."

"At the rate you and your friends are going, I believe you shall preceed me by some years."

Jo said nothing. Perhaps his words would prove true. Especially if she succeeded in her plans for revenge. Not that she intended to get caught.

Then a different thought occured. It was entirely possible her untimely capture might prove a boon instead of a boggle. Once she reached Stoneleigh, if she bided her time and the viscount let down his guard, her failure tonight might well turn into a triumph. Notwithstanding the fact it had been far more difficult to pull the trigger than she had expected, her vow to kill Stoneleigh could at last be fulfilled.

Then the viscount's hard dark eyes moved over her body. He was appraising every inch of her, assessing her slender curves and the peaks of her breasts. Jocelyn shivered. Stoneleigh was a cold, villainous, heartless man. She couldn't begin to guess what he might have in store for her once they reached his mansion.

She schooled her features into a mask of calm. She wouldn't let him win, she wouldn't!

One thing was certain: the next few hours would decide her fate. Soon both of them would know who the victor of this deadly game would be.

In the dark of the moonless night, the carriage trundled through the City, along Hampstead Road, past the village of Camden, headed for Hampstead Heath. Jocelyn looked out the window in time to see a sign for a tavern called the Blackleg Inn, then another for King's Bounty, an ale house down the road. It was quiet out here, the air cool and pleasant. Already the stifling smells of the London streets had disappeared, replaced by the scent of blooming flowers.

Most of the way, they had ridden along in silence, the viscount's broad shoulders propped casually against the seat, his head tipped back, his eyes half closed, but there was no doubt that he had been watching her.

"How long have you and your friends been following me?"

The unexpected question startled her from her reverie. She fixed her eyes on his face. "Long enough to know y' drink like a boozy sailor, gamble 'alf a bloody fortune at

the club—long enough t' know you're a thundering rake
who's tiffed 'alf the light-skirts in the City.''

His mouth curved up in what might have been amusement. "I take it you don't approve." His eyes ran over her
tattered waistcoat, the breeches that clung to her hips and
thighs. "But then a *lady* of your delicate sensibilities is
bound to find such a life repugnant."

Jo couldn't help it, she blushed.

"As for the women I've taken to bed—it might be interesting to discover just how much you know of that sort of
thing. Care to enlighten me?"

The color crept higher in her cheeks. "I know what
goes on between a man and woman. I'm not a bloody
fool."

"Fool enough to get caught while your friends got away
scot-free."

"Bugger off."

Stoneleigh chuckled, but the sound held little mirth.
They passed through an area of graziers in the suburbs of
the City, several cow and hog keepers, then a place of
nursery and market gardeners. It was quiet in the carriage,
except for the clank of iron wheels and the rhythmic clop
of the horses' hooves, then even those sounds faded.

They had arrived at Stoneleigh.

When a footman liveried in Stoneleigh red and gold
pulled open the door, Jocelyn eyed the opening wistfully,
but the viscount's big body blocked any chance of escape.

"I don't want to tie you up," he said, "but I will if I
have to. What's it to be?"

"Why the 'ell should I run? This is 'ardly bleedin' Newgate."

"Hardly." He caught her arm in a grip that left no
choice but to do his bidding, stepped down from the carriage and helped her alight. They crossed the gravel drive-
way onto the wide front porch, and unconsciously Jo's
steps began to slow.

In front of her the huge stone house, a hundred years
old and built in the French design, loomed three stories

high, with two great pavilions on either side of the entrance. Along each wing and across the front, tall mullioned windows rose up past the second floor, while the third was embellished by a slate hip roof and rows of tiny dormer windows.

"Impressive, isn't it?" Stoneleigh had paused, but instead of looking at the house as she was, he was looking at her.

"Looks a bit like a bloody mausoleum."

The viscount merely grunted, as if he knew it was far from the truth. "My great-great-grandfather, the first viscount, built it in the early seventeen hundreds. For a while he was ambassador to the King of France."

"Ye don't say?"

"Since you're so well informed, I'm surprised you didn't already know."

A faint smile crossed her lips. "I know a lot about your bloody bad habits, but not a flippin' thing about your soddin' blue-blooded family."

He gripped her arm once more. "Before this is over, you may well believe that I'll know an equal amount about you."

He tugged her forward, past the butler who held open the massive front door, and into the great hall. With its gleaming marble floors, exquisitely carved moldings, and lavish, mural-painted, barrel-vaulted ceiling, it was extravagant beyond anything she ever could have dreamed. She would have liked to stop and examine each beautifully crafted detail, but this time the viscount didn't slow.

"Where are y' taking me?" Digging in her heels, Jocelyn pulled him to a halt.

One corner of his mouth curved up. "Why, up to my chambers, of course. After all, I've tiffed every other light-skirt in London—why not you?"

Jocelyn gasped out loud. "How dare you suggest that I —that I—"

Rayne gripped the top of her arms and dragged her up on her toes. "You're no damnable gutter rat, though you do an extremely fine imitation of one. Who the hell are you?"

"I told you, y'll know that the second before I kill you." Jo glared up at him and the viscount glared back.

"Farthington!" he shouted, turning his attention to the small black-clad butler who stood nervously a few feet away.

The little man scurried forward. "Yes, your lordship?"

"Escort Miss . . . Smythe to a guest room. The one directly above my bedchamber. Have a bath sent up while I see she has something decent to wear."

"Yes, sir."

He threw a hard glance at Jo. "My men will be alerted that you are not to leave this house. I believe you and I have a good many things to discuss."

"I haven't a bleedin' thing to say to you that can't be said with a pistol."

"Try it, and you *will* be spending the night in Newgate." Her jaw clamped shut. "Now get upstairs and out of those wretched clothes."

Jocelyn stiffened her spine, lifted her chin, and turned toward the tiny gray-haired butler. He was staring at her with a look of contempt, his mouth pursed in utter disapproval. He relayed the viscount's wishes to another of the servants, tossed her another look of disdain, and started walking toward the stairs.

Jo didn't budge.

The butler took several more paces, his footsteps ringing on the black and white marble, before he realized she wasn't behind him.

"Would you be kind enough to follow me please?" he was forced to ask.

"I should be quite delighted," Jocelyn replied in her haughtiest, most proper drawing-room English. The startled look the butler flashed was surpassed only by one of annoyance on the handsome viscount's face.

"I look forward to our discussion, Mistress Smythe," he taunted, but Jo just kept on walking.

Chapter Two

RAYNE WATCHED THE GIRL climb the stairs, her posture correct, her movements graceful, and, except for an occasional tendency to swagger, her carriage as refined as any gently reared lady he had ever known.

Her clothes were a wrinkled mess, but her shiny black hair—slightly curly, cut short on the front and sides, a little longer in the back—would have been modish in the finest drawing rooms in London.

That she was the most intriguing bit of baggage he had run across in years, he couldn't deny. In fact, he found the irony of the entire situation quite beyond fantastic. After all, the lady had been trying to kill him. Now she was spending the night in his home, being treated as if she were a guest!

If it weren't so vexing, he might have laughed. What the hell had he done to deserve her wrath? Light-skirt or not, he was certain she hadn't warmed his bed. He would have remembered a face as fine-boned and lovely as hers. He would have remembered those clear blue eyes and thick black lashes.

He grinned, watching her climb the last few stairs in her snug brown trousers. He would certainly have remembered such a pert little derriere.

She was attractive, though not in the usual sense. She wasn't the classic, rounded, voluptuous sort of woman.

No, she was sleek, catlike, her body graceful and firm. Would she have killed him? He'd been a colonel in the army. He knew men—and women. Genevieve Morton might pull the trigger, but he didn't think this one would. He hadn't missed the way her fingers had trembled, the way she'd had to steel herself to attempt the deed.

Still, he couldn't be sure.

He watched as Farthington led her down the hall and up a second flight of stairs to the guest chambers on the third floor. It was too high off the ground for her to jump, and he'd be able to hear her moving around up there.

Rayne waited until she was safely inside, then climbed the stairs to the second floor and went into his sister's bedchamber at the opposite end of the west wing from his own suite of rooms. Alexandra was visiting friends in the country, but she would be home soon. Hopefully, not before tonight's mystery had been solved and his current handful of trouble had been properly attended and sent on her way.

Rayne crossed to his sister's huge white and gilt armoire, pulled it open and rummaged through armfuls of dresses: muslins, jaconets, bombazines, velvets, silks, and satins. Luckily, the girl upstairs and his sister were very nearly the same size, though Alex was probably bigger-busted.

The yellow muslin would do, he decided, seeing it against an image of glossy black hair, big blue eyes, and thick black lashes. He yanked the dress from where it hung, tossed it onto the bed, then pulled open several of his sister's bureau drawers and rummaged through the contents, pulling out a fine lawn chemise, a pair of white silk stockings, and two dainty satin garters.

He flashed a wicked smile, thinking his intimate knowledge of a woman's boudoir had often come in handy, grabbed a pair of kidskin slippers and started for the door. A glance in the mirror along the way, and he spotted a yellow satin ribbon the same hue as the dress.

It was foolishness, sheer folly to let the young woman's

unfortunate circumstances affect his sensibilities, still, he grabbed the ribbon and tossed it onto the pile.

Taking the stairs up to her room two at a time, he swung open the door without the good grace to knock and strode in. He heard her gasp, turned toward the sound, and saw her sink as low as she could beneath the bubbles in the small copper bathing tub.

"You might have bothered to knock." All trace of street jargon was gone.

"Why? Do you think I haven't seen a woman in her bath before?"

High color rose in her cheeks. Though her face had been darkened a little by the sun, her shoulders were as pale as ivory, and the swell of her bosom rose just above the water. Rayne chuckled to himself. Alex's breasts might be larger, but these appeared to have definite possibilities. His loins grew heavy at the thought.

"With your reputation," she said, "I'm sure you've seen a goodly number of ladies in their undress. But I am not one of them—nor do I wish to be."

He dumped the clothes on the bed. "I imagine you're hungry. When you've finished, you may put these on and join me in the dining room."

Jo said nothing, just tried to sink lower in the tub.

"Enjoy your bath." Thinking he wouldn't mind enjoying it with her, Rayne strode back out the door.

Downstairs once more, he poured himself a brandy and tossed it back, then another. He paced in front of the fire in his study, then checked his watch. God's blood, the chit should have been down before this.

"Beggin' yer pardon, milord." It was the upstairs maid, a young blond girl in her early twenties.

"Yes, Elsa, what is it?"

"It's Miss Smythe, milord. She's put up a fuss about her clothes. Says she won't wear the ones you give her."

Rayne set the brandy snifter down a little harder than he meant to. "Thank you, Elsa. I'll see to our guest." He stormed up the stairs and down the hall. When he jerked open the chamber door, he fully expected to see his sister's lovely gown in shreds, her undergarments tossed out the window.

Instead he saw the black-haired girl wrapped in a towel in front of a tall cheval glass mirror, holding the yellow muslin dress up in front of her and wearing such a wistful expression something squeezed inside his chest.

The moment she saw him, her look turned guarded and she tossed the gown away. "Where are my bleedin' clothes?" Unconsciously, her hands came up to where the towel tucked into the space between her breasts. He noticed several fading bruises and wondered how she got them.

"I had them burned."

"What!"

"Put on the dress."

"I want nothing from you."

"I said, put on the dress."

"Whose is it?"

"Since you know so much, I ought to let you figure it out, but I shall humor you and tell you it is my sister Alexandra's."

"You have a sister?"

"Exactly so. Now put on the dress."

Jo made no move.

"You look very fetching in that towel, Miss . . . Smythe. Even so, I would find it extremely entertaining to remove it and *assist* you into those clothes." He caught her intake of breath. "The choice is yours."

For a moment she just stared at him. Then she flashed him a mocking half smile. "As you wish, my lord."

Rayne didn't miss the fire in those ice-blue eyes. Still, he chuckled to himself as he turned and strode away.

Bloody bastard, Jo thought as she picked up the gown she had tossed on the high four-poster bed, but her fingers smoothed the fabric, so fine it seemed to caress her skin. In minutes she had pulled on the exquisite white lawn chemise, slid the delicate silk stockings up her legs and fastened them with the lovely satin garters. The slippers were a little too large, so she rummaged through the writing desk and stuffed a piece of wadded-up paper into the toes.

"Excuse me, miss, but his lordship sent me to button ye up." The little blond maid who had arrived with the bath stood in the open doorway, looking extremely hesitant to come in.

"I'll have to remember to thank him," Jo said bitterly, sure the servant knew the viscount had been in her room, that he had succeeded in enforcing his will where the blond girl had failed.

"Name's Elsa," she said, moving to Jocelyn's back to do up the buttons.

"My name is Jo." It felt strange to be talking in the soft smooth tones of refinement. Among her friends on the street, she had worked to lose the polish her father had instilled in her over the years. Now she discovered it felt good to play the part of a lady—if only for a night.

Funny thing was, it was harder than she had expected. After so many months of speaking nothing else, her gutter accent crept in at the oddest times, or whenever she was upset or angry.

Jocelyn glanced down at the lovely yellow dress. Cut in the latest mode, high-waisted, with a deep vee neckline and small puffed sleeves, the gown enhanced her slender frame and graceful curves unlike any she had ever owned.

It fit almost perfectly, she realized as the maid pushed the last of the buttons through the loops.

"Go ahead, have a look," Elsa said.

Jocelyn started toward the mirror, determined to see herself though she knew she shouldn't, then stopped as she spotted a length of yellow satin ribbon still lying on the bed. She picked it up, the texture smooth and so utterly feminine it made her fingers tremble just to hold it.

It made her remember a time when she had taken such

small things for granted. It made her uneasy to think that
Stoneleigh had been thoughtful enough to send it.

"Why don't ye let me fix the ribbon in your hair?" Elsa
asked.

She hesitated only a moment. "All right." Jocelyn
walked to the seat in front of the marble-topped vanity,
used the silver-backed hairbrush to comb through her
freshly washed curls, then let Elsa weave the ribbon
among them and tie it at the top of her head.

"Will that be all, miss?"

"Yes, thank you, Elsa." When the little maid left her
alone, Jo crossed the room to look in the full-length mirror. She looked lovely. Achingly, heart-stoppingly lovely.
Surely the beautiful young woman staring back from the
mirror couldn't be she. But it was, and for the first time in
months, a hard lump rose in her throat.

How long had it been since she had dressed in feminine
clothing? Two long, miserable years. Two years of living in
the gutter, of aching cold, and hunger pains gnawing at
her belly. Two years of threadbare castoffs bought from
the ragpicker with coins lifted from the pocket of a drunk.

Even when she'd lived at home, she had never worn
clothes as expensive as these, though she had gowned
herself quite prettily. She had sewn the dresses herself,
tutoring some of her father's students to earn money for
the fabric. And her father had always been pleased.

"You may not be dowered, my child. We may not have
the fortune to make the sort of match you deserve, but
you've noble breeding, and an inborn grace and beauty.
And you've a face and figure to be envied by half the
highborn ladies in London."

She could almost see his dear, sweet face, hear his gentle words of love and encouragement. Just thinking about
him made the ache in her throat grow tighter, made the
memories of all she had lost burn as bright as a rekindled
flame.

Jocelyn's resolve grew stronger. Stoneleigh had brought
them to this bitter end. Stoneleigh was the man responsi-

ble for all the anguish, all the terrible misfortunes she had suffered since her father died.

Whatever small measure of decency she discovered in the viscount didn't change things. And tonight, if God was on the side of justice, Jocelyn intended to make him pay.

"Good evening, your lordship."

Rayne allowed himself a lengthy perusal, taking in the gentle display of bosom and the graceful way she moved. A slow smile curved his lips. "What happened to the hoyden I left upstairs?"

"You may be certain she is here, but for the present, she shall remain at rest."

"The cat has sheathed its claws?"

"Something like that."

"Would you care for a glass of sherry or would you prefer ratafia?"

"I would prefer a flip, but I suppose I shall have to settle for sherry."

Rayne chuckled softly. "A flip, is it? Ale, brandy, and sugar. A sailor's drink right off the docks." He poured her a sherry from the decanter on the carved rosewood sideboard and handed her the stemmed crystal glass. "You certainly aren't dull, Miss Smythe."

"My name is Jocelyn. Since I'm playing the part of a lady this eve, I should prefer you to call me that."

"All right . . . Jocelyn." He fixed his eyes on her face. "If that is your name in truth, then I suppose it is a clue of some sort to what this business is all about."

"I doubt you would remember."

"Are you telling me we've met before? I can't credit I wouldn't recall."

"No, we've never met."

"Since we're being so cordial, why don't you call me Rayne?"

She took a sip of her sherry. "Why not? If memory serves, I've called you a good deal worse."

He laughed at that, recalling their fight in the carriage.

"So you have." He swirled the brandy in the snifter he cradled in his palms. "Are you hungry? Cook's had little notice, but I trust you'll find the fare far better than what you're used to."

A sadness swept over her features, then it was gone. "I'm sure I will."

Rayne led her to the sofa in front of the marble-manteled hearth and both of them sat down. "You look lovely this evening. The gown suits you even better than I imagined." Her graceful fingers smoothed the fabric. Rayne noticed her nails were cut short and there was no trace of dirt beneath them.

"Thank you. The dress is beautiful."

"Earlier—when I mentioned the meal we would be sharing—what was it you were thinking?"

"I don't know what you mean." Her thick dark lashes swept down to cover her eyes.

"I believe you do." He had never seen a brighter shade of blue.

"I was thinking of the others, my friends and the people I live with on the streets." She picked up an expensive cloisonné vase sitting on the Chippendale table at the end of the sofa. "I was thinking about this house and the lovely things in it. That this one piece of glass could feed and house many of them for the next several years."

He swirled the amber liquid in his snifter, then took a drink. "An odd sentiment, worry for the human condition, considering just hours ago you tried to take a man's life."

She stared at him, her eyes a cooler shade of blue. "Then I suppose it's clear I consider you quite apart from the rest of the members of the human race."

A muscle tightened in his jaw. He raised his glass in mock salute, "Touché," and took a sip of his brandy. The glass rang loudly as he rested it on the satinwood table in front of him.

"From what little you've said, I gather this charade you're playing is only partly false."

"What do you mean?"

"I mean that you are obviously a lady of some breeding, yet you would have me believe you actually reside with those two ruffians who accompanied you tonight."

"They're my family. Thanks to you, the only one I have left."

Rayne's hand slammed hard on the arm of the sofa. "Dammit, what is it I'm supposed to have done?"

"What's the matter, your lordship? Are your crimes so numerous you cannot keep track of them?"

"I've committed no crime that I'm aware of. Unless you are speaking of the crimes I committed in the name of war."

Jocelyn looked startled. "You fought in the war?"

"I was a colonel in the army."

"A man does what he must in order to defend his country."

"Then tell me what it is you believe I have done."

Jo set her glass down on the table and stood up. "Since I didn't succeed in killing you and am now here as your prisoner, I would like to do as you earlier suggested and enjoy something to eat."

Rayne stood up, too. When she started to walk away, he caught her arm. "You're obviously an intelligent woman, Jocelyn. Why won't you tell me what this is all about?"

"I fully intend to . . . when the time is right."

Rayne clamped his jaw, his temper nearing the edge. "If you know what's good for you, by God, you'll tell me now!"

Her eyes sparked blue fire and her hands balled into fists. "Go to bleedin' 'ell, your bloody lordship."

Rayne's grip on her arm grew tighter. "There are servants present. I'd advise you to watch that vicious tongue of yours. I am master in this house. Retribution for your misbehavior will be swift and hard, and whatever it is I choose to do, no one will gainsay me. Do you understand?"

Jocelyn stiffened her spine, but her insides had begun

to quake and, for the first time since they had arrived, she felt a shot of fear. In the light of the flickering candles, the tall muscular viscount looked dark and forbidding. The image of rough force and vast wealth seemed to scream at her from every hard muscle in his body.

In a voice a little like honey touched with gravel, he said, "Shall we dine, my dear Jocelyn?" and extended a powerful arm.

She forced herself to smile. "As you wish, my lord." Ignoring a fresh tremor of unease, she rested her hand on the sleeve of his superfine jacket and let him lead her away.

They entered the dining room, and the viscount pulled out the carved high-backed chair beside the one at the head of the table. The sumptous room was high-ceilinged, the walls flocked with gold, the floors warmed by rich deep Oriental carpets. A silver branch of candles lit the table beside a silver bowl floating with roses.

Awed by the magnificence of the room, Jocelyn let the viscount seat her, ignoring the growls that had begun in her stomach. She was used to existing on very little food, but the succulent smells wafting toward her from the pantry made her mouth water, and her stomach roared again.

The viscount frowned. As he took the seat beside her, candlelight flickered over a handsome face tanned dark by the sun and reflected the reddish highlights in his thick, dark, coffee-brown hair. His hands were big and strong, yet they moved with a casual grace she wouldn't have expected in such a large man. She found herself staring at them, remembering the times he had touched her with such implacable force, yet never hurting, almost gentle.

His shoulders were broad and looked to be well-muscled. Earlier she had noticed his waist was more narrow that she had first guessed. His brows were dark and nicely formed, and his eyes, a soft warm brown, were heavily ringed with gold.

Her eyes came to rest on his mouth, which still looked

harsh and angry, though his lips were full and sensuously curved.

She thought of another pair, not nearly as full, that had belonged to Martin Carey, the vicar's son. She'd been just fifteen when Martin kissed her, the only kiss she had ever shared with a man. She had been certain she was in love with the lanky, soft-spoken boy, that some day he would ask her to marry.

Maybe he would have. Instead, by the end of the year her father was dead, their charming little cottage on Meacham Lane lay in cinders, and she had been packed up and shipped off to her cousin's. She had never seen Martin again. One more casualty the viscount would pay for.

Jocelyn's stomach growled again, and the viscount swore a savage oath. "Why didn't you tell me you were very nearly starving? When was the last time you had something to eat?"

"Yesterday morning." She'd had to be careful sipping the sherry. On an empty stomach, the alcohol had gone straight to her head.

"Yesterday morning?" he repeated, incredulous. "Bloody hell! Ambrose!" he called to a servant. "We will dine immediately."

They supped on cold venison, roast fowl, and mutton pasties, some candied carrots and asparagus, and a bit of Gloucester cheese. The moment the silver-rimmed porcelain plate was set in front of her, Jocelyn tore off the leg of a small roast quail and dived in, ripping the meat from the bone with gusto and licking the juice from her fingers. In seconds she had cleaned the plate of every bite of the delicious food and drained the last of the wine from her goblet.

It occurred to her, somewhat belatedly, that if this was a test of how far her etiquette extended, she had just failed miserably.

She looked over at the viscount, saw his food was hardly touched and that he was staring at her with a mixture of pity and dismay.

Jocelyn straightened her spine. "I—I'm sorry. I guess I was hungrier than I thought."

"It's all right," he said gently. "I'd be quite that hungry, too."

The edge was gone from his voice. It sounded like rough velvet. When he looked at her the way he was now, it did funny things to the pit of her stomach.

"Would you like some more?"

She should say no, keep at least a portion of her dignity. Her tongue ran over her lips. "If it wouldn't be too much trouble."

With a slight nod of his head, her plate was swept away and a full one set in its place. A servant refilled her wineglass and set a silver tray of candied fruits in the middle of the table. She ate the second plateful, this time with a little more decorum, and finished at the same time he did.

"Feeling better?"

Now that her hunger was sated, the way she felt was foolish. Ridiculous for having let him glimpse a part of her world she hadn't meant for him to see. "I feel fine enough to leave, but I'm certain that isn't your intention."

"Hardly."

When she said nothing more, he shoved back his chair and came to his feet, towering above her. For the first time in her life she was grateful for the extra few inches she carried over other women.

"It's late," he said, pulling out her chair. "Come. I'll walk you upstairs."

Jo hesitated. "What will happen tomorrow?" She hoped it wouldn't matter. If things went as she planned, Stoneleigh would be dead and she would be safely away.

"We'll resume where we left off. I'll continue to hold you safe from the authorities until I discover what it is you have against me. However, my sweet, I warn you—I am not a patient man. If you don't tell me soon what this is all about, I'll be forced to turn you over to the constable. If you have any notion what it's like in a London prison—"

A whimpering sound escaped Jo's throat, and the viscount broke off. "I can see the notion scares you, and well it should. Why don't you consider telling me the truth?"

She shoved her chair back until it slid off the carpet and grated on the cold marble floor. "I told you, I fully intend to."

"When you're ready to pull the trigger."

Jocelyn said nothing. Stoneleigh rounded the table, took her arm, and none too gently led her upstairs. Inside her chamber, Jo found Elsa waiting to help her undress. An embroidered white cotton night rail had been laid out on the bed. It was hardly the garment in which to make one's escape, but she really had no choice.

"Thank you, Elsa," Jo said when the girl had finished removing her clothes. "Why don't you just leave those things in here? You can hang them up in the corner." She pointed toward a rosewood armoire, hoping the girl would leave the dress behind, but the little maid shook her head.

"Sorry, miss, but his lordship gave strict orders I was to bring these things to him."

Damn him! He was surely no fool. "Well, y' certainly wouldn't want to disappoint him."

"No, miss."

Elsa left and Jocelyn paced the floor, waiting for the hours to pass, praying the viscount would fall soundly asleep. The hour was extremely late; she couldn't wait too much longer. Walking over to the writing desk, she pulled open the middle drawer and lifted out the long silver letter opener she had spotted there earlier. It was thin and sharp on the edges, the handle solid and easy to grasp. It would make the perfect weapon.

She looked down at the way it nestled in her palm, and her stomach rolled. Shooting a man was one thing. Stabbing him was quite another. She thought of the blood, the way the knife must feel sliding through muscle and bone to reach a man's heart.

Sweet God in heaven, I can't do this! She swallowed hard and her hand began to shake. "I can't. I just can't."

You've got to! came a voice inside her head. *You owe it to your father. You owe it to yourself!* She thought of Sir Henry, of those last few terrible moments when he had raced back into the fiery flames. She thought of what Stoneleigh's cruelty had driven him to, his terrified screams as the blazing roof engulfed him.

She remembered their tiny thatched cottaged on Meacham Lane, saw the white picket fence, the butter-cups blooming out in front.

Then she saw the same house in ashes, nothing but the smoldering remains of a lifetime of dreams. She remembered her father's burial, the overwhelming sadness, re-membered the journey she had made to live with her cousin. She recalled the terrible year she had spent with him, the lewd remarks and lascivious glances, the hot hands he had tried to press on her body.

She thought of the nights she had spent on the road after she had run away, the cold and the hunger. She thought of herself sleeping in the gutter, of begging for food, of stealing, of the beatings she had suffered when-ever she had been caught. She thought of Brownie, dear, cantankerous Brownie, who had saved her from starvation and shown her how to survive in the harsh environment of the London streets.

"Stoneleigh," she said out loud, her grip growing tighter on the cold silver handle. The small oil lamp she had left burning on the desk flickered over the long thin blade. "You can do it," she told herself firmly. "You swore on Papa's grave you would avenge him, and you will."

Hefting the letter opener, gauging the weight and feel, she settled it in the folds of her nightgown and started for the door.

Chapter Three

RAYNE LAY AWAKE for a while, wondering about the strange events of the evening, the curious young woman upstairs. He could still hear occasional movement in the chamber directly above him, but eventually the sounds ended and he slept.

It wasn't until sometime later that some small noise awakened him. He wasn't sure what it was, but he knew he had heard it. Too many years on the field of battle, too many unwary men lying dead in their bedrolls from lack of caution for him to be caught unawares.

He didn't open his eyes, just lay there pretending to sleep. The sound came again from somewhere near the door. A knob turning. Footfalls. Soft rustling. Rayne's jaw clamped. The girl had come into his room.

He let her move closer, recognizing the light feminine steps, tentative but determined, the soft brush of fabric against her legs. He waited until she reached the bed, until she had walked up beside him. From beneath his nearly closed eyelids he could see her watching, studying his face, studying the curly brown hair on his chest. Her tongue ran nervously over her lips, then she stiffened her spine and her arm swept high above her head. The blade she held glinted silver in the last burning embers of the fire.

Rayne tensed, waiting for the knife to make its final

descent. He saw the slim arm tremble, the blade waver. His eyes opened wider, fastened on hers, saw the uncertainty, the blaze of conflicting emotion. Then she realized he had seen her, made a strangled cry of protest, and the blade arced downward toward his chest.

"Bloody hell!" Rayne's arm snaked out to block the blow. He caught her wrist in midair, twisted it until she winced, but still she held onto her weapon. He squeezed harder, determined to disarm her but fearful her slender wrist might break. Finally the knife tumbled free and clattered to the floor.

More furious by the second, Rayne rose up above her, twisted and brought her down on the bed beneath him, pinning her to the mattress with the weight of his long hard body. She struggled and fought, but both of them knew it was useless. In seconds his fingers encircled her wrists and he pinned them at the sides of her face.

"You bloodthirsty little vixen. I should have known better than to trust you." Even in his towering rage, he could feel her slender curves, the points of her breast pressing into the muscles on his chest. Her hips met his, he could feel her flat belly, the thrust of her small pelvic bones, and the anger in his veins began to heat his blood in another direction.

"Let me go, you bloody sod!" She tried to twist free, arched her back and thrashed her legs. Feeling the roughness of the hair on his calves, her eyes widened, and for the first time she realized he wore no clothes.

"You're . . . you're buck naked!"

Rayne's mouth curved up in a cold half smile. He chuckled, but the sound came out harsh. "You come in here to kill me and all you can think of is I'm not wearing any clothes? What did you expect, sweeting? That I would be one of those milksops who sleeps in a nightgown? Sorry to disappoint you."

Her small body stiffened. "I bloody well am disappointed. Disappointed my blade missed its mark and—dog that y' are—you're still breathin'."

"So the tables have turned once more." His eyes skimmed over her body, watched the way her breasts rose and fell with her labored breathing. "I wonder . . . could you really have done it?"

She twisted beneath him, her expression murderous. "You saw the knife."

Her body felt warm, the thin cotton barrier between them moving softly against his skin. Rayne felt a fresh flood of heat to his groin and his shaft began to harden even more.

"Where did you get it?"

"It's a bloody letter opener. I got it from your bleedin' desk."

"How careless of me. Then again, even had I known it was there, I wouldn't have believed you would use it."

"Just shows what a bloody fool you are."

"Yes . . ." he said, tightening his hold, "it would seem I have been at that." He smiled slowly, wolfishly. It was a smile that struck terror in the hearts of the men in his command. "Not anymore." Shifting her wrists so he held them above her head, both of them locked in the grip of one hand, he slid his other hand down her thigh and began to hitch up her nightgown.

"What . . . what are you doin'?"

"Getting a little vengeance of my own." He lifted his weight enough to jerk the nightgown up to her waist, shoved her legs apart with his knee, then settled himself between her thighs. "A little *sweet* vengeance."

She made a sound in her throat as his hand ran over her flesh, testing the firmness, feeling the smooth sleek muscle that wasn't at all like the soft plump flesh of other women's bodies.

"Don't. Oh, God, please don't."

He was hot and hard now, pulsing with the thought of being inside her. Would her passage be as sleek and tight as the rest of her? Would she writhe beneath him in passion, or struggle against him every hot driving inch of the way?

She jerked upward at the touch of his hand on her breast, but the nipple began to pebble between his fingers.

"You can't do this!" She bucked beneath him, trying to dislodge him, but it only settled him more solidly in place. "Dear God, you've taken everything else . . . please, I beg you, don't take this from me too."

Rayne's hand stilled where it cupped one small breast. It felt heavy at the bottom, gently rounded, ripe and tipping slightly upward. His shaft rode hard against her thigh.

"Surely, I'm not the first. You've been living on the streets, there had to be dozens of men who . . ."

But the tears that glistened in her pretty blue eyes, the terror etched on her face, and the trembling of her small slender body said there weren't.

"Bloody hell!" Rayne rolled off her, jerked the nightgown back in place and hauled her to her feet. "By God, you're going to make some sense or I swear I shall beat you within a bloody inch of your life!"

A small whimper came from her throat as he dragged her across the room, jerked open the door to his massive armoire and pulled out his burgundy velvet dressing gown. He let go of her to pull it on over his naked body, but she made no effort to run away.

Instead she lifted her chin and faced him squarely. "You may beat me if you wish. You can't make me tell you a single bloody thing—not until I'm ready."

"And were you ready this evening? Did you intend to tell me after you had delivered the fatal blow?"

Jocelyn nervously wet her lips. "I . . . I don't know." In truth she had forgotten all about it. She had sworn to let the viscount know in the final moments which of his sins he paid for with his life, but as she'd stood over him, all she could think of was how incredibly beautiful he looked in slumber, how strong and impossibly handsome. She had known he was solidly built, but she never would have guessed how finely muscled, how deeply etched each cord and sinew, how hard and well-honed he was all over.

She had raised the long sharp blade, but the truth was, if he hadn't opened his eyes and seen her standing there, she likely would have turned and walked away.

"You don't know?" he repeated, the full force of his hard brown eyes boring into her. "You don't know if you would have told me why it is you want me dead!"

Just when she thought he must surely raise a powerful fist against her, he surprised her with a sigh and raked a hand through his wavy dark brown hair.

"Damned but you are vexing." He gripped her arm and started for the door.

"Where are you takin' me?"

"Back to your room. This time, however, I intend to lock you in."

"Go to bloody hell." But he only dragged her up the third-floor stairs. One wide hand jerked open the door, and he shoved her inside. She could hear the grating of the key in the lock, then Stoneleigh's heavy footfalls as he stormed back down the hall.

He was an odd man, that much was certain. Nothing at all like she had imagined. Good Lord, any other man would have trashed her within an inch of her life—perhaps even killed her—for what she had tried to do. Any other man, she amended, would have tossed her in prison the moment she had accosted him on the street.

She thought of what had happened in his room. She could still feel the heat of his body as he pressed her down on the mattress, the tingling sensation of his hand moving over her breast. He could have taken her, but he didn't. She had felt his desire, seen the thick hard evidence all too clearly when he dragged her across the room.

She had seen men naked before—dead men stripped and left in the gutter, sick men who had sold their clothes for a last bite of food. But she had never seen one built the way he was, certainly had never seen one naked and aroused. It was a terrifying sight, she allowed, trying to imagine something so big and rigid thrusting inside her as she had heard men did.

Of course, she didn't know for sure.

And she wasn't about to ask Brownie—she knew he would tell her in the basest of terms, and she wasn't certain she wanted to find out. She still carried childish illusions of romance and love between a man and a woman. She wasn't ready to give those up quite yet.

Jocelyn sighed into the darkness. She was tired. So very tired. All she wanted to do was sleep—and get away from this house.

Away from Stoneleigh.

With a flash of clarity, she realized she no longer intended to kill him. That notion had faded with her last desperate effort, maybe even sooner than that.

She wasn't a murderer, that much was clear. Maybe Stoneleigh wasn't such a villain.

Then again, maybe he was.

She wished with all her heart she had never conceived her murderous plan, never vowed revenge against Stoneleigh, never tried to kill him, never wound up as a prisoner in his house.

She sighed again and sank down on the bed as the viscount locked the door. Tomorrow was another day. She would have to decide what to tell him or she would surely wind up in prison. But even if she dredged up his crimes to justify her hatred, she was certain it would not matter. Why should it? After all, what was a gutter waif to a man like Stoneleigh?

Jocelyn stretched out on the huge feather bed. It was deeper and softer than anything she had ever slept in. Lovely coral silk bed hangings swept down around her, and the big down pillow felt wonderful beneath her head. Tomorrow she would find a way to escape, to make her way back to London. By tomorrow night she'd be sleeping once more on the corn-husk mattress on the planks of her fourth-story garret above Boswell's ale house.

She snuggled deeper into the soft feather mattress, savoring each moment of delicious luxury. How beautiful it was here, how clean and pleasant. She wondered if the viscount knew how lucky he was to live in a place like this.

"Jo! Jolie! It's me, Tucker." From somewhere in her groggy sleep, Jocelyn heard a soft persistent rapping at the door. "Jo!" the harsh whisper came again.

She was off the bed in an instant, her nightgown jerked up to her knees as she streaked toward the opening.

"Tucker! How the bloody blazes did you find me?" They were speaking through the keyhole. Jocelyn prayed none of the servants were awake to overhear them.

"I followed 'is lordship's carriage till I seen he was takin' ye back to 'is 'ome. Then I run back to the garret hopin' to meet up with Brownie. He was upstairs, all right, a flippin bullet 'ole in 'im—bleedin' like a stuck pig. I patched him up the best I could, Jo, but 'e's in a bad way, 'e is."

"Sweet God in heaven."

"I had to come back for ye. I got lucky, 'itched a ride by 'idin' in the boot o' a carriage. I come in through an open window. Just 'appened to be downstairs when 'is lordship dragged ye up 'ere. He didn't 'urt ya, did 'e?"

"I'm fine, Tuck, it's Brownie who needs our help. How the bloody hell am I gonna get outta here?"

"Why don't ye climb out the window? I already been in the room next door. I could open the window and you could cross the roof and climb in."

"I don't know, Tuck, it's a flippin' long ways down."

"You can do it. 'Ell, I've climbed like a bleedin' monkey over 'alf the rooftops in London."

He had at that. Before he'd hooked up with Jo and Brownie, Tuck had been apprenticed to a chimney sweep. He'd run away, taken up a life of thievery to keep from starving, but not before he'd lost most of his fingers and several of his toes.

"All right, let's go." Jocelyn crossed the room, wishing she still had the pretty yellow dress and wondering how in blazes she was going to get to London in her nightgown.

She paused at the window, shoved it open, then leaned out over the sill. With the ceilings in each room as high as they were, it looked a bloody mile down to the earth. She glanced to the window next to hers. Tucker stuck his blond head through the opening and flashed her a cocky, reassuring grin.

"Nothin' to it, I tell ye. Just take yer time and don't look down."

She nodded and climbed up on the sill. The roof was constructed of smooth gray slate, and was steeper than it first appeared. Jocelyn took a step toward Tuck and the open window, then sucked in a breath as the icy stone bit into the bottom of her foot. She took another tentative step and then another.

Bloody nightgown, she thought as the wind caused it to tangle between her legs. But she wasn't about to take it off.

"Yer nearly there, Jo. Just a scosh bit farther."

A scosh bit still looked like a mile to Jo, whose legs had begun to tremble. She crouched down to lessen the thrust of the wind and continued taking slow, purposeful steps forward.

"Come on, Jo. Before some bugger looks up 'ere and sees us."

That was the impetus she needed. She couldn't put Tuck's life in danger as well as her own. She stood up again and moved forward. She had almost reached the window when the breeze surged forward, catching her nightgown, pushing it upward, baring a goodly portion of her lower anatomy. Jocelyn caught the hem and tried to shove it back down, stumbled forward several paces and nearly toppled over.

"For the love of Pete, be careful!" Tuck shouted.

Jocelyn worked to still her pounding heart and forced herself not to look down.

"Ye've almost got it." Tucker thrust out his hand, but Jocelyn caught only a glimpse of it.

She didn't want to lose her footing. She swayed a little, took another tentative step, fought a strong gust of wind that billowed out the gown, tried to catch the hem, felt the bottom of her foot slip, and shrieked as she started to fall.

"Jolie!"

Jocelyn pitched forward, landing hard on her side, her fingers clawing the slick gray stone, trying to find purchase. She saw the edge of the roof rushing toward her, made a last panicky grasp, and caught a raised slate tile that halted her slide off the roof. Trembling all over, she fought for control, her breathing ragged, her heart threatening to pound through her chest.

Slowly she pulled herself up, groping toward the window with her free hand. With a sudden harsh jerk, she felt a burning in her wrist and a jolt as if her arm were being wrenched from its socket.

When Jocelyn looked up, she saw Stoneleigh, bare to the waist, leaning over the windowsill, his powerful arm extended and locked around her wrist.

"Take it easy," he said, "I've got you." He hauled her over the sill and into his arms, and Jocelyn surprised herself by letting him. "You little fool," he said, his anger rising now that she was safe. "What the hell did you think you were doing?"

"Gettin' out of your soddin' 'ouse!" she said, but clung to him just the same. She was shaking all over, frozen to the bone, and fervently grateful just to be alive.

As if he had read her thoughts, his arms went tighter around her, pressing her against his massive chest. "Sweet Jesus, you very nearly got yourself killed."

Jocelyn pulled away, though some small part of her didn't want to. "I—I could have made it. We'd have been out of this bleedin' place and gone for good."

"You'd have made it, would you? You were a hair's breadth from winding up six feet under." He actually looked concerned, though she knew that could not be.

"What difference would it make to you?"

Rayne scowled. "Regardless of what you may think, I am not the ogre you believe."

She had to admit with some reluctance, her image of him had changed.

"Where is the boy?"

She glanced around for Tucker, grateful he had run when the viscount appeared. "What boy?"

"That little gutter snipe who convinced you to climb out on the roof."

"I had to escape," she said in lieu of an answer. "Brownie's been shot. He might die if I don't get to him."

"You mean that old gallows bird you were running with? The bastard robbed me—would have seen me dead. He deserves whatever he gets."

"He's my friend. I have to go to him."

"Tell me why you tried to kill me."

She only shook her head. Her image of him might have softened, but she was hardly ready to trust him. Besides, what good would it do? She didn't believe for an instant that if she told him, he would let her go.

"Then you'll stay locked up in this house."

Jo set her jaw. "No I won't. I'll find a way to escape."

"You'll stay, by God. You'll tell me the truth, or you'll stay until hell freezes over!" With that he gripped her wrist and dragged her across the room. Out in the hall he lifted her into his arms, though she squirmed against him, and carried her down the stairs.

"Is . . . Is everything all right, your lordship?" This from Farthington, who stood sleepily rubbing his eyes, his nightshirt hanging to just above a pair of knobby knees.

"Everything's just fine." Stoneleigh brushed past him. "You might keep an eye out for a wayward blond boy. He's bound to be hiding here someplace. Don't lose any sleep over it. Just be certain the silver is locked away."

Striding through the door to his chamber, he continued across the room and into the one adjacent, the one reserved for the viscountess when he married. He dumped Jocelyn onto the huge silk canopied bed, jerked down one of the golden cords that swagged back the heavy ice-blue curtain, and looped it around her wrists. In minutes he had tied her securely to the posts at the foot of the bed.

"If I tell you the truth, will you let me go?"

He looked at her face and read the lie about to spring forth. "No."

"Damn you, I have to leave!"

He leaned over her, his dark eyes blazing. "Listen to me, you little minx. It's nearly dawn. Already tonight you've tried to kill me twice and yourself once. You've got a lot of explaining to do before you get out of this house, and right now I'm not in the mood to hear it. I'd advise you to get some sleep. I certainly intend to."

With a last hard glance, he strode across the room to his chamber, jerked open the door, and slammed it solidly behind him.

"Damn you to bloody hell!" Jocelyn twisted on the bed, working to free the knots around her wrists but unable to. Every second counted, and she was tied like a pig in a poke! She glanced around, looking for something she might use to aid her escape. Instead she spotted the yellow muslin dress she'd worn earlier hanging from a hook near the door.

At least if she could get free she would have something decent to wear. "Where are you, Tucker?" she whispered out loud, wondering where the boy had gone. She felt certain that he would be back, that he would somehow discover her whereabouts, and when he did, he would help her escape.

It wasn't long before she heard him, or at least heard the grating of a key in the iron lock on the door. Tucker grinned as he shoved it open and held up a large metal key ring.

"Upstairs maid. Found it on the dresser in 'er room.

Figured the key was a better idea than tryin' the window again.''

"Far better," Jo agreed. "Hurry up."

It didn't take long for him to free her. And just a few moments more for her to slip into the yellow muslin dress. Tuck fastened just enough buttons to keep it on; Jocelyn grabbed the discarded white cotton night rail, a wrap against the chill and later perfect for bandages, and they were out the door and on their way. It was an hour's carriage ride to London, longer than that afoot. If they got lucky, they might hitch a ride.

"Stoneleigh's a light sleeper," Jocelyn warned. "We've got to be quiet." She started past his room, down the hall toward the massive front doors, but Tucker caught her arm.

" 'E's got servants near the front and rear. We'll 'ave to use the window I come in through."

Jocelyn nodded and let him lead the way. By the time they reached the window, she was so nervous she felt dizzy. She didn't breathe a sigh of relief until she had jumped from the sill to the ground. There was a footman posted by the entrance gate, but no one by the gate near the stables. They took that route and they were away.

As they raced across the grass toward Hampstead Road, Jocelyn thought of the man she had left behind. She would never see him again—unless he set the authorities on them. Even if he did, she wasn't worried. For one minor offense or another, she had been eluding the constable and his men for years.

In a way, she was glad their paths had finally crossed. His crimes remained the same, but she had found out a great deal about him—and learned even more about herself. Most importantly, her clash with him had somehow freed her, let her come to grips with the past so that she could now go on.

That thought saddened her. For years her vow of vengeance had given her a purpose, a reason to live each miserable day. Now, that reason was dead and the future loomed bleak and dreary. No dreams, no goals, no future. All she had was Tucker and Brownie.

Brownie. Right now the dear old rogue was all that mattered. She owed him her life. Now his was at stake and she had to help him. She would, she vowed, and once she did, she would find a way to go on.

Rayne stood at the window in his study for only a moment, just long enough to see his quarry slip through the rear gate and off in the dark, out of sight. He had known the boy would come back. Had known the two of them would find a means of escape.

It was exactly what he intended.

He left the study, determined to stay behind them on their flight back to the City, strode through the house in buckskin breeches, a pair of black Hessian boots, and a full-sleeved white lawn shirt. He went out the back door, heading straight for the stables. It took only a moment for the sleepy-eyed groom to saddle and bridle Trafalgar, his blooded sorrel stallion, another for him to swing up into the saddle and head off toward the road. He didn't intend to lose them; neither did he want to risk being seen.

Rayne thought of the woman he followed, and a muscle twitched in his cheek. She had offered to tell him why she wanted to kill him, but she would have said anything to help her friend. He wanted the truth, and this was the only way he could think of to get it.

He would follow her back to wherever she lived, find the scoundrel his coachman apparently had wounded, threaten him with the violence he hadn't been able to use on the girl, and force the two of them to tell him the truth.

His mind replayed the moment she had stood at the side of his bed in her prim little white nightgown. Would she really have stabbed him? He could still see the look on her face as she raised the knife—a mixture of anger, doubt, fear, and uncertainty. Pride and thwarted effort had provoked the attack. Still, he didn't know what crime she believed he had committed, couldn't know the workings of her mind well enough to be sure what she might or might not have done.

His own mind had been spinning since the moment he had first laid eyes on her, a scruffy black-haired waif with a pair of long shapely legs and a luscious little behind. What was it she believed him guilty of?

She was too old to be his by-blow, an illegitimate daughter of some wench he had long ago forgotten. Had he wronged her sister or mother? Jilted some friend who believed herself in love with him? Possibly, but he didn't think so. The hatred he had seen in her eyes was far too strong. She had said it had nothing to do with the war, some soldier of the opposing army he had killed or maimed.

"Damn," he said out loud just before he crested the rise above Hampstead Road. *What the hell could it be?*

"Easy boy." He drew back on the reins, forcing Tray into a walk. At the top of the ridge, behind the thick girth of a tree, he dismounted. Below him Jocelyn and the skinny blond boy were running behind a milk wagon headed into the City. They jumped onto the back, climbed into the bed, and ducked beneath the canvas tarp covering the milk cans. Rayne smiled to himself. They wouldn't be hard to follow. A nice easy ride into London and he would have his answers.

London. Genevieve. Damn. For the first time all evening it occurred to him that he had forgotten all about Lady Campden and the threats she had made. He heaved a weary sigh. He hadn't wanted to see her. Now fate had intervened and his course was set. Genevieve would do as she pleased; he had lost his opportunity to stop her. He hoped she wouldn't be foolish enough to expose their sordid affair to her husband, but if she did, so be it.

He thought of her bold, voluptuous beauty, and surprisingly, another dark-haired beauty came to mind. This one was younger, sleek and graceful, her breasts high and firm. Her eyes were a bright cornflower blue, her face fine-boned, her legs long and shapely. If she weren't such a vengeful little wench, he would find her damnably attractive.

He thought of her tiny waist, her tight little round behind, and his body stirred, his breeches growing taut across his loins.

Who was he kidding? The woman set his blood on fire. At supper, every time he had looked at her, he'd thought of how she had felt struggling beneath him in the carriage. After his tussle with her in his bed, he had thought of her supple skin, the long sleek muscles in her legs, the flatness of her belly. He remembered the way her breasts had felt in his hands, and wished he could have seen them.

When he had heard noises in her room, gone upstairs, seen the boy, and realized she was out on the roof, his heart had nearly pounded through his chest. She might have made it. She might even now be dead. It made his chest ache just to think about it.

He had dragged her in that window and wanted to throttle her. He had felt the peaks of her breasts through her thin cotton gown, the curve of her sweetly rounded behind, and had wanted to rip the clothes from her ripe little body and make love to her for hours on end.

If he was honest with himself, the truth wasn't all he wanted from the attractive little minx. And considering what she had put him through, he just might pursue the notion that lingered at the back of his mind.

A faint smile played on his lips. "We shall see, little vixen, if your trail of vengeance will wind up leading to my bed." Following the milk wagon along the dusty road, Rayne chuckled to himself and urged the horse into a gallop.

Chapter Four

THE WAGON RIDE seemed to take forever.

Jocelyn and Tucker had hardly spoken, both of them weary from the strain of the evening and their worry for their friend. Instead they had dozed, their heads propped on the sides of the rough wooden wagon. Every bone in Jo's body felt battered and sore, her muscles screamed with fatigue, and her limbs carried bruises from her scuffle with the viscount in his bed.

Her nap didn't last long, but it gave her some measure of strength, enough to dodge a broom wielded by the man who drove the wagon when he found them sleeping in the rear.

After that they made their way from the edge of town along the narrow streets and alleys leading to their garret above Boswell's ale house, not far from Drury Lane. Even at this late hour, the old run-down building was still noisy with patrons, gin-swillers mostly, men heavily bound to blue ruin. Jocelyn had grown so used to the noise she almost couldn't sleep without it anymore.

"Thank God we're nearly there," she said to Tuck as they headed down the dirty little alley to the rear of the building.

"I just 'ope Brownie ain't movin' 'round too much up there. Me patches weren't much better'n nothin'."

"As long as they slowed down the bleeding. That's the main thing."

"Wound a bit a rope around 'is arm, I did. Slowed the pumpin' some."

Jocelyn just nodded, her stomach feeling queasy at the thought of Brownie's lifeblood leaking away. Lifting the yellow muslin dress out of the dirty lane, she climbed the rickety stairs up the three flights to the attic and hurriedly pulled open the garret door.

Brownie lay on his mattress in the corner next to one Tucker had fashioned for himself. Jocelyn's bed rested on the floor on the opposite side of the room behind a make-shift curtain that was all the privacy they could afford. A tiny dormer window let in a meager amount of air, though that was mostly black and thick with soot, and their one great luxury—an old iron stove—sat on short squat legs near the door.

"Brownie," Jocelyn said softly, coming to kneel beside him. "It's me, Jo."

He gripped her hand with his, and she felt how cold and clammy it was. "I knew ye would best 'im. Got away clean, did ye? I'm proud a ye, Jolie gel."

"Tucker helped me escape. It's you we're worried about now." She pulled down the threadbare blanket that covered the black and silver hair on his brawny chest and looked at the red-soaked sleeve of his frayed homespun shirt. He had lost a great deal of blood. She could see that he was weak.

"The bastard didn't 'urt ye?"

"No . . . no, I'm fine." She lifted the makeshift bandage, nothing more than a chunk of Tucker's woolen blanket hastily folded and stuffed into the wound. The ball had gone straight through the fleshy part of Brownie's upper arm.

"Bloody rake the likes 'a 'im was probably too busy sniffin' at your skirts to keep 'is wits about 'im," Brownie grumbled.

Thinking of the moments she had spent in Stoneleigh's

bed, Jocelyn flushed. "I wasn't wearin' skirts, remember?"
She pulled the night rail from around her shoulders and
started tearing the soft white cotton into strips.

Brownie's gray eyes moved over her body. "Well, by the
looks o' ye in that fine yellow dress, it's fer certain yer
wearin' 'em now."

The pink in her cheeks grew brighter. She hoped he
wouldn't see it in the dim yellow glow of the candle. "He
burned my clothes."

She felt his muscles stiffen beneath her hand. "The sodden blighter stripped ye, did 'e? How the 'ell did ye make
'im mind 'is manners? I'll wager the bastard was as 'ard as
a thunderin' stone once he got a look at yer ripe lit'le
body."

"Brownie, would you please lie still? The viscount was a
perfect gentlemen. He . . . he provided a bath and gave
me clean clothes. Nothing untoward happened."

Brownie's knowing gaze met hers. "Ye always was a
terrible liar, gel."

"Dammit, Brownie! I'm tellin' y' not a bleedin' thing
'appened. We fought, is all. Then Tucker came and broke
me outta 'is bleedin' house, and 'ere I am."

He chuckled softly and seemed to relax. "I take it ye've
decided not to kill 'im."

"I found out it doesn't matter anymore." Brownie
started to say something else, but Jo put a hand to his lips.
"Please, Brownie, just lay quiet. It's important to keep up
your strength." She turned to Tuck. "Hand me that water
can. I need to get him cleaned up."

Tucker nodded and went to fetch the can.

Outside the door, Rayne stood in the hallway. He had
followed the girl and the skinny blond boy through the
outskirts of London and into the City, leaving Tray stabled
behind an inn. As the streets grew narrow and dirty, as the
smell of open sewers and uncovered drains filled the air,
he began to feel more and more uneasy. And more and
more worried for Jocelyn's safety.

Surely a woman of her obvious breeding couldn't be living in a place like this! But it seemed very clear that she was.

She was easy enough to follow in her bright yellow dress, even on a moonless night like this one. Past taverns and coffeehouses, their huge wooden signs swinging in the breeze above the dark narrow streets; past ragged shoeless beggars asleep in the gutters; past drunken men arm in arm with bawdy, half-clad strumpets, Jocelyn hurried along. Several times he'd been worried that she might spot him, but she'd been so concerned for her friend she had never looked back.

Now he understood her disguise, why she had been wearing men's breeches. In this part of town a woman in skirts made a target for every ruffian and blackguard in every darkened doorway, every courtyard and alley she walked past.

Just watching her racing along the streets made his chest grow tight with fear for her.

And the farther she went, the seedier the district became. He knew this part of the City, these narrow, crooked streets near Drury Lane. Years ago he had come here to fetch a wayward soldier back to duty, a young boy who had lost a friend in battle and fallen in with bad company to drown his sorrows. Rayne had extracted the boy, though he'd had to fight half the drunks in the Red Cock Tavern to do it.

He had come here a couple of times after that for his own amusement, or more correctly, that of his best friend Dominic Edgemont, the Marquess of Gravenwold. There was a dark side to Dominic's nature, a side that once in a while demanded release. Gravenwold knew where to find it, and Rayne occasionally joined in.

But it wasn't the place for a woman.

He followed Jocelyn and the boy along the Strand, down several dark lanes near Great Queen Street and Long Acre, until they finally turned into a rookery between St.

Martin's Lane, Bedford Street, and Chandos, which thieves called the Caribbee.

Sweet Jesus. The building she went into was as seedy as any he had seen. The windows in the ale house were dirty, the boards on the porch old and broken, the alley in the rear full of stinking refuse and overrun with rats. Rayne climbed the rickety stairs not far behind them, then listened on each floor for movement in one of the rooms. On the fourth floor he could hear Jocelyn's voice through the flimsy garret door, but he couldn't make out what she said.

His jaw hardened with resolve. He wanted this whole ugly business put to an end. Quietly opening the door, he pulled out the pistol he'd shoved into the waistband of his breeches, a show of force he hoped would gain him the truth, and stepped inside the room.

It was small and airless, with a pair of broken cane-backed chairs, a squat iron stove, and a wainscot table with an old iron candlestick sitting in the middle. A jagged shard of mirror served as a looking glass, and a red linsey-woolsey curtain partitioned off one corner.

It was a hovel far worse than he could have imagined, yet strangely enough, there was a homeyness about it, and it was immaculately clean. Maybe it was the way the old yellowed newspapers were stacked so neatly on the table beside the cracked coffee mug, or the tiny square of delicately embroidered curtain that fluttered at the window, or maybe it was the chipped blue-flowered plate that served as decoration on one wall.

Whatever it was, it renewed his determination to find out the truth about this beautiful, intriguing young girl. He cocked the hammer on the gun.

"Very touching." All of them jumped, turned and stared in his direction. "Personally, I believe dying might be the wiser course—considering the years you'll be spending in prison."

"You!" Jocelyn stared at him in horror.

"Exactly so."

"How . . . how did you find us?"

"You may thank the gown you stole for making it exceptionally easy. A bit like following a beacon in a storm."

"Ye can do what ye want with me," the injured man said, "but let 'er and the laddie go." He tried to push himself up from the pallet, but Jocelyn pressed him back down.

She eyed Rayne's pistol, then her gaze swung up to his face. "I'm not leavin'—'is bloody lordship or no." Ignoring Brownie's protests, Jocelyn bent over him and continued to clean the wound as if Rayne hadn't spoken. The boy seemed uncertain exactly what to do, but he didn't try to run away.

"You—boy—what's your name?"

"Tuck . . . Tucker, sir, I mean yer lordship."

"Sit down over in that chair."

"Yes, sir." Tucker crossed to the chair and sat down warily.

Rayne uncocked the weapon and shoved it back in his breeches. So much for his show of force. "How is he?"

Jocelyn glanced up, but only for a moment. "He's lost a lot of blood."

Rayne crossed the room to her side, knelt, and began to examine the wound. It was clean but still oozing liquid. "Too bad you're such a tidy little housekeeper. Cobwebs are often just the thing to help stop the bleeding."

"How would you know?"

"I know a lot about bleeding . . . and dying."

Tucker leaped to his feet. "There's cobwebs aplenty out in the 'all. I could get 'em in a minute."

Bright blue eyes came to rest on Rayne's face. "Would it really help?"

"It might."

"Go get them, Tuck."

As Tucker came away from the chair and raced out the door, Jocelyn dabbed more blood from the wound, then folded a clean square torn from the white cotton nightgown to use for packing, working steadily until the boy's return. When he handed her a big gob of grayish-brown spiderwebs, she flashed a look of uncertainty but began to spread them carefully across the wound.

"There's some sort o' ruckus goin' on out there," Tucker said. "I'm goin' back and 'ave a look. Place the likes o' this, ye can't be too careful." He cast an eye at Rayne, who nodded.

He didn't really care if the boy came back or not; he had his hands full with these two. Besides, if trouble of some sort were brewing, it was best to know what it was. "Go ahead."

The boy hurried away, and Jo finished dressing the wound, wrapping the bandage carefully, then splitting the end and firmly tying it off.

"Thank ye, ducks." Brownie squeezed her hand. "Ye've got me feelin' more chipper already."

"I'm glad to hear it," Rayne said, his voice once more cold, "because you and I have some things we need to discuss."

"He's injured—leave him alone," Jo started, but the door flew open and a wide-eyed, terrified Tucker raced in.

"We gotta get outta 'ere—the bleedin' buildin's afire!"

"What!" Jocelyn's head jerked up.

Rayne strode to the door and pulled it open. Already orange-red flames soared up through the rickety stairwell. He closed the door against the choking black smoke that rushed in. "Is there another way out of this place?"

"Aye," Tuck said. "Opposite end o' the 'all. Stairs leadin' down through the tavern."

"You and Jocelyn go ahead. I'll bring your friend." He crossed the room and slid an arm under Brownie's shoulder. Together they came up from the mattress, only to be stopped short at the sight of Tucker's futile urgings, Jo's frozen limbs and terrified face.

"She's afraid o' fire," Tuck said, his voice high and urgent. "Won't move a muscle."

"Bloody hell!" Propping Brownie against the wall with a savage oath, Rayne grabbed the threadbare blanket the older man had been using, strode to where the girl stood frozen, and draped it over her head and shoulders. "You've got to help me, Jo," he said. "If we don't get out of here soon, none of us is going to make it."

She moved her head up and down as if she understood, but didn't start walking.

Rayne gripped her shoulders. "Jocelyn, did you hear me!" It was the tone of command he used on his troops, and it cracked across the room more loudly than the fire outside their door. "We have to move and we have to move now! I'll carry Brownie. You just hang onto me, do you understand?"

She nodded. "Yes."

Returning to Brownie, Rayne bent over and heaved the stout older man across his shoulders. With Tucker leading the way and Jocelyn's arms around his waist, they started out the door. By now, flames had completely engulfed the back stairway.

Coughing and sputtering, laboring for breath in the hot choking air, Tucker led them unerringly off through the thick black smoke and down the stairs that came up through the tavern. The heat in the building stifled the air in their lungs. Their clothes grew damp with perspiration, and the sweat-soaked fabric plastered itself against their skin. At the second-floor landing just above the ale house, they stopped, a wall of red-orange flame blocking any farther descent.

"This way!" Rayne raised a booted foot, kicked open one of the bedchamber doors and went in, closing it soundly behind them. He walked straight over to the window. "We'll have to jump from here. Brownie can you make it?"

"It's me arm what's 'urt, not me arse. Long as I land feet first, I'll be finer'n a just tupped whore."

"Jocelyn?" Rayne jerked the blanket off her head. Her eyes were glazed, her face so pale her skin looked nearly translucent.

"I'll go first and 'elp the others." Tucker hurried forward.

"Good boy." Rayne shoved open the window, realized the side of the building not two feet away was already engulfed in flames, and helped him up on the sill. For the first time he noticed the young boy's hands. Nothing but a mass of scars, a thumb and forefinger all that remained of one hand, a thumb and two fingers left on the other. The rest were burned to stumps and partially melted together. He felt a pang of sympathy but forced it down. "Jump."

Tucker flew from the ledge, landed with a tumbling roll and jumped easily to his feet. He turned and grinned up at them. Jo went next without a word of protest. She seemed unable to speak. She landed with a groan, pitched forward and sprawled, but brushed herself off and climbed to her feet. By now the flames had burned through the door and the room was so thick with smoke they couldn't see. The air was unbreathable and clogged with huge floating cinders.

"Yer next, gov'nor," Brownie choked out.

"Not a chance." Rayne shoved the brawny man onto the sill, steadied him a moment, let go, and Brownie launched himself into the air.

As soon as he was clear, Rayne climbed through the window, his large frame nearly filling the opening, then he was leaping through the smoke and flames, hitting the ground with his knees bent, landing easier than he had expected, able to keep his balance and stay on his feet.

"She's comin' down!" Tucker yelled as the roof crumpled in with a shower of fire that reached several stories higher. At the same instant, the flaming walls of the building broke apart and began to arch outward, the fire increasing with the surge of wind. Rayne swung Jocelyn into his arms, and Tucker and Brownie raced beside him out of the way. Behind them the wall hit the ground, sending a shower of bright orange sparks into the black night sky, and the circle of onlookers scattered.

The four of them stopped a ways down the alley, all of them breathing hard, their hearts still raggedly pounding.

"You two all right?" Rayne asked Brownie and Tucker. The older man looked pale, but a wide grin split his face.

"Fer a bleedin' blueblood, ye ain't no cowheart."

"Ye coulda left us." Tucker eyed him strangely. "After what Jo said, I didn't figure ye fer no bloody 'ero."

Ignoring this last, Rayne set the girl gently on her feet. Her face and clothes were covered with soot, her short black hair a tangle of curls around her face, but the color had returned to her cheeks. "All right?" he asked.

She nodded. "Yes. I'm fine, just . . . I'm sorry I was so much trouble."

"It's all right."

"No it isn't, but I . . ." She glanced away, unwilling to say any more. "If anyone should be afraid of fire, it ought to be Tucker."

"How did it happen?"

"He was apprenticed to a chimney sweep when he was four years old. His mother died and his father sold him for a week's worth of gin. He ran away a couple of years ago. Now he lives with us."

Rayne had heard stories about that sort of thing. Young children small enough to climb up the chimneys were stripped naked and forced to sweep them clean. Some of them burned to death; others, like Tuck, were often badly maimed. Laws had been enacted to protect the children from such cruelty, but so far none of them had really been successful.

He glanced at the boy, who looked decidedly uncomfortable and more than eager to change the subject.

"Looks like we ain't the only ones gettin' the worst o' it." Tucker pointed toward an area behind the crumpled remains of the fire-swept ale house. The run-down section was a maze of dilapidated buildings, many uninhabited except by riffraff off the streets. There were courtyards within courtyards, alleys within alleys, pockets of rubble that should have been razed long ago.

Engrossed in watching the new set of flames, Rayne turned at the sound of Jo's voice.

"Sweet God—it's the orphanage!" Before he could stop her, she had hoisted her skirts and begun to run madly down the block, Tucker right behind her.

"Stay here," Rayne instructed Brownie, who appeared too weak to argue. Taking off at a run, Rayne followed his quarry once more, wondering what insanity kept him from leaving this place of filth and despair and heading back to Stoneleigh.

And knowing without doubt that he would not.

Up ahead, Jocelyn darted into an alley that skirted the block-long blaze, and Rayne followed, emerging just in time to see the sign that read FOUNDLING HOSPITAL NEW ROW LANE go up in flames.

"Good God." Children in dirty nightshirts, some in nothing at all, streamed through the open front doors. They were barefoot, screaming and crying, their faces soot-blackened, their eyes wide with fear as they turned to look back at what had once been their home.

Rayne moved closer. "Are all of the children out of the building?" he asked one of the parish nurses, a broad-hipped older woman with a pox-scarred face and graying, mouse-brown hair. But even as he said the words, he saw several children thrust their heads through a second-story window and begin to cry for help.

"Merciful Lord above!" The woman began to sob out hysterical cries of doom, which Rayne ignored, urging her instead toward a makeshift bucket brigade. Engine companies were rounding the corner, draft horses racing full tilt, brass bells clanging, whistles blowing, but there wasn't time to wait for their arrival.

Not and save the children.

Rayne grabbed a bucket of water on its way down the line, doused his shirt and breeches, and started for the open front door. Around him people shouted orders, stumbled past him into the street, or sat on the cobblestone crying. As he made his way forward, he searched the bedraggled throng. Where the hell was Jo?

She had made it this far, she could go on—she had to! Jocelyn stood at the bottom of the smoldering staircase, gazing up as smoke filled the hall. Tucker had already gone upstairs. She had to follow. She had to help him bring the children down.

The curtain a few feet away burst into flames, and Jocelyn fought down a wave of nausea. Her feet felt leaden, her arms and hands bloodless and numb. It took every ounce of her will just to stand at the foot of the stairs and watch the flames lick the walls down the hall. They were the same blazing orange as she remembered, destroying with the same terrifying abandon. In her mind's eye, one blaze meshed with another. She could almost see the timbers falling, hear the screams of agony coming from inside the parlor.

"Jo!" Stoneleigh's voice broke the trance. "Get the hell out of here!"

"I—I have to help the children. They're trapped up there. Tucker has already gone up."

"I'll get them."

"You? But why should you—"

"For God's sakes, Jo, they're children! What the hell kind of man do you think I am?"

Before she could answer, he gripped her arm and spun her around. "The longer you stay here, the harder it's going to be."

She nodded and started for the door.

"Are you sure you can make it?" he asked.

"I'll make it."

It wasn't nearly as hard going out as it had been going in —perhaps because she wanted to leave so badly. Perhaps because Stoneleigh had said he would save the children. In the long hours of this ghastly night, she had come to believe that he could accomplish nearly anything.

She knew he would save them, just as she knew that

her hatred of the viscount had been a mistake. Not for one moment more could she convince herself that Stoneleigh was the ruthless, uncaring man responsible for her father's death.

Out in the street, Jocelyn stood watching the burning structure, gnawing her bottom lip, wringing her hands and counting the mounting seconds Tucker and the viscount had been fighting the growing flames.

She nearly swooned with relief when she saw them come out, both of their faces black with soot, each of them carrying a child in his arms and grinning from ear to ear.

Jocelyn started smiling, too. She had lost the last few meager possessions she owned in this world, but the children were safe. She and Brownie and Tucker were safe. All because of Stoneleigh.

When he and Tuck walked up beside her, Jocelyn smiled at them, then impulsively hugged her young friend. Tuck cleared his throat and backed away.

"I'll see t' Brownie," he said, leaving the two of them alone.

She looked up at the tall handsome man, feeling a surge of gratitude that brought a hot ache to her throat. "You got them out."

"I told you I would."

"Yes . . ." Tears stung her eyes and she had to glance away. She felt so weary. So bone-achingly weary. Her head pounded fiercely, her lungs still burned with the remnants of the thick black smoke she had breathed, and her hair was plastered damply to her cheeks. She glanced down at her hands, saw they were black with soot and that streaks of black ran up her arms.

Then her eyes fastened on the beautiful yellow dress.

It was ripped and dirty, soot-blackened and burned. One of the puffed sleeves hung in tatters, and even the delicate embroidery over her breasts, which earlier had looked so incredibly feminine, was now streaked with mud and soot.

"My dress," she said, her mind somewhere along the way having laid claim to the extravagant clothing that was the most precious thing she had ever owned. "It—It's ruined."

Her pain-filled eyes met a concerned pair that were gold-rimmed brown, and the tears she had fought to hold back began to slip down her cheeks. "It was so pretty," she said on a whisper that drifted away with the wind. "So pretty."

The tears began to fall freely, and her body shook with sobs she couldn't seem to stop. She cried for the tiny garret room they had lost above the ale house—the first they'd ever had with a stove. She cried for the pain Brownie suffered, for the children without a home, but mostly she cried for herself. For the bitter empty life that stretched ahead.

"It's all right, love, you've got every reason to cry." The viscount's deep voice reached her ears, and for the first time she realized he had pulled her into his arms. "Don't worry about the dress. I'll see that you get another." But it wasn't about the dress, and both of them knew it.

The kindness in his voice and the comfort he lent only made her cry harder, her arms going around his neck as she clung to him like a harbor in a storm.

"Easy, love. Just take it easy. Everything's going to work out."

It would, Rayne knew. He would see to it. This poor, lovely girl touched him in a way no one had in years. He would help her. He wouldn't leave her fighting to survive in the streets. "In the meantime—why don't you tell me why it is you hate me so much?"

Chapter Five

"**W**ILL YOU TELL ME?" Rayne tipped her chin with his fingers. Behind them the smoke and flames against the dull backdrop of dawn looked ashen and grim.

Jocelyn nodded. "Yes."

He saw something different now in the clear blue eyes that assessed him, something forthright and possibly even relieved. Rayne believed this time she would tell him the truth.

In the meantime, however, there were the children to see to, crying, cold, and hungry, with nowhere to go and no shelter to protect them.

While the fire was brought under control, Jocelyn helped the parish nurses with their forty ragged charges. Rayne had gone off with one of the parish officials to solve the problem of where the children might find shelter. Once it was decided they could be moved temporarily to the Workhouse at Bell Yard, he set about finding transport, hiring every vacant hackney coach and wagon he could flag down, then barging into one inn after another to round up food and blankets.

"You've been a godsend, my lord." Ezra Perkins, chief officer of the Foundling Hospital, a thin-faced, gangly little man with receding hair, shook Rayne's hand until he finally had to extract it. "I can't imagine what we should have done without you."

"As soon as you're ready, I'll help you and your staff relocate. We'll find a building better suited someplace else."

"Thank you, my lord. You've no idea how grateful we are."

"I'm glad I could be of assistance." Rayne also agreed to donate whatever was needed in the way of beds, blankets, clothing, and food to get the new home started.

He smiled to himself. Grimy, sweaty, his clothes ragged, dirty, and covered with soot, he felt more useful, more alive, than he had in the last three years. "If there's anything else you need, just let my solicitor know. Now, if you'll excuse me, Mr. Perkins . . . ?"

"Why, yes. Yes, of course."

With the problems of the moment well in hand, and plans put forth for the new Foundling Hospital, Rayne worked alongside Jocelyn and Tucker, loading the blanket-wrapped children into the rented wagons and carriages and sending them off to their temporary home. The sun had come up, but the day had turned overcast, and a chill wind swept in from the north.

"Why don't you wrap one of those blankets around your shoulders?" Rayne said to Jo, who looked even more ragged and dirty than he.

"I'm too tired to be cold." A barefoot little boy named Stevie clung to her neck as she lifted him into a commandeered bread wagon, the back already filled to capacity with other blanket-bundled children.

"I don't want to go," the child said, his small lips pursed, tears streaking wetly down his face.

"I know it's hard to leave your home, Stevie, but the other children will be going with you."

"You'll still come to see us, won't you?"

"Of course I will. Just as often as I can." She kissed his soot-blackened cheek and settled him in with the others.

" 'Bye, Jo," a little girl with strawberry curls called out.

" 'Bye, Carrie." Jocelyn waved farewell as the coach

rolled away, then surreptitiously brushed a tear from her cheek.

Rayne watched her a moment, reached out and turned her chin with his hand, forcing her eyes to his face. "I'll see they're well cared for. You mustn't worry about them."

"That's very kind of you."

"I'm happy to do it. I'm glad I was here to help." She flashed him the same sort of look he had seen on her face before, not quite surprise, but something close to it. It bothered him, the opinion of him she worked to overcome. "You must have come here often," he said, determined to ignore a prickle of irritation.

"I love children. These are even more dear, since they've no one else who cares for them." She took a weary step toward the last waiting wagon, stumbled and swayed, and Rayne caught her up in his arms. "What . . . what are you doing?"

"The children are safe, the fire has very nearly burned itself out, and you are exhausted. Since now is obviously not the time for our little discussion, I'm taking you home."

She pressed her hands against his chest. "I can't go with you—not without Brownie and Tucker. They've no place to stay, and Brownie's injured."

Rayne sighed with defeat. He should have known this would happen. "All right, they can come, too. But I'm warning you—no more tricks, no more deceit, no more roof-climbing, and no more running away."

Jocelyn smiled wearily. "We've nowhere to go, why should we run?"

Rayne only shook his head. After rounding up a last stray carriage for their trip back to Stoneleigh, then searching out Brownie and Tucker, he helped them all climb wearily aboard. Tucker sat on the roof with the driver; Brownie and Jocelyn took a seat inside with him. Just outside the City, Rayne stopped to retrieve Trafalgar from the inn where the stallion had been stabled.

All of them slept after that. Rayne woke up once to find Jocelyn's head propped on his shoulder. He turned in the seat, slid an arm around her waist and settled her comfortably against his chest.

He awoke once more with the sudden halt of the carriage, his arm fitted snugly beneath the warmth of her soft upthrusting breasts, her head cuddled into his shoulder. His body must have sensed her presence for he was rock hard and throbbing, pressing uncomfortably against the front of his breeches.

He glanced up to meet Brownie's cold black eyes, which held a message that was clearly one of warning.

"Take it easy, old man." Rayne eased Jocelyn away from him. "I don't intend to take anything the lady's unwilling to give."

Brownie eyed him a moment more, but some of the tension seemed to drain from his body.

"What is it?" Jo asked, stretching her cramped muscles as she slowly came awake.

"Nothin' t' worry about," Brownie said. "Long as 'is lordship keeps his bleedin' yard in his breeches."

Rayne merely grunted and swung open the carriage door.

"Me'n the lad'll be sleepin' in the stables." Brownie leaned heavily against the side of the hackney coach.

"There's no need for that. Your arm needs tending. Jocelyn will want—"

"The stable will suit. I ain't much for frills. Tucker can see to me wound."

"But Brownie—" Jo began.

"That's the end o' it, gel."

She could see it would do no good to protest, and in a way, she couldn't blame him. The lavish three-story mansion was intimidating at the very least. Within its sumptuous walls, Stoneleigh's powerful presence would loom even larger than it did already.

"There are rooms above the carriage house," the viscount said to Brownie. "My chief groom and his sons live there. There's a place to bathe in the stables, and I'll see that you're given clean clothes."

Brownie nodded. He and Tucker set off toward the rear of the house, and Jo let Stoneleigh guide her up the stone steps to the massive front doors. At the look of disbelief on the butler's face when they entered in their torn, soot-covered clothes, she found herself hiding a smile.

"There was a fire at the orphanage," Stoneleigh said by way of explanation to the startled group of servants in the entry. "Miss Smythe and I were fortunate to arrive in time to help."

He gave no explanation as to what they were doing there in the first place, just a look that warned them not to ask.

Amazing, she thought, watching the tall man from beneath her lashes. Even covered with dirt and grime, his face smeared with thick black soot, there was an air about him. A tone of voice that demanded respect, an erectness in his bearing that left no doubt he was in command.

Farthington snapped his fingers, and the servants swarmed to do his bidding. Baths and clean clothing all round. Footmen to search out something for the two men in the carriage house. Jocelyn was assigned a bed-chamber on the second floor, just down from Stone-leigh's.

"I'll send Elsa to you," he said as they stood outside her door. "Bathe, get some sleep, and I'll see you this evening at supper. Afterward we'll have our talk."

"All right." It sounded so simple. Just go upstairs and be coddled and pampered, fall asleep for the day in one of those deep feather beds, then come downstairs for a sumptuous meal and the finest wine the viscount's blunt could purchase.

Then she would merely explain . . . what? That his lordship's ruthless actions had been responsible for the death of her father? For the terrible years she had been forced to live in the streets? Or was there some mistake? Some other explanation for what had occurred?

Whatever the case, her course was set. She had given her word, and she intended to keep it. Stoneleigh would soon know the truth.

It went pretty much the way she had imagined, a luxurious bath, a long, dreamless sleep beneath clean linen sheets, then dressing in another of his sister's expensive gowns, this one of pale pink lawn sprigged with roses. It fit her as well as the first, and Jocelyn found herself curious about the woman who was, at least in form, a mirror of her own slender frame. Of course, she knew she would never get to meet her.

The viscount would hardly introduce a street urchin to a lady of quality the likes of his sister.

Jocelyn sighed with resignation, wishing things could be different, but grateful for the way it had all turned out. Once Elsa had helped her dress, she left her chamber, ready for the evening ahead. Oddly, she found herself looking forward to it. Since she had come to the City, she had dreamed of this encounter. Of course, in her dreams she'd extracted revenge. Now, she just wanted to hear the viscount's side of what had happened, wanted her past laid to rest so her life could go on.

At the bottom of the wide sweeping staircase, the viscount stood waiting. "I've sent supper out to the others, so you needn't worry about them. We can check on them later, if you like."

He was dressed in a pair of beige breeches, a chocolate-brown tailcoat, wide white stock and snowy cravat. If she had thought him handsome before, after the danger they had shared, the way he had come to her rescue, now she thought him devastating.

"Thank you. I appreciate your helping them." She accepted his arm and suddenly felt shy. So this was what it might have been like to stand in one's parlor and receive a gentleman caller. To have a Season in London and be escorted about town on the arm of a handsome *gallant*.

This is as close as I'll ever come, she thought, and reveled in the moment.

"My sister's clothes seem to suit you. When we return to the City, I'll take you to visit her modiste, see that you are outfitted properly."

"Outfitted? But I couldn't possibly—"

"Why don't we talk about that later? Supper is ready. I'm sure you must be starving."

She was. Earlier she had been too tired to eat more than a bite of the cold meats, fruit, and cheese he had sent up to her chamber.

She smiled at him. "I promise this time I won't forget my manners."

He smiled back. "I'm not one bit worried about it."

The meal wasn't nearly as formal as the last. Just a comfortable seating in a drawing room in the rear of the house, two wing-backed chairs positioned at a small white-clothed table set with silver. Below the marble-mantled hearth behind them, a low fire warmed the grate, a soft yellow glow flickering over the silver-domed platters set before each place.

"We call this the Ruby Salon," Stoneleigh told her, referring to the flocked red-velvet walls. The ceilings were high, with heavy, ornately carved wooden beams. The furniture was mostly in shades of deep red or gold, with gilded accents and plush dark ruby-red carpets.

"It's lovely, my lord." Like the rest of the house, it was elegant in the extreme.

"I think it's time you called me Rayne." He seated her in the overstuffed chair across from him, then took a seat himself.

"All right . . . Rayne." She smiled. "I believe it suits that stormy temper of yours."

He chuckled softly. "Raynor is my real name. Raynor Augustus. Something from one of my forebearers back in medieval times."

Jocelyn pulled her white linen napkin from the silver ring beside her plate and carefully arranged it in her lap.

SWEET VENGEANCE 65

"My name is Jocelyn Asbury." She watched the viscount carefully, awaiting his reaction, but his expression did not change. A servant stepped in and removed the silver dome that covered a steaming Wedgwood plate, then faded into the shadows.

"You're looking at me as though that name should mean something. Should it?"

"I'm not certain. Not anymore. Before all of this happened, I believed you were so callous a man that you might have simply forgotten. Now I—"

"Now you're beginning to believe you might have made a mistake."

She hoped so. It suddenly occurred to her exactly how much she wanted to be wrong. "Yes."

He reached for her hand, where it rested on the table, and gave it a gentle squeeze.

"D-Do you think Brownie's wound will heal all right?" she asked, not yet ready to broach the subject at hand. Belatedly, it occurred to her that a proper lady would hardly pursue such a topic during the course of a meal. Fortunately, the viscount seemed not to mind.

"Infection is always a threat, but you cleaned it well. Odds are he'll be fine."

"You've seen such wounds before?" She took a bite of fish. The partridge looked succulant, the whiting was poached to perfection, and the candied carrots still bubbled in its thick rich juice. All of the food looked delicious, yet knowing what lay ahead, she wasn't sure she could swallow a single bite.

"I was a colonel in the army. Thirteenth Light Dragoons."

"The calvalry?"

"Yes. But much of the time I was stationed on the Continent. Special envoy to General Bergen-zach. My mother was Austrian, you see. I speak the language. I'd spent a good deal of my childhood there."

"Your mother was a member of the Austrian nobility?"

He nodded and took a bite of partridge followed by a

sip of wine. "She was a countess. My grandfather was a close personal friend of the Emperor Joseph. Since one of Pitt's aims at the time I was commissioned was to expel the French from the Austrian Netherlands, my connections proved quite valuable."

"Surely you weren't involved in the fighting."

"I fought at Stockach, Magnano, and Zurich. I took a musket ball at Marengo and they shipped me home for a while."

"The scar on your shoulder," she said, remembering far too clearly the muscles across his bare chest when she had seen him naked. Her cheeks grew warm, and a smile of amusement curved the viscount's lips.

"Exactly so." He wiped his mouth with his napkin. "When the fighting ended with the Peace of Amiens, I believed I'd finished with the whole ugly business, but a year later I was called back to duty. I was returning to Austria when my ship fell under attack. I took a saber wound in the side and spent a year in a filthy French prison, before I escaped and made my way home."

"You were in prison?"

"A subject I would rather not discuss."

"Yes . . . of course. I hardly blame you." She could easily imagine the vile conditions he must have suffered.

"Have you followed the war?" he asked as she pretended to eat but merely shoved the food around her plate.

"You noticed the newspapers up in our garret . . . I suppose you're surprised I can read."

"I suppose. It appears you are a woman of many surprises."

Jocelyn wasn't sure that was a compliment, but the warm look in his eyes said it might be. They continued to converse throughout the meal, the viscount working to put her at ease, giving her time to gather her thoughts, Jocelyn falling deeper and deeper under his charming spell.

"I thought you were starving," he said when he realized his plate was empty while hers had hardly been touched.

"I'm afraid I hadn't much appetite after all."

"So it would seem." He tossed aside his napkin and rose to his feet.

"I would very much enjoy a cigar with my brandy. It's hardly fashionable in the presence of a lady, but—"

"I shouldn't mind at all." She set her napkin aside as Rayne came up behind her chair. "My father often smoked a pipe after a meal. I quite enjoyed it." She felt a momentary pang at the memory, but firmly tamped it down.

They took brandy and sherry in a small salon off the viscount's study, Rayne seating her beside him on a forest-green tapestry sofa in front of a slow-burning fire.

"Well, Miss Asbury, I believe we've spoken more than enough about me. I think it's time you told me about yourself. I'd like very much to know what all of this is about."

With a silent prayer for courage, she leaned back against the sofa and took a sip of her sherry. "It's hard to know where to begin . . . Marden, I suppose."

"Marden Manor?" He drew on the cigar he clamped between his strong white teeth, then released a plume of smoke into the air.

"Marden Village, actually." A cluster of thatched-roofed buildings grown up at the edge of one of the viscount's huge estates, one of many such holdings he owned. "I was raised in a small cottage on Meacham Lane at the far end of the village."

"I'm afraid I'm not familiar with it. My family spent very little time at Marden."

"I was born in the cottage. My father's name was Sir Henry Asbury. He was a scholar. He tutored children of the landed gentry who lived nearby, as well as the vicar's son and a few of the children from the village. Not many, of course."

Still no flicker of recognition. "I take it he also tutored his daughter."

"Yes. My mother died of childbed fever when I was ten years old. Papa and I were left alone." She kept watching him, waiting for some glimmer of remembrance, some faint memory of what she discussed. There was none.

"Three years ago my father fell on hard times. The older children he'd been tutoring went away to school, some of the others stopped coming. Money got scarce. Paying the lease on the house became a problem. My father traveled to Stoneleigh to see you about it. he—"

"Your father came to me?" He leaned toward her. "When?"

"I told you—a little over three years ago. The summer of '04."

He pondered that a moment, took a long thoughtful draw on his cigar. "Go on."

"My father begged for an extension. We could raise the money sooner or later, he said. We just needed a little more time. You denied his request. After that you refused to see him. He went to Marden to speak to your estate man, and they ordered him off the property. My father was devastated. By then I had started to take in washing . . . we needed the money so badly."

She sighed. "Perhaps I shouldn't have, I don't know. It only seemed to make him feel worse. He couldn't eat, started losing weight, couldn't sleep. I was so worried. . . . I told him we could make it—I told him, but he—" Her voice broke on the last.

"It's all right, love. Just take it easy." Rayne crushed out his cigar in a crystal ashtray near his elbow, then urged the stemmed crystal glass of sherry up to Jo's lips. She took a long, calming sip.

"Better?"

"Yes."

"I know this is hard, but I want you to tell me the rest."

She glanced away. "I planned to. I've *got* to, but . . ." But the tightness in her throat would not ease.

"I know this is upsetting, but I really need to know."

She nodded, took another sip of sherry, and steeled herself to do battle with the terrible memories.

"The days were a nightmare after that. My father started drinking. He would sit in the house for hours, just staring straight ahead. The day the sheriff came to evict us, he was worse than I had ever seen him. He kept babbling about the past, talking about things that had happened years ago. When I went outside to speak to the sheriff, my father must have gone a little bit crazy. He must have because h-he . . . because h-he . . ."

Rayne reached over and gripped her hand. "It's all right, Jo, this is all in the past. Soon you'll be able to put it to rest."

She nodded. The warmth of his fingers helped to ease her tension, thaw a little of the icy chill she felt around her heart.

"While I was out on the porch, my father poured lamp oil over the furniture and draperies. He set the house on fire, then he came out to face the sheriff. He said he would destroy everything we owned before he would let you take it from him."

I'll burn every blasted stick of wood, every scrap of paper in that house before I'll let that bastard have it!

Oh, my God! Papa what have you done?

"I tried to run back in, tried to make them let me go, but the place went up like tinder. Papa stood on the porch for the longest time. I was crying. It wasn't until he saw his beautiful books begin to burn that he realized what he had done."

She could see it now just as clearly as if the fire were raging there in the viscount's small salon. The fire at the ale house had brought it rushing back, all the hurt, the terrible pain.

"When one of the inside walls fell in, he started shouting, saying all sorts of crazy things, calling you vile, filthy names worse than any I've heard on the streets."

When she didn't go on, Rayne squeezed her hand, the reassurance lending her strength.

"Before anyone could guess what my father intended, he turned and raced back inside the house. I suppose he finally realized the enormity of what he had done, but I'll never really know. I only know that he ran through the open door and into the flames. I could hear him screaming as the ceiling caved in."

Unconsciously she pulled her hand from his. "It was the most anguished, inhuman sound I've ever heard."

She didn't realize she was crying until Rayne eased her into his arms. "It's all right, love." He cradled her head against his chest and she started crying harder.

"H-He was such a gentle man. He never asked for anything. H-How could you just turn him away?"

"I didn't," he said softly. "My father was viscount then."

"Your father?" She pulled away to look at him, her eyes enormous in her pale oval face. "But I thought . . ."

"You thought what?"

"I don't know. E-Everything was so mixed up." She hiccoughed softly and fresh tears slipped down her cheeks. "I'd never seen the viscount, of course, and till then neither had my father, but I hated you for what you had done. I might have confronted you then—"

"My father," he corrected. "You might have confronted my father. He died in December of 1804. That's when I inherited the title."

The enormity of her mistake hit her like a blow. *His father.* Not Rayne, but the man before him. "Sweet God, I nearly killed you!"

"You didn't. That's what matters, and all of it is behind us."

"If I had—dear Lord, if I had—"

"Listen to me, Jo. Our misunderstandings are almost over. I want you to tell me the rest."

She accepted the handkerchief he pulled from the pocket of his waistcoat, dabbed at her eyes, blew her nose, and took a shaky breath. "Two days after the burial, I was sent off to live with my cousin in Cornwall—Barclay Peters and his wife, Louella."

"I take it that didn't work out."

She sighed and mopped at her tears. "It wasn't too bad at first. I was lonely, of course, and the workload was heavy. It wasn't until I turned sixteen that things began to worsen. After that, every time his wife went out of the house, Barclay couldn't keep his hands off me. God, I hated him. Finally, I ran away."

"That's when you came to London."

She nodded. "I thought I could take care of myself. I thought I could find a job of some sort. I was such a bloody fool."

"I suspect this is where Brownie comes in."

"By the time I met Brownie, I'd spent the two pounds I'd set off with—all the money I had in the world. I couldn't find a job. No one wanted to hire a single woman with no vouchers. Even my schooling didn't help."

"What happened then?"

"I was starving. Sleeping in the alley. I stole food to live on, but I wasn't much good at it. I took a terrible beating from the owner of the Red Cock Tavern when he caught me stealing a kidney pie out of the kitchen. Brownie found me that night in the alley, nursing my cracked ribs and battered face. He took me under his wing, taught me how to get by. I never could have made it without him."

Rayne smiled at her with a mixture of warmth and regret. "Then I guess I owe him a very great debt."

Jo's head came up. "What . . . what do you mean?"

"I mean that I want to make things up to you. I don't know exactly what happened between your father and mine, but I'm going to find out. My father was not an evil man, Jocelyn. There must be more to the story, and I intend to discover what it is. In the meantime, I want you to rest here, get your strength back. I've got some business in the City. In a day or two, we'll talk again."

Jocelyn smiled up at him. For the first time in years she

felt unburdened. Surely somehow things would work out.
Rayne had promised and she believed him.

It wasn't her first mistake.

It surely wasn't her last.

Chapter Six

RAYNE DID INDEED HAVE business in the City. On Lombard Street he spoke with his solicitor, then sent word to William Dorset, his estate manager at Marden. Dorset had worked for the Garrick family for the last twenty years. The lands at Marden earned a small fortune each growing season, and though the place was run with little thought to progress, Rayne was satisfied with Dorset's work and the money the man helped him earn.

Finances, however, were not the reason for the letter Rayne sent. William Dorset would know exactly what had gone on between Sir Henry Asbury and Augustus Bartlett Garrick, Third Viscount Stoneleigh. And Rayne wanted badly to discover what it was.

He saw little of Jocelyn over the next few days and even less of her two friends, though he suspected she spent a good deal of time with them. Instead, he ordered his solicitor to arrange for his inspection of several pieces of property at various locations in the City. The one that best suited his purpose was a small, elegantly furnished town house on Maddox Street, just off Hanover Square.

With its exquisite drawing room, spacious bedchambers, brocade Hepplewhite sofas, and rose silk draperies, he was certain Jocelyn would love it.

That is, if she agreed to become his mistress. Rayne felt a tightening in his groin just to think of it. Since the moment he had seen her in her snug men's breeches, his attraction to her had been growing. For the past two days, he had ached with it. The problems between them had all been cleared up; he wanted Jocelyn Asbury in his bed, and he intended to see her installed there.

Unless, of course, she refused, which he didn't really think she would.

Not in her uncertain circumstances.

But just to be on the safe side, he intended to show her the town house. Compared to her burned-out hovel above Boswell's ale house, how could any sensible female refuse?

That night when he returned to Stoneleigh, he told Jocelyn she'd be traveling with him into the City the following morning. She had been living in his home too long already. Sooner or later the scandalmongers were bound to catch wind of an unattached female having taken up residence at Stoneleigh. For himself, he didn't really care, but he had his sister to think of. Alexandra would soon be returning from her sojourn in the country, and he wanted no unseemly scandal attached to her name.

Besides, the sooner he had Jocelyn installed as his mistress, the sooner he could seek his pleasure in her bed.

Rayne smiled inwardly, pleased at the path he had chosen. Jocelyn would be well cared for—and with any luck at all, so would he.

"Well, what do you think?" They were standing in the foyer beneath a crystal chandelier, Jocelyn looking radiant in his sister's pale peach muslin day dress. He chuckled softly. Alexandra would wangle two expensive new gowns for each of the ones he had borrowed, but seeing Jo in them was worth every shilling.

"I think the place is quite lovely. Whose is it?"

"Why don't we go into the drawing room?" He took her arm and led her over to the sofa. Once they were seated, he captured a slender hand. "Are you certain you like it?"

"Of course I like it. It's magnificent. But what has any of this to do with me?"

"How old are you, Jo?"

"Eighteen the end of last month."

Her age was no problem. "I'm going to be frank with you, Jocelyn. In return, I expect you to be equally honest with me."

"All right."

"First of all, I want you to know that whatever the truth, it will make no difference between us." *It will only make things easier and help to salve my conscience.*

"Whatever is it, my lord?"

"The evening we met . . . the night you came into my chamber, I got the distinct impression that you were—" Rayne searched her face. "Have you ever been with a man, Jo?"

She looked at him oddly. "Of course I have. I've been living with Brownie and Tucker. They may not be aristocrats, but they're men, just like any others."

He hadn't credited that. The boy seemed too young, and the older man . . . well, he'd acted almost fatherly toward her. It bothered him to think of them together, though he knew it shouldn't.

"Then you've slept with both of them?"

She looked decidedly embarrassed. "I know it was hardly respectable, but I hadn't much choice. Besides, it was often very cold. You see, we had only moved into the garret a few weeks earlier. Before that we lived in a basement. The old iron stove was quite a luxury for us."

"You don't mean you all three slept together?" He tried not to sound disapproving. After all, the woman had done what she had to in order to survive. Still . . . "I'm sure you had very little say in the matter, but—"

Jo bristled, her back going rigid, her chest puffing out like a small angry hen. "I'm sorry I've offended your bloody sensibilities, *y' lordship*. If y' didn't want the truth, y' shouldn't 'ave asked."

"I'm sorry. You're right, of course, and I apologize. I

shouldn't have expected you to be a virgin—not after all you've been through."

Her face flamed scarlet. "What—What do Tucker and Brownie have to do with me bein' a virgin? Surely you're not thinkin' . . . you don't mean to think that they—that I—that we . . . ?" Abruptly she came to her feet. "I think I'd like to leave now." She stood ramrod straight in front of him, hands balled into fists, glossy black hair curling around her pretty face. He knew he shouldn't, but in spite of himself, he laughed.

"You *are* a virgin." He gave another bark of laughter. "I wouldn't have asked, except when I had you in my bed I thought—"

"I said I want to leave."

She turned and started for the door, but Rayne came off the couch and caught her in two long strides. "Take it easy, sweeting. I didn't mean to offend you. I just needed to know how to proceed."

"Proceed with what?" At the mutinous look on her face, some of his self-assurance slipped. Maybe this wasn't going to be as easy as he thought.

"Why don't we sit back down?"

She did so, reluctantly, even warily.

"I told you I was going to be frank. I didn't mean to insult you, but at least now I know where I stand."

"And just where is that?"

"I would like to become your protector, Jocelyn. You could live right here in this house. Brownie and Tucker could live here—work here, if that's what they prefer— make this their home, too."

She looked more wary still. "In exchange for what?"

"Sharing my bed."

The pink returned to her cheeks. She eyed him from beneath her thick black lashes. "Not the way I did with Brownie and Tucker," she said softly.

"No . . . I want you, Jo. The way a man wants a woman. You *do* understand what that means?"

She fidgeted beneath his close regard, shifting uneasily

on the sofa. "I've seen 'em coupling in the alley. I've seen men naked. I've seen *you*—remember? I'm not a bloody fool." She was still upset. He could hear it in the street slang that hadn't quite left her voice.

"I would be gentle with you. Teach you how to pleasure me, and give you pleasure in return. It's all very simple, really." Damn, she was going to say no. He should have wooed her more carefully, taken his time.

But he'd wanted her so badly.

He said nothing more, just let her mull over his words. When she spoke, there was uncertainty in her voice, a hint of fear, but mostly resignation.

"Brownie told me a long time ago that the best I could hope for was a man who would take me to mistress. He says I've been lucky so far, that it's a wonder some bleedin' whoreson hasn't already tupped me good." She looked up at him and a fresh surge of color tinged her cheeks. "At least that's what Brownie says."

"I'll take good care of you, Jo. You won't want for anything. You'll have beautiful gowns, a nice place to live, plenty of money to spend."

"Why me?" she asked.

Because your sleek little body is all I've thought about for days. Because all I can dream of is hoisting your skirts and driving myself inside you.

"Because you're beautiful and innocent. Because you're kind-hearted and caring. Because you're not afraid to stand up to me." It occurred to him suddenly that these words were also the truth. "Because I think of you and my body aches for yours."

She swallowed so hard he could see it. "I—I'll have to ask Brownie."

Brownie. There was a rub he hadn't thought of. And just when he'd been sure she was going to say yes. "Are you certain that's wise? After all, the man is extremely protective."

"Brownie's also very practical. We ate more than one meal out of a garbage bin this year, and now our home is gone. He's bound to say I'm better off bein' swived by you than some bird-witted bloke off the street."

He fought a grin of amusement. "Yes, well, I suppose I do have some redeeming qualities." He hoped to God she found him at least a little bit attractive.

"Oh, you do," she said. "Most assuredly. You're brave and kind, and you're extremely handsome."

"I'm glad you think so. It will certainly make things easier." He slid a little closer to where she sat next to him on the sofa. "But just to be certain this is going to work out, why don't I kiss you?"

God, he'd been wanting to do that for days. Just the thought of her lush pink lips beneath his sent the blood rushing hotly through his veins.

He cupped her face with his hands, lowered his head and took her mouth. Her lips were softer than he had imagined. And warmer. He wanted to plunge his tongue between her teeth, to taste the satiny sweetness inside, to unbutton her gown and fill his hands with her small up-thrusting breasts.

Instead he nibbled her bottom lip, used his tongue to tease the corner of her mouth, then molded her lips to his. He drew her gently against him, and Jocelyn came willingly, sliding her arms around his neck, kissing him back, though her efforts were tentative and decidedly those of an ingenue. He stroked her back and felt her tremble. Already he could hear her shortened intakes of breath, feel the tension beginning to flow through her body. With her fiery nature, he had guessed she would be responsive. Now he was certain.

Breathing even harder than she, Rayne was the first to pull away. "My God, but you're sweet."

Her fingers traced the line of her kiss-swollen lips almost in wonder, then she smiled up into his face. "If that is the way it will be, I think I shall not mind so much."

"It will be even better. That I promise you."

On the trip home, Jocelyn was pensive and so was Rayne. If all went well and Brownie could be appeased, tomorrow he would send word to his solicitors to make the final arrangements on the town house. By as early as the day after tomorrow, he could have Jocelyn Asbury warming his bed. Rayne felt a surge of heat and a tautness low in his belly. Just thinking about the girl made him randy as a bloody goat.

He grimaced. He'd been too damned long without a woman.

Which reminded him that at least he'd heard nothing from Lady Campden—or her husband. Genevieve had apparently come to her senses and kept quiet about their affair, thank God.

He glanced at the woman on the carriage seat beside him. She was nothing like the voluptuous women he usually found attractive. Jocelyn was all slender grace and smooth muscle. Over the years, her body had responded to her need for survival, much as his had during the war, growing solid and supple, with little excess flesh.

In the years since he had left his regiment, his own body had remained surprisingly fit and trim. Especially so, considering the punishment it had received—the hard drinking, the late night hours, the dozens of nameless, faceless women.

He was rich as Croesus, the owner of several vast land holdings and a number of lesser properties too numerous to name. He was a nobleman, a powerful force to be reckoned with among the fashionable members of the *ton*. He gambled a bloody fortune, drank himself senseless several nights a week, and spent the rest of his time in some woman's bed.

And he'd felt useless and bored every moment of every day since his return to London.

In truth, his idleness was killing him. He would rather have stayed in the army, but his duty to his family, his title, and lands came first. He was bored—and jaded—and the only thing of interest he had uncovered in the past three years was perched on the seat beside him.

This unfortunate young woman with the taut little body

and china-blue eyes intrigued him. He wanted Jocelyn Asbury, wanted to search out her mysteries and learn her most intimate secrets. He wanted to explore her sensuous curves, to take her hot and hard, and drive her crazy with wanting him in return.

Tonight, if luck rode with him, she would agree to become his mistress. Rayne found himself pacing his bedchamber, waiting for the hours to pass, as nervous as a schoolboy for the first time in years. It was crazy and he knew it, but damn, he wished this agony would end.

Jocelyn entered the Red Salon wearing a diaphanous silver gown more beautiful than any she had ever worn before. She had protested accepting the dress. It wasn't right that she continue to usurp his sister's clothes. Rayne had merely laughed and said Alexandra had been pressing him for a new wardrobe; now she would have it.

Jo saw him rise from the sofa at her entrance. He had never appeared more handsome, his long muscular legs encased in cream breeches cut in the new longer fashion he usually wore, his broad shoulders seeming even broader in a finely tailored gold brocade waistcoat and forest-green tailcoat. As he walked in her direction, his brown eyes assessed her, darkening in a way that made soft heat slide through her body. Then his sensuous lips tipped up in a smile.

Jocelyn's gaze settled there, searching the finely chiseled curves, unable to think of anything but what those lips had felt like moving over hers. Just the memory of the way he had tasted made her insides go soft and buttery.

She had replayed the bold sweetness of that kiss a dozen times on the carriage ride back to Stoneleigh that afternoon, remembering with clarity the way it felt to be held in his powerful arms. Solid muscle, unrelenting strength tempered with gentleness, and passion barely restrained—that was the way she saw him now, and her stomach turned liquid every time he looked in her direction.

"Good evening, my lord." She sank into a curtsy for the first time in years, rose, and saw the pleasure on his face.

"Come here," he said in his honey-touched-with-gravel voice. She walked to him, and Rayne took her hand. When he lifted it and brushed it against his lips, goose bumps feathered across her skin. "You look lovely."

"Thank you."

He poured her a sherry, and a brandy for himself, then led her to a place on the sofa. They talked about the weather, just as they had before, and a little bit about the war, but her mind kept straying to the subject they had come to discuss. Why didn't he ask for her decision?

Rayne cleared his throat, looking nervous for the first time since she had met him. "I'm not a patient man, Jo. How much longer do you plan to keep me in suspense?"

Thank heavens, the waiting was over. It made her insides churn to think of it, yet she had known from the start she had no other choice.

"Brownie says yes—provided we can come to terms."

A dark brown brow arched upward. "Terms?"

She nodded. God in heaven, what if he didn't agree? She thought of returning to her life on the streets, thought of the burned-out hovel she had once called home, and prayed Brownie was right and Rayne would concede.

"Brownie says to ask you for a settlement—in writing— in advance. He says you could tire of me in a fortnight, then where would I be?"

"I hardly think a fortnight will suffice for what I have in mind, but his point is well taken. How large a sum does he want?"

"Five thousand pounds."

"Five thousand—"

Jocelyn bit her lower lip to keep it from trembling. She'd known this would never work. Brownie must have been mad! Still, she couldn't back down now. "Brownie says a man ought to pay for his folly."

"Is that so? What else did Brownie say?"

Jocelyn went pink from her throat to her shoulders.

"He said a swell o' your likes is a lot more agreeable while his rod is 'ard and 'e's got the blue ache in 'is breeches."

Rayne flashed a look of amazement, then one of amusement mixed with chagrin. "I think I shall be very glad when you've come under my protection instead of Brownie's. The first thing I insist on is no more unladylike discussions with your two blackhearted friends."

"He also says you should provide a lease on the house for two years after you've gone."

"I believe I can manage that. Anything else?"

He hadn't said no yet. At least not flat out. Maybe Brownie was right after all. "A monthly stipend for clothes and other items I might need."

"I would have given you a generous allowance, Jocelyn. I'm not a miser."

Would have? Did that mean she had pressed him too far? "If y' don't think this is fair . . . I mean, I've never . . . I'm not sure how to . . . I mean it's bound to be hard to decide my worth. If you like, I could ask Brownie to come in and you could discuss it with him."

"It's hard, all right," Rayne grumbled beneath his breath. He fixed her with a hot brown stare that made her pulse race harder than it was already. "But I believe the value you have placed on yourself is more than fair. I'll see the papers drawn up in the morning. By the day after tomorrow you'll be installed in your new home."

Jocelyn's stomach clenched. By the end of the day she would no longer be a virgin. "Then I guess it's settled." She stood up and extended her hand. Rayne stood, too, clasped it firmly and drew her into his arms.

"I believe a kiss would better seal our bargain."

Especially *this* kiss, she thought, as his mouth claimed hers. This was no gentle brushing of lips, but the demanding kiss of the man who would bed her. Jocelyn gripped Rayne's shoulders, torn between the hot, melting sensations that were snaking through her body and fear of the hard length pressing so boldly against her. He tasted of brandy and fine cigars, and his lips were warm and tempting.

She was trembling when he broke away. The viscount's expression looked fierce, his eyes hot and possessive.

"I believe it is I, my lovely waif, who have made the better bargain."

Voices in the entry greeted her the morning they were set to leave for London. A woman's voice, sweet and excited, Rayne's full of surprise and husky laughter. Jocelyn froze at the top of the staircase as both of them glanced up, the handsome viscount and the willowy auburn-haired girl who hugged his neck.

"Good morning," the young woman said, looking up at Jo with a smile. "Rayne, you didn't tell me we had company."

"Given the fact that you're home three days early and haven't let me get a word in edgewise, I've hardly had the chance."

In that moment, Jocelyn realized what she should have guessed from the start: the beautiful young woman was Rayne's sister. And she would hardly appreciate him bringing his soon-to-be mistress into her home.

"Introductions would be easier, Jocelyn, if you would make your way down here with the rest of us."

"I—I . . . yes, my lord." She wished she could vanish like a wisp of Rayne's cigar smoke, but it was far too late for that.

"Jocelyn, this is my sister, Alexandra."

The pretty girl smiled. She looked to be somewhere near her own age, Jo thought, maybe a year or two younger.

"It's a pleasure to meet you," Alexandra said.

"It's lovely meeting you, too." Jo felt the girl's green eyes moving over her, taking in the pale pink muslin day dress she must have recognized as one of her own, and a wave of embarrassment washed over her. "Your brother was kind enough to loan me some of your things. I hope I haven't put you at an inconvenience."

She glanced a bit wide-eyed at Rayne. "No, no. Of course not." Alexandra had the same slender frame and above-average height as Jo, but was a little bigger busted and a little fairer, with a smattering of freckles across her nose. She was lovely in the extreme, with high cheekbones, big green eyes, and lush rose lips with the same chiseled curves as her brother's.

"I'll explain everything later, Alex," he said in his no-nonsense way which came out more as a command. "In the meantime, suffice it to say that Jocelyn is the daughter of Sir Henry Asbury. She's had a bit of misfortune of late, but things are beginning to work themselves out."

Alexandra nodded as if she understood, which she could not possibly. She flashed a bright warm smile. "We drove straight in from the country. I'm absolutely starving. Have you two already eaten?"

Jocelyn thought of what "starving" usually meant to her, a stomach gnawing with pain, her mouth watering uncontrollably at the slightest whiff of food. The word meant nothing like that to this sheltered young girl. Still, there was something of warmth and good nature about her that made Jo's uneasiness fade.

"I'm afraid we're just leaving," Rayne said, for which she felt grateful. Good Lord, what on earth could she say to the girl? "Cook has chocolate and cakes set out in the solarium. I've a good deal to do in the City, so I'll be away for a couple of days."

Jo knew exactly what he had to do—move her into his town house and initiate her into his bed. Her stomach began to churn.

"That is," he corrected with a pointed glance at his sister, "if you think you can behave without my being here to act as chaperone."

"Of course I can. Miss Parsons will be with me. You know what a stickler she is for propriety."

"Exactly why I hired her. Even at that, I believe you take a great deal of advantage."

Alexandra looked crestfallen.

"Never mind. Just behave yourself. Give those poor blighters who fall at your feet a crumb of pity now and then, and I'll be home by the end of the week."

The two of them hugged again. Jocelyn said her goodbyes, and they made their way out the front doors.

Brownie and Tucker were waiting, looking cleaner than she had ever seen them, their brown twill breeches and loose-sleeved linen shirts neatly pressed and without a single hole. Brownie's arm was healing nicely; Tuck's hair had been trimmed, and seeing them so well cared for made a hard lump rise in her throat.

"Ready?" That from Rayne, who helped her into his elegant black barouche, the Stoneleigh bear and serpent crest gleaming boldly on the door.

A trunk had been packed with the clothes she'd been wearing, and Elsa had been sent ahead that morning to act as her lady's maid and put things in order. They were off to the City, and though her stomach swirled with butterflies at the events that lay ahead, Jocelyn felt more hope for the future than she had known in years.

Then she looked at the viscount, noticed the thick bands of muscle along his neck, thought of him naked, thought of the power in his solid arms and shoulders. She thought of the night she had stolen into his room, could still see the thrust of his rigid shaft as it rode high and hard against his belly.

Recalling the sailor she had once watched from the shadows of an alley, the rutting grunts and pumping of his bare buttocks as he plunged into a drunken whore, Jocelyn's insides churned. She had survived starvation and poverty, she would survive this, too. Still, the sterling future that she had envisioned suddenly looked a little bit tarnished.

* * *

Alexandra Garrick stood at the mullioned window in the entry, watching the Stoneleigh carriage pull away. She'd been gone for three weeks, packed off to Marden like an unruly child, and all because of that silly business with Lord William, the Earl of Crayfield's second son. For heaven's sake, it had only been the tiniest little kiss, but Rayne had seen them and he had been furious.

God's truth, if she hadn't witnessed her brother's magnificent temper a thousand times, she might have feared for poor William's life! Well, what did it matter; she was home now, in plenty of time for the Season.

In fact, she'd come back from Marden early, knowing her brother's anger would have long since faded and hoping he might have already begun the rounds of balls, routs, ridottos, house parties, and receptions of the year. Instead he'd been preoccupied, busy with business—or so he had said—and his beautiful house guest, a girl just a year or two older than she.

Alexandra had been surprised to find the girl in residence at Stoneleigh, considering she had no chaperone. And the way Rayne had looked at her! Everyone in the *ton* knew her brother had a penchant for women. Faith, they practically threw themselves at him. But he had never brought one of them home!

And what of the girl? With her gentle warmth and sincerity, Jocelyn Asbury was as far from the sophisticated females her brother's taste usually ran to as England was from Wales.

Alex felt a mischievous grin coming on. The whole thing was deliciously shocking. Faith, she was glad Miss Parsons had been busy unpacking.

"The man may be your brother," the stiff-rumped old spinster would have said, "but he's nothing but a rakehell and a scoundrel. I say he's a bad influence on a young impressionable girl."

Hardly a bad influence, Alex thought. In fact, since her father's death, Rayne had been overly strict—at times an absolute tyrant! He worried for her, threatened any man who came near—but he loved her and she loved him.

Alexandra stepped away from the window. Rayne had seemed different today, more his old self, as he had stood beside the pretty black-haired girl. There was a lightness in his bearing, something even in the way he smiled.

She hadn't seen him like that since he'd left the regiment. Then he'd been a man with a job to do, a man with a purpose. Then Christopher had died . . . and Papa. And Rayne had been forced to come home.

Maybe the woman would be good for her brother. Alex hoped so. Just as he worried for her, she had been worried for him.

Chapter Seven

"A RE YE SURE YE'VE THE STOMACH for this, gel?" Brownie set the currycomb aside and stepped away from the dapple-gray gelding he had been brushing, one of a matching pair that pulled his lordship's fancy carriage.

"It can't be as bad as all that," Jo said softly, but Brownie could see she wasn't so sure. "Most women do it, sooner or later."

The lass had come out to the stable where he and Tuck had been working. They had decent rooms overhead and the fullest bellies they'd had in years. Still, he was worried about Jo and the sacrifice she was about to make.

Brownie grunted. "Depends on who's plowin' ye, I guess."

Jo's chin came up. "The viscount isn't the terrible man I thought he was, Brownie. He's been kind and considerate, and more generous than any man I've ever known. How many men would have risked their lives for us the way he did?"

She pulled a golden stem of straw out of the manger and twirled it between her fingers. "Besides, you said yourself, the best I could do was to find a protector. Living on the streets the way we were, there was very little chance of that."

" 'E won't stay, ye know." He hated to say it, but in the past two years they had learned enough about the viscount to know it was the truth. Stoneleigh kept 'em, one after another, until he grew tired of 'em, then he was off chasing some new piece o' tail. To Brownie's way a thinking, the man had already swived more than his share of wenches. What the bloody hell did he need with Jo?

He picked up the currycomb and began once more to brush the horse. "What about babes, gel? 'Ave ye thought o' that?"

Jo smiled softly, almost wistfully, reminding him of the gentle, frightened girl he had found that night in the alley.

"I've thought of it, Brownie. The night you and I talked about setting some sort of terms. I love children, and with the money the viscount's agreed to, even if I should end up carrying his babe, I'll be able to take care of it. And I don't think he's the kind of man who would abandon his own flesh and blood."

Brownie grudgingly nodded. "Ye've the right o' that, I suppose. Still, I know ye weren't raised t' this sort o' thing. I know it don't sit well with ye."

"No it doesn't. But picking a man's pocket doesn't sit well with me, either. Nor stealing money from some drunken cove in the street. I learned a long time ago that people do whatever it takes to survive."

"Do ye know what 'e'll expect o' ye?"

"Some, I guess."

"Do ye want me t' tell ye?"

She looked like she might say yes, then shook her head. "No. I'm frightened enough as it is."

"Most women come t' accept it. Doxy or wife, they get used to it. I've known plenty who enjoyed it." He grinned, exposing a gap in his bottom row of teeth. "Some blokes is better at it than others. The morts I've tupped 'ad no complaints. Who knows, his bloody lordship's 'ad 'is yard in enough wagtails t' know what the 'ell 'e's about. Mayhap, he'll teach ye t' like it, too."

Jo's pretty cheeks went red. "Perhaps." But when she glanced nervously away, his worry increased tenfold.

"Ye've been like a daughter t' me, gel. Fancy clothes

and a clean place t' live ain't the whole o' it. Ye change yer mind, ye just tell me. I'd slit 'is lordship's bloody throat before I'd let 'im lay a bleedin' 'and on ye.''

Jo smiled softly, her hand coming up to his shoulder. "I've made my decision, Brownie. The viscount's agreed to our terms. He's done his part—now it's my turn.''

Brownie just nodded. It galled him to think of his lovely little lass spreadin' her legs for the bleedin' viscount. To his bloody lordship, she was just another light-skirt, but he and Tucker knew her worth—and it was solid gold.

"'E ain't good enough for ye lass, but I'll abide by ye decision.'' Brownie lifted her chin with his fingers. "Ye just remember—ye need me, I won't be far away.''

Seated at the long mahogany table in the dining room of his newly acquired town house, Rayne swallowed a bite of roast capon. A few feet away Jocelyn lifted her wineglass. Her fingers trembled on the long crystal stem.

"Nervous?''

She smiled at him bravely, but her eyes glanced away. "A little.''

After their arrival, they had spent the day unpacking, putting away Jocelyn's meager possessions, the dresses he had commandeered from his sister, the clothes and sundry items he had brought along for himself. Afterward he had taken her on a brief round of shopping.

"There's nothing to be afraid of, Jo. We're going to take things nice and easy. I'm not going to hurt you.'' Well, that was almost the truth, for he couldn't prevent the pain she would feel just this once. Of course, he wasn't about to tell her that. At least not yet. She was nervous enough as it was.

"Are you finished with your supper?'' He glanced at the gravy congealed on her plate, at the vegetables long since grown cold, which Jocelyn had scarcely touched.

"Yes. I guess I wasn't very hungry.''

"So I gather.'' God's blood, he was hungry enough for the two of them, but it wasn't food he wanted. He could hardly keep his eyes off the soft mounds rising above her ice-blue satin-trimmed gown. Her face looked pale, but her raven-black hair appealingly framed her cheeks, and her shoulders appeared as smooth and silky as the fabric of her dress. "Shall I call for dessert?"

"No. Not unless you'd like to have some."

Thinking of the dessert he had in mind made his shaft grow thick and heavy beneath the table. Damn but he wanted her. Maybe he should have paid a visit to Madame Du Mont's, then he wouldn't be so bloody tempted to rush things.

"I had a wonderful time today," Jocelyn said a little later, making nervous conversation. "I hope I thanked you properly."

You very soon will, my love. "You thanked me profusely every five minutes."

She laughed at that, the sound so sweet a ripple of heat shot through his body. Their day together had gone swiftly, the joy of watching Jocelyn's pleasure every time he bought her the slightest trinket making the hours fly past. The evening, however, had seemed endless. He'd been hard from the moment she had entered the drawing room, hard off and on all through supper.

Now, at the thought of the pleasures that lay ahead, Rayne took control of his wayward manhood, tossed his napkin down on the table and slid back his chair, coming eagerly to his feet.

"It's been a very long day, my love." And he planned for an even longer evening. "It's time we retired upstairs. Elsa should have your bath drawn and your nightclothes laid out," a filmy white lace gown he had bought her at a little shop on Bond Street. He couldn't wait to see her in it.

Jocelyn wet her lips. "All right."

He wished she would try to relax. Maybe even enjoy herself. Dammit, he felt like a wolf about to make his supper of a hapless lamb.

He took her arm, and she trembled as he led her toward

the stairs. "I'll give you a few minutes to make yourself ready, then I'll join you in your chamber."

At his reference to the room they would share, he felt her stiffen. Dammit, this wasn't going at all the way he had planned.

"As you wish, my lord." Jocelyn climbed the stairs and disappeared into her bedchamber.

Rayne paced the carpet for what seemed hours but in truth was less than twenty minutes. Then he climbed the stairs to the suite adjoining hers. After a long hot bath he hoped might ease his tensions but only fueled his raging passion, he drew on a burgundy brocade dressing gown.

He glanced at the clock. Jocelyn had had plenty of time to make ready and, he hoped, perhaps even begin to feel some of the anticipation he felt. He rapped softly on the door, pulled it open without permission, and stepped inside her room. Jocelyn stood in front of the window, wearing the white lace nightgown. She turned at his approach, the nightgown floating softly around her ankles, and Rayne sucked in a breath.

She was everything he had imagined and more. She was small and exquisitely slim, but sweetly curved and utterly feminine. A white satin ribbon had been woven through her jet-black curls, scallops of lace trailed down the vee between her breasts, and small white clusters were all that hid her nipples from his view. Lace veiled the tantalizing cleft of dark hair at the juncture of her thighs, but the curves of her hips were exposed through the sheer gauzy fabric, as well as her long shapely legs.

At his slow, deliberate perusal, blooms of pink rose in her cheeks, and her hands came up to cover her breasts.

"Don't," he said in a voice gone rough, "you look lovely." Sweet Jesus, far more than that. She was all sleek muscle and graceful curves, her wavy black hair framing a fine-boned, achingly beautiful face. "Who would have believed, my lovely little waif, those old clothes of yours hid such an incredibly beautiful woman."

The flush in her cheeks grew more pronounced as he

moved closer. When his hands came up to her shoulders, he felt her tremble.

"I—I'm afraid I haven't the faintest idea what to do."

He smiled at that. "To begin with, try to relax." He left her a moment, crossed the room and poured them each a snifter of brandy. "Here, maybe this will help." It might, he thought, but he didn't want her numb and senseless. He wanted to feel the passion he knew was there inside her. He wanted to tap it, then drown himself in the outpouring of his labor.

Jocelyn sipped the brandy, but her body remained stiff and unyielding, and her eyes followed each of his movements.

"Come here."

Jo stepped closer, and Rayne drew her into his arms. He sensed her reluctance, though she tried to disguise it, and the moment his mouth touched hers, he realized how different this kiss was from the last. Jocelyn's lips were just as soft and lush, her breath just as sweet as before, but the arms around his neck felt tense and brittle, the ripe, sweet mouth that opened to his tongue felt taut with resignation.

She was in his arms out of duty, resigned to her fate like the lamb to the slaughter he'd imagined. Damn, but it wasn't supposed to turn out this way.

Determined to force a response, Rayne deepened the kiss, and Jocelyn allowed the invasion of his tongue. But there was no answering warmth, no rapidly pounding heartbeat, no sharp intake of breath. Sliding her gown off one shoulder, he admired a small pointed breast, cupped it with his palm and began to massage her nipple. The crest grew taut and he felt her shiver, but it was with fear, not lust.

Rayne inwardly groaned, fighting the ache in his groin. Damn, why hadn't he thought of this? He'd been so damned sure he could arouse her, been certain she'd be the fieriest of vixens in his bed. What an arrogant, conceited bastard he was. The girl was an innocent, by Christ, not some seasoned whore! He had known her only days, yet he'd expected her to be mad for him. What an addle-pated bloody fool!

Rayne broke away to look into her upturned face and saw that her bottom lip trembled. "This isn't going to work, is it?" he said softly.

"W-What do you mean?" Jocelyn's fingers grew tight on his arm.

"You aren't ready for this, Jo. It isn't time for this to happen." Of course he could always just take her. It was obvious she would let him. His body would be satisfied—in time things might work out.

"Don't say that. It's just that I'm n-not certain yet what to do."

"Jo—"

"Please, Rayne." A note of desperation stole into her voice as her eyes searched his face. "All I need is a little more time. I can learn to please you. I know I can. Please—" She broke off on this last and her eyes grew shiny with tears. "I—I can't go back there. You've got to give me a chance."

Rayne looked at her and his heart turned over. His hand came up to her cheek. "Listen to me, Jo. The papers are already signed. You'll never have to go back to the streets, do you hear? Never."

Her chin rose stubbornly. "I won't take somethin' I 'aven't earned."

Rayne smiled gently. "I'm not asking you to. I'm telling you that we're going to wait. I want you, Jo. That hasn't changed. But I want you to want me, too."

"I don't understand."

He ran a finger along her cheek, then settled his hands at her waist. They nearly went around her. "Do you remember the last time I kissed you?"

"Yes . . . I remember."

"You enjoyed it, didn't you?"

"Yes . . . but this is different."

"It isn't different—at least it shouldn't be. When the

time is right, that's the way you'll feel when we make love."

Jo fell silent. It was obvious she didn't believe him.

"You railed at me once for my vast experience with women—half the light-skirts in London, I believe you said. If you're convinced that's true, then the least you can do is trust me to know what I'm doing. Will you do that much for me?"

She smiled at him, the first real smile he had seen, and some of her tension seemed to ease. "Yes."

Rayne kissed her gently. "Take off your nightgown."

"What?"

"You said you would trust me."

She wet her lips, but lifted her chin and slid the lovely gown off her shoulders. It pooled in a soft white circle at her feet.

"Your body is beautiful, Jo. Never be ashamed of it. Learn to enjoy it. Now, come to bed."

"But you said—"

"I said you weren't ready, and you aren't. All we're going to do is sleep together. I won't even take off my robe." He didn't dare. As it was, he ached with every heartbeat, and God knew he wouldn't get a wink of sleep.

Jocelyn walked in front of him over to the massive four-poster bed, and he admired her tight little round behind. He must have groaned aloud, because Jocelyn turned to look at him.

"Did you step on something? I hope Elsa didn't drop one of my hairpins."

Rayne chuckled softly. "No, my love, the pain I'm feeling is a little bit higher off the ground." He took her hand and pressed it against his hardened shaft. Startled blue eyes swung to his face, and Rayne frowned. "I thought you said you'd seen me."

"I—I did, but you're even bigger than I remembered. How will all of that . . . I mean, are you certain that we'll fit?"

"We'll fit, love. That I can promise."

Jocelyn climbed into bed and Rayne followed her up. He nestled her back against his chest, but kept her away from his groin where his body still rose up hot and rigid. He made no further move to touch her.

He could feel the tension in her body, but eventually her breathing evened out and Rayne relaxed a little himself. He had made a difficult decision, one he would pay for every night until he'd possessed her luscious little body.

He glanced at the woman who at last slept peacefully beside him. He had soldiered for years. When he wanted to, he had more self-discipline than any man he knew. He smiled grimly. He would need it—every bloody ounce. But some male instinct told him that awakening Jocelyn Asbury to the flames of passion would be worth it. He cuddled her sleeping figure against him and finally went to sleep.

Jocelyn drifted in that hazy awareness just before waking, a smile on her face as she snuggled against the solid warmth beside her. Since she had met the viscount, times she'd been cold and hungry seemed to fade into the mist of a distant bad dream. Beneath her now wasn't a lumpy corn-husk mattress gouging her ribs, but a soft feather bed.

The sheets were the finest linen, the pillows downy and soft. And she was warm. It seemed years since she'd been this warm. And something else was happening, she thought, noticing a soft, spiraling sensation that fluttered in her belly and tingled along her skin. It felt incredibly good, this feeling, immeasurably pleasant.

Jocelyn's eyes flew open as she realized the marvelous sensations were emanating from the area of her breast, and that Rayne's big hand cupped the fullness while his fingers teased her nipple.

"Rayne?" she whispered, uncertain whether to pull away or let him continue, to trust him as she had promised.

"Easy, love." He cradled her back against his chest, as he had when they had fallen asleep. She could feel the thick bands of muscle and the sensuous slickness of his silk brocade robe still resting between them.

Rayne kissed the nape of her neck, and her heart skittered sideways. He made no other move, but his hand continued its magic until her nipple puckered and tightened and her breath caught in her throat. Rayne nibbled an earlobe and her body arched backward, her hips pressing into his groin.

That was when she felt it, that same threatening length she had touched the night before. She thought of the sailor in the alley, thought of Rayne's solid flesh shoving into her that same way, and her whole body went rigid.

Rayne must have felt it because he stopped caressing and eased himself away.

"I'll send Elsa up to help you dress," he said. "I thought we might visit my sister's modiste, then perhaps spend the evening at the theater."

"You're taking me to the theater?" She could scarcely believe it.

"What did you think? That I would keep you locked up in this house?" He grinned. "Or maybe you thought I would chain you to the foot of my bed."

She flushed, because it wasn't that far from the truth.

"Whenever you're ready, you may join me downstairs." He started to walk away, then stopped and turned. "By the way, from now on you are Jocelyn Asbury Wyndam, two years a widow, just recently in from the country."

"But why do we have to—"

"I want to make this as easy for you as I know how. As a widow, you'll be able to move about more freely. I shall have to hire you a proper companion, one who clearly understands her role in this little drama, but that shouldn't be too difficult."

"Jocelyn Wyndam," she repeated.

"Unless you'd prefer something else." She shook her

head. "Good. Then up and out of that bed. We've a very busy schedule."

Jo just nodded, her mind absorbing the notion of the person she had just become.

Her first day as Mrs. Wyndam was a day like nothing she could have imagined. From Charing Cross to Whitechapel, they strode the stone walkways beneath huge signboards with bright-painted letters, stopping at one glass-windowed establishment after another. Pelham's Clockmaker Shop, Wedgwood's China Shop, Deard's Bauble Shop, Betty's, the St. James's Fruitier—she had but to look at an object and she found it in her possession.

At a chairmaker's shop, she admired a beautiful mahogany rocker, and the next thing she knew, Rayne was laying down more coin.

"I only said it was lovely," she said. "I didn't mean for you to buy it. You've already bought me enough." Lord, the viscount's blunt seemed endless!

He chuckled softly. "My beautiful Jocelyn, I gamble more in a single evening than the sum total I've spent on you. Let me worry about the money; you just enjoy yourself."

At Lady Claridge's, one of the City's most fashionable modistes, he spent a second small fortune. Gowns of the finest muslin, kerseymere, and cambric lace; a gossamer creation of silver tissue embroidered with sapphire threads, a rich plum sarcenet tunic dress, a satin spencer; a taffeta mantelette, and a fringed silk cape. There were slippers and parasols to match, and bonnets of every description.

And even as he lavished her with gifts, he played the gentleman—or at least as much of a gentleman as the viscount could be.

"She has lovely breasts," he told Lady Claridge, who wasn't a lady at all, or so Rayne said. Jocelyn flushed to her toes. "They may be small, but they're exquisitely formed. As much as I hate to share them, it *is* the vogue. With your expertise, I'm certain you'll show them off to their greatest advantage."

"Of course, milord." Garbed in a fashionable gown of India muslin, wearing a wig that covered her short-cropped mouse-brown hair, the tall woman tapped a length of measuring tape thoughtfully against her chin. "A deep vee, I should think. It will make the most of her . . . assets."

"And her legs," Rayne said, "she has the longest, most incredibly shapely legs."

"A split," said Lady Claridge, "very long, very provocative—very chic."

Jocelyn hardly approved of the way he took command, or the intimacies he made no attempt to hide, nor was she prepared for the strange effect of his words. Every time Rayne mentioned her body in such an intimate fashion, something warm tugged low in her belly.

And the way he looked when he said it—as if his eyes ravished her even as his body had not.

She thought of that look now as they strolled along the street, the viscount's muscular arms laden with boxes. If she had been paying more attention to where she was walking and less to the handsome man beside her, she might not have collided headlong into a gentlemen of his lordship's acquaintance, a blond man nearly as tall as he.

"Good grief!" The blond man caught her just as she stumbled and started to fall, sparing her what would have been a painfully embarrassing jolt on the bottom.

"Harcourt," the viscount said, handing his boxes to a footman from his carriage, then taking Jo's arm and sliding it protectively through his own. The scowl on his face said the blond man wasn't one of his favorites.

"Stoneleigh." Appraising blue eyes raked Jo from head to foot. Though he was leaner than Rayne, more sinewy than muscular, he was handsome. Softly curling golden-blond hair, a straight patrician nose, and well-defined chin added to the promise of a firm male mouth. "So this is

what's been keeping you away from the tables. I can't say
I blame you.''

"This is Mrs. Wyndam, a friend of the family's just in
from the country.''

Harcourt made a magnificent leg. "A pleasure, madam, I
assure you.''

"Stephen and I went to Cambridge together," Rayne
said to Jo. "You might say we're very old friends.''

"You might," Lord Harcourt said. "More accurately, you
might call us rivals." He smiled, but it looked a little bit
thin. "We've boxed, played any number of high-stakes
card games, matched our best-blooded horses . . . In
fact, Rayne and I are often at odds—though never when it
comes to appreciating a beautiful woman." His eyes slid
down to her breasts. "In that, I have always found his
lordship's taste impeccable.''

"I'm glad you approve," Rayne said coldly. "Now if
you'll excuse us, it's been a very long day. It's time we
were leaving.''

"Of course. Will you be attending the Gladstone's soiree this evening, Mrs. Wyndam?''

"No," Rayne answered for her. "Mrs. Wyndam is still
getting settled. It may be some time before she gets out
and about.''

"I'm sorry to hear that.''

"I'm certain you are," Rayne said none too kindly, but
Harcourt only laughed.

"Good day, my lord," Jo said, feeling the tug of Rayne's
arm.

"Good day, Mrs. Wyndam. I look forward to the day our
paths cross again.''

"I'll just bet he does," Rayne grumbled as he stepped
into the street and jerked open the carriage door before
his footman could do it for him.

"I gather you don't like him.''

"We don't much like each other.''

Jo sank wearily back against the seat. "Why not?''

"Hard to say, really, it goes back so far. In college we

were always playing pranks on each other. As we got older, the rivalry grew more fierce. What Harcourt said about the ladies . . . we've often been attracted to the same women."

"Recently?"

Rayne nodded. "An actress by the name of Rosalee Shellgrave. She was Stephen's mistress . . . for a while."

Jocelyn looked up at him. "You stole her away from Lord Harcourt?"

He shrugged, his superfine jacket rustling against the seat. "I suppose you could say that. I didn't know how much Stephen cared for her until it was too late."

"No wonder he doesn't like you."

He turned to face her, his eyes suddenly dark. "Stay away from him, Jo. There is nothing he would rather do than lure you into his bed."

"Because he thinks I'm spending time in yours?"

"Exactly so. Now, if you don't mind, I'd prefer we discuss something more pleasant than Stephen Bartlett."

Jocelyn looked out the window. A gentleman stepped from a glistening black carriage, and a woman selling lavender pressed a small bunch under his nose. A blind man begged for alms at the bookseller's shop next door.

"What happened to her?" Jo asked. "To the actress, Miss Shellgrave?"

Rayne sighed wearily. "I'm afraid I found her less than amusing in a very short time." Jo frowned. "You needn't look at me that way. I settled an enormous sum on her, and she's quite happy with her latest protector."

Jocelyn said nothing.

"If it will make you feel any better, had I known how much she meant to him, I would have let Stephen keep her. *Now*, may we discuss something else?"

Her gaze drifted back out the window. The viscount was a hard man, as she had known he was. Arrogant in some ways, spoiled in others. Yet there was great humanity in him. And she had known few men who were strong enough to admit they were wrong.

Still, the callous way he cast off his unwanted lovers bothered her. Would her own fate be the same?

An apple cart spilled in the street, and Rayne's driver cursed the man roundly. Jocelyn smiled to think she had said far worse.

"What time will we be leaving for the theater?" she asked.

"I believe we'll save the theater for tomorrow night." Rayne slid an arm around her waist and pulled her closer, his shoulders so broad they brushed the side of the carriage. "That is, if you don't mind."

She sighed with relief. "Hardly, my lord. I never would have guessed how much work is involved in assembling a lady's wardrobe."

"My sister enjoys every moment of what we went through today."

"Well, you may rest assured that I do not." She flashed him a sidelong glance. "Speaking of which, shouldn't you be concerned that Lady Claridge might . . . might somehow be indiscreet?"

"You needn't worry. I've availed myself of the lady's talents many times in the past. She's the height of discretion."

Many times. Many mistresses. Rosalee Shellgrave and how many others? Jocelyn's insides balled into a hard tight knot. She would soon join what seemed to be legions. Jocelyn rode the rest of the way in silence.

Chapter Eight

THEY ARRIVED BACK at the town house just as dusk was falling.

"From now on we'll sleep in my room," Rayne said as he led her upstairs. "The bed is larger, the windows bigger, and there's a far better view of the garden."

Jocelyn glanced down at her hands, intertwined against the front of the pink muslin day dress she hadn't yet changed out of. She wanted to turn and run, to tell him she had changed her mind, that she didn't want to make love, didn't want to be another of his conquests. It didn't seem fair that her life and those she cared for most hinged once more on the viscount and his whims.

Still, there was Brownie and Tucker to think of, a place for all of them to live, and food to fill their empty bellies.

"Are we going to . . . is tonight the night?" she asked, her eyes coming up to his face.

"No, tonight is *not* the night, more's the pity. Tonight I shall merely continue where we left off this morning. You enjoyed that, didn't you?"

The heat rose in her cheeks. What good would it do to deny it? "I—It was very pleasant."

"Good. Tonight I'll use my mouth as well as my hands and we'll see if you enjoy that too."

Jocelyn made a sound low in her throat. "Y-Your mouth?"

He nodded. "For days I've thought of nothing but kissing your lovely breasts."

Jocelyn swallowed so hard she was certain he could see it. "If you'll excuse me, my lord, I find it's exceedingly warm in here. I believe I shall change into something a little more comfortable." She started for the door, her legs a little wobbly. Rayne's deep voice stopped her cold.

"Good idea. A chemise, I should think, will be enough. Rest for a while, bathe if you like. I'll rouse you when supper arrives."

Rest, she thought. How could she possibly rest when all she could think of was the viscount's beautiful mouth fastened on her breast? And his tongue. Sweet God, what would it feel like if he touched her with his tongue? She was frightened, yet in a way she was not. Her path had been chosen, a course she was helpless to change, and with each passing day she was less certain she wanted to.

Jocelyn crossed the room, her long legs flying as if she could run from the notion.

Rayne watched her go and a corner of his mouth curved up. It wasn't warm this evening; in fact, he had noticed a bit of a chill. His smile grew broader. Jocelyn wasn't immune to him—not in the least.

All day long he had gone out of his way to touch her—briefly, of course, just a gentle caress now and then. Several times he had felt the quickening of her breath, the too-rapid flutter of her heart. Jocelyn was responding—the wait would well be worth it.

Rayne called for a bath—healthy or not, he couldn't get enough of them, not since his days in the army. Jocelyn seemed to feel the same, and he wondered if her time in the filthy London streets had been the cause. His valet, a man named Burbage who came with the house, brought him a linen towel and, while he dried himself, proceeded to lay out his clothes.

"All is in readiness, milord," said the balding, stately servant.

"Thank you, Burbage." He glanced at the trousers, white linen shirt, brocade waistcoat, and cravat laid carefully out on the bed. "Just the breeches and boots. I won't be needing the rest."

The valet looked at him oddly, but dutifully put the extra clothes away and left the room. Outside the window darkness had fallen, leaving the garden below lit by soft burning lamps. The chill in the room had been banished by a grate of glowing coals.

Bare to the waist, Rayne crossed the room, rapped lightly on the door to Jocelyn's chamber, then pulled it open. She was sitting on the window seat, wearing only her thin lawn chemise, turning the pages of a book.

"What are you reading?" he asked softly, his eyes locked on the curves revealed beneath the sheer white fabric. Heat pooled low in his belly and his body went rock hard.

She glanced up from the volume, her eyes surveying his chest, measuring the width, the solid planes and valleys, the swath of curly brown hair. "W-Wordsworth and Coleridge."

"Ah, the *Lyrical Ballads.* Where did you find it?"

"Downstairs in the library. Do you enjoy reading?"

"On occasion. Usually I prefer more active pastimes. Hunting, riding, shooting. Boxing is a favorite. But then you know about my box club and our gatherings at Lord Dorring's . . . that is where you and I had the good fortune to meet."

Her eyes slid down to the bulge of his sex, pressing hard against the front of his snug-fitting pants. Her uneasy look bespoke her doubts.

"Not all women have this effect on me, Jocelyn, I assure you. Before your defenses go up, why don't we eat?"

It was the most erotic meal Rayne had ever consumed: Jocelyn wearing only her thin chemise, he bare to the waist, most of the time unmercifully aroused, both of them sitting just inches apart on the sofa.

"You still aren't eating," he said when he looked up and

caught her watching him from beneath her thick black lashes. "I won't have you starving just because you're afraid I'm going to bed you."

From a tray of cold meats and cheeses, oysters, and palm-sized mutton pasties, he tore off a bite of cold partridge and brought it to her lips. "Here, give this a try."

She opened her mouth, and her soft full lips slid over his fingers. They were damp and warm, and the ache in his groin grew more fierce. She took a second bite from his hand, then another.

"Now it's your turn," he said, his voice rough and husky. "How about feeding me an oyster?"

Jocelyn smiled, beginning to relax a little and enjoy the game. Though Rayne sat beside her half naked, her nervousness had fled, and resolve replaced any fear she might have had. Resolve . . . and a warm, pulsing sensation that slid hotly through her body.

Rayne accepted the oyster, tilting his head back, catching it on his tongue. She fixed her gaze on his mouth as he swallowed, and noticed the sensuous movement of his lips.

"Why don't you try another?" she said, meeting his bold look squarely. She didn't miss the flash of fire she read in his gold-rimmed brown eyes.

"Yes . . ." he said. "Why don't I?"

The way he said it made the heat slide lower, expanding, making the room feel suddenly warm. She couldn't help but admire him. She had never seen a man so finely muscled, with thick bands of sinew across his chest, narrower bands rippling down a stomach as flat and hard as a washboard.

Rayne opened his mouth and slowly sucked the oyster from her fingers. His tongue felt slick and warm where it curled against her skin, the feel of it making her tingle. Before she could pull away, he gripped her wrist and brought her palm to the base of his throat. She could feel the long thick tendons moving up and down as he swallowed.

When he let her go, instead of pulling away, she moved her hand lower, though it trembled a little, sliding it through his curly brown chest hair, her eyes still fixed on his face.

Rayne reached for the strap on her chemise and slid it off one shoulder. The feel of his fingers brushing her skin made her shiver, but this time it wasn't with fear. She had made the decision to accept him in her bed. In return he had promised her time and asked for her trust. Jocelyn intended to give it.

The second strap slid down, baring her to the waist. "Do you have any idea how much it pleases me to look at you?"

She could feel his steady heartbeat. "It pleases me to look at you, too."

Rayne's look grew even hotter. "If I didn't want to touch you so badly, I could be happy just feasting my eyes on you. As it is . . ." He reached for her, and his palm cupped a breast.

He lifted it, molded it. His fingers felt rough against her skin. Jocelyn's heart thundered madly. Rayne used the edge of his thumb to tease her nipple, making it pucker and tighten. She felt light-headed, the room once more overly warm. Rayne kissed her gently, stroking her flesh, kneading it, making her tremble. Her breast grew heavy and achy. Each of his fingers burned like tendrils of flame.

When he lowered his head and took the small taut bud into his mouth, Jocelyn's breath caught on a whimper and her head fell back against the sofa. Lacing her fingers in his hair, she arched upward, and Rayne began to suckle gently. He circled her nipple with his tongue, laved it, tugged on it with his teeth, and Jo felt an answering tug low in her belly.

He nipped and tasted and kissed. Sweet saints—her body seemed to burn! One minute she was bathed in flames, the next she tingled as if the fire had frozen. She might have let him take her there and then if it hadn't been for the unwelcome knock that sounded at the door.

Rayne's dark-haired head came up. "What the bloody hell . . . ?"

"Excuse me, your lordship," came Burbage's tentative voice muffled by the heavy wood. "It's your sister, sir. I'm afraid there's been an accident."

"Oh, Rayne." Jocelyn straightened on the sofa, pulling her chemise back in place.

"I've got to let him in," he said. "You had better get your wrapper." As she hurried from the room, he walked to the door and pulled it open.

"What's happened? Is Alex all right?"

"I believe so, sir. But she's broken her ankle. The surgeon is with her. Apparently it was he who sent word through your solicitor."

Damn, he'd been so caught up in his pursuit of Jo, he'd neglected to leave word where he could be reached. Of course his solicitor, Frederick Nelson, always knew where he was. "How did it happen?"

"Riding, I believe, my lord. I'm afraid that's all I know."

Wearing a blue silk paisley wrapper, Jocelyn hurried across the room to Rayne's side. "What's happened?"

"Alexandra seems to be involved in another misadventure. I'm afraid I'll have to leave."

"Is she all right?"

"Apparently she's broken her ankle." He released a weary breath. "She's a handful, I can tell you. God only knows how this might have happened. My father should have taken her across his knee instead of encouraging her reckless behavior. Now I may have to."

Jo caught his arm. "She's too old for that, Rayne. Especially coming from you."

He grinned wickedly. "A woman is never too old for a thrashing. Not if she needs one. You might keep that in mind."

Jocelyn tilted her chin. "And *you* might keep in mind that your sister is a lady. She deserves to be treated as one."

Rayne only grunted and strode toward his wardrobe to

pull on a white linen shirt. He headed for the door just a few minutes later, when Brownie sent word that his carriage had been sent around.

"If all goes well, I'll be back day after tomorrow." He dragged her against him and kissed her as if he'd be gone a fortnight. Jocelyn found herself clinging to his neck, her body molded against him.

He grinned down at her roguishly. "Don't forget where we left off. I assure you *I* won't."

And then he was gone, his carriage clattering out of the courtyard at the rear of the house and off down the narrow back street that fronted the stables. Jocelyn leaned out the window and waved down to Brownie and Tucker, assuring them as she had before that she was all right.

Brownie waved back and so did Tuck. If she weren't so tired, she would go down and see them. As it was, all she wanted to do was curl up in bed. Besides, her body still throbbed with the remnants of Rayne's touch. Now that she knew how wonderful it could be, she wanted to savor it, to replay the sensuous evening and all that had occurred.

On top of that, she didn't want to say something that might upset her two friends—something, for example, about her still-unbreached maidenhead. She didn't want Brownie to worry any more than he already had. And in truth, after the feelings Rayne had stirred this eve, it was only a matter of time. The viscount would take her the moment he believed she was ready.

Thinking of the fires that had raced through her blood, Jocelyn found to her amazement she looked forward to the day he would.

"Good heavens, Rayne, you scared me to death." Alexandra would have leaped to her feet had she been able. "I didn't expect you home for several more days."

He stood in the door to the salon like an angry bull. "You didn't think that when I received word you had broken your ankle I would bother to see if you were all right?"

She licked her lips, suddenly gone dry. "Who—Who told you I broke my ankle?" She flicked a glance at the young man sitting beside her on the sofa, nervously wringing his hands. Other than that one movement, Peter Melford sat frozen, staring up at Rayne's furious features, unable to utter a sound.

"I received word through my solicitor. Apparently the surgeon sent a message—an urgent message. So urgent, in fact, that I was forced to tear myself away from a very pleasant encounter to rush to your sickbed." He turned a hard look on the boy, the late Lord Townsend's second son, who sat beside her. "Instead I find you lounging in the salon in the middle of the night with a man. A little late for callers, wouldn't you say, my dear little sister?"

She tried to laugh, but her brother's fierce expression cut her off. "Lord Peter was with me when I fell from my horse." ·

"And when, pray tell, did that happen?"

"Yesterday. He just stopped by this evening to check on my welfare."

"At this hour?"

Peter Melford jumped to his feet. "I was on my way home, your lordship. I was worried. I meant no disrespect."

Rayne ignored him. "And where is Miss Parsons, your overpaid chaperone?"

"Right here, my lord." She stood ramrod straight in the doorway, her mouth pinched together in a disapproving line. "Unfortunately, I had the headache. I retired before this young man's arrival or he would not be sitting here now."

Rayne fixed his eyes on Alexandra. "And your ankle?"

"The message must have somehow gotten confused. In the beginning we thought it was broken, but it turned out to be only a sprain."

Rayne turned his attention to the sandy-haired young

man who now stood nervously in front of him. "I believe
we would all be best suited if you would take your leave,
Lord Peter."

"Yes, my lord."

"You may also retire, Miss Parsons. I shall see to my
sister." She arched a satisfied brow, as if for once they
were both in agreement, then turned and marched from
the room. As soon as Lord Peter had left, Rayne nodded to
the butler, who slid the massive drawing room doors together, leaving the two of them alone.

"I'm sorry, Rayne, I really am. I didn't mean for you to
worry."

"Tell me how it happened." He stood in front of her,
his face implacable.

"I—I went riding. Lord Peter and I, that is. And his
sister Melissa, of course."

"Of course," Rayne said with a deceptive calm that
didn't fool her for an instant.

"We were racing. The fence was just a little higher than
I thought. Sasha cleared the jump without a problem, but
I lost my seat. Silly, wasn't it? It shouldn't have been a
problem."

"The problem you have, little sister, is not with the
fence, but with me. I am giving you fair warning. Either
you begin to behave like the lady you were raised to be, or
I shall march you into your chamber, turn you over my
knee, and treat you like the spoiled child you've become."

She would have stood if her leg had not been swathed
in bandages. "Don't you dare threaten me, Rayne Garrick.
I'm a grown woman. I won't let you treat me like a baby."

"If you want to be treated like a woman, start acting
like one. And that most certainly does not include receiv-
ing gentleman callers in the middle of the night."

"It isn't even midnight. Besides, Lord Peter is just a
friend."

"Lord Peter is a lovesick swain, just like the rest of
them. I swear, Alexandra, one day all this hotheadedness
is going to come back to haunt you."

"And what about you, big brother? Why must I act the model of decorum while you behave any way you bloody well please?"

"Because I'm a man, that's why. And you had bloody well better stop swearing!" Rayne bent over her, his dark eyes skewering her to the sofa.

Alex's mouth twitched; she couldn't help it. He'd said the very same swear word she had. He must have realized it, because his own lips twitched and then both of them burst out laughing. Rayne's tone was deeper, of course, but there was something of a family resemblance in the huskiness of the two.

"I'm sorry, Rayne, truly I am. I didn't know the surgeon had sent for you. I would have told him not to."

"He would have sent word, Alexandra, because he knew if he didn't, I'd have his head served up on a silver platter." He bent forward, slid an arm beneath her knees and lifted her up.

"I'm not trying to be hard on you, Alex. I just want what's best for you. The scandalmongers are just waiting for a young woman to make a slip. They can ruin you, Alex. You don't want that, do you?"

She shook her head. "I promise I'll be more careful."

"Good girl." He stopped at the doors, slid them open, then crossed the hall and climbed the stairs.

"How is your mistress?" Alexandra asked, and Rayne paused.

"And what precisely do you know of mistresses?"

"Only that you've had quite more than your share."

Rayne sighed. "I swear Alexandra, I'll be glad when you are married. Then your poor unfortunate husband can deal with you. Perhaps he can figure a way to keep you in line."

Alex didn't tell him she intended to wait a number of years before she let that happen. She smiled and let him carry her on up the stairs.

* * *

Jocelyn knelt in the garden behind the town house. It was small and very formal, with box hedges and tulips and lovely potted geraniums. Lavender bloomed in one corner, scenting the air, and where she worked among the roses, the ground beneath her fingers felt damp against her skin.

Jocelyn loved the garden. She had tended the yard at their cottage on Meacham Lane, which was surely not as elegant as this, but blossomed with color through most of the year. She missed it once she left. She only just realized how much now.

"Mornin', Jolie." That from Tucker, who came down on his knees in the soft earth beside her.

"Good morning, Tuck."

"What ye doin'?" The wind blew strands of his pale hair into his eyes, and he brushed them away with the stump of his hand.

"Weeding. The roots are becoming clogged. I want to give the new growth plenty of room to breathe." Roses were her favorite. The delicate satin petals, the intense reds, ivory whites, and delicate pinks. Throats of fire in some.

"His lordship expects ye to do 'is gardenin'? I should think warmin' 'is bleedin' bed would be enough."

Jo's cheeks grew warm. "He doesn't expect it. I love to garden. I've been doing it since I was a little girl." Her mother had taught her. Later she and her father had worked in the garden together.

"Is 'e treatin' ye all right?"

She nodded. "I couldn't ask for better care. He's taken me shopping—his lordship has bought me dozens of lovely things. But what about you, Tuck? Are you happy here?"

"Me and Brownie like workin' in the stables. We couldn'ta stood bein' locked in the 'ouse."

"I think Rayne knew that."

"Maybe. Or maybe 'e just wanted t' keep us away from ye."

"You're welcome in the house any time. You know that, Tuck."

For a moment he said nothing. " 'Ow can ye stand it, Jo? 'Aving 'is bleedin' 'ands on ye? It flippin' well makes me sick t' think of that whoreson touchin' ye. I wish I'd shot the bastard meself that night. Then ye wouldn't 'ave to be lickin' 'is boots."

Jocelyn came to her feet, and Tucker stood up, too. "Don't say that, Tuck! For bloody sakes, the viscount risked his life for us. He's been good to us, given us food, clothing, provided this beautiful home."

"And what do ye 'ave to do for it—be 'is bleedin' whore, that's what."

Jo stared at him as if she had never seen him. For an instant tears stung the backs of her eyes. "In a way I suppose that's true, but in another way . . ." How could she explain the feelings Rayne stirred in her? She didn't understand them herself.

"The viscount made a bargain. He's been kind, more than kind . . . and patient." She raised her eyes to his face. "The truth is, his lordship hasn't even touched me."

Tucker scoffed. "Why not? 'E don't think you're good enough?"

Because he wants me to desire him, and God help me, I do. "Because he wants things to be right between us. He's a good man, Tucker. Surely you can see that."

He grumbled something she couldn't hear while his eyes slid down to the toe of his boots. Jo didn't remind him they were the first new pair he had ever owned.

" 'E says 'e'll find me a position. See me indentured to a tradesman."

It cost money for such a position. But she already knew how generous Rayne could be. "What do you think you'd like to do?" It went unspoken that with his maimed hands, most trades were closed to him.

"Ye don't really believe 'im, do ye?"

"Yes, I do."

Tucker shrugged his shoulders. "Me pap was a baker. If it come down to it, I guess that's what I'd want to be."

His father. A man who had sold his own son.

"I don't recall much o' me folks," Tuck said, "but I can still smell them pasties comin' outta the oven. Fresh bread still makes me think o' me mother."

"I think you would make a fine baker, Tuck."

"O' course, it wouldn't be for a while . . . even if 'is bloody lordship keeps 'is word."

"I'm sure he will. The viscount always does what he says." That was the truth, Jo realized. A few weeks back she wouldn't have believed the viscount could be a man of honor. Finding comfort in the notion, Jo bent down once more and began to dig up the earth.

"Will 'e be coming back soon?" Tuck asked.

Jo felt a curling warmth in her stomach. "Tonight," she said softly. "He sent word he'd be here late this eve."

Tucker just nodded, and Jocelyn continued her work. But her hands trembled a little as she sifted through the earth. Rayne would arrive this evening. From the moment of his departure, she had found herself looking forward to his return.

Her stomach fluttered at what the evening might bring.

Chapter Nine

STANDING AT THE CURB in front of Lord Dorring's town house, Rayne stepped into the sleek black landau he had chosen for his trip into the City.

No markings glittered on the doors, nothing to blatantly reveal who he was or raise speculation as to where he was going. He had rarely concerned himself about propriety; now he found himself strangely unwilling to hear Jocelyn's name linked with his in the same degrading tones the *ton* reserved for women like Rosalee Shellgrave or even Lady Campden.

It would happen, of course, sooner or later. But Rayne intended to spare his soon-to-be mistress for as long as he possibly could.

"Maddox Street, Finch," he called to his coachman. "Make haste, I'm in a hurry." He settled himself against the seat as the carriage lurched off, on his way at last to see his lady.

He had been restless to get there all evening, lost several large hands of whist he should have won, all because his mind kept straying to Jo and their heated encounter of a few days before. But tonight was Tuesday. He hadn't missed a meeting of the Pugilist's Hand in the last two years. If he did so now, the men were bound to speculate. Harcourt was a member. He would relish the opportunity to carry tales of his recent introduction to the lovely Mrs. Wyndam.

God's breath, the girl hadn't yet been bedded! He wasn't about to throw her to the wolves!

The carriage arrived a few minutes past eleven, an early departure from Dorring's, but not really remarkable. What *was* unusual was the small amount of brandy he had consumed, the little, in fact, he had been drinking since he had met the black-haired minx who had accosted him at gunpoint.

After his return to London, he had been gambling in the extreme, drinking and whoring out of boredom. Since that fateful night in front of Dorring's town house, he most certainly hadn't been bored. Rayne thought of Jocelyn and smiled. He hoped she would be waiting.

Then again, it might be interesting to climb naked into her bed while she lay sleeping. Her defenses would be down, she might accept his caresses, even respond. If she did, he could take her, drive himself into her tight little body and capture the essence of her that had eluded him since the moment of their first fiery encounter.

Rayne sighed, knowing such thoughts were futile though his body had already begun to grow hard. *Discipline,* he cautioned. *When she is ready, you will know, and it will be all the sweeter.*

The carriage rounded the corner onto Grosvenor, then turned down the narrow lane at the rear of his town house. His groom was waiting, directing the landau and horses into the carriage house, Brownie working beside him.

"Good evening, Brownie," Rayne called out as he climbed down to the cobblestone floor.

"Evenin', gov'nor,"

"How fares our lady?"

"She's been waitin' for ye. Nervous as a cat, she is."

Rayne nodded, hiding his disappointment as he stode the stone walkway toward the house. Jocelyn wasn't asleep. Neither, it seemed, was she the bundle of sweet

anticipation he had secretly hoped. Ah, well, time would
solve the problem. Of that he had no doubt. He should
visit Madame Du Mont's, give his body some ease. Yet he
knew that he would not.

Rayne entered at the back of the town house, strode
down the hall, handed his hat and gloves to the butler,
then made his way into the drawing room. After what
Brownie had said, he expected to find Jocelyn seated on
the sofa, but there was no one there.

"She's upstairs, milord," the butler said with a too-smug
curl of his lip.

"Thank you." He would have to do something about
these servants. He didn't like their bloody-minded atti-
tudes. He could just imagine the way they must treat
Jocelyn when he wasn't around.

Rayne climbed the stairs two at a time, wondering if he
would find her sleeping after all, almost wishing he
would. He opened the door to her chamber and again
knew only disappointment.

"In here, my lord," Jocelyn called softly, and the sweet
sound of her voice sent a ripple of heat through his body.

Determined to ignore it, he strode through the open
door into his bedchamber and came to a halt just a few
paces inside the room.

"Good evening, my lord." Jocelyn stood beside a large
copper bathing tub filled with steaming hot water. "I
thought you might enjoy a bath before we retire." She
was wearing the white lace nightgown he had bought her.

Rayne's stomach clenched. He eyed her from head to
foot, caught her slightly altered breathing, the too-rapid
pulse in the hollow of her throat.

"Yes," he said, his voice a little rough, "I believe I
would like that very much." He moved toward her, hopeful the invitation he read in her bright blue eyes was the
one he wanted, fearful that if he moved too quickly, he
might break the spell and frighten her away.

Jocelyn smiled softly. "Why don't you let me help you
undress?"

His mouth went dry. Jocelyn walked toward him, white lace floating behind her, jet-black hair gleaming in the glow of the candles and the light of the slow-burning fire.

Since the moment he had seen her in the sheer lace gown, he had been rigid with desire, heavy and aching, and worried more than a little that if she went too far and then tried to stop him, he might not be able.

"Are you certain about this, Jo?"

"I would be far more certain, my lord, if you would kiss me."

Rayne groaned and swept her into his arms. She came there willingly, pliant and responsive, kissing him back, opening to the pressure of his tongue.

Take it easy, he warned himself. *Don't push her too fast.* But he didn't really want to go slow. He wanted to sweep the gown off her svelte little body, to kiss her breasts and her belly, to lower her onto the floor, open his breeches and drive himself inside her.

Instead he broke away to kiss the line of her jaw, to catch a delicate earlobe between his teeth, to trail kisses along her shoulders.

"Your bath, my lord," Jocelyn whispered breathlessly.

"Yes . . ." It would give things a chance to slow down, allow him to cool the simmering heat that raged through his body.

At least that was what he hoped until he stripped off his jacket and waistcoat and tossed them away, then felt Jo's fingers working the buttons on his shirt. He unfastened his cuffs with unsteady hands, shrugged the crisp white linen off his shoulders, then reached for the buttons at the front of his breeches.

Jocelyn's fingers found them first. He noticed they were shaking, but he didn't dissuade her. Instead he tilted her face up, bent his head and kissed her, his shaft so thick and hard he feared he might explode. The strain eased as the buttons came undone. Jocelyn glanced away.

"Your boots," she whispered.

Rayne sat down in a nearby chair and pulled them off,

then removed his breeches. Naked, he walked to the tub and climbed in. Jocelyn's cheeks colored prettily as she knelt at the rim, unmindful of the water that dampened the white lace gown, turning it nearly transparent.

"This had better be a very short bath," Rayne said, "or you, my love, will find yourself joining me, nightgown and all."

She laughed softly. "I bathed earlier, my lord. I should prefer to join you in bed."

She saw the heat of desire in his eyes, and for the first time she looked uncertain. "T-That is . . . if you wish it as well."

Rayne cupped her face between his hands, pulled her mouth down to his and kissed her. "My lovely Jocelyn, you have no idea how much I wish it."

She smiled a bit tentatively, then took a deep breath. Reaching for the sponge lying on the floor beside her, she soaped it and began to wash his broad back. Beneath the water he shifted against his aching arousal. Jocelyn raised the sponge, trickled water across his shoulders, leaned forward and began to wash his chest. He could feel the weight of one soft breast as she bent over him, the peak just brushing his arm.

She soaped the muscles across his chest, rinsed them, then soaped his stomach and rinsed that, too. When her fingers paused at the edge of the water, Rayne captured her wrist and gently dragged her hand below the surface. She let go of the sponge and it floated up among the soap bubbles, but her hand remained below, moving lightly over him, judging the size and shape and feel.

"We're made to fit together, Jo. Your body will soon grow accustomed to mine."

"Rayne?"

"Yes, love?"

"Would you kiss me again?"

He almost smiled. Whenever she grew frightened, she trusted his kisses to ease her fear. So far they had, and this one appeared to be no different. He used his tongue with extra care, teasing the corners of her mouth, urging her to respond. She did so tentatively at first, then with more and more abandon. It severed the last thin thread of his control.

Heedless of the water he sloshed over the side of the tub, he came to his feet, naked and aroused, soap bubbles sliding down his chest.

"Rayne!"

He chuckled softly, reached for her, dragged her against him and kissed her. Sliding an arm beneath her knees, he lifted her up and started walking. The white lace gown was drenched in an instant. So was the carpet as his big wet body strode across the floor toward the massive canopied bed. He came down with Jo in the middle of the soft feather mattress, careful not to hurt her, ravishing her mouth while his hands found her breasts.

She stiffened only for a moment, then she was kissing him back, threading her fingers through his hair, arching her slender body against him.

Jocelyn started to tremble and it wasn't from the dampness or the cold. Rayne's hard-muscled frame pressed against her. She could feel the sensuous contours, the thick bands of sinew across his shoulders, the washboard ridges of his stomach. One of his powerful hands was laced in her hair, while another cupped her buttocks to hold her against him, his fingers massaging, teasing, making the place between her legs throb and burn.

Sweet God in heaven. She had never felt such fiery sensations, never been so swept up, never blazed so totally out of control. Rayne took her mouth, plundered it, possessed it. His tongue drove her to frenzy. Beneath her fingers the muscles of his damp chest flexed and tightened, and her nipples grew so hard they ached wherever they rubbed against him.

As if he sensed her need, he slid the gown off her shoulder, baring a breast, lowered his head and took her nipple into his mouth. Jocelyn felt a jolt of fire, felt the heat flash through her body, and moaned low in her throat. Rayne suckled gently and heat throbbed hotly in her belly. He kissed and laved, opened to take more of her into his mouth, tugged, and nipped, and tasted, setting her blood aflame. When he pulled away, the sudden loss felt so poignant, it made her want to weep.

He was only removing her nightgown, drawing it over her head, then tossing it away. In seconds he was kissing her again, his lips caressing, demanding, his tongue plunging into her mouth. His hand felt like fire where it moved across her flesh, then it was sliding through the triangle of soft black curls at the juncture of her legs, spreading the petals of her sex, his finger slipping inside her.

Jocelyn cried out at the heat that raced through her body. Tongues of fire spiraled upward, blotting thoughts of anything but Rayne and the magic he created. She was wet there, she realized, as he used that wetness to stretch and prepare her, sliding a second finger inside, easing both of them out and then back in.

She was frightened, she was wary, she was embarrassed.

She was none of those things.

She wanted his fingers inside her, though until now she wouldn't have believed it. She wanted him to stroke her, to fuel the flames of heat roaring through her.

"Rayne," she whispered, straining against the hard muscles flexing across his chest, pleading for something, knowing it was that thick hard length of him that she had been so afraid of, needing it yet fearing it at the same time.

"Easy, love. Just take it easy." He kissed her again, slowly, deeply, while a hand massaged her breast. "You're ready for me, Jo. Can you feel it?"

"I'm ready. Dear God, Rayne, surely I'm more than ready."

Rayne made a sound low in his throat. Then he was parting her legs with his knee, positioning himself above her, kissing her breasts, suckling, then returning to her mouth and easing his tongue inside. At the very same instant, she felt his hard length sliding inside her, so thick

and hot that for a moment she was once more afraid. But
his kisses teased and taunted and his muscles rippled
against her breasts, and in seconds she was spreading herself wider, urging him onward until he reached the barrier
of her maidenhead.

"There'll be pain, Jo. But only just this once. I'll try to
be as gentle as I can."

Her body tensed, awaiting the moment, the tearing of
her flesh. Instead his fingers cupped a breast and teased
her nipple, his tongue climbed the walls of her mouth,
and his lips—God, his lips drank from hers until they
seemed to possess her very soul. Jocelyn felt a surge of
heat, opened like a flower in the sun, and Rayne drove
himself home.

Ragged pain tore through her. Jocelyn cried out, but the
sound was swallowed by his kiss.

"I'm sorry," he said from where he poised above her,
his brow creased with concern. "I wish there had been
another way." She saw the price of his care in the sheen
of perspiration at his temples, the damp hair clinging to
his forehead.

"I'm all right. The pain lasted only a moment." She *was*
all right, she realized. She was always all right as long as
she was with Rayne.

"Thank God." He kissed her again, long and deep, and
the moment she relaxed, her body flooded with warmth.

Slowly Rayne began to move, gently testing, careful not
to hurt her. Surprisingly, the pain did not return. All that
remained was the weight of Rayne's hard-muscled body
and the rigid hot length of him buried deep inside her.
She might have felt vulnerable and invaded; instead she
felt tenderly breached.

Rayne increased his movements, the rhythm growing
faster, surer, deeper. His muscles strained and her own
began to grow taut. Pleasure rippled over her; fire seemed
to swirl through her veins. What on earth is happening?
she thought wildly. Then the thought spun away on a
wave of incredible heat.

With each long, powerful stroke, flames roared through her body. Her limbs felt disconnected; her breasts felt hot and cold, heavy and achy and tingling. She was trembling all over, consumed by the feel of Rayne's big hard body, the bands of muscle flexing and moving above her. Damp heat engulfed her, catching her up in the fire and the yearning, the fury and the passion, gripping her like some powerful force she didn't understand but that seemed to beckon her onward.

"Let it come," Rayne said softly, feeling the tension in her body. "It's what you want, love. It's exactly what you need."

Trusting him, she closed her eyes, letting the tide sweep over her. In seconds she was surging through waves of shimmering heat, breaking through the silver foam, rising upward, upward, cresting the wave, letting it lift her, carry her on toward the distant horizon. She cried out Rayne's name, and the wave broke over her, her body shaking, the taste of pleasure heady, so impossibly, incredibly sweet.

She felt him shudder as he clutched her against him. His head fell back and a growl caught in his throat. It was the most incredible moment she had ever known, the most exciting, the most fearsome.

She was breathing hard as she spiraled down, and so was Rayne. He held himself above her for a moment, then he eased himself away and cradled her in the curve of his arm.

Neither spoke for a time. They just lay there listening to the soft sweet thudding of their hearts beating nearly in unison. When her world had once more righted itself and her pulse had slowed, Jocelyn turned on her side to face him.

"Why didn't you tell me it would be this way?"

Rayne chuckled softly. "How could I explain?"

She smiled at that. "I suppose it wouldn't have been easy. It was far too lovely to put into words. Thank you."

"Thank you? For what?"

"Such a wondrous gift. I shall never forget it as long as I live."

He laughed again, the sound even deeper. "This is only the beginning, my love. You have a thousand more such gifts in store."

A thousand gifts. A thousand nights? She hoped so. She found she desperately hoped so.

"Most women don't find their pleasure the very first time. I knew you were a passionate woman, Jo. But you are a treasure."

Jocelyn smiled and curled against him. When his arm brushed her breast, she started, surprised at the fresh rush of heat that swept through her body. In the candlelight, she arched a brow at the sight of Rayne's thick shaft, once more hard against his belly.

"I know you're probably sore," he said in a voice like rough velvet. "Maybe I should sleep in the other room."

"I believe, my lord, I should like you to kiss me."

"But surely you know that if I do—"

"Unless, of course, you don't want to."

"Good God, you *are* a treasure." With that he rolled her beneath him, coming up on his elbows, his body looming over hers. A delicious long kiss, and he slid himself inside her, catching her up on the same wave of pleasure he had carried her on to before.

It was bliss unlike anything she had prepared for. Passionate. Beautiful. And poignant. Surely what they'd shared was as special for Rayne as it was for her, Jocelyn thought. Surely he had feelings for her, different from what he felt for any of his other women.

The thought made her uncertain future seem hazy and distant. She was happier than she had ever been. She wouldn't let the fears she harbored deep inside ruin the pleasure Rayne had brought her. She would keep them buried in her heart, and surely one day they would disappear.

* * *

By morning Jocelyn's uneasy thoughts had all but faded away. She awoke when a ray of sun slanted in through the curtains. Stretching and yawning, she smiled, thinking of Rayne and the pleasures of the night before. She turned to the place beside her, but he had gone. On the pillow where his head had lain she found a single red rose.

Jocelyn's heartbeat quickened. He had brought it in from the garden. Carried it in just for her.

Gloriously happy, she rolled onto her back, bringing the rose beneath her nose and inhaling the subtle sweet fragrance. He had gone, but he hadn't forgotten. And soon he would return.

He arrived before nightfall, sweeping into the house as he always did, setting the servants into a dither. He ordered supper served upstairs, and Jocelyn flushed to imagine what the household must be thinking. At the table they said very little and ate even less. Then he was kissing her, crushing her against him, turning her around to unbutton her dress. He carried her over to his big four-poster bed and they spent the night making love, sleeping only briefly, then waking to start all over again.

"You've the most glorious hair," he said to her during the hours before dawn. "Black as night. So incredibly thick, yet still soft and silky." His fingers sifted through it, brushing it back from her face. "I would love to see it long and spread about your shoulders."

Jocelyn smiled softly. "Then I shall grow it long just for you."

Rayne bent down and kissed her. "That would be a splendid gift—one I would surely treasure."

Then he was pulling her into his arms again, kissing her mouth, exploring it, trailing moist kisses along her shoulder to her breast.

In minutes she was damp and writhing beneath him, the covers tossed away, Rayne's tall frame pressing her down in the mattress. He slid his hardness inside her, filling her, making her feel complete, and Jocelyn reveled in the pleasure and closeness, the joy that Rayne always brought her.

Jocelyn's life would have been the stuff of dreams if she hadn't worried constantly that it would soon end. Brownie repeatedly warned her, reminding her gently what they both knew of Rayne's past women.

"Sooner or later, the bloom will be off the rose, lass. Ye had better prepare yerself for it."

Jocelyn found herself strangely unwilling to listen. Though part of her knew it must surely be true, another more hopeful part said that nothing as sweet as the two of them shared could possibly be the same as what Rayne had shared with other women.

She clung to that hope fervently and tried to push aside her fears.

If only Rayne's sordid past would let her.

Instead, reminders continued to surface. Like the night they attended a masque at Vauxhall Gardens. Jocelyn had been looking forward to it, excited about dressing as Cleopatra in an extragant off-the shoulder, silver-trimmed gown. Rayne wore his regimental uniform, his shoulders looking broader than ever beneath a pair of gold colonel's epaulets.

Under bright paper lanterns they had waltzed together, as Jocelyn had never done, then strolled into the darkness of the gardens.

Rayne kissed her gently, cupping her cheeks with his hands. He had just pulled away when a cold male voice drifted over them.

"Having a pleasant evening?" Stephen Bartlett, Earl of Harcourt, garbed as Peter the Great, stood on the path beside a lady in a red velvet gown with a thick white ruff and wide panniers.

Jocelyn couldn't see the woman's face beneath her scarlet domino, but her red-tinted lips were finely carved, her body ripe and very nearly bulging from the bodice of her dress.

"Very pleasant, thank you," Rayne said brusquely, "or at least it was."

Jocelyn wore a domino, too, a white one edged in silver, but Harcourt appeared to see right through it.

"And the charming Mrs. Wyndam. One would have no trouble recognizing your lovely . . . attributes in any disguise." He smiled at Jo. "May I present Lady Campden? I don't believe the two of you have met . . . though her ladyship and the viscount are well enough acquainted."

"Quite well enough," the lady in the red gown said. She studied Jocelyn with a too-thorough glance, then turned to Rayne. "So *this* is your latest . . . amusement. She appears to be quite lovely, Rayne. No wonder we've seen so little of you lately."

Rayne's hand covered Jocelyn's fingers as she unconsciously gripped his arm. Her hands had suddenly grown cold, and Rayne's hold tightened protectively.

"Mrs. Wyndam is practically a relative. Her father and mine were friends." That was a lie if ever there was one. Still, it was part of the story they had concocted to avoid a scandal. She was surprised he had gone to so much trouble. "I'm seeing to her welfare until she's settled in."

"How utterly . . . convenient," her ladyship said. She smiled savagely, her lips blood-red in the moonlight. "Since she's such a good friend of the family, I insist she come to Campden House. Lord Campden and I are holding a small soiree a week from Saturday next. It would be our pleasure if both of you would attend."

"I believe Mrs. Wyndam has already made plans," Rayne said smoothly.

"I shall cancel them," Jo said, the woman's arrogance firing her temper. "I should be quite delighted to attend."

For a moment Rayne looked angry. Then acceptance crept into his features, and maybe a hint of respect. Lady Campden had thrown down the gauntlet. Jocelyn had merely picked it up.

"Until Campden House, then." Harcourt made a leg, an amused grin lighting his handsome face.

"I suppose I shouldn't have done that," Jo said as they walked the pathway toward his carriage. "I don't know what came over me. I hope you're not too angry."

He chuckled. "I'm none too pleased, I can tell you. You've thrown me to the hounds and yourself to the wolves, but it was bound to happen, sooner or later."

"What do you mean?"

"I mean her ladyship is an old flame of mine, and Stephen wants badly to seduce you."

"I can handle myself, you may be sure." She stopped on the path and turned to face him. "I promise I shan't embarrass you—if that is your concern."

"Hardly," he scoffed.

"Then it must be the lady." Uncertainty crept into her voice. "I know I lack certain of her ladyship's . . . endowments. Surely I haven't her experience. If you've an assignation with the woman—if you've grown tired of me already—"

"Jocelyn, my love"—Rayne turned her toward him and brushed a soft kiss on her mouth—"you are without doubt the most delightful little minx to cross my path in years. I've only begun to sample your charms; I've hardly had time to grow tired of you. It's wolves like Harcourt who worry me."

"Harcourt! Surely you don't believe I would be interested in a man like him? Why he's—he's—"

"He's what, love?"

He isn't you. "Not my sort, is all."

One corner of his mouth curved up. "I'm very glad to hear it." He kissed her then, so soundly her knees went weak.

Still, she couldn't quite wipe the incident from her mind. Lady Campden was another of Rayne's score of women. That she still felt something for him had been obvious, yet apparently he no longer held feelings for her.

What of her own precarious position? Every hour she spent with him, she gave up a bit more of herself. She was falling in love with him—more every day. But how did Rayne feel? How would she feel if he left her?

It was a terrifying thought, and yet she knew that it could happen.

With every passing day she prayed that it would not.

Chapter Ten

IT ISN'T LOVE, Jocelyn told herself firmly as she lay content and sated beneath the gold silk canopy on Rayne's four-poster bed. Though Rayne had left early that morning, his male scent lingered, the smell of pine soap and a hint of tobacco mixed with the potent aroma of their wild night of pleasure.

It isn't love, it isn't! she repeated for the hundredth time. It was only the newly awakened passions, the unexplored feelings Rayne had unleashed, which she'd never had to deal with before.

All the confusion she had begun to feel, all the fear that suffused her heart, they were nothing more than raw, untried emotions. Sooner or later she would bring them under control.

At least that was what she told herself, even though the rational part of her, the thinking, logical part, told her to beware. As she had from the start, Jocelyn forced the thoughts away, swinging her long legs onto the thick Aubusson carpet, grabbing her beautiful pink silk wrapper and pulling it on, then strolling to the window to gaze down at her lovely little garden.

Rayne cared for her, she was sure he did. He had been good to her, better than any man she had ever known. He pampered her, catered to her every whim—what more could she ask?

Jocelyn turned the brass latch, shoved open the mullioned window and sucked in a breath of sweet clean air. The factory soot didn't suffocate this part of the City. Here life was rich and bountiful, filled with joy and laughter, the hours she spent with Rayne uncommonly sweet.

And no man ever more dear.

She spun at the knock on her door, turning just in time to see him stride in.

"Get dressed," he said, "we're going for a drive in the park. I've something of a surprise for you."

"All right." Filled with happiness that he had returned so quickly, Jocelyn hurried into her bedchamber to find Elsa waiting to begin her toilette. When she had finished half an hour later, Rayne waited at the foot of the stairs.

"What's this all about?" Jo asked.

"I ran across a friend, is all. A painter I met when I served in the army. He has an easel set up in the park."

Lifting her yellow muslin day dress out of the way, a favorite Rayne had ordered to replace the one she had lost the night of the fire, she took his arm and they headed for his carriage.

"I also happened onto the Marquess of Gravenwold." He was Rayne's best friend. "According to Dominic, Lady Campden's spread word of your arrival to half the *ton*. They'll be attending in regimental numbers for her soiree on Saturday."

"I wish I'd kept my mouth shut."

"So do I, but I suppose that's somewhat selfish. You'll probably enjoy yourself." He turned her chin with his hand. "All I ask is that you stay away from Harcourt."

"I told you, the man holds no appeal."

"You don't think he's handsome?"

"Well, certainly he's that, but—"

Rayne's eyes turned dark. "I mean it, Jo."

Jocelyn only smiled. It felt good to know he was jealous, if only just a bit. It was comforting that he should feel some of the same disturbing things she did.

She glanced out the window, beginning to enjoy herself. Beneath an azure sky more beautiful for its fluffy white clouds, Hyde Park sparkled with newly budded leaves and colorful flowers: crocus, tulips, and buttercups. Earth and damp leaves scented the air, cicadas hummed, and bees drank nectar from the throats of beckoning blossoms.

"There he is." Rayne pointed toward a man seated by a small serene pond. "His name is Thomas Keeley."

They climbed down from the carriage and crossed the damp grass to the lean graying man with a long pointed brush between his fingers.

"I'm glad you're still here, Thomas." Rayne shook his friend's slightly paint-smudged hand.

"I'll be painting here all week." Thomas turned an appraising look on Jo. "A lovely creature, Rayne. Have you brought her to sit for a portrait?"

"A portrait?" Jo said. "You want him to paint my picture?"

"Actually, Thomas paints miniatures, when he isn't doing landscapes." Rayne reached across the table and picked up a tiny gold-framed locket. The delicate face of a beautiful blond woman had been carefully painted on the front. Minute pearls ringed the edge, and three tiny diamonds formed stars above the lady's head.

"It's done in enamel," Rayne said. "Every color is separately applied, then fired." He handed her the small piece of jewelry, the thin gold chain draping across her palm.

"It's beautiful."

"Would you like Thomas to do such a portrait of you?"

She glanced back down at the locket. "I would rather have your face painted on the front."

Rayne laughed at that. "I don't think that's a very good idea. I can just image what Harcourt would have to say if he found out."

Jocelyn laughed, too. "I suppose you're right, but still . . ." Her gaze strayed out over the water, then to the easel where a lovely painting of the pond had almost been finished.

"Do you suppose Mr. Keeley could do a painting of the pond on the locket? It's so very lovely here."

Rayne swung his glance in the painter's direction. "Thomas?"

The graying man smiled, then nodded, a look of approval crinkling the lines of his face. "I've never been asked before, but yes, I believe I can do it. I also believe, my friend, that you are in the company of a very special woman."

Rayne's handsome features softened. "That comes as no surprise, I assure you. It's a fact I discovered quite some time ago."

Jocelyn flushed at his words, praying with all her heart that he meant them. A short while later the transaction was completed. The viscount led her back to the carriage and instructed the driver to return them home.

He didn't stay long. Alexandra had been pressing him to enter the Season's round of parties, already in full swing, and he couldn't put her off any longer.

"If all goes well, as soon as you've been introduced at Lady Campden's soiree, you'll receive invitations to other of the Season's affairs. If you should decide to go, I shall endeavor to attend as often as I can."

"I can't image myself in such circumstances, but perhaps in time—"

"Unfortunately, I can only too easily imagine it. I just hope you'll continue to welcome my company once you're the toast of London."

It was flattery, pure and simple, but Jocelyn adored it, just as she did the locket he presented to her a few days later.

"It's lovely." Holding it up by the thin gold chain, she examined the gold-rimmed circle in the lamplight. "Mr. Keeley captured the landscape perfectly, and the tiny diamonds look so beautiful nestled among the clouds." She held it out to him, fighting a mist of tears. "Please, Rayne, help me put it on."

He did so, the beautiful locket cool against her throat,

while his hands at the nape of her neck felt so very warm. That same heat shone in his eyes, a hunger that never seemed to leave him—or her.

"I love it, Rayne." *But not as much as I love you.* The thought terrified her, yet she couldn't deny it was true.

Maybe it was part of the reason for the fight that began that next day.

Rayne had gone out early; he had some unfinished business, he said. On his return, he sent word upstairs she should join him in the study. There was something they needed to discuss.

Jocelyn's stomach tightened. *Sweet God in heaven, was this the moment she had been dreading?* Was he going to tell her he had found somebody new? Her hands were shaking by the time she reached the study, her secret fears surfacing.

"W-What is it?" Entering the wood-paneled, very masculine room in a pale pink jaconet gown, she fluttered the small matching fan.

Rayne glanced up from the *Morning Chronicle* he had been reading, closed the paper and set it aside, then pushed back his chair, rounded the desk and took her hands.

"Why don't we sit down?" He was dressed impeccably in a burgundy tailcoat and light gray breeches, a white piquet waistcoat and cravat.

"Oh, Rayne, what is it? Whatever is wrong?"

"Nothing is wrong, my love. It's only that I've just been speaking with William Dorset, my estate manager at Marden. We met at my solicitor's office earlier this morning."

"I don't understand."

He led her across the room to a tufted leather sofa, urged her to take a seat, then sat down beside her.

"William has been with the Garrick family for more than twenty years. He was at Marden the day your father came. He knew of Sir Henry's earlier visit to see my father at Stoneleigh. He told me exactly what happened."

Jocelyn's throat went dry. She didn't want to think about the past. She was happy, so incredibly happy. She didn't want her father's memory to come between them.

And yet some part of her could not let it go.

"What did he say?"

Rayne shifted on the sofa, his tall frame moving with a hint of unease. "Try to remember the way things were back then. You were a young girl, Jo. You saw your father as a hero—everyone does. But no man is perfect, certainly not Sir Henry."

"I—I don't understand what you're saying."

"William says your father brought much of his destruction upon himself. He says Sir Henry began to drink *before* he lost his pupils. That he started at the time your mother died. William says that as the years went by, his drinking worsened, and that was the reason his pupils began to leave him, the reason he could no longer afford to pay the lease on the cottage."

"But that isn't true!"

Rayne captured her hands. "William says your father was drunk the day he came to Stoneleigh. My brother Christopher had died only the week before, and my father was locked in his study, overcome with grief. Your father burst in, ranting and raving something about being tossed into the streets, and my father ordered him removed from the house. Later, when he arrived at Marden demanding to remain in the cottage, it was William who turned him away. William says that if the circumstances today were the same, he would do it again."

Jocelyn jerked free of his hold. "He's lying! My father was a good man—kind, considerate. Your father's cruelty was his ruination—and mine!"

"After Sir Henry died, my father insisted William check into your guardianship. Your cousin and his wife spoke to him personally, and at the time he believed they would care for you well. Even at that, they were given a small monthly stipend to offset the cost of providing for you. It was done as a gesture of appreciation for the years of service Sir Henry had given the people of Marden before his decline."

Jocelyn surged to her feet. "I don't believe you. It can't be true, it can't be!" She turned away from him and walked to the window. Flowers bloomed in the garden, but Jocelyn barely saw them. She didn't realize she was crying until Rayne came to the place beside her and eased her into his arms.

"Can you not remember some of these things? In the back of your mind, does it not ring with a certain amount of truth?"

She shook her head, her cheek moving back and forth against the thick hard muscles beneath his shirt.

"Sometimes the facts are difficult to accept, Jo. I would have spared you, but I believed this was the only way to set things right between us."

She said nothing more, just straightened her spine and pulled away from him. "You have told me what it is you believe. My opinion happens to differ."

"Jocelyn—"

"On the other hand, you have been kind to me . . . and generous. I should like some time, my lord, to think about what you have said."

Rayne nodded, his expression grim. "Then you shall have it. Remember, Jo, this is all in the past. The problem belonged to our fathers, not to us."

He paused for a moment. "Tomorrow evening is Lady Campden's soiree. You have until then." He smiled softly. "If you have not come to grips with this and set it away from you, then upon my return I shall carry you up to our rooms and make love to you until you have."

Jocelyn said nothing, but she couldn't deny the warm thread of heat that Rayne's words sent through her body. She watched him leave, thinking of all that had happened between them, of her father and what William Dorset had said.

Was it true? Was her father really to blame for the terrible things that had happened? She didn't want to believe it, but if she searched her mind and heart, she knew that at least some of what Dorset had said was the truth.

Her father had begun drinking after her mother died. But he had stopped not many months later. Or had he? She remembered finding bottles of gin in the cupboards that she hadn't known were there. She remembered finding one beneath a box hedge in the garden. But she had rarely seen him drunk.

At least not until that last year. But that was because of Stoneleigh—wasn't it?

She tried to think, tried to remember, but her mind refused to grasp the sequence of events. She had been busy with her friends, the other young girls in the village, busy daydreaming of Martin Carey, the vicar's son. As always when she tried to remember, her mind seemed a jumble of disconnected memories, her thoughts mixed up with the fire and the screams and the roof caving in.

Maybe Rayne was right. Knowing him as she had begun to, she found it difficult to believe his father had been other than a good man. But so was her own father. No one could convince her of anything else.

The real question was, did any of it still matter?

Her father had been dead three years. The third Lord Stoneleigh was also dead. What had happened between the two men was past. Rayne believed it shouldn't affect them. Jocelyn agreed it was their happiness now that was most important.

Her mind still spinning, she left the study and climbed the stairs, heading up to her bedchamber to change out of her pretty pink dress. She would spend the day working in the garden. Tomorrow afternoon Rayne would return.

From this moment forward, she vowed, she would put the past behind her, turn her thoughts to the present and the future. Rayne was all that mattered. Rayne. And the fact that she was desperately, passionately in love with him.

* * *

"Why can't I go with you and Mrs. Wyndam tonight?" Alexandra stood in the entry as the Stoneleigh butler held open the door.

"It just isn't done, Alexandra." Rayne pulled his sister a discreet distance away. "I won't mince words with you, Alex—the woman is my mistress, as I believe you already know. It isn't yet common knowledge to the members of the *ton*, but sooner or later word will creep out. When it does, I don't want your name connected with the two of us."

"But—"

"That's the end of it, Alexandra."

Her bottom lip curled down in a pout. Then she grinned. "Give Mrs. Wyndam my regards."

I intend to give her far more than that. "I shall." Rayne accepted his hat from the butler and made his way out the door. From the moment he had left Jocelyn standing in his study, he had regretted his leaving. He should have had it out with her then and there, then dragged her upstairs to his bed.

Jocelyn was such a passionate little creature, he had no doubt he could make her see the folly of letting the past come between them. At the time, he had thought that giving her a chance to come to grips with her feelings was the wisest course.

Now he worried that her anger might have been turned against him once more, that all her old resentments and misdirected vengeance might resurface.

He wouldn't stand for it, of course. He would have the matter laid to rest, and soon—and Jocelyn once more ensconced in his bed. Still, he wanted to see that special warm glow in her eyes when she looked at him, wanted to feel her fingers slide into his hair as she kissed him. He wanted her warm and willing as she took him into her sleek little body.

Rayne smiled, feeling a mixture of anticipation, determination, and just a hint of trepidation. She would be expecting him. He had sent word ahead of the time of his arrival. He reached the house and searched for her in the drawing room, but she wasn't there.

"She's in your study, milord," the butler said.

Rayne's brow went up. "My study?" Had he really expected her to be waiting in his bed?

"A footman delivered a message of some sort. She was placing it in on your desk."

"Thank you." Rayne walked down the hall and into the book-lined, walnut-paneled study. Jocelyn was bending over his desk, clutching something in her hand.

"Rayne!" At the sound of his heavy footfalls, she whirled toward him, her hand coming away from the desk, pointing in his direction. He caught a flash of silver from the object she gripped in her fingers.

The shot came hard and fast, slamming into his chest, echoing into the room, the pain and the blackness hitting him like a vicious blow to the head.

"Rayne!"

It was the last word to enter his mind as he slumped forward onto the carpet, the fingers over his heart slick and red with blood, knowing his love had killed him. *God, oh God, not Jo.* Disbelieving, yet certain—wishing his soul had departed before he found out. He closed his eyes and let the darkness engulf him, but with each of his shallow heartbeats, he felt the anguish of her betrayal, worse than pain of the bullet, far worse than dying.

And then the pain was no more.

"Rayne! Dear God, Rayne!"

The silver tray slid from her fingers, the message from his sister falling away as Jocelyn raced to kneel beside him, her eyes wild with the horror of what had happened, with the sight of Rayne's blood leaking from his body onto the floor.

She whirled at a soft sound behind her, heard the thud of something heavy on the carpet. It was a pistol, still hot and smoking. She fought to see from where it had come, tried to blink back her tears, but saw only the billowing curtain in front of the open window.

Then the servants were swarming in, shrieking and wailing as they spotted the viscount's fallen body.

"Someone please help him!" Jocelyn cried, heedless of the scalding wetness on her cheeks, deathly afraid it was already too late.

"She did it!" The butler pointed a finger in her direction. "She's the one who shot 'im."

"What?" Around her the room seemed to spin.

"It was her—the viscount's whore! She come into his study and waited for him. She's kilt him, I tell you."

"Look there!" cried one of the scullery maids. "There's the gun she used! Somebody grab 'er!"

"But I didn't do it!" *I love him!* "I wouldn't hurt him!"

"Get her!" cried the butler. They started coming toward her, footmen in livery, servants in black and gold, house maids. She looked for Elsa, hoping the woman she knew best among these strangers would come to her defense, but her little maid was nowhere near.

"I—I didn't do this!" But the pistol rested at her feet, and the viscount lay dead or dying.

Seeing him there so pale and lifeless, a sob welled in her throat, but there was no time for it. Jocelyn spun toward the window. Then she ran.

"Stop her!"

But Jo had run for her life before. At the sill, she hoisted her pale blue muslin skirt, climbed over, and leaped to the ground some distance below. She landed with a jolt, scraped her knees, climbed to her feet and started running again.

The stables—Brownie and Tucker would help her—she only had to reach them.

She slid to a halt, clutching the corner of the building for support. Dear God, what if the constable believed her friends were involved in the shooting? What if Tucker and Brownie were thrown into prison? What if they were hanged?

Tears blinded her, and she wiped at them with the back of a hand.

Sprinting away from the town house, Jocelyn barely heard the voices behind her as she raced down the block and ducked into an alley. An aging donkey pulling a one-horse cart plodded along in front of her. Jo dodged the cart, streaked past the back of a moss-covered church, tried the door, found it locked, and kept on running. She burst onto Grosvenor Street, crossed St. George, passing a row of merchants selling brooms, shoelaces, socks, then a woman selling apples.

"There she is!" someone shouted, and a fresh jolt of terror clutched her heart. "The black-haired whore in the pale blue dress. She's a murderer, she is!"

Jocelyn's heart leapt into her throat. *A murderer! Sweet God, Rayne must truly be dead.*

Her throat closed up, and as much as she feared for her safety, her mind whirled with thoughts of him. Had no one been able to help him? Was he in pain? Was he asking for her? How could she have left him? They were thoughts that tortured her mind as she flattened herself against the wall of the alley, gasping for breath, her lungs burning, her sides aching.

On Brook Street she turned east again, desperate to reach her old neighborhood, terrified that they would catch her first. Into another alley, this one rotten with sewage, the smell overwhelming, the stench of a dead cat, her slippers sliding on the muck of stagnant water, the wet seeping in, ruining the soft blue kid leather.

Rayne had bought them for her. *Rayne.* His name echoed in her mind, and the pain was overwhelming. *Please don't leave me!* It was the last thought she had as she rounded the corner of an ale house and ran headlong into three of the constable's men.

Chapter Eleven

"How is he?"

Alexandra looked up to see Catherine Edgemont, Marchioness of Gravenwold, walking beside her handsome dark-skinned husband down the second-floor hall of the town house. The tall, imposing man was Rayne's best friend.

"Oh, Catherine." Standing just outside her brother's door, Alex went into the red-haired woman's arms and they tightened around her. More tears came, the flood an endless stream since Rayne had been shot.

"It's all right, Alex," the beautiful woman soothed. "Dominic and I are here, and we intend to stay until your brother is back on his feet."

Alexandra tried to smile at the hopeful words, but her lips seemed unwilling to cooperate and a sob caught in her throat.

Gravenwold turned to the short gray-haired surgeon. "I presume you're Dr. Chandler."

"That is correct."

"What can you tell us of Rayne's condition?"

"I'm afraid it doesn't look good. It's a chest wound, you know. Very messy. There's considerable pain, as you might imagine. We were able to extract the lead ball, but the bleeding's been quite extensive. He's weak, and extremely distraught over . . . what has occurred."

"Have they been able to piece together what actually happened?"

"Somewhat. He's been awake off and on. The constable questioned him as much as he dared, considering the severity of the injury. He also questioned the servants and Alexandra, of course. Which disclosed the fact that the woman who posed as Jocelyn Wynham had earlier been with the viscount at Stoneleigh. Her real name is Jocelyn Asbury."

A muscle ticked in Dominic's cheek. He knew about the woman. Rayne had spoken of her at length the last time Dominic had seen him. "What else have they learned?"

"Theophilus Finch, the viscount's coachman, claims the woman tried to kill his lordship twice before. Once just outside Boodle's, and again outside Lord Dorring's, when the viscount arrived for his weekly game of cards."

Catherine handed Alexandra a handkerchief, and she dabbed it against her eyes. "Farthington, our butler, says Rayne brought the woman in right off the streets," Alexandra said. "The night she arrived, she was wearing a pair of ragged men's breeches. Rayne borrowed several of my gowns just to clothe her. He bought her this house. He treated her like a lady, for God's sake—and look at the way she's repaid him!" Alex started to cry again, and Catherine hugged her once more.

"Where have they taken her?" Dominic asked.

"Newgate, I imagine." The doctor's face looked grim. "The coachman insists there were two men also involved. The servants here believe them to be the same two the viscount had recently taken into his employ."

"Where are these men now?"

"Gone. Vanished practically into thin air. Regretfully, there is no evidence to suggest they were anywhere near the scene at the time of the shooting."

"Rayne said nothing to implicate them?"

"No. He's only mentioned the girl." The doctor removed the quizzing glass he had been wearing, letting it dangle from the thin black band around his neck. "If you've other questions, maybe his lordship can give you the answers. He's been asking for you."

Dominic took an anxious step toward the door. "Is it all right to go on in?"

The graying man stuffed the quizzing glass into the pocket of his blue-striped waistcoat. "Be as brief as possible. Don't say or do anything that might upset him."

Dominic took a steadying breath, lifted the latch on the bedchamber door and strode in.

As quietly as he could, ignoring the metallic smell of old blood and the acrid odor of sickness, he sat down at his best friend's bedside. Rayne's usually dark-tanned face looked waxy pale, and his breathing sounded shallow and raspy. His eyes were closed, and tendrils of reddish-brown hair clung damply to his forehead and temples. Already the freshly applied bandages on his chest had begun to soak through with blood.

"Dominic?" It was not much more than a whisper, and Dominic's stomach clenched at the raspy, pain-filled voice.

"I'm right here, my friend." He clasped Rayne's wide tanned hand, but the answering grip felt weak and unsteady.

"I'm . . . glad you've come."

"I got here as fast as I could."

Rayne moved his head in the semblance of a nod. "It was Jocelyn," he said thickly.

"I know."

"Where . . . have they taken her? No one would tell me."

"Newgate, most likely. That would be the usual course."

The line around Rayne's mouth grew whiter than it was already, and his face looked gray and grim. "She . . . blamed me for . . . what happened to her father. Long story. Remind me to tell you . . . sometime."

"I'll do that." Dominic swallowed against the tightness

that had risen in his throat. "Just as soon as you're back on your feet."

Rayne gave a second slight nod of his head. His eyes slid closed. "I don't want her . . . to hang. I know I . . . shouldn't care. Part of me would even . . . like to see it. But another part . . ." He opened his eyes with an effort and looked into Dominic's face. "Get her out of there, Dom. See she's sent away somewhere. Do whatever it takes."

Dominic wanted to argue. He wanted to see the woman rot in hell for what she had done. "Are you certain that's what you want? The woman tried to kill you, Rayne." *May even yet succeed.*

"I can't stand to think of her in there . . . in that god-awful place. I know what it's like . . . in a place like that."

"She belongs in there. She's got to pay for what she's done."

Rayne came up on an elbow so swiftly, Dominic hadn't the chance to stop him. "Promise me, damn you! No matter what happens—promise me!"

"All right, Rayne—take it easy." He eased his friend back down. "You know I'll do it. Anything."

"Thank you." Rayne relaxed on the bed. "There's . . . just one more thing."

"Of course."

"If this goes the worse . . . if I don't make it—"

"You'll make it, damn it!"

"If I don't . . . promise me you'll watch out for Alexandra."

The ache in Dominic's throat grew more painful. "That goes without saying. She'll move in with Catherine and me. As a matter of fact, we'll be staying here with her until you've recovered."

Deep brown eyes fixed on his face. "Is that really going to happen? I want you to tell me the truth."

Dominic's hold on Rayne's hand grew tighter. "The truth is, a lot of it depends on you. I know what kind of

fighter you are. If you want to lick this thing, you will. I
want you to. All of us do. But you've got to want it, too."

"What . . . makes you think I don't?"

"We've been friends a long time, Rayne. I know how
you felt about the woman. I saw it in your face whenever
you mentioned her."

Rayne's eyes slid closed once more. For a long time he
said nothing. When he finally spoke, Dominic had to lean
close to hear him.

"I told you a man was a fool to fall in love." Then his
grip on Dominic's hand grew slack, and he drifted into a
fitful, pain-filled sleep.

Jocelyn Asbury pulled the tattered woolen blanket more
closely around her shoulders. It was cold in the tiny dark
cell, so incredibly cold. She shivered, feeling the wetness
between her toes, her slippers soaked clear through from
the pool of stagnant water that covered the rough stone
floor. The air smelled fetid and damp. The odor of human
excrement and unwashed bodies nearly overwhelmed
her.

With only the light of a single small candle, it was dark
in the cell she occupied, alone except for the roaches and
spiders, but her journey into the depths of the prison had
revealed a multitude of thieves, footpads, cutthroats, prostitutes, and beggars. The starving and the homeless, the
ruthless and those just fighting to survive, all of them
were wearing out their lives like a tattered woolen shirt.

Now, once more, she was one of them.

Jocelyn sank down on a battered three-legged stool and
lifted her wet freezing feet onto one of the rungs. Except
for a soggy straw mattress and the chamber pot in one
darkened corner, the stool was the only item in the room.

She tucked her thin muslin skirt beneath her, trying to
stem the cold, trying in vain to stop her teeth from chat-
tering. She still wore her pale blue muslin dress, torn now
in several places, the row of embroidered flowers beneath

her bosom hanging limply below, with several more dangling from the hem.

That she wore the gown at all was a miracle, or at least a miracle in the form of a dear friend named Brownie, whom she suspected had paid the garnish—money for the guards to ensure a minimum of care.

Pay or strip was the rule. Brownie had arrived even before she had been dragged in, the constable's men handling her roughly, one of them blatantly fondling her breasts.

"Some bloke paid ye garnish," a beefy guard had told her with a leer. "Wish to Christ he 'adn't. 'Ad a mind to see what ye 'ad beneath yer foine lady's clothes."

But the money had been paid and the guard had been true to his word and left her alone. There was coin enough for a cell to herself, to ensure a bit of food, moldy and full of weevils, but sustenance just the same, and even a single small candle. Coin enough that she wondered where Brownie had stolen it.

She wondered where he was and if he and Tucker had escaped the fury brought on by the shooting.

She thought of Rayne and wondered if he was dead.

Her throat closed up as she remembered his pale, still body, his shallow breathing, his lifeblood leaking onto the carpet. She thought of him and her heart ached and she wanted to cry, but she couldn't. Not one droplet had fallen from the moment she had been taken by the constable's men. She had been too numb for tears, too bleak, too desolate.

Even now, as she heard footfalls approaching, she felt too dazed to rouse herself. The big iron key grated in the rusty lock.

"Get yerself out here, me foine lit'le piece. It's a visitor ye be 'avin'."

She gripped her blanket, suddenly hopeful, and walked through the door, her heart thrumming loudly in her ears. Was Rayne all right, then? Had he told them the truth of what had happened? Had they come to set her free?

Her pulse beat wildly as they led her toward the front of the prison, past the underfed and overcrowded, along the dank and filthy corridor that smelled worse than any Southwark gutter, her hands trembling with uncertainty, yet her heart alive with hope and expectation.

Then she saw that her visitor was Brownie, saw the tight-strained creases on his dear life-worn face, and knew that her hopes were dashed.

"Brownie!" She ran to him as the guard closed the door behind them, locking both of them in, and the stout man caught her against him. Tears threatened, but now was not the time to let them fall.

"Are ye all right, gel? They 'aven't 'urt ye, 'ave they?"

Yes, she wanted to scream. *My heart hurts. The pain is nearly unbearable.* But she couldn't tell him of the terrible ache she felt. Couldn't tell him that her grief and the terror of her confinement were nearly overwhelming.

Instead she shook her head and pulled away to look at him, forcing herself to smile. "No, they didn't hurt me. It was you who paid the garnish, wasn't it?"

He grinned, though not with mirth. "Got it from 'is bloody lordship 'imself. Me and Tuck meant to foist it if ever things went wrong. Well, they bleedin' well did."

"I-Is Rayne . . ." Her chest constricted. She bit her lip to keep it from trembling. "I-Is he dead?" Every beat of her heart seemed to slow as she waited for the answer.

"Not bloody yet," Brownie said. "Ye nearly kilt 'im, but he's a strong un', 'e is."

"I didn't shoot him!" *I love him!* "I never would have hurt him. I thought you knew that."

Brownie eyed her a moment. "Ye didn't shoot the blighter?"

"No, of course not." *And he's still alive!* Her heart seemed to beat with a strong steady rhythm for the first time in days.

"If ye weren't the one, who the bloody 'ell was?"

"I—I don't know. God's truth, I've wondered, but now

that I've come to know him, I can't believe anyone would want to hurt him."

"Well, someone bloody well wants 'im dead."

Who *had* shot Rayne? She'd been too numb to wonder. There was Stephen Bartlett, of course, maybe even the actress, Bartlett's mistress. Or perhaps Lady Campden in some sort of jealous temper.

"I don't know who did it, Brownie, but if Rayne isn't dead, he can tell them it wasn't me." She clutched his arm, feeling a fresh shot of hope. "Don't you see, Brownie? This is all a terrible mistake, and as soon as Rayne gets better, he'll straighten everything out."

The ray of hope grew brighter. Rayne would get well. She would be out of this hellish place, Rayne would come for her and everything would be just as wonderful as it was before.

Brownie cleared his throat. He looked a little uncertain, but Jo didn't care. Rayne was alive. Alive! It was the only thing that mattered.

"I'll see the guard gets more blunt. Enough to keep ye safe till things get cleared up and ye can get out. Hide these last few coins fer ye'self. Ye never know when they might come in 'andy."

She slid them down the front of her dress. "You said you took the money from the viscount. How did you know where it was?"

"Weren't 'ard to figure. 'E was bound to keep a few quid someplace, most likely in 'is study. Wouldn't 'ave touched it if things 'ad worked out between you and 'im."

"They don't know you stole it, do they? You and Tuck aren't in trouble, too?"

"'Aven't seen the lad. 'E must o' took to the street same as me, just as soon as 'e seen there was trouble."

Brownie poked a finger between the buttons of his course linen shirt and scratched an itch on his stomach. "Don't think they're lookin' for us, though. Constable believes yer the one guilty o' the deed. But ye can bet I'll keep an eye just the same."

"Everything is going to be all right, Brownie. All we have to do is pray for Rayne to get well."

The beefy man rested a gentle hand on her cheek. She could feel the calluses and the groove of an ancient scar.

" 'Aven't prayed for nothin' in years, gel. But if it'll get ye outta this 'ell 'ole, I'll pray till me knees is bloody."

Jocelyn smiled for the first time since that awful shot had been fired in the viscount's study. She leaned into Brownie's hand and covered it with her own. "Rayne will get well, I know he will. When he does, he'll take care of everything."

Brownie said nothing, just turned at the sound of the big metal key opening the lock on the door. In silence Jocelyn moved past him, following the guard back toward her cell.

"Yer mighty popular, missy. Couldn't be yer hoistin' them foine lady's skirts o' yer's, could it?" It was the guard again.

Three days had passed since Brownie's visit. "Someone else is here?"

The guard turned the key and jerked open the heavy iron door. He was a fat man, balding, with a fringe of dirty brown hair, little pig eyes, and a beard.

"A gentl'man, this time. Handsome bloke, he is. Ye best be mindin' yer manners."

A gentleman. Not Rayne; he couldn't possibly have come. Had he sent someone in his stead? Had they finally come to release her? Again hope soared. She followed the guard down the corridor, working her fingers nervously through her hair, wishing she could somehow make herself presentable.

They passed the place the guard had taken her before, leaving the common side of the prison and entering the masters' side. The criminals here were a cut above those on the other side—or at least they had more blunt.

"In here," the guard said, jerking open a low wooden door.

The room was well-lit, she saw, aglow with tall candles and furnished with a stout wooden table and chairs. She stopped as she spotted the black-haired man standing with his back to her on the opposite side, his hands clasped tightly behind him. He turned at her approach.

Gravenwold. It had to be. Dark eyes, dark skin. Rayne had spoken of him often. Heart thundering, Jocelyn sank into a curtsy, terrified that something had happened.

"Do you know who I am?"

"Lord Gravenwold," she said, moving toward him, "Rayne's friend."

"That's right."

"He isn't . . . he isn't—"

"No. At least not yet." Hard black eyes fixed on her face with a look so cold she shivered. "But even as we speak, his life hangs in the balance."

She grabbed the back of a wooden chair and clung to it for support. "Dear God in heaven."

"Such concern. I wouldn't have expected it. But then if you hadn't been a talented little actress, Rayne would not be lying near death."

"W-What! Surely you don't think I shot him!"

The skin grew taut over his high cheekbones. "Your act is extremely touching, Mrs. Wyndam . . . or is it Miss Asbury? But the fact of the matter is, my friend has been gravely wounded, and you, madam, are to blame."

"But I didn't shoot him! Once Rayne is well, he'll be able to tell you what happened." She leaned across the big wooden table, imploring him to see that she spoke the truth. "Rayne can tell you himself that I was not the one."

"I'm afraid, Miss Asbury, that you've miscalculated on that score. You see, his lordship has already regained consciousness on several different occasions. He clearly named you as his assailant."

"But Rayne wouldn't do that! He couldn't!"

"I assure you, he has."

"I don't believe you. You're lying! I thought you were his friend."

"I am his friend. I'm also a man who believes in justice. If it weren't for Rayne, I would gladly see you hang."

She sank down on the chair, trembling all over, fighting a sweep of nausea and trying to gather her thoughts. "If you believe I'm guilty, then why have you come?"

"To put it bluntly, I'm here to give you a choice: You may remain here in the masters' side of the prison to await trail for attempted murder, assuming Rayne recovers, or you may plead guilty, receive a ten-year sentence—life imprisonment should he die—and be transported for your offense."

"T-Transported?"

His look remained hard. "Jamaica, most likely. Since the importation of slaves is no longer allowed, there's a considerable demand for convict labor."

"But I—I didn't shoot him," she said weakly.

"If that is the truth, then I would suggest you stand trial. If you're innocent, you'll be acquitted."

Trial or transportation. Jocelyn's throat closed up. *God, oh God, this couldn't be happening!* But it was.

She wanted to protest, to tell him how unfair all of this was, but the ache in her throat kept the words locked away. When had life ever been fair to her? Certainly not since her father died. Things had been different since she had been with Rayne. Now it seemed even he had turned against her.

"If you would like some time to decide, I shall return in a day or two and you may give me your decision then." The marquess started around the table toward the door.

"No." Jocelyn wet her lips, suddenly so dry she could barely speak. "You may have my decision now." As if she really had one. How could she risk standing trial when no one knew who the real culprit was? When she had no way to prove her innocence? Going to trial would be hopeless. She had no evidence, the servants had condemned her, and even Rayne believed her guilty.

"I'll accept your offer of transportation. We both know I have no other choice."

The marquess's thick black brow went up. He eyed her a moment, then bowed stiffly, his face an emotionless mask. "As you wish. I shall attend the details myself." He started walking again, his burgundy tailcoat and stark white shirt in contrast to the rough gray walls of the prison. Passing her wordlessly, he nodded to the guards, who pulled open the low wooden door.

"I should like you to know, my lord," Jocelyn said to his tall retreating figure, "that I did not shoot his lordship. He was . . . extremely dear to me. I had hoped that he might . . . harbor certain warm feelings in return. After what he has said, it is obvious to me that he does not now, nor did he ever. Still, I wish him Godspeed in his recovery. I pray you will tell him."

The marquess said nothing, just ducked his dark head beneath the low wooden frame and continued out the door.

As the rotund guard strode back in, Jocelyn lifted her chin and forced herself up from the chair. It took all her will, all her formidable determination, not to sink down onto the cold stone floor and succumb to her despair.

Her eyes filled with tears, but she wiped them away, determined the guard would not see them.

"Ye've a new cell, ducks. Pretty fancy fer a murderer."

"The viscount isn't dead."

"Same as—you shoot one o' them foine English bluebloods."

Jocelyn said nothing, just let him guide her down the corridor and into her new, slightly less dismal cell. But inside, her heart was breaking. She had been so hopeful—so naive. She had trusted him, looked up to him as she never had another man. She had loved him.

The price for it was going to be the highest she had ever paid.

"How is he?" Dominic asked Catherine as he joined her in their bedchamber, just down the hall from where Rayne lay in a feverish sleep.

"As good as can be expected, under the circumstances. His fever's still high. We've been bathing him in cold water." Her husband looked tired, she noticed, and worried for his friend. Catherine's heart went out to him.

"Is the doctor still with him?"

"Yes. Alexandra's at his bedside. Poor thing's had even less sleep than we have."

Still wearing the burgundy tailcoat he had worn to the prison, Dominic crossed the room and pulled the curtains, trying to cut out some of the bright late afternoon sunlight.

"Maybe we can get a few hours of sleep before supper," he said, returning to her side.

"I hope little Randall is sleeping all right. This is the first time he's been this long without us."

Dominic tilted her chin with his hand. "Our son is doing just fine. He has an excellent wet nurse, and a nanny who spoils him rotten. It's his mother and father who can't seem to get along without him."

Catherine smiled into his splendid dark eyes. Then her warm smile faded. "Did you see her?"

Dominic nodded. "I don't want Alexandra to find out. I know she wouldn't approve. Neither do I, for that matter, but it's what Rayne wants, so that is the way it will be."

"What did she say?" Catherine asked.

"Exactly what I would have expected. That she is innocent of the charges." Dominic sank down in an overstuffed chair in front of the hearth, and Catherine walked up behind him. She settled her hands on his broad shoulders and began to massage the tension from the muscles in his neck.

"I take it you didn't believe her."

"I told her if indeed she was telling the truth, she should remain here in London and wait to stand trial."

"And?"

"She accepted the offer of transportation instead."

"Then she must be guilty."

"She's guilty, all right. Rayne told the constable she

turned the gun on him the moment he stepped into the study. They'd had a disagreement the day before, something to do with her father." He raked a hand through his sleek black hair. "Rayne is no fool. I can't believe she duped him so completely."

"Are you certain there can be no other answer? No chance that Rayne and the servants could be mistaken?"

"God knows I wish there were. But the evidence seems conclusive."

"Did you have a chance to speak to the magistrate?"

He nodded. "And the captain of the *Sea Demon*. They'll be transporting a load of women prisoners to Jamaica the end of the month."

Catherine sighed. "I feel so terrible for him. From what you've told me, I think Rayne was half in love with her."

"She certainly took him in."

"All that hatred bottled up inside her. She must be twisted in some way."

"She seemed perfectly normal to me." He shook his head, a sleek black lock of hair falling softly over his forehead. "She said he was very dear to her. That she wished him Godspeed in his recovery. She asked me to tell him."

"Will you?"

"I don't know. I don't want to upset him any more than he is already."

"I just hope he can hang on until his fever breaks. The surgeon believes if that happens, he'll have a fighting chance."

Dominic just nodded. When he arose, Catherine slid her arms around his neck. "Make love to me, Dominic. Make me forget all this sadness—at least for a while."

He didn't answer, just kissed her hungrily, needing to ease his own pain as well. Then he was lifting her up, carrying her across the room toward the big feather bed.

The strength of their loving would renew them. Catherine wished she could lend some of that strength to their friend.

Chapter Twelve

WEARING A COURSE BROWN LINEN SKIRT and simple white homespun blouse, clothes she and the others had been given for the long sea voyage ahead, Jocelyn stood at the rail of the ship, *Sea Demon.*

The hundred-foot, full-rigged brigantine plowed clumsily into the open sea. It was a battered old tub, stripped of all but necessities, the hold converted to sleeping quarters where a hundred twenty convict women had been crammed in.

Dry-eyed and emptyhearted, Jocelyn watched the distant shoreline become a fading speck on the horizon, no more than the merest dark shadow above the blue-gray sea. The distant ridge spoke nothing of home or the people she had grown to love, wrenched away from her now just as her family once had been.

What she would suffer, she could not know. What cruel treatment she would receive for her supposed crimes, what hardships she must bear for the next long years, she could only imagine. But this time she was no green girl to wind up starving in the streets, no innocent young virgin to succumb to the promise of future, of happiness . . . of love.

Jocelyn felt the wind caress her skin, sweep her hair against her cheek, and thought of another such gentle touch. The brush of warm fingers on her breast, the feather soft press of firm male lips.

Rayne.

His lies had convicted her. He had abandoned her, betrayed her. And yet she missed him with a searing pain that was worse than any agony she had ever suffered, any misery she might suffer yet.

Why had he done it? What had he gained?

Only one answer surfaced, and it was as galling as the rest. The viscount's interest in her had waned, just as Brownie had warned her. Though he had certainly not planned his own assault, it hadn't taken long for him to seize the opportunity it presented. The shooting was an easy way for him to be rid of her. And by far the cheapest.

The five thousand pounds and the lease on the house were no longer a problem. She was exiled from the City. Brownie and Tucker had gone underground, and even if they hadn't, they would never dispute the word of a nobleman. It would do them no good if they did.

Rayne had abandoned her, just as he had the others. But for all her pain, all her despair, her heart still ached for him. Or at least for the bittersweet memories she still carried. She worked to bury thoughts of him, as she had from the moment the black-eyed marquess had come to her in the prison.

And yet she could not forget.

"You've ten more minutes!" the first mate called out. Above his head sailors climbed into the rigging. Sea gulls circled the stern, screeching and cawing, and a cold wind whipped the huge canvas sails. "Ten more minutes, then it's back to your quarters."

They had been told the rules: Two hours each morning and two each afternoon, they would be brought up in groups and allowed to walk the foredeck. The rest of the time, they must remain in the hold. There were bunks down there, shoulder-wide and stacked seven deep, with barely a foot of room between them. A long wooden table ran the length of the hold, and sooty whale-oil lanterns provided what dim yellow light they needed to see.

The women were all dressed alike, though they came in every size, shape, and color. Most were English, but there were also Scots, Welsh, French, Italian, several blackamoors, and even a lone Spanish woman. They were thieves, beggars, prostitutes—or worse. Old, young, feeble, strong, they all had one thing in common—the courts had found them guilty.

"What's yer name, ducks?" A buxom older woman with a mane of thick white hair strolled up to the rail beside her. "They call me Dolly. Dolly Whitehead." She extended a thick fleshy hand, and Jo shook it.

"Jocelyn Asbury."

"What ya in fer?"

For a moment Jo didn't answer. "Attempted murder," she finally said, with an unconscious squaring of her shoulders.

The woman named Dolly just chuckled, rippling her flabby girth. "Wouldn'ta pegged ya for somethin' like that. Ya hardly look more'n a girl."

Jocelyn thought of Rayne, deathly pale and slumped on the floor. "I didn't really shoot him. It was all a mistake."

"Sure it was, lamby. Just the way it was with the rest of us gels."

She started to deny it, but what good would it do? None, she knew, and prayed in time she would accept the hand fate had dealt her.

She wondered how long it would take to accept Rayne's betrayal.

"How many weeks till we get to Jamaica?" she asked the heavy older woman, searching for a change of subject.

"Somewhere's 'round six, I figure. God willin' and a stiff wind at our tail."

Six weeks, maybe more. In their cramped and dismal quarters it would seem more like six years.

"Time's up, ladies! Let's move it now. Get yourselves below."

"I suppose we best be goin'." As Dolly started to walk away, Jocelyn turned to see a tall brawny seaman coming toward her. He was bare-chested, except for the red scarf tied around his thick neck, barefooted, and sun-browned the color of polished teak. Muscles bulged in arms as big as a stout tree branch; his course black hair had been braided into a queue.

"Better snap to, lassie. Cap'n's real finicky about his rules bein' broken."

Jocelyn nodded, grateful for the note of friendliness in the man's deep voice. Something about him reminded her of Brownie, and she smiled at him with warmth.

The big seaman smiled back, taking in her wavy black hair and bright blue eyes. "You wouldn't be the Asbury woman, would you?"

"I'm Jocelyn Asbury."

"I'm Meeks," he said. "Second mate aboard this ship. Cap'n's give orders to see you get special treatment. An extra blanket, a little extra food and the like. He asked me to keep an eye on you."

"Why is that?"

"Gentleman come to see him. High and mighty aristocrat. He paid the cap'n to see you safely to Jamaica."

Gravenwold. Rayne's conscience. Did the viscount really believe spreading his blunt here and there would make up for the terrible damage his lies had done?

"I'm not a fool, Mr. Meeks," Jocelyn replied. "I'll take whatever extra I can get and not regret it for a moment. I've no one on this earth to look after me but myself, and I learned a long time ago, 'Pride goeth before a fall.' "

The sailor grinned even more broadly. "Not all of it, I'm thinkin'. I suspect you've a good bit of it along that stiff little spine a yours." He chuckled to himself, rippling the muscles across his chest. "You best get goin' now. You can come up after supper for a while, if you've a mind to."

"Thank you, I'd like that."

"I'll have to fetch you. Otherwise, the men will think you're travelin' to the fo'c'sle to give 'em a taste of scut."

Jo flushed. She couldn't help it. Rayne had pulled her out of the seamy side of life; it was hard to accept that she had slid back in.

"Beggin' your pardon, miss," the second mate said, and Jo noticed that his lantern-jawed face had turned red, too.

"It's all right, Mr. Meeks."

" 'Tisn't right, miss, and you won't be hearin' it comin' from me lips again. Off with you now, before Mr. Dearling gets wind of you."

"Who's Mr. Dearling?"

"First mate and master-at-arms. Best stay away from him, lass. He can be a mean one, he can."

Heeding the second mate's words, Jocelyn walked among the women returning down the ladder into the musty belowdecks' enclosure.

In the dim light of the hold, some of them sat at the long wooden table playing cards; others reclined in their tiny, suffocating bunks. As Jocelyn approached the berth she had earlier been assigned—one of the choicest, she realized—it was occupied by somebody else. The black-haired, dark-skinned Spanish girl Jo had noticed when she first came aboard propped her bare feet on the extra blanket Mr. Meeks had mentioned.

"I'm afraid you'll have to move," Jo said. "That's the bunk I've been assigned. If I recall correctly, yours is the one on the top."

The pretty girl's dark eyes narrowed. "I think it is *you* who are mistaken. The bunk on the top—she is yours."

In the last three years, since her father died, Jocelyn had been down this disturbing path more than once. It wasn't the bunk or even the pillow and blanket. It was the fact that if one of the women took something of hers, others would try to do the same. She stepped toward the woman on the bed and leaned close.

"The bleedin' bunk is mine," she said, purposely sliding

into the thickest cockney she knew. "Move y' lazy arse outta it, before I move it for y'."

The Spanish woman's eyes went wide. She edged her way out of the narrow bed and came to her feet in front of Jo. She stood a little bit shorter, but she was heavier, more lushly built.

"I am warning you, *puta*. The bunk, she is mine." She propped her hands on her hips and tossed back her raven-black hair. "I have no love for you, *Inglés*. It would please me to teach one of you a lesson."

Jocelyn stiffened, her hands unconsciously balling into fists. "Just y' bloody well try it."

For the first time the Spanish girl looked uncertain. Her fists were clenched, but her eyes darted nervously around the room as if she were searching for someone.

"Stop it—the both of yas—right this minute!" That came from Dolly Whitehead, who stepped between the two women. "Conchita, you get back up in that bunk where you belong. Jo—you take yourself off for a walk, such as ya can down here in this stinkin' hole. We gotta put up with each other for the next six weeks—maybe longer. This ain't a good beginnin'."

Jo half expected the Spanish girl to turn on the older woman. Instead she looked chagrined.

"Go on now," Dolly urged, and the young girl hoisted her skirts and climbed to the bunk at the top.

Jocelyn started walking, more than willing to keep her end of the bargain.

"Don't pay Chita no mind," Dolly said, coming up beside her. "She's got that hot Spanish temper, ya know, but for the most part she's a good girl."

"I take it the two of you are friends."

"Of a sort, I guess. We met in prison. Kinda took to each other, mother and daughter like. She's real lonely, ya know."

Aren't we all, Jo thought, but didn't say so.

"She's in for stealin', but the truth is, her damnable temper's the reason she's here. She come to England with her mama, but the old bat run off and left her. She was doin' a fair job of fendin' for herself, workin' as a chambermaid till she and the mistress of the house come to disagree."

"Don't tell me," Jo said with heavy sarcasm, "she tried to steal the lady's bed."

Dolly laughed. "Weren't that. Seems the woman come down a little too hard on her young'un's. Beat 'em with a birch rod till they bled. Chita loved them children. She knocked the holy bejesus outta the woman. Told her she had best leave them kids alone. They come for her the next day."

"I see." Jo fell silent. If Chita loved children that much, she couldn't be all bad.

They reached the front of the hold, heard the frothing of waves against the hull through the thick damp timbers, and paused.

"I'll see she keeps outta your way, I promise ya. You won't have to worry about her givin' ya no more trouble."

Jo sighed. "If there's one thing I don't want any more of, it's trouble."

Dolly smiled as she left. Jocelyn noticed the remnants of pox scars dotted her throat and disappeared beneath the collar of her blouse. Jo walked for a while longer, weaving her way among the throng of women, her mind on the Spanish girl who had also been betrayed. At least they had that much in common.

She grew pensive as she thought of Rayne, her chest growing tight with the too-familiar ache. Why had he done it? How could he abandon her so completely? Which woman did he share his bed with now? The questions were endless.

When she returned to her tiny airless bunk, wedged in between six other women, she climbed up feeling heartsick and lonesome, memories of Rayne still clouding her mind and heart. Images of their days together engulfed her. Rayne in his soot-blackened clothes lifting a helpless child into the back of a wagon. Rayne laughing at some-

thing she had said, the sound of his voice rich and warm.
Rayne hauling her across the roof to safety, his hands incredibly strong yet immeasurably gentle.

She thought of him as he had been the night she welcomed him to her bed, so tall and impossibly handsome.
She hadn't forgotten a single detail of his face, a line of his
hard-muscled body. In the darkness of the hold, she felt as
if she could reach out and touch him, could feel his thick
chest pressing her down on the bunk, the heat of his
mouth as he kissed her.

She tossed and turned, alternately burning for him and
hating him, always hungering for him, always missing him.

In the darkness, she touched the locket she wore beneath her thin white cotton nightgown. She had hidden it
from the guards by poking a small hole in the hem of her
dress and stuffing it inside. She wore it now beneath her
clothes, and every time she touched it, she thought of
him. She should get rid of it, she knew, rid herself of the
painful memories it wrought, but she could not bring herself to part with it.

Her hand slid lower, down to her breast, and for a moment she pretended it was Rayne's hand touching her,
caressing her. She bit her lip against the trembling that
started in her body and the jolt of desire that came so
swift and hot through her veins.

It was all she could do not to move her hand lower, to
touch herself as he had, to soothe the terrible ache that
thoughts of him brought. But she knew the heat would
not leave her. Only Rayne could douse the flames.

Only Rayne.

Jocelyn turned her head toward the rough wooden wall
of the ship. Rayne's handsome face smiled down at her,
his brown eyes warm and gentle. Rayne.

For the first time since she had left the prison, Jocelyn
started to cry.

"It's good to see you, Dominic. I'm glad you stopped by."
Dressed in fawn breeches and a white linen shirt, Rayne

led his tall dark friend over to the brown leather sofa in front of the hearth.

"I hoped I would hear from you." Dominic sat down on the sofa. "When I didn't, I decided I had better find out why."

"I guess I have been keeping to myself a bit," Rayne evaded. After his fever had broken, he had begun the long, tedious road to recovery. As soon as he'd been able, he had moved from his town house back to Stoneleigh on Hampstead Heath. He didn't want to remain in the rooms he had shared with Jocelyn.

He didn't want to remember.

"I hope you know how much Alexandra and I appreciate the way you and Catherine stepped in and took care of things."

"You would have done no less for me. That's what friends are for."

Rayne crossed stiffly to the carved walnut sideboard, his wound still not completely healed. He picked up a crystal snifter. "Brandy?"

"Sounds good."

Rayne poured them both a glass, handed one to Dominic, then seated himself in the overstuffed chair across from his friend.

"You're certainly looking better than you were the last time I saw you." Dominic sipped his brandy. "Alexandra must be taking good care of you."

Looking better? That wasn't exactly the truth. He looked healthier, of course; the pallor had gone from his skin, and he'd regained some weight. But there were smudges beneath his eyes, and his cheeks remained hollow and pale, the tan long faded from his usually sun-browned complexion.

He had stayed indoors more than he usually did. His back ached constantly where the lead ball had exited his body, and he hadn't been able to sleep.

"You're right about Alex." Rayne smiled. "She watches over me like an old mother hen. My father used to say, something good comes of everything. Alex has been so worried about me, she hasn't had time to get into trouble. That young buck Peter Melford has been paying her court, but other than that, she's been relatively subdued.''

"As you say, something good comes from everything."

Rayne nodded and took a drink of his brandy. Dominic watched him, assessing him, it seemed. The marquess set his crystal snifter down on the Chippendale table in front of the sofa a little harder than necessary and leaned forward.

"All right, Rayne, we can banter back and forth all evening—I'm more than willing, if that's what it's going to take—or you can tell me what the hell is going on."

"I'm afraid I don't know what you mean."

"Don't you? You've been back on your feet for some time, yet you haven't made a single appearance in Society. I know you're still not quite up to snuff, but you haven't been to a prize fight, a horse race, haven't even spent an evening gambling at White's or Boodles. Tell me what's going on."

Rayne swirled the snifter he cradled between his wide palms. "Nothing . . . at any rate, nothing I can't handle."

"What exactly does that mean?"

Rayne took a long deep swig of his drink. "I'll be honest with you, Dom, the easiest part of this whole damned thing was surviving the gunshot. It's the rest of it that's been bloody hell."

Dominic sipped his brandy. "You want to talk about it?"

"Not really. I can't imagine it would do any good."

"Why don't you give it a try?"

Rayne toyed with his glass, then took another long, deep drink. "All right. The truth is, I'm having a deuce of a time with this whole bloody business. Jocelyn . . ." Rayne cleared his throat. "Jocelyn meant a lot to me. More than I cared to admit at the time. Now that she's gone, I keep thinking about her. I can hardly eat, rarely sleep. I

keep seeing her beautiful face, thinking of what she suffered in the past, imagining her in that god-awful prison. I
know what a hellhole it is."

"We did the best we could by her. Besides, she isn't in
there now."

"No she isn't. She's locked away on some damned old
brig with a hundred and twenty other women, most of
them the scum of the earth. They live like animals on one
of those ships."

"Captain Boggs has a reputation for fairness. They say
he's the best of the lot among those in the trade."

"The trade of transporting criminals." Rayne rested his
head against the back of the chair. "Ah, God, Dom. I can't
stand to think of her that way."

Dominic set the brandy snifter aside and came to his
feet. "Listen to me, dammit, you've got to stop this. The
woman tried to kill you! She very nearly succeeded. We
both know she'd tried it before. You told me yourself the
two of you had been fighting about her father. You saw
her pull the trigger, for God's sake!"

Rayne stood up, too. "That's another thing. On the rare
occasions when I do fall asleep, I keep dreaming about
what happened that day in the study, except that in my
dream things are different. I walk into the room, Jocelyn
turns, and her hand comes up—but in my dream the shot
is fired and *then* she shouts my name. *After* I've been hit,
not before. I can see the horror on her face before I fall. I
can see the anguish she feels for what has happened to
me. Why would she look that way if she were the one
who shot me? Why would she cry out my name?"

"It's only a dream, Rayne."

He raked a hand through his hair, and both of them sat
back down. "She told you she was innocent."

"What did you expect her to say?"

He pondered that. "I saw her, dammit! I saw her pull
the trigger. What other explanation could there be?"

"The truth is, the woman is guilty. You've got to face it,
accept it, and get on with your life."

Rayne leaned back against the chair. "God, how I hate her. As much as I once cared for her, that is how much I hate her for what she has done."

"Let it go, Rayne. Hatred and vengeance are what caused all this sorrow in the first place."

Rayne nodded, just the slightest inclination of his head. "I know you're right, but . . ."

"But it's easier said than done. I understand, my friend. I believe, if I stood in your shoes, I would feel much the same." Dominic finished his brandy and set the snifter aside. "I'd better be going. There are several hours of daylight left, and I promised Catherine I'd get home from the City as quickly as I could."

Rayne forced himself to smile. "As I said, I appreciate your stopping by."

"You'll get through this, Rayne. Time will take care of things. It always does."

Rayne sighed. "I suppose you're right. A little drinking, a friendly game of cards, and a buxom wench might be just the thing."

Dominic smiled. "It usually is."

"There's a house party at Lady Townsend's tomorrow eve. Alexandra has been pressing me to take her. I suppose I could oblige."

"An excellent idea." As they headed to the door, Dominic clapped Rayne on the back. "You'll get over this, my friend. Just give yourself the chance."

Rayne nodded. "Give Catherine my love."

Dominic shook Rayne's hand, turned and walked out the door. Rayne stared after his tall retreating figure, remembering Dominic's words, trying to stop the terrible churning inside him, the nagging doubts, the unbearable pain.

Was it hate he was feeling—or love? How could two such conflicting emotions be so closely interwoven? Love, hate, anger, tenderness, passion. Which of those did he feel for Jo?

He wondered where she was and what she suffered. He

wondered if she thought of him, if she might regret what she had done.

He wondered if Jocelyn felt any of the roiling, aching, tortuous emotions she had aroused in him.

The first storm hit the third week out. After the first several hours the hold was slippery with vomit, the slop jars filled to overflowing, the men on deck too busy hauling canvas and battling the towering waves to empty them.

Jocelyn threw up several times but finally contained her queasy stomach. At the urging of some of the others, she tore a strip from the tail of her blouse and tied it over her mouth and nose so she could breathe without gagging.

By the fourth agonizing day, some of the women were too weak to leave their bunks, so Jocelyn and the others had taken to tending them. They'd been allowed on deck only once since the storm began. The seas were just too heavy, the men afraid an errant wave might wash one of them overboard into the foaming surf.

Since it was too dangerous to light a fire in the galley in such rough weather, food rations had thinned from a nightly strip of salt pork and biscuits and a morning bowl of burgoo—cornmeal mush and molasses—to weevily hardtack twice a day, with a ration of rusty dried beef thrown in for supper.

Jocelyn's extra rations, previously provided by Mr. Meeks during their walks in the evenings, were now merely stacked on her plate. At the looks of envy she received, Jocelyn gave in to her nagging conscience and shared the food with the sickest of the women. Most of the time it just came back up. The bunks were full of moaning, emaciated bodies, and until the weather broke, it appeared things would stay the same.

Thankfully, the seas began to calm the afternoon of the fourth day. The women who were able were led up on deck, while sailors doused the hold with saltwater to get rid of the noxious smell.

The second day of normalcy found most of them back

on their feet, even Conchita, who had suffered the worst bout of seasickness Jocelyn had ever seen. The Spanish woman's dark complexion had turned an ashen gray and her cheeks looked hollow and wan.

Jocelyn had fared better than most, and the voyage was nearly half over. Surely, she reasoned, she could survive the rest. At least she thought so until the captain ordered the women out of the hold earlier than usual the following morning.

"All right, ladies, gather 'round!" Silas Meeks bellowed orders from the first mate. "Quiet up, now! Mr. Dearling requires a word. Quiet—or it'll only go the worse!"

Jocelyn stood near the rail beside Dolly Whitehead, who stood next to a thinner, sallow-complexioned, slightly unsteady Conchita Vasquez.

"What do you suppose has happened?" Jo whispered to the broad-hipped woman.

"I—I don't know. Maybe they're just gonna tell us when we're gettin' to Jamaica."

"Maybe," Jo said, but she didn't really think so. The way the crew was muttering, the way Mr. Meeks was standing there looking so grim, didn't bode well.

"Silence!" Dearling ordered. He was a slender, sandy-haired man who looked no more than thirty. Mr. Meeks had told her the man had once been a lieutenant, an officer in His Majesty's Navy, but he had been drummed from the service. He looked harmless enough, but Silas had confided that the man was a "bucko mate"—an officer known for his cruelty.

"You women know the rules," Dearling was saying, and an uneasy shiver slid down Jo's spine. "You know the captain will not allow them to be broken." The women began to shift nervously and mumble among themselves.

"Next to water," Dearling continued, "food rations are the most important commodity on board this ship. Should worse come to worse, stealing them could be tantamount to murder. That being the case, it has come to our attention that one of you has broken into the stores."

At Dearling's nod, two burly seaman, one with an ugly tattoo on his arm and another with a heavy black beard, began to make their way among the crowd of women. Dozens of anxious watchers stepped out of their way, looking profoundly relieved as the men moved on.

Jocelyn noticed that Dolly Whitehead had begun to wring her thick-fingered hands.

"If they knew who did it," Dolly whispered, "they wouldn'ta waited till now." But her shoulders were shaking and she kept nervously wetting her lips.

Jocelyn watched her, watched the men approaching, the women parting like the Red Sea in their haste to get out of the way, and suddenly her heart lurched in her chest.

Oh my God! For the first time it occurred to her that all the time Conchita had been sick, she had never wanted for food. She had only been able to keep the meagerest portion down, but Dolly was always there with something more, enough to keep her going.

Jocelyn's eyes fastened on the tattoo riding on the big seaman's arm as he strode the deck, coming to a halt directly in front of her. For a single terrifying moment Jocelyn thought they had come for her, but instead they gripped Dolly's arms and began to drag her, wailing and fighting, toward the stern.

"Mrs. Whitehead," Dearling pronounced, his speech always formal. "After a thorough investigation of the matter of the theft of ship's rations, we have discovered it is you who are guilty of the crime."

Dolly said nothing, but her aging body quaked in fear.

"For an offense of this magnitude there can be no leniency. You will be tied to the mast and flogged like the common thief you are."

"No!" Dolly tried to break free, but the men held her thick body fast. "I only done it so's she wouldn't waste away. I thought she was dyin', don't ya see? I couldn't let her die!"

Standing next to Jocelyn, Conchita whimpered, the sound pitiful, coming from the once haughty girl.

"Dolly—she did it for me," Chita said as they dragged the buxom woman toward the mast. "I cannot let them do this to her. She is too old." Conchita started forward, her face deathly pale, gray smudges beneath her dark-lashed eyes. She swayed unsteadily, and Jocelyn gripped her arm.

"You can't do it. You're still too weak. It's liable to kill you."

"I do not care. Dolly, she is my friend. I do not have many. I must help her as she tried to help me."

She started forward again, but Jocelyn stepped in her way. "I'll go. I'm young and strong and I haven't been sick. Ten lashes isn't all that much." She thought of Brownie. "I've a friend who's taken fifty."

"You—You would do that for me . . . for Dolly?"

Jocelyn didn't answer, just strode toward the aft of the ship, pushing between the rows of women, praying to God her courage would not desert her.

Chapter Thirteen

"SHE DIDN'T DO IT!" Jo called out, her voice loud and clear. "I did!"

Tied to the mast, the back of her blouse torn open to reveal the pockmarks on her veined, translucent skin, Dolly jerked her head around.

Dearling stiffened. "I beg to differ," he said, "but it matters naught to me if you wish to take the old woman's place." He smiled so evilly, Jocelyn winced. "Cut her down."

"Are—Are ya sure, ducks?" Dolly whispered as her arms swung free and she stumbled in Jocelyn's direction.

"I'll be all right."

"I won't be forgettin'." Then she was swallowed up by the surging mass of women, winding her way toward the rail and her small dark friend.

Jocelyn's wrists were bound, her hands dragged over her head and tied to the mast. Dearling himself came down to tear open the back of her blouse and the thin cotton shift she wore beneath. She could sense his lecherous smile as surely as she felt the cool salt air.

"I believe I shall do the honors myself." Dearling took the whip from a stout seaman's hands.

For the first time, Jocelyn noticed there wasn't just one strip of leather but a group of them. *Cat-o'-nine-tails. Sweet God in heaven.*

She stealed herself, but even as she did, when the terrible blow finally came, the pain was so sharp that a sob escaped and her knees buckled beneath her. Red welts rose on her back and a trail of blood dripped onto her skirt. *Dear God, how would she survive nine more?*

She was shaking all over, terrified she would cry out, her skin ablaze with fiery heat. She heard Dearling shake out the lash and closed her eyes, her fingers unconsciously biting into the smooth wood of the mast. It creaked as the ship swayed. The long leather thongs made a rustling sound against the deck.

"Hold, Mr. Dearling!" Silas Meeks stepped forward from the crowd of sailors and strode toward the uniformed man. "You said it matters naught who takes the old woman's place." With his feet splayed, his wide chest bare and bulging with muscles, he fisted his hands at his waist, fixed a smug look on Dearling and grinned. "I'll stand in for the lass."

Jocelyn turned her head until her eyes locked with his. She knew she should protest, but for the life of her, she could not find the courage to speak.

Silas Meeks ended her dilemma with an even broader grin and a wink.

"This is highly irregular," Dearling said, clearly disgruntled.

"Cut the girl down!" Captain Boggs had come to the upper rail, his dark blue uniform spotless. He stood shorter than Dearling, older and balding, but obviously a man of authority. The first mate opened his mouth to protest, received a dark look of warning from the captain, and turned to do as he had been told.

In minutes Jocelyn had been freed and Silas Meeks stood tied to the tall cypress mast. With the captain looking on, the blows were swift and clean, slicing open the big seaman's back until his sun-baked skin ran red. But Silas remained on his feet, giving up no more than a pain-filled grunt or two. Afterward several of his shipmates, clearing awed by his courage, cut him down and helped him to his quarters in the foc's'le.

"I cannot believe it." Chita waited at the base of the ladder leading into the hold as Dolly helped Jocelyn down. "I have never seen a woman more brave."

"Not nearly as brave as Mr. Meeks." Jo grimaced at a jolt of fiery pain and moved toward a bench at the end of the long wooden table.

"He is a fine man, no?"

"He is a fine man, yes," Jo said.

"And you are a very fine friend." Chita's black eyes filled with tears. "I was wrong to treat you as I did. I hope you can find it in your heart to forgive me."

Jocelyn reached for the younger woman's hand. "Friends are supposed to forgive each other."

Chita smiled softly, Jocelyn smiled, and Dolly spread salve on Jocelyn's back.

Maybe her new life wouldn't be so bad, Jo mused. Already she had made three new friends. Then she thought of Brownie and Tucker, the friends she had left behind, who were as close to her as family. Rayne had taken them from her just as surely as if he had killed them.

Rayne.

She imagined his handsome face, but his look was no longer gentle. It mocked her for a fool. She had hated him in the beginning. Her hatred of him now was even stronger. The anger and hurt grew inside her, festered and swelled. She knew that Rayne was the one person on this earth whom she could never forgive.

"Good afternoon, your lordship."

"Good afternoon, Frederick. I know you're busy. I won't require much of your time."

Frederick Nelson, the viscount's man of affairs, eyed the tall man in front of him. Though his lordship was dressed as impeccably as ever, today in a dark brown tailcoat with a brown velvet collar, he looked different since his injury, a bit thinner, his face a little pale. But there was

something else, Frederick noticed, something more difficult to define.

If the viscount was a hard man before, now he was a
man honed of steel.

"Why don't we sit down?" Frederick moved behind his
Sheraton desk as Stoneleigh strode to one of the black
leather chairs in front of it. There was an edge about him,
a restlessness, a blaze of suppressed anger that glinted in
the depths of his cool dark eyes.

"What brings you here, my lord? I hope it is not grave
news." Frederick adjusted his wire-rimmed spectacles and
picked up the pencil on the green felt blotter in front of
him.

"No, nothing like that. But there is a matter of some
importance that I need you to look into."

"Of course."

"I've decided to expand my land holdings. I'm interested in something out of the country. The Caribbean, I
believe. From what I've heard, there's a great deal of profit
to be made there."

"Quite so. The West Indies has earned a fortune for a
number of wise investors. As a matter of fact, a few of my
clients and many of those represented by my colleagues
are currently involved in enterprise there. It shouldn't
take more than a couple of months to obtain a list of
properties for you to consider. I shall need the particulars,
of course, the type of land you're interested in, the
amount you wish to spend. In three or four months—"

"Three or four weeks is more what I had in mind."

"But I couldn't possibly—" The ink in Frederick's pen
pooled in a nasty black puddle where it pressed against
his writing tablet.

"Surely there are men here in London with holdings
they would be willing to sell—if the price were right."

"Why certainly, my lord, but as an investor, you would
be wiser to bide your time, make the soundest investment
possible."

The viscount smiled thinly. "I'm not in the mood to

bide my time. I intend to be a landowner in the West Indies in the very near future."

"The Indies . . . yes. There ought to be something available."

"I'm particularly interested in Jamaica."

"Jamaica! B-But the sugar planters are having a deuce of a time there."

Stoneleigh shrugged his massive shoulders. "Then I'll just have to grow something else."

"B-But your lordship, what do you know about—"

"Just find the property, Nelson. The sooner the better. There'll be a bonus in it for you. You may rest assured it will be the larger for every day you spare."

Frederick swallowed. "Yes, my lord."

Stoneleigh came to his feet, and Frederick noticed the gold-headed cane that had never been a part of his dress before. He wondered if it concealed a blade, as many of them did, or if the viscount had taken to carrying it because of his injury. "I'll expect to hear from you as soon as possible."

"Yes, my lord. I shall begin our search this very afternoon."

"Good." Stoneleigh strode to the door, his long powerful strides a little slower than the last time Frederick had seen him. Once or twice he leaned a bit on the cane. "Don't fail me, Nelson."

"Have no fear, your lordship. The task is as good as complete."

When the viscount nodded and strode out the door, Frederick collapsed in his chair. Good God, the man's voice held the edge of a rapier; his face could have been cast in stone. Frederick didn't intend to disappoint him. In fact, he pitied the man who did.

He thought of the shooting the viscount had barely survived. What was it he'd heard had happened to the woman?

Frederick's insides clenched, then suddenly turned to

water. If he remembered correctly—the woman had been sent to Jamaica.

"You've grit, lass. I'm thinkin' you'll be fine." Silas Meeks stood framed in the open door of the Sword and Buchaneer Tavern.

It was a low-ceilinged, smoky affair, but according to Silas, a place far better than the sort some of the other women would encounter. Except for the few who remained aboard *Sea Demon,* headed for Barbados, the rest would be auctioned off, sold to the highest bidder for back-breaking labor on the distant plantations.

The cream of the crop, Silas had told her, were spoken for ahead of time: the youngest and strongest, the least likely to make trouble . . . the most comely. Those women went to owners in cities like Kingston, Mandeville, and Port Antonio, to work in homes, shops, and taverns.

Amazingly, she and Chita had both wound up working for Barzillai Hopkins, the owner of the Sword and Buchaneer as well as a dozen other ale houses, grog shops, and bawdy houses along the quay. They had become fast friends since the incident on the ship, and though they didn't work together, they saw each other often in the course of various errands or while filling in when one of the women got sick.

Unfortunately, Dolly Whitehead had been less lucky. Her fate remained unknown, a whim of the auction block.

Jocelyn looked up at the big brawny seaman who stood in front of her. "I'll be fine, Silas." She smiled a bit forlornly. "I'm a survivor. I'll get by somehow. I always have."

"You're a rum one, lass. It's been a pleasure to know you."

"I'll never forget what you did for me."

Silas shrugged off her words. "I'd best be goin'. Ship sails on the mornin' tide. We've taken on a load'a pimento, logwood, and rum. We'll deliver the rest of the women to Barbados, fill the balance of the ship with hogs-heads'a sugar, and set sail for home."

Before he could leave, Jocelyn stood on tiptoe and kissed his weathered cheek. "Good-bye, Silas."

The big man's face turned red. "Take care, lassie." With a last fond glance, he turned and strode out the door.

"Devil take it! What the hell's goin' on here!" Barz Hopkins, a dish-faced, evil-eyed man with the most lecherous grin she had ever seen, walked up beside her. When he wasn't shouting, he was grinning. Or pinching one of the women's bottoms.

"Move your arse, girl! There's men's tankards to fill, and a leg of mutton to serve to the hungry. Get a move on, or I'll give you something to dawdle about!"

He meant it, she knew. He had cuffed her more than once. He took no back-talk from anyone, kept a birch rod out in the kitchen, and used it less than sparingly. Jocelyn had welts on her legs and bottom to prove it.

"I'm sorry, Mr. Hopkins. I was just saying good-bye to a friend."

"And good riddance. A man can't get a good day's work out of you lazy wenches as it is. Don't help havin' a burly ol' salt like Meeks lookin' over your shoulder all the time."

Which meant that Hopkins had given her a wide berth whenever Silas Meeks had been in the tavern. Now she had lost her protector. Once again she had no one to depend on but herself.

"Ale, wench! And hurry. A man could die'a thirst in here." Jocelyn turned away from Barz Hopkins and hurried to do the loud sailor's bidding. She was getting used to the noise, the bilious odor of stale tobacco, and the rancid smell of sweaty, drunken men.

By the end of the first month, she had also grown used to sleeping on a straw mat on the floor in the attic, twelve-hour workdays, and fending off the drunken men's advances.

She hated the ankle-length full red skirt and white ruffled petticoats she was forced to wear, hated even more the low-cut blouse that showed far too much of her bosom. The beautiful gold and enamel locket Rayne had given her rode safely once more in her hem, but she constantly battled to keep some sailor from lifting her skirts or trying to kiss her.

Barz Hopkins remained her greatest fear. His lecherous grins had grown even more constant, and her bottom was black and blue with bruises from his indecent pinching. Worst of all, day by day Barz's temper seemed to be growing shorter—and Jocelyn was very much afraid she knew why.

She sighed as she crossed the room. It was crowded in the tavern this eve, the room hazy with smoke beneath the heavy wooden beams, and noisy with boisterous laughter. It was a big place on a corner across from the wharf, with doors leading in from two different streets. There was a taproom, a dining room, a gallery upstairs with small curtained booths for use by the whores who worked the second-floor brothel, and rooms above the dining room for overnight guests.

"What's keepin' ye, wench!" This from a British sailor off a boatload of men ordered to duty at nearby Fort Charles.

Jocelyn hurried in the brawny, bearded seaman's direction. "I'm sorry to take so long. It's just that we're so busy."

She set three pewter tankards of rum in front of the sailor and his friends and had started to walk away when the seaman slid an arm around her waist and hauled her onto his lap.

"I told you I'm busy!" Jocelyn tried to pry herself free, but he held her fast. "Let me go!"

The men howled with laughter. "I've plenty of coin in me purse," the man said. "More'n enough to pay for ye time."

Jocelyn stiffened. "I'm not interested." She shoved at his chest, as solid as a chunk of steel. "There are plenty of others who are."

The bearded man caught her jaw between his fingers. "None so comely, I'll wager. I've a mind for silky black hair and eyes as blue as the sea."

"And a pair o' tits like two ripe mangoes!" one of the others called out, bringing another coarse round of laughter.

Below the overhanging gallery upstairs, Rayne stood in the darkness, watching the display in silence. A muscle bunched in his jaw, and his fingers bit into his scarred wooden chair.

He had occupied the same seat last night, watching unnoticed among the crowd of rowdy men as Jocelyn worked serving drinks on the opposite side of the tavern. He might have left this eve as he had the last, satisfied with the severity of her sentence, satisfied that, in a different way, she suffered just as he did.

He might have, if he hadn't seen the sailor's beefy fingers grope her bosom, hadn't seen the repulsion and despair in her beautiful bright blue eyes.

He might have gone. Now he could not.

Rayne slid back his chair and stood up, then started shoving his way through the crowd toward the three men sitting at the battered wooden table. He could hear their raucous laughter and crude remarks, see Jocelyn's face turn red as one of the men fondled her bottom. When the sailor tried to kiss her, forcing her mouth down to his wet sticky lips, she jerked free a hand and raked her nails down his cheek.

"You little hellion!" A ringing slap echoed across the tavern. The seaman raised his arm again, but Rayne caught it in midair, his fingers biting into the work-honed flesh.

"Let her go," he warned softly, his voice as hard as granite.

"Rayne . . ." It was not much more than a whisper, the merest breath of air. Jocelyn sat frozen on the bearded sailor's thighs while the rest of the tavern began to fall silent.

"I said, let her go."

The brawny man released her, and Jocelyn stumbled away. He shoved back his chair, slamming it into the wall, and started forward. "The little whore is mine." The sailor swung, his teeth clenched in anger.

Rayne ducked the heavy blow and threw a hard punch to the sailor's middle, doubling him over, but the big brute came up swinging. Rayne dodged the first two punches, but a third connected with his jaw, rocking him backward, then his fighting instincts took over. He bloodied the sailor's nose, threw a punch that cracked his jaw, and landed a fist in the tough sailor's stomach. It took three more battering blows, but finally the burly man sagged to his knees. A hard right to the jaw and he hit the floor with a groan, his eyes rolling back in his head.

Jocelyn stood a few feet away, looking pale and shaken. Rayne reached for her arm and dragged her toward him. Even as remnants of the fight pumped through his veins, he noticed how soft her skin felt, how silky her hair was as it accidentally grazed his cheek.

"W-What are you doing here? Why are—"

"Why am I still alive and breathing?" He made a rude sound in his throat. "What's the matter, sweeting? Disappointed?"

She stared at him as if she were seeing a ghost.

"Devil take it! What the hell's goin' on here?" shouted Barzillai Hopkins, the homely, sour-faced man who owned the tavern. Rayne knew all about him. He had made it a point to know.

"Get your arse back to work, girl. You've caused enough trouble here." He raised the birch rod and brought a stinging blow across the back of her legs, making her suck in a breath. "You can count on more o' that later. Maybe you'll learn to mind your manners."

"I—I'm sorry for the trouble, Mr. Hopkins." She started to hurry away, but Rayne caught her arm.

"Stay here," he said, turning his attention to the innkeeper, fury pumping once more through his veins. "I want a word with you, Hopkins."

"Who the devil are you?"

"In private."

Hopkins's protruding eyes appraised him from head to foot, taking in his tailored fawn breeches, expensive Hessian boots, and fine lawn shirt. One look at Rayne's fierce expression and he nodded. "You'd best follow me."

Chapter Fourteen

JOCELYN WATCHED THEM GO, then numbly sank down in one of the chairs vacated by the three hastily departing sailors.

Dear God in heaven. Rayne.

For a fleeting instant, joy had flooded her heart at the sight of him, well and whole and as handsome as ever. With it came the wild, insane hope that she might awaken from this terrible nightmare, that Rayne had finally come for her.

But one look at those hard brown eyes told her it wasn't the truth.

Her stomach clenched and her heart pounded wildly. She shuddered, as she remembered his fierce look of hate.

It was obvious now that Rayne hadn't lied to the authorities. He truly believed her guilty. It was there in every harsh line of his face. Every unforgiving glance, every tense movement, said how much he despised her. He had judged her and found her guilty.

She didn't know how he could, after the moments they had shared, the love she had felt for him; couldn't imagine him condemning her without a chance to explain. But there was no doubt that he had.

And she hated him for it. More than she would ever have believed.

Anger and pride kept her bearing erect, just as it kept her from pleading her innocence. That and the fact it was clear he wouldn't believe her if she did. She saw him reappear, standing half a head taller than the others, his thick brown hair glinting auburn in the light of the whale-oil lamps. When he turned and started walking in her direction, Jocelyn's mouth went dry.

Why was he here? Hadn't he done enough already? What more, in God's name, did he want?

He crossed the room, looking neither to the right nor left, his hard expression giving the usually boisterous patrons a moment of pause.

He stopped a few feet in front of her. "Go up and get your things. You're leaving."

"What!"

"I said get your things."

"I'm not going anywhere with you."

"You're leaving—one way or another—you may be certain of that." He meant it. She could see it in his eyes. He would drag her out if he had to.

"What about Mr. Hopkins? What about my sentence?"

Rayne smiled, the line of his mouth looking thin and cruel. "Never fear, my sweet, nothing has changed. Nothing . . . except that from this day forward, you will serve your time working for me. Now get your things."

Jocelyn gripped the back of the chair, her body going rigid. She could barely find the strength to move until Rayne hauled her toward him.

"Go!" he roared, and she nearly stumbled in her haste to obey.

On trembling limbs she wove her way through the crowd, climbed the two flights of stairs to the attic, and snatched up her few belongings: her shift and night rail, the plain brown skirt and homespun blouse she had worn on the voyage, a pair of sturdy brown shoes, a brush and comb Chita had given her, and of course the locket hidden along with Brownie's coins in the hem of her red gathered skirt.

There was a tiny bit of soap and a few other items, but nothing of consequence. With unsteady hands she used the skirt to bundle them up, tying the items inside, then hurried back down the stairs.

She paused before she reached him, surveying his immaculate clothes, noticing that his body looked leaner than it had before, his muscles even harder. She noticed there wasn't a hint of warmth or gentleness in the rigid lines of his face.

"Where are we going?" she asked when he took hold of her arm. Her stomach fluttered at the once-familiar heat of his touch, and something tightened in the pit of her stomach.

"I've a room at the King's Inn. We'll spend the night there."

Jocelyn came up short, halting him just outside the tavern. "If you believe for an instant—if you have any idea of taking up where you left off—"

"Don't be a fool." He started dragging her along the boardwalk again, forcing her to run to keep up with him. "Unless you wish to travel in the dark, we'll be staying in town until morning. Tomorrow we leave for my plantation, Mahogany Vale. It's a good day's ride from the city."

"You own land in Jamaica?"

He flashed a cold, mocking smile. "A recent acquisition."

Jocelyn felt a chill creep down her spine. "I assume that means you don't believe my punishment was harsh enough. That you've decided to take a personal interest in seeing justice done."

He chuckled mirthlessly. "You may assume anything you wish. As far as I'm concerned, I'm here to try my hand as a planter, nothing more."

"Of course. How could I possibly believe you've any ulterior motives." Who was this stranger? How could she ever have trusted him? How could she have loved him?

Rayne said nothing, just continued along the boardwalk at a grueling pace, heedless of the unwieldy bundle of clothes she clutched to her chest. It crossed her mind that she might try to escape, but she didn't know the country, had no place to go, no one to turn to—and the penalty for failure was too great.

They rounded a corner, crossed the street, and eventually reached the King's Inn, a two-story, white wood-framed building with a balcony around the upper floor. Still gripping her arm, Rayne dragged her into the lobby and up the wide white-banistered stairs. He paused in the hall outside his door, inserted the key and unlocked it, shoved her inside and followed her in.

Rayne strode toward her. He grabbed the tiny bag that held her clothing, tossed it onto the high tester bed and untied it, then began to rummage through the contents.

"What do you think you're doing?"

"Making sure you don't have a weapon." He turned toward her, jerked her close and ran his big hands over her breasts, along her waist, and down her body.

"How dare you!" Jo stumbled backward, her face flushing hotly with embarrassment.

"I dare anything I please, and you had better get used to it." Cold brown eyes bored into her. "I don't intend to spend every waking hour watching my back, Jocelyn. If you even think of threatening me, this time there will be no reprieve. You may be certain that you will hang."

She might have laughed if the whole thing weren't so frightening. "I'll try to keep that in mind."

"The chaise should do for a bed . . . unless you'd prefer the floor."

Jocelyn surveyed the small single-armed couch beneath the window, then the comfortable four-poster in the middle of the room. She looked at Rayne, saw the hard mocking glint in his eyes, and lifted her chin.

"For the past four weeks, I've been sleeping on the floor above the tavern. Before that I slept in a narrow cot in the center of a row a foot apart and seven deep. The chaise will seem a luxury, I assure you." She smiled with bitter resentment. "You have my most humble gratitude."

Rayne's jaw tightened. He turned and began to unbut-

ton his shirt. "I suggest you get some sleep. The day will
be a hard one tomorrow."

Jocelyn scoffed. "You wouldn't know what a hard day
is." Head held high, she walked behind the screen in the
corner and began to change into her nightclothes.

Rayne watched her go. Crossing the floor to a satinwood table along the wall, he poured himself a brandy
and tossed it back, then poured himself another. He set
the snifter down and finished undressing, his movements
a little slow since the tension of the evening had renewed
the pain in his back. Then he climbed beneath the clean
linen sheets.

The room was large and airy, the inn the finest in Kingston. The bed was firm, the feather mattress soft, and the
smell of fresh-cut lilacs in the vase on the Queen Anne
table scented the late night air.

It was peaceful here, quiet except for the occasional
rattle of passing carriage wheels or the clop of horses'
hooves on the street below the window. It was restful, but
the last thing on Rayne's mind was sleep.

He was listening to sounds in the darkness, the rustle of
Jocelyn removing her clothes. He could hear the whisper
of fabric against her skin as she discarded each piece,
could imagine her long sleek limbs moving gracefully as
she stepped out of her skirt.

He didn't need to see behind the screen to know exactly what she looked like standing there naked. He remembered every luscious curve, every creamy inch of her
skin. Her beautiful face had haunted him for weeks. His
body had burned with memories of her smooth pale flesh
writhing beneath him.

On the voyage here from England, those memories had
strengthened his hatred. He'd recalled every warm embrace, every heated moment they had shared, and convinced himself that each of them had been a lie. He had
even come to believe that she hadn't been a virgin. Pucker
water, he surmised, alum used to tighten a woman's pas-

sage, and maybe the blood of a chicken. It was an old trick, but a good one.

Now he knew without doubt his instincts from the start had been correct. Jocelyn might be capable of murder, but she was no whore. Even in the dingy old tavern, she had played the role of lady, struggling against all odds to keep that part of herself that she had once given to him.

How strong her hatred must have been to give up something she valued so highly. Then again, maybe that was the single part of her performance that she had not planned.

Rayne heard Jocelyn's slim bare feet cross the floor, and the same heavy tightness he had known each night since she had been gone clutched his chest. The chaise creaked as her slender shape curled up on the cushions, and it occurred to him that he had forgotten to set out a blanket.

God's blood, it was hardly cold. And even if it were, after what she had done, what was one more night of discomfort? He lay there awhile in the darkness, listening to her movements, hearing her shifting, trying to get comfortable on the narrow padded chaise. Still, he did not stir.

An hour passed, maybe two. Jocelyn's breathing grew deep and even, telling him she finally slept. He listened to it, imagined the gentle rise and fall of her breasts, remembered what it had felt like to touch them, and his body grew hard and throbbing.

With a low muttered curse, Rayne climbed out of bed, jerked off the light satin counterpane and crossed to where Jocelyn lay sleeping. He tossed it over her curled-up form and stormed back to bed.

Feeling better somehow, and wishing like hell he didn't, he closed his eyes against the image of Jocelyn lying on the narrow chaise. How could someone who looked so innocent be capable of murder? It was a question that nagged him, just as it had from the moment he'd awakened in his sickbed.

He glanced toward the place where she slept, only a few feet away. He was scarcely afraid of her, though God help him, he probably should be. He was twice her size and a well-seasoned soldier. She never would have succeeded in the first place if he hadn't trusted her so completely. Aside from that, though she might want him dead, she wasn't a fool. His threat alone would be enough to deter her.

Still, he was too long a soldier not to take care. He wouldn't let his guard down—at least not completely.

Rayne's thoughts drifted, and he began to succumb to the exhaustion overtaking his body. With an ear cocked toward any unwelcome movements Jocelyn might make, he slept. Through the long hours of the night, no worries plagued him, no nagging doubts. He knew where Jocelyn was and that she was safe.

He awoke to find himself more rested than he had been in weeks.

Jocelyn stirred, a little too warm beneath the ice-blue satin counterpane. She tossed it aside, trying to recall how it had gotten there, then realizing Rayne must have done it, jerked her head in his direction. He wasn't in bed. In fact he wasn't even in the room.

Grateful for the time to compose herself, she scrambled behind the hand-painted screen, quickly used the chamber pot, and completed her morning ablutions. She dressed in her simple brown skirt and blouse, her serviceable brown leather shoes, and had just finished combing her shoulder-length hair when Rayne opened the door and strode in.

"You're ready, I see. Good. Gather your things and let's go."

She rolled them in the red skirt this time and followed him out of the room. Recalling his fancy gilt-trimmed carriage, she was surprised to see instead a heavy flat-bed wagon, the cumbersome conveyance loaded to the sideboards with supplies and equipment. There were long lengths of lumber, kegs of nails, hammers, saws, canvas;

and foodstuffs: sacks of flour, cones of sugar, tins of coffee, rice, beans, even several odd pieces of harness.

"You're serious about this land of yours," she said, somewhat amazed.

"As a matter of fact, I am."

He gripped her waist, his hands as warm and strong as she remembered, and started to help her climb up on the big wooden wheel.

"Jo! Jocelyn!" Running full-tilt down the street, Conchita Vasquez raced toward her, red skirts flying out behind, thick black hair cascading to her waist.

"Chita!" Jocelyn jumped down from the wagon wheel and the women hugged fiercely. "I didn't think I'd see you before we left Kingston. How did you find me?"

"Old sourpuss, he say you were gone. He say some crazy rich planter pay him a fortune to let you go. I figured if the man had that much money, he would be staying at the finest hotel in the city."

Jo went still, and Chita's head jerked toward the big man towering above them. "Conchita, this is his lordship, the Viscount Stoneleigh."

Chita's big black eyes grew round. *"Madre de Dios."* She sank into a curtsy, which looked somewhat ridiculous in her gaudy tavern clothes. "I—I am sorry, Your Grace. I did not think . . . I should not have said that."

Rayne smiled faintly at the form of address meant for a duke. "It's all right, Chita. This isn't the first time someone has called me crazy."

"I-I did not mean it that way," Chita said. "I just thought—"

"I can imagine what you thought." He turned to Jo. "We've a long way to go, Jocelyn. Say good-bye to your friend."

"You'll be all right, won't you?" Jo asked, seeing tears on the pretty girl's cheeks, which had been looking a little pale of late.

"I will miss you, just as I do Dolly. Now I have no one."

Jocelyn knew exactly what she meant. "I'll miss you,

too." The women hugged again, and tears burned the back of Jo's eyes. "Stay away from old sourpuss."

"I will try." Chita clutched her hand. *"Vaya con Dios."* Turning away with a look of despair, the dark-skinned girl raced back toward the tavern, stopping to wave one last time. Then she disappeared around the corner.

Jocelyn raised her eyes to Rayne's face but couldn't read his expression. He gripped her waist a little too hard, steadying her as she climbed up on the wheel and into the wagon.

Around them the streets of Kingston were crowded this morning, alive with tradesmen, sailors, wealthy planters and their wives, and black-skinned slaves in their simple white cotton garments. Most of the men wore baggy trousers and wide straw hats, while the women dressed in plain skirts and blouses and covered their heads with scarves. Donkeys roamed the streets, their backs laden with wicker baskets piled high with fruits and vegetables destined for the Jubilee Market.

It was Sunday, market day for the island. Though Jocelyn had seen almost nothing of Jamaica, she had been on errands to the market several times. It was a colorful place, bustling with natives hawking their wares, slaves selling items from their own small gardens, fishmongers, and craftsman marketing furniture made from the beautiful hardwoods of the island—mahogany, satinwood, rosewood, Spanish elm.

Rayne climbed up on the wagon, grimacing slightly as he settled himself on the seat. It was obvious he was still not completely recovered from the shooting, and in spite of herself, Jocelyn felt a surge of pity.

He stretched his long legs out as best he could in the cramped wagon boot and picked up the reins, slapping them against the horses' rumps until they leaned into their traces.

"Is Mahogany Vale a sugar plantation?" Jo asked as the heavy conveyance rolled along.

"It was a sugar plantation, though the elevation was a little too high to be much of a success."

"Then why did you buy it?"

"I said it *was* a sugar plantation. Since sugar prices are down, I plan to grow coffee."

"Coffee?"

"Exactly so." He sat no more than three or four inches away, one long leg propped up on the wagon boot, his heavy-muscled arms nearly brushing her shoulders. She could feel the heat of his powerful body, and her own slender frame began to grow warm.

"W-Why have you decided on coffee?" she asked. Anything to take her mind off what she had been thinking.

He flashed her a hard look, debating whether or not she deserved an answer.

"Blue ruin," he finally said. "Gin. The bane of the lower classes. With Society campaigning against it, coffeehouses have sprung up all over London. Coffee's been tried on the island before, not to any great degree, but the little that's been grown has been successful." They rounded the corner, turning off King Street, heading for the edge of town. "I just plan to do it on a grander scale."

Why was it that didn't surprise her? Probably because Stoneleigh wasn't the kind of man to do anything that was less than monumental.

"Where, exactly, do I fit in?"

He didn't bother looking in her direction. "Mahogany Vale isn't a large plantation. There are only fifty workers there now, plus the house servants, and half a dozen Portuguese indentured servants who came over three months before I bought the place. But there's a great deal to be done."

He turned toward her, his eyes raking her, a corner of his mouth curling sardonically.

"Under other circumstances, the fact you've spent time in my bed might allow you certain . . . privileges."

Jocelyn bristled.

"As it is, you will labor right alongside the rest of the

workers. You will work the same hours, eat the same food. You'll be treated no differently than anyone else."

Jocelyn's teeth clenched so hard she could barely speak. "Has it ever occurred to you, *your lordship,* that I might not be interested in your so called 'privileges'? Nor do I wish to be reminded of the loathsome hours I spent in your bed."

Rayne hauled back on the reins, bringing the horses to a halt along an empty stretch of road beneath an overhanging mahoe tree, its bright yellow blossoms just beginning to redden. He set the brake and wrapped the reins around it, and Jocelyn suddenly went tense.

"I've often wondered about that. At the time, I believed you enjoyed it—overmuch, in fact. I can clearly recall the way you moaned and clung to my neck, the way you wrapped those long slender legs of yours around my back to draw me deeper inside you. Now you tell me you loathed it. After what's happened, I suppose I should believe you. And yet I wonder—"

He broke off as he dragged her against him.

"What—What are you doing?"

"Let's just say I'm satisfying my curiosity." Then he was bending her backward, his mouth coming down over hers, his tongue thrusting hard between her teeth.

Rage and humiliation washed over her. Jocelyn pounded his chest and tried to break free, but he held her as tightly as a rabbit in a snare. She could feel the muscles bunching in his thick arms and shoulders, the steady rhythmic beating of his heart. His lips were warm and firm, his thighs hard where they pressed against her own, and his tongue—dear God, his tongue was slick and hot and searing her mouth with its every movement.

Heat roared through her, blinding hot waves that stunned her with their impact. She wanted to shout her denial, cry out her fury at the power he still held. She wanted to feel nothing but emptiness when he touched her, nothing but loathing. Instead she felt a wild hot pas-

sion careening through her body, a wave of heat and longing that spoke of the times he had touched her before.

God, oh God, oh no. She wanted to hurt him, to rake
her nails down his cheek and call him every loathsome
name she could think of. She wanted to slap him and rail
at him for destroying her life, her world.

Instead she slid her arms around his neck and kissed
him back, her tongue touching his, a soft moan catching
in her throat. She felt his fingers working the buttons on
the front of her blouse, the fabric parting, his tanned
hands sliding inside to cup the upthrusting fullness of her
breast.

"Rayne . . ." At the soft sound of his name, his movements stilled.

He continued to hold her against him, but the touch of
his hand grew harsh and rough, and she winced. Rayne's
thick chest rumbled with bitter amusement.

"It wasn't all pretend, was it, Jo?" He laughed again, the
sound so cold Jocelyn shivered. "How does it feel, my
love, to want a man you despise?"

Heat burned her cheeks, hotter than the bright Jamai-
can sun. She wanted to tell him he was wrong, that once
she had loved him. She wanted to say she was innocent,
that she would never have hurt him. But one look in those
hard dark eyes, one glance at his unforgiving profile, and
she knew he wouldn't believe her. His mind was made up
—he had already judged her guilty.

"You're just a man," she said. "Just a man like any
other. What I feel for you is nothing more than lust. The
very same emotion you once felt for me."

"The emotion that very nearly got me killed. Believe
me, I haven't forgotten."

"Lusting after the fairer sex was always your strong suit,
I believe."

"And yours, my sweet, was always lying through your
lovely white teeth." He picked up the reins, released the
brake, and urged the horses once more into motion. The
wheels rolled sluggishly and the harness jangled even

louder than the buzz of insects on the leafy, overgrown mountain path.

Bastard! Bloody stinking bastard! But Jo didn't say it. She couldn't afford to. Just as he had almost from the moment of their first meeting, Rayne held all the cards. She would do his bidding, be at his beck and call in order to survive. She wasn't about to let him goad her into doing something foolish, something that might add years to her sentence—something that might get her hanged.

She glanced at him from beneath her lashes, taking in his unflinching profile. That he could still affect her after what he had done enraged her. He was handsome and charming, a man profoundly experienced in the art of seduction. That she had fallen in love with him wasn't surprising—that she still felt drawn to him, still felt this overwhelming attraction, seemed astonishing beyond belief.

Still, it was the truth. It had happened the moment he had touched her, maybe even the moment he had appeared in the tavern.

It angered her, galled her, but it would not be her undoing. She might desire him, but she knew him now for the man he really was, and she would be wary.

And sooner or later, Rayne would grow tired of his vengeful games. A rural plantation was hardly a manor house in London. His comfortable life would lure him away and she would be free of him. She still faced her unjust sentence, but she could endure it. She didn't know what the future might hold, but as long as she was alive, there was a chance that she could be happy.

They traveled the narrow dirt road on its winding path through the mountains, the countryside more beautiful than Jocelyn could have dreamed. In places she could see the ocean, the most incredible turquoise-blue, and long stretches of white sandy beach.

They passed through several small settlements where whitewashed cottages sat beside the road, their front yards surrounded by tiny picket fences heavy with climbing roses.

Rayne said little along the way, but his back was as rigid as hers, anger still riding hard on his shoulders. Her own anger waned fairly quickly in the face of such towering beauty. The day was just too stunning, the air too sweetly scented, the sky too pure a blue. When Jocelyn saw a butterly with a six-inch wing span, she forgot her anger at Rayne and pointed excitedly, jumping to her feet with such enthusiasm she nearly toppled from the wagon.

Rayne's hard arm caught her and he hauled her back down on the rough wooden seat. "What in bloody hell do you think you're doing—trying to get yourself killed?"

"Did you see that?" She pointed once more toward the graceful, disappearing insect, her eyes alight with wonder.

For a moment Rayne looked grim, then amusement lifted the edges of his mouth. "That's a swallowtail butterfly."

"Good heavens, it was incredible. The biggest butterfly I've ever seen."

He released a gruff chuckle, his brown eyes suddenly lighter. "Wait till you see the size of the lizards."

Jocelyn almost smiled. Rayne chuckled again and urged the wagon forward, the horses leaning into their traces to tackle the steep mountain slope. Jocelyn sat in silence as it rumbled along the narrow, twisting road toward the small plantation that sat on a branch of the Yallahs River.

They reached it several hours later. By that time Rayne's stiff demeanor had returned, and Jocelyn wasn't certain whether it was caused by the pain of his injury or his anger at her. She ignored it as she took in her surroundings: the blue cloudless sky, a brighter hue even than the sea; the mountainous, heavily foliaged peaks in the distance; the gentle slopes and tiny secluded valley that was Mahogany Vale.

As they drew near, small black and white spots became workers on the hillside bent to their tasks, and wooden carts pulled by donkeys made their way across the freshly tilled black earth fields.

Jocelyn had expected a huge, white-columned plantation house. Instead she was surprised to see a comfortable hip-roofed, two-story wood-framed structure with wide porches in front and a screened-in balcony running the length of the house upstairs. As they pulled into the yard, she was even more surprised to find the white paint was peeling, the porch sagged a little, and the flower beds were badly overgrown.

"I told you it needed work," Rayne said a bit defensively at her look of disbelief. "The workers have already cleared most of the fields. We'll be starting on the house as soon as the ground has been readied for planting."

"I'm afraid I've no idea what one plants to grow coffee."

"Slips taken from full-grown coffee shrubs. I've a shipment coming in from Haiti." He cast her a hard, mocking glance. "Since the planting, picking, hulling, and sorting will all be done by the workers, you'll find out about it firsthand."

With that last biting remark, he jerked rein on the horses, bringing the wagon to a halt in front of the house, and jumped down, wincing as he hit the ground harder than he had intended.

Jocelyn felt a momentary surge of triumph that his mocking attitude should be thus rewarded. Then she saw the beads of perspiration that had formed across his forehead and instantly felt contrite. When Rayne rounded the carriage and reached up to help her down, she ignored his outstretched hands and jumped to the ground by herself.

The lines of his face grew hard. "As I recall, you didn't find my touch all that loathsome back there on the road."

Jocelyn met his dark look squarely. "Any fool can see you're in pain. I only meant to spare you. Now, if you'll show me where I may put my things, I shall lay them away and return prepared to work."

For a moment Rayne said nothing, just fixed his eyes on her face as if he tried to read her thoughts. Then he turned and strode off toward the front of the house. "Follow me."

Chapter Fifteen

RAYNE LED JOCELYN into the house, then let her walk past him into the entry. The house he had purchased looked far less run-down on the inside, in no way elegant, of course, but the furnishings had once been expensive and the paper on the walls complimented the Oriental carpet on the smooth hardwood floors.

The wood-frame structure was colonial in style, with a drawing room on one side, a dining room on the other, and a handsome staircase in between. A smaller withdrawing room faced the rear of the house, along with an intimate solar and a study where the former owner had conducted the business of running his plantation.

"Your quarters are upstairs," Rayne said, breaking into her thoughts. "Second door on the right. If you need anything, ask the chambermaid. She's usually somewhere at hand."

Clutching the same small bundle of clothes she had brought with her from the inn, Jocelyn looked up at him. "You want me to stay in the house?"

"I want you close enough so I can keep an eye on you. As far as working the rest of the day, I believe tomorrow will be soon enough for you to begin your labors. In the meantime, I'll have cook send up something for you to eat."

When he said nothing more, Jocelyn crossed the foyer, lifted her skirt up out of the way, and climbed the stairs.

Rayne watched her go, her lithe form moving gracefully. He caught the sway of her hips, a glimpse of slender ankle, heard the rustle of her skirts against her legs. When she turned at the top of the stairs, her small pointed breasts moved gently beneath her blouse, and his blood began to thicken in his veins. He thought of her sweet soft lips, and his stomach clenched, an ache pooling low in his groin.

Bloody hell! The woman had the most incredible effect on him. He couldn't look at her without wanting to hoist her skirts, couldn't hear the sound of her voice without wanting to plunge his tongue inside her mouth. He hadn't meant for her to sleep in the house. God's breath, he hadn't meant to bring her back with him at all!

Or had he?

Wasn't that, in truth, the very reason he had come to this bloody island in the first place?

Everyone had tried to dissuade him. Particularly Dominic and Catherine, and especially his sister.

"For heaven sakes, Rayne," Alexandra had pleaded, "you're putting your life at risk for that woman. Can't you see that?"

"Alex may be right," Dominic agreed. "You underestimated the woman before. You can't be certain what she's capable of."

"I'm hardly afraid of her. She caught me unawares is all."

"That isn't the point!" Dominic had argued, but Rayne had been determined.

He had to confront her, had to lay his doubts to rest. He needed to see her face, he told himself. One look in those clear blue eyes and he would see the loathing she had hidden from him so well. One probing glance would unmask her treachery, then his mind could accept the truth of what had happened and leave him in peace.

He had been so sure, so obsessed with the notion, so

unflappably determined to put things to rest. He had
crossed an ocean to accomplish the feat, had bought a
bloody plantation! But when the final moment came, it
hadn't gone the way he had planned.

He remembered that moment now as she closed the
door to the bedchamber down the hall from the large
room he had taken at the opposite end. There had been
surprise in those big bright eyes, then the flashing blue
anger he had seen a dozen times since he had met her.
And maybe a moment of fear. But the hatred was dis-
guised, just as it had been before, by a look of innocence
and despair and even a hint of pain.

It was there, by God, it had to be! She had betrayed him
—he had watched her pull the trigger! It was there, lurk-
ing in those bright blue eyes, hidden by a woman with a
twisted desire for vengeance, a woman who had mastered
the art of deceit.

And when it appeared, Rayne intended to see it.

So he had paid the tavernkeeper, Barzillai Hopkins,
twice what he should have in exchange for her servitude
—and was now paying even more dearly.

Rayne strode into the office study, reached for the bottle on the shelf behind the desk and poured himself a
liberal dose of rum. He downed it in a swallow and felt the
fiery liquid burn a path into his stomach. As hot as it was,
it didn't match the fire that still raged in his veins. The fire
that burst into flame every time he saw her.

He sank down on a high-backed leather chair behind
the stout mahogany desk. He had spent many a night at
this desk already, going over the books, reviewing the list
of workers who lived in the small thatched cottages built
of woven wood plastered with mud.

He had bought the failing plantation and settled himself
in the house long before he had gone that first night to
the tavern. Needing time to prepare himself, he had
worked long hours in the fields beside the workers, clearing away the rotting cane. He had bought the place sight
unseen, nothing more than an excuse to justify his jour-

ney. But during the course of his research on the island and its economy, his interest had been piqued. With a little effort, what might he make of the place? How could he turn the old place around?

At first the notion of a coffee-growing enterprise seemed absurd, but little by little the idea took root as solidly as the old cane crop once had, and now he could not shake it. The hard work challenged his body, though it heightened the pain in his back, and the thought of success drove him on as nothing else had since the war.

He poured another glass of rum. It was hardly his favorite, but he had been working so hard, had gotten so involved in his plans for the place and buying more of the needed supplies, that he hadn't thought to buy brandy.

He grimaced as he tossed back the fiery liquid and felt the warm glow of numbness settle in. He had slept well last night. Exhaustion had deadened his dreams, and he'd been able to ignore the throbbing ache of desire that had plagued him from the moment he had spotted Jo working in the tavern.

Last night he had slept. Tonight it wouldn't be so easy.

Rayne listened for footfalls upstairs and imagined Jocelyn's feet padding across the carpet. He could still recall the heat of her mouth beneath his in the wagon, feel the shape of her small upthrusting breasts. Perhaps he should summon Dulcet to his quarters. The alluring octaroon housekeeper had been making eyes at him since the moment of his arrival.

"I belong Massa James," she had said, referring to the former owner. "I please him well. Now I belong to you."

Rayne surveyed her heavy breasts and narrow waist. She had liquid-brown eyes and high cheekbones and a mouth that was as lush as any he had seen. His body needed easing—why the devil shouldn't he accept what she so freely offered?

Rayne sighed. Dulcet could soothe his body, but not his mind. Only Jocelyn could do that—and only with the truth.

Lies were all he'd get now, but sooner or later she'd admit her deceit. Once she revealed her betrayal, he would be free.

Standing beside the high tester bed, Jocelyn stripped off her dusty clothes and tossed them on the rose chintz counterpane. She was weary from the bumpy road and her uncomfortable seat on the wagon. Yet even with Rayne there to dampen the moment, she had enjoyed it— every sweet-breathing minute.

She drew on her night rail and walked to the window. The air was so incredibly clean up here, the sky so filled with stars. What would happen if she went outside? she wondered. Would someone try to stop her? It was silent in the house, the servants retired for the evening. She didn't own a wrapper, but if she were quiet, perhaps no one would see her.

Knowing she shouldn't, but lured by the cool night air, she left the room and descended the stairs. She wouldn't go far, just sit for a while in the darkness, absorbing the night sounds and fresh mountain breeze.

She moved into the shadows and sat down on a low rock wall surrounding the overgrown garden. It was peaceful out here, so still and restful. In minutes she was caught up in the quiet, something she had missed since her childhood in the country. The sound of an opening door went unnoticed, as well as the crunch of gravel beneath a pair of heavy male boots.

"I thought I heard something. I might have known it was you."

Jocelyn leaped to her feet, squeaking in surprise at the sound of Rayne's voice. "I—I wasn't sleepy yet. It was so pretty out here, I just . . ." How could she explain what it felt like just to breathe the sweet clean air? "I wasn't going anywhere."

Though she could barely see him, she could feel the sweep of his eyes down her body. "What the devil are you wearing? Surely you haven't come out here in your night-gown?"

Unconsciously, she took a step backward. "No one saw me. It's dark out here and there's no one around."

"Except me."

She had no answer to that.

"What are you doing out here?"

"Looking at the stars. I've always loved the constellations." She pointed to the heavens. "That's Canis Major. And there—that's Taurus the Bull."

He grunted. "So it is."

"It's beautiful this time of night . . . and so quiet. Not like the City . . . or the tavern. There never seemed a moment of peace."

"You shouldn't be out here."

"I suppose not. I'm surprised you didn't lock me in."

"The island itself is your prison. There is no place for you to run."

She stiffened. He still wasn't ready for the truth. She could hear it in his voice. She wondered if he ever would be.

"If that is the case, then you won't mind my sitting here a little while longer." She sank down on the low rock wall where she had been resting. "I like watching the fireflies —they keep me company."

Rayne caught her arm and pulled her back to her feet. "You keep parading around half naked, and one of these men will be keeping you company." *Or I will.* "If you think *I* rode you hard, you'll soon discover there is quite a difference."

She jerked free of his hold, her cheeks burning hot with embarrassment. "Your concern is touching, my lord."

Rayne peered at her through the darkness. "I meant what I said—it isn't safe for a woman out here alone. Our workers may not pose a problem, but there are others nearby who could. I don't want you wandering around at night by yourself."

Surely he wasn't worried? Jo scoffed. Worried something might happen before he'd taken his bloody revenge.

She stood up and started back toward the house.

"We'll be starting work early," he said.

Jocelyn just kept walking.

Used to long days of labor, Jocelyn awoke before sunrise, disoriented for a moment by the mosquito barr hanging from the bed and the feel of the soft feather mattress.

She sighed as she remembered where she was, then allowed herself a minute to soak up the feeling of comfort she had been denied for so long. She stretched and yawned into the darkness of the room, not yet gray with the light of dawn. Finally, she lifted the covers and rolled to the edge of the bed to light a candle.

She hadn't slept well last night, though the bed was soft and the room far better than the dismal servants' quarters she had expected. Still, her night had been fraught with dreams of him, the conversation they'd had out in the darkness and all that had happened since his arrival.

It angered her, this hatred she saw in his eyes—and frightened her far beyond that. During the night, she had awakened damp with perspiration, dreaming he towered above her wild with rage, his big hands wrapped around her throat as he slowly choked the life from her body.

She tried to tell him that she hadn't shot him, but he only squeezed harder. "If you didn't do it, who did?" he had roared.

It was a question she had asked herself a thousand times since that fateful afternoon, the list of potential villains growing longer and ever more confusing.

She knew Rayne had enemies. She'd spent nearly two years gauging his movements, been witness to half a dozen tavern brawls, seen him woo and jilt a score of women with little regard for their feelings. He had told her himself that Lady Campden had once been his paramour and that her husband had always been jealous.

Add to the list Stephen Bartlett, Lord Harcourt. And of

course Rosalee Shellgrave, the actress who was once Stephen's mistress—before she had been Rayne's.

There was a last name she was loath to mention, even in the silence of her mind. A thin, blond boy with badly burned hands. At first she had denied the possibility. Then she recalled the subtle shift in their relationship, the strange way he'd behaved ever since she had begun wearing dresses and acting like a lady. Had Tuck developed some kind of schoolboy infatuation? Could he possibly have been jealous of Rayne? Did he believe in some way that he was protecting her, maybe even saving her?

Jocelyn's stomach clenched at the thought, and she prayed it wasn't the truth. Even if it were, her conviction for the crime would keep him safe. It was small consolation for the tremendous injustice, but it eased her mind a little just the same.

Jocelyn finished dressing, ran a comb through her hair, and picked up the candlestick she had lit to brighten the room. Pulling open the heavy wooden door, she stepped out into the hallway. The house was dark, or at least it appeared so until she passed the study downstairs. Yellow light leaked from beneath the door and she could hear movement within.

Surely Rayne wouldn't be up this early.

Curious who it might be, but unwilling to risk finding out, Jocelyn continued outside to the building that housed the kitchen. Working indoors in the steamy, constantly overheated room was the least favorite task she could set for herself, but she wasn't about to wait for Rayne to put her to work. She wasn't about to let him find fault with her or anything she had done.

For several long moments Jocelyn stood unnoticed in the kitchen doorway. Huge black kettles bubbled on a hand-fashioned, white-brick stove beside a big brick oven. Steam hissed from a teapot, and vegetables and fruits sat in stacks on long wooden tables: corn, cassava, sweet potatoes, mangoes, sour sop, and jack fruit. Already it was hot inside the room, but the smells were pleasant, odors of simmering meats and fresh-baked bread.

"Bread done," said a tall cocoa-skinned woman with long-boned limbs, high cheekbones, and a full-lipped smile. "You want I should get dem?"

"Dat chore too much boderation." A short black woman, dark as coal, with a girth three times the size of the other, jerked open the oven's iron door. "I d-weet."

Jocelyn couldn't help smiling at the heavy *patois*, English Creole, the woman was speaking. Even after her weeks in Jamaica, she could barely make out what the speaker was saying.

"Hallo," said the tall woman, whose speech was much easier to understand. "You girl come with new massa?"

"Yes. My name is Jocelyn."

"Jo-ce-line?"

"Jo will do, if that's easier."

She grinned, displaying a mouth full of white. She was pretty, Jo realized. Exotic and willowy, yet big-breasted, and sensual in a way far different from most other women.

"I am Dulcet and dis woman is Gwen. I am house-keeper and Gwen is cook. The two dere are Robin and Bluejay."

Jo turned to see two young girls giggling behind their hands in the corner.

"Stop dat!" Gwen said. "I goine swat you, you don' git to work." The smiles were gone in an instant, the two young girls once more soberly slicing away at a pile of ripe cassava.

"Dey neber goin' learn." Gwen shook her wooly-haired head and pulled out a second loaf of bread. Jo's mouth watered at the succulent aroma.

"You massa's girl?" Dulcet asked.

"No."

Dulcet smiled broader. "Good."

Jo didn't like the sound of that, or the way the woman had looked when she'd spoken of Rayne. But her smile was warm, and as soon as Jocelyn pitched in to help, they accepted her as if they had long been friends.

"Bebo sick today." Dulcet bit into a piece of the mango she sliced, then licked the sweet from her long brown fingers. "Gwen my friend. Massa say okay to help." There was that look again, sort of a flush that darkened the high bones in her cheeks.

"I gather you like him."

"Massa hondsome mon." She grinned. "Big hands. Strong body. Big steek."

"Big steek?" Jo repeated.

On the opposite side of the table, fixing boiled green bananas and rice, Gwen's huge middle shook with mirth. She made several lewd gestures with her blunt-fingered hands that made it clear Dulcet meant *big stick*, and it was Jocelyn's cheeks that turned red.

"She want mek wi d-weet," Gwen said, and though Jo had no idea what separately each word meant, she got a pretty good idea Dulcet wanted Rayne in her bed.

If it hadn't been for the embarrassed look on the pretty girl's face and the fact she obviously hadn't been there yet, Jocelyn's jealousy might have surfaced. As it was, she found herself grinning, then all three women broke out laughing. God, it felt good to laugh.

Rayne watched the women from the doorway. He'd been standing there for some time, mesmerized by the sight of Jocelyn's smiling face.

In his dreams he saw her that way, laughing and talking with carefree abandon, but during the day his rational mind took over and blotted out any warm memories he still held. That she was up and already working surprised him, though it probably shouldn't have. She had always been a willing worker, pitching in more than she had to around the town house they had shared.

She bent over a long wooden table, slicing green bananas. Her face was flushed from her laughter and the steamy heat of the kitchen, and damp tendrils of shiny raven hair clung tenaciously to her cheeks. She stretched a bit, working to get the kinks out of her back, and her breasts thrust forward enticingly. He imagined exactly where her nipples might be, and a surge of heat tightened his groin.

She stretched once more against the uncomfortable position, and his mind strayed from the sensuous picture she made to the time she had mentioned her labors in the kitchen of an East End tavern.

"It was the worst job I ever 'ad," she'd said, her cockney sliding in with the unpleasant memory. "I 'ated the bloody 'eat and the smoke and those never-endin' stacks of dirty dishes. God's truth, I would rather be a thief."

He had laughed then. He wasn't laughing now.

Neither was Jo. She had seen him standing in the doorway, and all of the women had fallen silent.

"I—I didn't think to see you up for quite some time, my lord. I figured the kitchen could always use some help."

"Yes . . . I recall how much you enjoy that sort of work." Unconsciously she grimaced, and Rayne's mouth curved into the faintest of smiles. "However, I think it best you forego your labors in here for a while. I've something else in mind for you."

"Of course." She started to unfasten the apron she had tied over her skirt.

"You might want to leave it. This job gets pretty dirty."

She lifted her chin. It was obvious she believed he had something dire in store for her. He should have. Dammit to hell, he bloody well should have!

"This way." He led her out behind the kitchen, walking briskly toward the large patch of earth being cultivated in the rear. Tall stalks of corn waved in the breeze, and melons climbed long low vines along the neatly ordered rows. A black and white mutt scampered past one of the dark-skinned workers, who chased the animal away with the threatening end of his hoe.

Rayne stopped at the edge of the vegetable garden beside a short, well-built black-haired man no more than six and twenty.

"Jocelyn, this is Paulo Baptiste. He's the man in charge of the garden and the grounds around the house."

Paulo rose from where he knelt, dusting the rich dark soil from his hands. *"Bom dia, senhorita."*

"Jocelyn speaks French and English, but no Portuguese, I'm afraid." Sensing the younger man's interest, Rayne felt an unwanted twinge of jealousy.

"It's a pleasure to meet you, Paulo." Jocelyn extended a slim-fingered hand, but the Portuguese man saw the dirt on his own and merely shook his head.

"The pleasure is mine, I am sure." He was a strapping fellow, for his lack of height, with intelligent eyes and an easy disposition. Rayne had liked him from the start, had recognized his gift for working with the soil, and his ability to manage the workers.

"Jocelyn is extremely good with flowers. I thought perhaps she could do something with our miserable beds."

Jo's eyes swung to his face. "You're letting me work in the garden? But I thought—"

"I know what you thought, Jocelyn, and you may rest assured that if those beds didn't need attention so badly, I would have put you to work clearing the last of the cane fields."

The thought *had* crossed his mind. God knew she deserved it—that and a whole lot worse. But seeing her watching the fireflies last night, hearing her laughter as she worked in the kitchen, sent the notion right out of his head.

"Paulo will show you the hothouse and the potting shed. You'll find the tools you'll need for weeding. Make me a list of the plants you want, and the next trip into town for supplies, I'll see that you get them."

She watched him with eyes that searched his face. "All right."

Rayne merely nodded. The look of pleasure she had flashed at the task he had set made his chest grow tight.

Damn, he wished she wouldn't look at him that way. It made his mind cloud with feelings that long should have died. It made all his nagging doubts resurface.

It made him want her with a passion that nearly matched the anger he felt at what she had done.

Bloody hell! Rayne turned away from the sight of Jocelyn strolling beside the small dark Portuguese off toward the potting shed. Already she was laughing at something the younger man said, and already Rayne regretted the decision that had thrown them both together. Damn her to hell for the vixen she was!

Determined to forget her if it took every ounce of his will, Rayne strode off toward the stables. Like most of the outbuildings, the barn was old and in need of repair. The roof leaked, and cobwebs clung to the rafters and climbed the walls in every corner. It smelled of animals, manure, and straw.

Crossing to a stall at the rear, Rayne opened the door and coaxed out the big black stallion he had taken to riding since his arrival. Knight was the finest animal on the place, the only horse of any breeding that hadn't been sold before he got there. Rayne saddled the animal himself and swung up into the saddle. His back spasmed with pain; he winced, then ignored it.

He needed to survey the work being done in the fields, needed some clean fresh air. He needed to purge the hot coil of lust that had tightened low in his belly.

He would work till dusk if he had to, let exhaustion cleanse his mind of this hellish desire. If that didn't work, he'd consider taking Dulcet to his bed.

He would do it, he vowed. He would do whatever it took to keep his mind and body from its feelings of need for Jo.

Wearing a bonnet one of the Portuguese women had loaned her, Jocelyn worked all day beneath the bright Caribbean sun. She should have been hot and tired and irritable after such a day of labor, but she wasn't.

Every moment out of doors had been a joy, a feeling almost as good as being free. Paulo Baptiste had been helpful and kind. She discovered he was an indentured servant, not a convict as she was.

"I sell myself into bondage," he had said. "For the chance of a new life. In only five years I will be a free man. I will have earned enough money for a fresh start in America."

"That sounds wonderful, Paulo." And it gave her hope. Maybe someday she could make a fresh start somewhere else.

She was thinking along those very pleasant lines while she undressed and pulled on her white cotton night rail. She had just drawn back the rose chintz counterpane when she saw it, a huge, hairy-legged black spider nearly as big as her hand. The scream came unbidden, even before she turned and raced to the door. It flew open before she reached it, and Jocelyn collided headlong with Rayne. His arms went around her when she stumbled, and he caught her against his chest.

"What is it? What's happened?"

She was shaking all over, and feeling suddenly foolish at the scene she had caused. "I'm sorry. There's a spider is all. It's just that it—it's so bloody big!"

Rayne's mouth curved up. She couldn't believe it, but he actually smiled. "I'm afraid they're a hazard of the island. They're harmless, but they're definitely big. You ought to see the size of the lizards."

Jocelyn bit her lip. She tried her best not to laugh, but suddenly the urge was just too great. She looked at Rayne, saw the glint of mischief in his eyes, and both of them grinned. Then they were laughing, holding onto each other, their bodies shaking with mirth. It was just as it had been before, the same as a dozen happy times they had shared.

In that one moment, more than anything on this earth, Jocelyn wanted Rayne to know the truth of her inno-

cence. She looked up at him, saw the way his smile had
faded and a dark smoky glint had come into his eyes.

"Rayne, I didn't—"

His kiss cut off her words, so swift and hot her knees
nearly buckled beneath her. If it hadn't been for the moment of laughter they had shared, she might have tried to
stop him. Instead she opened her mouth to invite his
tongue, felt the silky softness, felt the hot demanding ur-
gency, and leaned against the hard wall of his chest. Steel
muscle rippled, his heart pounded fiercely beneath her
hand, and fiery heat slid through her body.

Rayne's hands moved down her back to cup her bottom, and he settled her against him. She could feel his
solid length, remembered what it felt like thrusting inside
her, and moaned low in her throat even as her fingers
sifted gently through his hair.

She felt him stiffen, felt him pull away, and knew hunger like a starving urchin. When she glanced at Rayne's
face, gentle and laughing only moments before, she
winced at his undisguised fury.

"I'm not a fool, Jocelyn. I know that is what you believe. I know that I once behaved that way, but you may
rest assured I will not play the fool for you again."

"Rayne, please. If only you would—"

"Don't," he said. "Not another word."

"But I—"

He gripped her arm. "It is all I can do not to strike you.
Consider yourself fortunate I've contained myself thus
far." She didn't doubt he meant it. It was there in every
angry line of his face. With a last hard glance, Rayne
turned and stalked out the door.

Jo stared after him until one of the houseboys arrived to
dispatch the spider, then the room fell silent and she was
left alone.

With a heart still pounding and a heaviness in her
breast, she lay down on the bed and stared up at the thin
mosquito netting. Tears stung the backs of her eyes, and
her throat felt hot and achy.

For one brief moment Rayne had been the man she had known and loved. The laughter in his face had suffused her heart with hope and swept her into the past as if they had never left it.

Then the laughter had faded and passion had surfaced. She hadn't been immune—and neither had Rayne. His fury had been aroused by that passion, a desire he seemed even more unwilling to submit to than she. And yet it was there. Her body still throbbed with the need he'd aroused. Her mind held images of his hard frame pressing against her.

With a bitter sob, Jocelyn clenched her fist and slammed it down on the mattress beside her. If only he would listen! Once he had been a man of reason. Hot-tempered to be sure, but rarely without good cause. Now his fury blinded him. He believed her guilty, and he wanted to see her punished.

Yet there had been that single instant of laughter. That one gentle glance that betrayed some inner feeling not yet dead. Was it possible more of those feelings still lingered? Perhaps they were there, buried just beneath the surface. Perhaps if she waited and prayed. If she earned a little of his trust, in time he would listen.

Maybe in the time he remained on the island, he would come to believe her.

If he did, she might yet find the chance to be free.

Chapter Sixteen

RAYNE DRANK HIMSELF into a stupor that night, then worked sixteen hours the next day fighting a blinding headache. For the next three days he went out of his way not to encounter Jo. It crossed his mind to wonder how she and the handsome dark Portuguese were getting along, but he forced the notion away.

Each night, he drank more heavily than he intended, but it was the only way he could fall asleep. Riding his horse along the trail above the plantation, he had seen Jocelyn's slender figure bent over the flower beds, just a small black-haired dot among the overgrown grass, and yet he would have known her anywhere. A wagonload of bedding plants had been brought in from Kingston along with fresh supplies, and already she had them blooming pink and red beneath the nurturing sunlight.

Twice he had seen her surrounded by the workers' children. He had heard her laughter and that of the little ones. He remembered the foundlings in the workhouse, the love she had felt for them, the caring. It didn't fit the image he carried of a woman twisted with hatred, yet he knew that image must be true.

He had seen her aim the pistol, seen the silvery flash of the muzzle just before the shot rang out. He could still feel the slickness of blood on his fingers, the agonizing blaze of the bullet.

The pain in his back was a constant reminder, and yet . . .

Driving himself like a madman from dusk till dawn, Rayne took his meals in his study or carried them into the fields wrapped in a cloth in his saddlebags. He had regained most of the weight he had lost, the hard work had thickened his muscle, and the hours in the sun had burnished his skin to the hue of a tall Spanish elm.

By the end of the week, the last of the fields would be cleared and tilled, though the shipment of coffee slips had not yet arrived. They were due into port the first of next week.

Sitting at his desk, Rayne glanced at the clock on the mantel. Nearing midnight and he still couldn't sleep. He closed the ledger on his desk and refilled his glass with more of the brandy he'd had brought in with the last load of supplies.

He still felt far too sober, and just minutes ago he had heard Jocelyn speaking to Dulcet as she climbed the stairs, her voice throaty and laced with amusement at something the taller woman said. They had stayed up late, sewing new garments for the children, enjoying the task, it seemed, though it hadn't yet been assigned.

In his mind's eye, he could see her. A vision in the lacy white gown she had worn for him the night he had taken her maidenhead, her hair glistening like a raven's wing in the soft yellow glow of the lamp. Her skin was the color of ivory and every bit as smooth. She had come to him with a smile on her face, welcoming his advances, lulling him into believing she desired him.

He laughed at the bitter twist of fate, certain now that indeed that much was true. Her body had betrayed her, just as she had betrayed him. He thought of the kiss they had shared in her room. She had wanted him. He did not doubt he could have taken her.

Rayne tossed back the brandy and shoved back his chair. Sitting there brooding would only make things worse. Instead he rounded the table, lurching a little as he moved, and crossed to the door leading into the hall. Hours ago he'd untied his neckcloth, now he jerked the long white length from around his throat and began unbuttoning his shirt. It was open to the waist by the time he reached the landing and started down the upstairs' hall.

He might have made it to his room if he hadn't heard the movement, seen the candlelight seeping from the space beneath her door. As it was, the soft yellow rays drew him like a beacon, his dark hand reaching for the latch with a will of its own. Then he was lifting it, shoving open the heavy wooden door and stepping into the dimly lit interior.

Jocelyn glanced up from where she sat reading by the flickering light of a stout white candle, and her eyes went wide at the sight of him. She snapped the book closed, set it down on the small pie-crust table beside her, and slowly came to her feet.

"What are you doing in here?" she asked as he moved forward into the room.

She wasn't wearing the white lace nightgown, but he wasn't disappointed. After the night he had seen her out in the garden, her prim white night rail seemed somehow more enticing.

"What do you want?"

"What do I want?" Rayne heard himself say. "I don't believe, my love, that you are unable to guess." He bumped into a chair near the foot of the bed and spat a violent curse.

"You're drunk." She took in his nearly unbuttoned shirt and the slight muss of his hair. "Get out."

He chuckled without mirth. "Why should I? It isn't what either of us wants." Jocelyn stiffened, though he could see he had spoken the truth. It was there in the quickened pulse at the base of her throat, the way she unconsciously moistened her lips.

"You're wrong. This is my room. You don't belong in here. You never will again."

He arched a dark eyebrow. "Is that so? Why don't you come here and we'll find out?"

She only backed away. "You aren't thinking clearly. If you try to come near me, I'll fight you, and the others will hear. Is that what you want?"

"What I want, my dear sweet Jo, is for you to remove your nightgown and climb up on that bed. I want you to spread your legs and welcome me inside you with the same sweet passion you showed me before."

He didn't miss the fury in her eyes. He wanted her anger. He had come here to get it—and more.

"I told you to get out, and I mean it." She picked up the book she had been reading and hurled it in his direction. It hit one of the bed posts and bounced harmlessly onto the floor.

Rayne merely chuckled. "I've always admired the fire in you, Jo. I believe it's what made you so passionate in bed." He moved toward her, the alcohol haze clearing a bit at the desire coursing hotly through his veins. Already he was hard and aching, bulging against the front of his breeches.

Jocelyn spun away from his grasp, picked up a flowered porcelain water pitcher and hurled it at his head. He ducked at the last possible second and it shattered on the floor.

Rayne smiled coldly. "You'll have to do better than that, sweeting." He darted to the right and Jo darted left, spinning away from him and sprinting for the door. The bulky nightgown clung to her long slim legs, slowing her down, and he caught her in two swift paces.

"Let go of me!" She tried to pull away, but he held her fast.

"You've got spirit, my love. I like that. But I've got something you want—and I intend to see that you get it."

"No." She stubbornly shook her head, tumbling her glossy black hair while her eyes remained fixed on his face. For the first time she looked afraid, and a knot balled hard in his stomach.

"Frightened? You needn't be. I don't intend to hurt you. I only mean to see you warm my bed."

"No, damn you!" When Jocelyn tried to jerk free, Rayne caught the top of her nightgown and ripped it to her waist. She backed away from him wide-eyed, holding up the tattered remnants of fabric to cover her breasts.

He glanced from her trembling figure down at the fine gold chain he had accidently caught in his hand. The clasp was broken, the chain draping lifelessly over his palm, but the locket remained intact, the delicately enameled pastoral scene exquisite, the tiny diamonds taunting him from among the fleecy clouds.

If he had been torn between anger and desire for her before, now he was enraged.

"What is this, my love?" he mocked, daring her to comment. "A keepsake? Or a trophy? A reminder of how well and truly you had me fooled!"

Jocelyn made a whimpering sound in her throat as he clenched the locket in his fist and hurled it against the wall in the corner. It landed with a clatter, and Jo cried out as if she were in pain. Blind with fury, Rayne crossed the few paces between them and caught her before she could run.

"You owe me. I intend to see that you pay."

"Let me go!"

But he had no such intention. Instead he half carried, half dragged her toward the bed and shoved her down on the soft feather mattress.

"You have your trophy. Now I'll have mine." Using his body to hold her in place, he ripped the shredded gown from her shoulders, then stripped it off her body. Naked and exposed beneath him, Jocelyn finally stilled. He found himself looking into her big blue eyes, saw the anger she didn't bother to disguise, and something else.

There was pain in her expression, anguish and bitter despair. As if some last precious hope had been stripped from her along with her clothes. He couldn't stand to see it, couldn't believe he had lowered himself to this.

Bloody Christ—he wasn't some kind of savage!

He let go of her wrists, but he didn't move away, just stared into those anguished blue pools and wished he could see them light with love and laughter as he had once believed.

"Why, Jo?" he said, his voice raw with pain. "Why?"

Her eyes searched his, glistened with a mist of tears. Then he was lowering his head, brushing her lips with the gentlest of kisses. His tongue slid along her bottom lip and he felt it tremble. He would taste her sweetness, he vowed, just this one last time, and then he would leave.

With the lightest caress, he settled his mouth over hers and felt the softly rounded curve of her lips. Just a moment more, he told himself, just this one last time.

Tendrils of shiny black hair brushed his fingers and he smoothed it away from her cheeks with an unsteady hand. He meant to pull away then, to go and leave her alone. Instead he felt her fingers slide into his hair, urging him closer, felt her lips part beneath his, and the tentative touch of her tongue.

Below him on the mattress her body arched upward, her small ripe breasts pushed into his chest. She tasted of wild mountain berries. Her skin felt as smooth as the petals of an orchid.

Rayne groaned low in his throat, and the last of his control slipped away. He was plunging his tongue into her mouth, taking her lips, then kissing her eyes, her nose, her cheeks. He filled his hands with her breasts, caressing them, working the peaks until they pebbled. He could feel her slender, fine-boned fingers sifting through the hair on his chest, pushing the shirt off his shoulders. He ripped the last button free in his haste to be shed of it, then unfastened the front of his breeches, allowing the heavy weight of his sex to spring free.

Jocelyn's hands were there, even as he moved above her, guiding him toward the core of her, urging him inside. He could feel her trembling, feel the heat of her body, and flames of desire roared through him.

222   Kat Martin

His tongue laved a dusky pink nipple; he tugged it
gently with his teeth and heard her moan. Then he was
parting her thighs, touching the soft slick petals of her
sex, sliding his finger inside to ready her for the single
hard thrust of his shaft.

She wanted it. He knew by her wildly thudding heart,
the arching of her hips, and he reveled in the power he
still held.

And so did Jo.

She sensed Rayne's burning hunger and the knowledge
made her own passions soar. She felt his fiery touch, the
slick wet heat at her core, and her trembling body jerked
upward. She wasn't thinking clearly, hadn't been from the
moment she'd seen the anguish on Rayne's face, his raw
aching need for her, the pain he'd kept so carefully locked
away.

Her fingers bit into the thick bands of muscle across his
shoulders, kneading them, feeling their incredible power.
He kissed her again, and fiery heat engulfed her, banked
for so long she'd forgotten the rapture, the wildly fierce
sensations. Sweet God, how could she? This was what she
wanted. What both of them wanted. It felt so right,
though with what lay between them, she knew that it was
wrong.

Still, she could not deny it. Not when the pleasure was
so heady, the fire so hot and sweet and consuming. Not
when the closeness erased the pain and the heartbreak of
the past, if only for this brief time.

"Rayne," she whispered, but his hard kiss silenced her.
It was no longer gentle, nor was gentle what she wanted.
She wanted him to come into her, to fill her, to pound and
pound until he drove away this terrible gnawing hunger,
this incredible aching need.

And he did. With one solid thrust he filled her, his hard
body joining them as if this one single act encompassed all
the times they had shared before.

Rayne! In the eye of her mind she cried out his name
and prayed that his heart would hear her.

She didn't want to need him. She didn't want to love him. She wanted to hate him, to free herself from the bondage he forced upon her, but she couldn't. Not now. Certainly not in this sweet, eternal moment. Not while each driving stroke, each pounding thrust, sent her higher and higher, farther out into that place of pleasure and light and fulfillment. Not while she was once more with the man she loved.

She felt the tension in his muscles, and his passion drove her on, pounding into her deeper and harder, urging her onward and upward. Then she was there, swirling among the reds and the golds and the silvers, feeling such a rush of joy that she thought for an instant she might die of it.

In that moment nothing mattered but the feel of him, the thrill of their coming together. She gave herself up to the fire, felt a second rush of pleasure, felt Rayne shudder and stiffen above her, felt the wetness of his seed as he plunged himself inside her, then both of them began to spiral down.

It took a long while to drift back to earth, an even longer time for her mind to accept what had happened. She did so reluctantly, and only when she felt Rayne's withdrawal, saw him standing above her, buttoning up the front of his snug black breeches. His expression was inscrutable, a cool mask of indifference that hurt more than the jeering taunts he had made when he had first come into the room.

For a moment he said nothing, just looked at her as if she were someone he might have met once somewhere else.

"It is obvious my assumption about your needs is correct." He bent down to retrieve his shirt, crumpled in a heap on the floor, straightened, and pinned her with a cold, expressionless glare. "From now on I will take you as hard and as often as I like. You may as well get used to it."

Jocelyn jerked as if she had been slapped. "If—If you

think for an instant that I will let that happen, you are a
bigger fool than you believe.''

His mouth curved up in a bitter half smile. ''We shall
see, my love.'' He lifted the latch and pulled open the
door.

"I'm warning you, *my lord*, should you try to force me,
this time I *will* put a lead ball in your chest!"

Rayne's dark brows drew together in a frown. He
seemed to mull over her words, which made no sense in
the context of what he believed. Then his bottom lip
curved sardonically.

"I cautioned you once about threatening me. I meant
exactly what I said. And should you try to leave, the authorities will have you in hand in a fortnight. I suggest you
accept your lot and make things easy on both of us." With
that he stepped out in the hall and slammed the door.

Jocelyn stared after him, unable to believe what had
happened. Her body felt limp and sated, yet part of her
already throbbed for more of his touch. How could she
want a man who so obviously despised her? How could
she have been duped by a single desperate glance?

With fingers that trembled, Jocelyn touched her kiss-
swollen lips, still tender from Rayne's passions. Her heart
felt leaden. Her throat burned with the tears that threatened to overwhelm her.

Getting up off the bed, she numbly crossed the room
and knelt on the hard wooden floor at the edge of the
carpet. In minutes her fingers closed over the locket
Rayne had hurled with such contempt. With hands that
trembled and a bitter ache in her heart, she held it up to
the light of the candle. The fine gold chain was irreparably
broken, but the beautiful enameled locket gleamed as
beautifully as ever. Jocelyn's fingers closed around it and
she clutched it to her breast.

She wanted to weep and wail, to sob out her heart and
her broken dreams. She wanted to, but she did not.

Still the pain was there, deep and scalding, hurting her
heart and soul. It was lessened only by that one revealing

glance, that instant of gentleness that just as before had risen unbidden and unwanted in Rayne's dark eyes.

Because of it, he hadn't forced her.

And in the instant before he released her, she had known that he would not.

She tried to tell herself she had just imagined it. That she had played the fool, that he cared nothing at all for her and he never had. But when she closed her eyes, she could still see it, that anguished flash of pain, that desperate moment of need.

And because she couldn't shake the notion it truly existed, the despair she felt did not take root as deeply as it might have. It was there, yes, piercing and painful, dull and aching just below the surface. Then she would remember that look and hope would rise anew. She wouldn't admit defeat, not yet, and she knew from years of bitter experience that in the morning she would feel better.

The sun would shine and she would spend her day working in the garden. The simple pleasure would be sweet and untainted. She would take what she could get and it would be enough.

Paulo Baptiste watched the master's pretty lady bend to her task, her long slim fingers sifting through the rich black earth of the flower beds. Even if his lordship denied it, Paulo knew the woman belonged to the viscount as surely as if the priest had spoken the vows. It was there in the way he looked at her, the possessive way he touched her, even his protective male stance.

And Jo looked at him much the same, though neither of them knew it. Each of them did his best to remain aloof from the other. Paulo wondered if it would do either of them any good.

"Bom dia, menina."

"Bom dia, senhor," Jo said. Paulo was teaching her a little of his language. Besides Portuguese, he also spoke

Spanish, and later, he'd declared, he would teach her that, too.

"You did not wear your bonnet today." Paulo stood frowning, then crouched down beside her. "You do not fear the harshness of the sun?"

She smiled at him. "I needed to feel its rays today. I wanted to absorb some of its warmth."

Paulo eyed her uncertainly. "Yes, I can see you are a little pale. You are sure you are not sick?"

"I'm fine, Paulo. But thank you for asking." Paulo was as close to a friend as Jocelyn had made since her arrival. Dulcet and Gwen were friendly, but the language barrier made it difficult for them to converse, and knowing the way Dulcet felt about Rayne, there was little Jo could say.

"You are lonesome, no? I have seen it in your face while you are working."

She pulled a weed from beneath a short bushy shrub and tossed it onto the pile with the others. "In a way, I suppose I am. It would be nice to have another woman to talk to, someone to share things with." She thought of Brownie and Tucker and how much she missed them. She thought of Conchita and Dolly and wondered how they faired.

"A woman of your years should be married. What you need is a husband and children."

"I'd love to have children. Who knows . . . perhaps one day, if I'm lucky I'll find someone."

Paulo's jet-black eyes searched her face. "I think already you have found him. I have seen the way you watch him—the way he watches you."

Jocelyn flushed. "You don't understand."

"I understand when a man wants a woman. If I did not see that same look in you, I would think of claiming you for myself."

Jocelyn's head snapped up. "Surely, you don't mean that. I thought you and I were friends. I thought—"

"It is clear, *querida*, exactly what you are feeling, but I

am a man, just like any other. I have needs, just as he has.
If you were not his woman, I would make you mine."

"But—"

"Do not say more, *meu bela.* Your eyes tell me what is
in your heart even if your pretty mouth will not say the
words."

Jocelyn said nothing more, but unconsciously her gaze
searched for Rayne. At least he hadn't returned to her
room. In fact, he had gone to great lengths not to come
near her. Even if he wouldn't admit it, he was just as upset
about what had happened as she was. Considering he believed she had shot him, probably more.

Several times she had thought to search him out, to tell
him the truth about the shooting. But she felt certain he
wouldn't believe her. Rayne was convinced. The servants
had accused her, she had no proof, and in leaving, it appeared she had run away.

And Rayne certainly hadn't bothered to find out the
truth.

"Do not work long without your bonnet," Paulo said,
his handsome dark face stern. "In this you will do as I
say."

Jocelyn almost smiled. He was a strong man, protective,
gentle, and kind. He would make some lucky woman a
good husband. In a corner of her heart she wished it
could be her.

Conchita Vasquez bent over the chamber pot in a corner
of her tiny room behind the kitchen and heaved up the
contents of her stomach. The bouts of nausea had usually
stopped by this late in the morning, but the smell of a
three-day-old parrot fish baking in the kitchen had sent
her running for her room.

Madre de Dios, sometimes she felt so ill, she wished
she could just lay down and die. Of course, old sourpuss
would not let her. Even after she told him about the babe,
he would make her work until her belly was so swollen
and heavy she could hardly move. Chita sagged with a

sudden shot of fear. *Dios mio,* would he toss her out in the street?

"Chita! Get down here, you lazy whore! You've a passel of work to do!" That was cook's old gravely voice. The woman was as heartless as her master.

Chita poured water into the basin on her scarred wooden dresser, rinsed the bad taste from her mouth, then washed her face and dried it on the apron over her skirt.

"Chita!"

"I am coming!" She shoved open the door to the kitchen of the Blue Boar Inn, and the fishy smell assailed her. It was all she could do to force the bile back down.

Stepping away for a moment, she spotted the big man she recognized immediately as the one who had purchased Jo's contract.

"Señor Viscount!" she called out to him, hurrying across the taproom in his direction. "Could you tell me please, how is my good friend Jo?"

He eyed her from head to foot. "Your friend is fine. But you'll soon see that for yourself."

"Jo is coming here?" She beamed up at him. "You are bringing her back?" *Por Dios,* it would be such a relief to have someone to talk to, someone to be with her when her time came. Already she was so frightened!

"I'm afraid not." Chita's bright smile faded. "Get your things. You're going to join her."

"Join her? You are taking me with you? You are taking me to Jo?"

His handsome face closed up, his expression turning bland and unreadable. "There is a great deal of work to be done on Mahogany Vale. We needed a few extra workers. Now do as I say, and get your things."

"*Sí. Sí, señor.*" Uncertain whether to be grateful or frightened, Chita hurried back toward the kitchen. Whatever awaited, it couldn't be worse than the fate she faced with Barz Hopkins. Or could it?

What would Stoneleigh do when he discovered her condition? Would he beat her? Make her give up the child? *Dios mio.* She made the sign of the cross and swallowed the fresh surge of bile in her throat.

Chapter Seventeen

"DULCET, HAVE YOU SEEN JOCELYN?" Rayne stopped the tall willowy housekeeper at the base of the stairs.

She smiled at him, soft invitation in her night-black eyes. "Jo out in kitchen with Gwen. Gwen make coconut sweet bread. Jo come in from work to taste it."

Rayne merely grunted. "Tell her I wish to see her. I'll be working in my study."

"Yes, massa." She started down the hall toward the rear of the house, then stopped and turned. "You are sure you not wish Dulcet come tonight? Mek wi d-weet. Make you very hoppy mon."

Rayne took in her seductive curves and plump, heavy bosom and felt a twinge in his groin. Part of him would like that more than a little, but another part felt reluctant. He wasn't quite sure why, but until he knew for certain, he would wait.

"Your offer is certainly tempting, Dulcet. But now is not a good time. Maybe sometime in the future . . ." He left the rest unfinished.

Dulcet looked at him with a hint of regret, then smiled. "I wait. When you need, I come."

"Thank you." God, the sun must be addling his senses! The woman could satisfy his needs as well as any, and enjoy herself, into the bargain. What the hell was the matter with him? Still, he did not change his mind. Instead he walked into his office and sat down behind his mahogany desk. Jocelyn knocked softly and entered a few moments later.

"Dulcet said you wished to see me."

He pointed toward a box piled high with bolts of fabric, India muslin, bombazine, jaconet, silks, and lace. "I'm tired of seeing you dressed in rags. You told me once that you had sewn your own clothes. I want you to spend a few less hours in the garden and fashion yourself something decent to wear. I shall expect to see you dressed properly whenever you're inside the house. Do I make myself clear?"

She was torn, he could see, between his demanding tone of voice and the beauty of the shimmering cloth.

"If that is your wish, my lord, obviously I have no choice but to obey."

"Exactly so." He hadn't missed her thinly veiled sarcasm or the unconscious squaring of her shoulders. She made it sound like she was doing him a favor, and amusement tugged at the corners of his mouth. "I'll have the houseboy carry the box up to your room."

She merely nodded and turned to walk away.

"One more thing."

"Yes?"

"A friend of yours will be joining our small compliment of workers."

"A friend?"

"The woman you introduced me to on the street in Kingston. Conchita Vasquez."

Jocelyn's mouth fell open. "Conchita is here? At Mahogany Vale?"

"Paulo Baptiste is seeing her settled in the servants' quarters. I thought you might like a moment to visit."

Jo broke into a grin. "Might? God's breath, I can hardly wait!" She picked up her skirts and started to race out the door, then stopped and turned. "She's all right, isn't she? Hopkins hasn't mistreated her?"

"The woman looked healthy enough to me, but I really wouldn't know."

"How did you find her? Why did you—"

"We've been needing a few more workers. I remembered the girl looking fit and stout. I figured she would do as well as any."

It wasn't the truth, and the look in Jocelyn's eyes said she knew it. Bloody hell, what in God's name had possessed him? So what if Jo was lonely? So what if he had seen her wistful expression and known she was missing her friends? Dammit, she was supposed to be unhappy. She was supposed to suffer for what she had done!

"Thank you, my lord."

He wanted to hear her call him Rayne, as she had that night in her room. He wanted to take her again, possess her, pound into her right there on the desk, and he despised himself for his weakness.

"That is all," he said brusquely. "You may leave." He knew his arrogant dismissal would gall her, and Rayne felt a jolt of satisfaction. Looking back at his work as if she weren't there, he waited until the door closed solidly behind her, then let out a slow breath of air.

He still wasn't certain why he had done it. Regret for his drunken escapade up in her room, perhaps. He really wasn't sure. Then again, part of him had meant what he'd said to her that night. She belonged to him, and though he would not force her, if he wanted her again and she wanted him, he would not hesitate to take her.

He only prayed that if he did, the powerful attraction he still felt for her would not grow stronger. That it would not destroy the protective shield he had carefully set between them.

By God, he might want her, but that did not alter the fact that she had nearly killed him!

Rayne shoved back his chair, walked to the shelf behind his desk, poured himself a brandy and tossed it down. The truth was that beneath her gentle facade, Jocelyn Asbury still blamed him for the death of her father. Whether or not she was ready to admit it, she secretly hated him, just as she had from the start.

He warned himself never to forget it.

"Conchita!" Jocelyn raced into the tiny bedchamber upstairs in the servants' quarters.

"Jo!" The Spanish girl dropped the blouse she had been folding, opened her arms and rushed to embrace her friend.

"I never thought to see you again," Jo said. "I was so worried what might happen to you."

"As I worried much about you." They hugged again, then Jo stepped away.

"Are you all right? Hopkins didn't hurt you?"

"A beating or two, *nada mas.*" She grinned, her teeth flashing white against her dark complexion. "I tell him I have the pox. I say if he try to press the sailors on me, I will tell them and they will kill him for trying to sell them a pox-infected whore."

Jocelyn laughed. "No wonder he left you alone."

"I was not sure how much longer I could fool him, but *si,* he left me alone."

"What have you heard of Dolly?"

Chita shook her head, long black hair rippling down her back. "I have heard nothing. I pray that she is well." She clasped Jo's hand. "What of you? The viscount, he treats you well?"

"Stoneleigh is the man I'm accused of shooting. He brought me here to see that I'm properly punished."

"Madre de Dios." Chita crossed herself. "He has beat you?"

"No."

"He has ravished you?"

"No." Her cheeks went red. "I suppose that was what he meant to do, but . . . in the end, he didn't force me." They had never spoken of such personal things, but Jocelyn needed a friend so badly it all just seemed to tumble out. "I was in love with him once."

Chita's black eyes widened with surprise, then she nodded. "I too was once in love—or at least that is what I believed. It is very painful, no?"

"Yes . . . it is."

"I am glad he did not hurt you. Me, I could never be in love with such a man." She shivered. "He is a hard man, I think."

"I didn't shoot him, Chita. I wish so badly I could tell him. I wish he would believe me, but I don't think he will."

Chita's face looked grave. "In this I believe you are right. The viscount has much anger at you. As we journeyed here, I could see it in his face whenever I mentioned your name. It made me afraid for you."

"Sometimes it makes me afraid, too." She smiled forlornly. "At other times . . . I see something in his eyes that makes me think he still cares."

"Then you must wait, *mi hermana*. If you speak too soon, you will only anger him more. If that happens, he will never believe you speak the truth."

Jocelyn sank down on the bed. "That's what I've been thinking." She forced a smile she didn't feel. "Enough of my troubles. What of you? The last time I saw you, you were looking terribly thin. I can see you've put some weight back on, but you still look a little too pale."

Conchita sat down beside her, took Jo's hand and placed it on her gently rounded stomach, looked up and promptly burst into tears.

"Oh, my God!"

It didn't take long to unravel the story.

"He was a friend of the man I worked for," Chita said tearfully, "the son of a local squire. Each time he came to the house, he would seek me out. I thought he loved me. He was so handsome . . . and I was such a fool."

Jocelyn squeezed her shoulder. "We're all fools sometimes. You mustn't torture yourself." She handed Chita a handkerchief, and the Spanish girl blotted her tears.

"I am afraid to have this baby, and yet already I feel love for it."

"I think it's only natural for you to be afraid." Jocelyn hugged her. "When the time comes, I'll be with you, and I know you'll make a wonderful mother."

"What—What will *he* do?"

Indeed, what would Rayne do when he found out? "He won't send you away." At least she didn't think he would. "He can be a hard man when he believes he has been wronged, but he would never hurt a young woman who had fallen on bad times."

Nor make her get rid of the baby.

Still, Jocelyn wasn't about to tell him, at least not yet. Instead she suggested they find a way for Chita to work for Paulo in the vegetable garden.

"The work is not too hard and Paulo is a kind, caring man. When time for the baby grows near, we can speak to Rayne. I'm sure he'll let you work inside the house."

Secretly she hoped throwing Paulo and Chita together might result in a courtship. Paulo spoke Spanish, had lived for a time in that country, and it appeared he needed a woman. Chita certainly needed a man.

The following day she approached Rayne in his study, hoping he'd let Chita work with Paulo. Listening from behind a stack of papers on his desk, he seemed only mildly concerned.

"There's as much to do there as anywhere else. If Paulo agrees, that will be fine."

"Thank you, my lord." Since Chita was only four months along, the labor wouldn't hurt her. Once she grew round with child, Rayne was bound to notice. Jocelyn prayed that what she'd told Chita was true and he would understand. "And thank you for bringing her here."

Rayne's face turned hard. "I told you before, more helping hands were needed. Chita's were as good as any."

"Yes . . . that is what you said."

"Now I'd suggest you get back to work. Paulo has been

lenient with you so far. If I see you shirking your duties, you may rest assured that I will not be so easily taken in."

Jocelyn felt a wave of anger. "Have you yet found me lacking, my lord? Do you really believe I would give you the least cause to complain? And if I did play the laggard, what would my punishment be? A flogging perhaps? Or another brutal round in your bed?"

Rayne's handsome face paled beneath his suntanned skin. Then a flush of fury swept his features. "There are times I look at you and I could lay the whip to your traitorous flesh myself."

It was Jo's turn to pale.

"But you need not fear—the beating you deserve will not come from me. As to the time you've spent in my bed, I'd be a fool to regret it since it is obvious that you enjoyed too. Nor will I promise it will not happen again."

His dark eyes raked her from head to foot, and a cold mocking smile curved his lips. "I would suggest a hasty return to your flowers, my sweet, or it may happen again right here. I should like nothing better than to press you down upon my desk, spread your long shapely legs, and ravish your scheming little body."

With a cry of outrage and a sob caught in her throat, Jocelyn picked up her skirts, turned, and raced toward the door. Her heart hammered wildly, thudding in fear at the anger she had seen on his face—or was it the desire that had blazed in his eyes?

Shaking all over, she didn't slow down till she reached the vegetable garden. Across the long rectangular patch of earth, Chita stood beside Paulo in the shade of a palm where she had left them. Not until she heard her friend's soft laughter did she stop, working hard to bring her emotions under control. Paulo was grinning at something Chita said, his black eyes smiling.

Jocelyn had sensed his attraction to the pretty Spanish girl almost at once, and Chita had not been immune to Paulo's proud masculinity. Seeing them together, happy and laughing, Jocelyn felt an unexpected pang of envy.

Once she and Rayne had laughed like that. Once they had been happy. It might not have lasted forever, but she never would have guessed that it would end like this. She turned away from the pair and walked wearily back toward the flower beds she had been weeding at the front of the house.

With every day that passed, Rayne's hatred seemed to swell instead of fade. He trusted her less. He despised her more. Just being in her presence seemed to drive him beyond all reason. How could she ever hope to make him see?

With the prospect growing ever more dim, Jocelyn did her best to avoid him. The few times she saw him, he was always aloof, his glance always cold and mocking. Though he worked like a madman during the day, driving himself to the point of exhaustion, late in the evening he sat brooding, consuming far more liquor than he should.

She could hear him down in his study, or climbing the stairs to his room in the wee hours of the morning, a little unsteady on his feet. His overindulgence worried her, reminding her all too clearly of what had happened to her father. Drink had turned Sir Henry bitter and uncaring, dim and lifeless, long before the night he had died.

In her heart of hearts, Jocelyn couldn't bear the thought of Rayne's life wasting away like that, and yet there was nothing she could do.

It was late in the afternoon the following week when the coffee plantings arrived. Mahogany Vale bubbled with excitement as the heavily laden two-horse drays rolled in.

All of the workers gathered around to assess the contents: heavy bags of seed, stout little seedlings with their pointed dark green leaves, and the odd-shaped cuttings that would be the boon or bane of the beautiful old plantation.

Jocelyn found herself as caught up in the fervor as the others. Wearing a new peach muslin dress, one of the simple but attractive gowns she had fashioned for herself from the cloth Rayne provided, she wandered away from the house to stand among the crowd as the wagons drew near. He rode at the head of the column, his big hands easily controlling the team of stout bay horses whose ears had perked up as soon as they had rounded the final bend toward home.

Jocelyn couldn't help but admire how tall and fit he looked, how incredibly handsome. Working out of doors seemed to suit him, which she never would have guessed, his energy as boundless as his determination. She wouldn't have suspected this side of him, but she couldn't deny the appeal it held for her. He was kind to his workers, concerned for their welfare, and always willing to lend a hand no matter how difficult the task—or how loathsome. In truth, it appeared the handsome viscount was twice the man she had ever believed.

"It is exciting, no?" Conchita asked, walking up beside her. She noticed Paulo stood close at hand.

"Yes, I suppose it is. For Rayne's sake, I hope it succeeds."

"You can say that after what he has done? After all you have suffered?"

Jocelyn merely shrugged. "He believes I am guilty. There was a time I felt much the same about him."

"Lady, lady!" Jo felt a gentle tug on her skirt. "Hold me so I can see?" There stood Tooney and Mike, two of the workers' children Jocelyn had met when she'd first arrived. They were darling little boys, one pudgy, one thin, less than a year apart in age, Tooney three and Mike four.

Jocelyn reached down to the round-faced smaller child and hoisted him up on her hip. Paulo lifted Mike up onto his wide shoulders.

Mike grabbed hold of Paulo's thick black hair to balance himself. "Take it easy, *moco,* you had better not wiggle so much."

The little boy grinned from ear to ear. "I see good from up here."

Paulo just smiled.

"Massa! Massa!" Little Tooney grinned and waved in Rayne's direction.

When he caught the source of the sound, Rayne smiled and waved back, then he noticed the child sat perched on Jocelyn's hip. Something flashed across his features at the sight of it, something Jocelyn couldn't have named in a thousand years and yet it made her heart turn over. Their eyes met, held, then Rayne jerked his gaze away. Jocelyn felt numb and shaken, and an ache had risen in her throat.

She followed Rayne's movements as he strode to one of the wagons and climbed up to where a short, balding man wearing spectacles and a bright plum tailcoat sat beside a dark-skinned driver.

"All of you! If I could have your attention!" The crowd, already beginning to quiet, fell silent at Rayne's command. "We've all worked hard for this. Not a man among you has shirked his duties. We've cleared the fields and tilled the soil in readiness for this day and finally it has come. The plantings have arrived, and with them, the man beside me. His name is Bertrand Spruitenberg. He is here to help us with the coffee."

A Dutchman, Jo thought as she assessed the jaunty little man. Probably once from Java. No one knew more about coffee than they did.

"I'll expect you to follow his orders, second only to mine. If we all do just as he says and continue to work as hard as we have been, there will be nothing to gainsay us. I believe there is every chance that we will succeed."

A cheer went up from the workers, and it occurred to Jocelyn how much they respected the man who had taken up the reins of their failing plantation.

In a sad, heartbreaking way, she respected him, too.

"Lady, lady! Please to put me down now."

Jocelyn laughed. "Seen enough already, have you?" She set him back on his feet. "I'll tell you what. Gwen's got some cane sticks in the kitchen. I saw them there this morning. Why don't we go and get you one?"

The little boy grinned with pleasure. "One for Mike, too?"

"Of course one for Mike. You can bring it back to him."

Tooney nodded vigorously and clutched Jo's hand. With a last glance at Rayne, who already bent to the task of unloading the wagons beneath the palm-frond cover shading the floor of what had once been the sugar shed, she started toward the kitchen at the rear of the house.

Even with Tooney smiling and talking beside her, she couldn't forget the tender expression she had seen on Rayne's face when he had noticed her holding the child. What had he been thinking? she wondered. And what would it take to make him look at her that way again?

Rayne worked beside Bert Spruitenberg from dusk till dawn for the next ten days. Testing several methods of growing, they seeded a portion of the freshly tilled fields, planted year-old seedlings in another section, and cuttings made from the upright branches of full-grown plants in another.

It was a gargantuan task, yet he reveled in it, more certain with each passing day that his plan would succeed. He'd become so accustomed to the long hours of labor, he had forgotten not everyone was conditioned to working that way. Eventually the game little Dutchman looked so ragged Rayne was forced to relent.

"I know the pace has been grueling," he said to the graying man seated on the sofa. "But the progress has been worth it." Through the window in his study, he could see a portion of the newly planted fields, and pride swelled inside him at what they had accomplished.

They had left the fields early today, eaten a hasty meal, then retired to the drawing room to enjoy a cigar before Rayne went to work in his study.

"Why don't you rest for a couple of days?" Rayne said. "Go into town, if you like. The King's Inn is a pleasant place. You may charge the room to me."

The little Dutchman looked relieved. "That's a fine idea, I don't mind telling you. Coffee may be a mighty nutrient of the brain, but planting it is a calamitous fatigue of the body."

Rayne chuckled. Like many an Englishman back home, the Dutchman was convinced that coffee contained properties that expanded the mind's ability to think and revitalized the body. Growing it, however, was not the same as drinking it.

"I'll have one of the boys drive you in tomorrow morning. If you're back in a couple of days, that should be sufficient."

"If it wouldn't be inconvenient, I should like to leave this evening." He grinned. "It's been far too long since I've enjoyed the pleasure of feminine company."

Taking a draw on his cigar, Rayne blew a wreath of smoke into the air. "All right. I'll have Paulo find someone to take you."

"You're certain you won't join me? A willing wench might be just the thing."

It might indeed. "Too much to do." Rayne got up from his overstuffed chair.

"You mustn't worry about the planting," Bert said, standing up to join him. "It's progressing right on schedule. Faster even than that."

Rayne clapped the man on the back. "Rest assured, I appreciate all you've done."

But it wasn't the planting that Bert had mistakenly assumed was on Rayne's mind. It was the Dutchman's words about the company of a woman. In the past ten days, Jocelyn had made herself scarce, and Rayne had been so busy, he'd had little time to ponder her rare appearance, though he had thought about her often.

This afternoon he had seen her working among a patch of yellow crocus, handling each vibrant blossom with infinite care, and just as it had when he'd spied her holding the child, something tightened inside his chest.

It was maddening, this power she held over him. He had to put an end to it, and soon. He had put off facing her, convinced the right time would somehow miraculously be at hand. But the moment had not come, and he had waited long enough. It was time he confronted her, put to her the question of the shooting and forced her to admit the truth. Once she did, he could set her away from him, stop having the dreams that continued to plague him, and bury the painful incident in the past.

Once he had accomplished what he'd set out to, he would see her gone from Mahogany Vale, settled with someone else to serve out her sentence. Not with Barz Hopkins—he could never stomach that. But there had to be someplace she could go, someone who would consider the past she had suffered and treat her fairly.

If not on Jamaica, then on some other island.

In truth, every day he put it off, every moment he avoided the confrontation, was tearing him apart. There wasn't an hour of the day he didn't wonder where she was and what she was doing, didn't try to catch a glimpse of her working among the flowers or laughing with the children she had befriended.

It tortured him, and yet he could not seem to stop.

Rayne crossed the room, opened a carved walnut sideboard and pulled out a decanter of brandy. He wouldn't drink much, he promised, just enough to steady himself. He wanted to be clear-headed when he looked into her eyes. He wanted to be ready for the lie he was certain to see, the hatred she felt for his father, which had somehow spilled over onto him. He wanted her to see his determination and finally admit the truth.

He wanted this over and done with.

Rayne filled the snifter and downed a shot of brandy, the fiery liquid soothing as it began to calm his nerves. Another shot and he would seek her out.

He glanced out the window. Dusk had begun to fall; the workers would be dispersing, heading toward their thatched mud cottages. Jocelyn would be coming in—if not, he would find her.

Tonight, he vowed, he would put his heartache to an end.

Chapter Eighteen

JOCELYN FINISHED WATERING a pot of newly planted pink geraniums, pleased with the progress she had made.

Wiping her damp hands on the apron she wore over
her lavender dress, she started toward the potting shed to
put away the large tin watering can she had been using.
She had finished with the flowers early that morning, then
changed into fresh clothes to help take care of the children.

A woman named Magda usually saw to the toddlers still
too small to accompany their mothers into the fields, but
Magda's monthly flux had come, and she was feeling
poorly. Jocelyn had gladly volunteered, loving the chance
to spend time with Tooney and Mike and the rest of the
little ones. As the sun dipped low, the mothers had come
to claim their weary offspring. Alone once more, Jocelyn
had decided to water the freshly planted flowers at the
front of the house one last time.

Now, finished with the task, she made her way back to
the potting shed, which sat off by itself behind the vegetable patch.

As always, it was cool and immaculate in the long, rock-
walled building, every tool in place, the benches wiped
clean, the dirt floor swept with a corn-husk broom.

As the last rays of sun slanted through the rafters below
the thatched roof, a mountain breeze swept in through an

open rear window. Jocelyn caught the scent of earth that clung to the spades, shovels, hoes, rakes, and myriad other gardening tools, along with a whiff of violets, blooming in tiny dishes on one shelf. She had just set the watering can down on a workbench when she heard a noise behind her and the sound of an opening door.

"I thought I might find you out here." Rayne stepped into the fading sunlight, auburn highlights glinting in his hair. He wore snug buff nankeen breeches and a white lawn shirt open at the throat. His high black boots were still dusty from the fields.

"I was just finishing up before I went in to supper." She tried not to notice how handsome he looked, how incredibly masculine.

She tried to ignore the way his breeches rode his hard-muscled thighs, the sinews standing out along his neck, hinting at the power beneath his shirt. She tried, but she couldn't help a prickle of heat at the memory of the muscles across his chest, the way they had flexed and moved when the two of them made love.

"I'm almost through with the beds around the house," she said, hoping he wouldn't notice the tremor in her voice. "I hope you're pleased with what I've done." Though she willed it not to, her heart beat faster and a trickle of dampness slid into the space between her breasts.

"I'm more than pleased with your work. Unfortunately, it isn't flowers I have come here to discuss."

"If it isn't my work then w-what is it?" Her eyes searched his face, but a shadow from the rafters darkened his features. There was tension in his stance, his feet braced apart as they had been when he faced that sailor in the tavern.

"The time has come, Jocelyn, for us to deal with the past. I sought you out this eve to talk about the shooting. I didn't intend to discuss it here, but as I think on it, perhaps this is best. Here, at least, we are away from prying eyes and listening ears."

Jocelyn swallowed hard. "Yes . . . the shed is quite private. Paulo is very particular about who's allowed inside."

She could barely force out the words. Her mouth had gone dry and her hands had begun to tremble. Had he come to hear the truth? Was this the opportunity she had been praying for almost from the moment of his arrival? Hope soared, and yet she felt wildly afraid.

"About what happened . . ." she said. "I was hoping the time would come when we might discuss it."

Something in Rayne's manner subtly shifted. When he stepped out of the shadows, she saw the harsh lines across his forehead, the tautness along his jaw. A cold, deliberate purpose had settled in his eyes, and her heart lurched sideways in her chest.

"I hardly think the matter is open for discussion. Both of us know what happened—I was shot in the chest at fairly close range. The injury was a grave one. I very nearly died. I've come to hear whatever it is you have to say about it."

Jocelyn's eyes ran over him, taking in his rigid posture, his jaw clamped hard against her words. His eyes had turned unfathomably dark, and the line of his mouth looked grim.

It struck her like a blow that he had come not to learn the truth, but prepared to refute her denial. He was certain she would lie, certain she was guilty—just as he had been from the start. Already he had steeled himself against her.

Just as before, Rayne had already condemned her.

Fury and despair welled up inside her, cresting like a wave. Pain and anger engulfed her, swamped her and left her feeling weak. The anguish she felt closed off her words, the truth he would never believe and she could not now bring herself to speak.

She wanted to lash out at him, to strike against the terrible certainty she had refused to face before now— that nothing she could ever say or do would change his mind. Inside she felt like dying. She ached with the sense of hopelessness, of heartbreak, failure, and loss. Her life stretched out before her, a black yawning pit with no future, nothing but bleak despair and bitter loneliness.

"Come, my dear Jo, I've traveled four thousand miles to hear you say it. We both know you did it. What remains is for you to explain how you plotted and planned. Can you not find the courage either to refute my words or at last admit the truth?"

Still she said nothing. Rage and humiliation had pushed her beyond the power to speak, even to reason past this single agonizing moment. She had waited so long, had dared to hope, even dream. Now her hopes were dashed.

"You want the truth?" she finally bit out, summoning her courage, though inside, her heart was breaking. "The truth is I hated you from the start. I waited until I knew your guard would be down, then lured you into your study. When you got there, I pulled out the pistol I had hidden in the pocket of my skirt and I shot you!"

The agony on his face was unmistakable, yet it could not eclipse her own. She wanted to hurt him, to punish him as he punished her. "That's what you want to hear, isn't it? That's what you came here for. To hear me say I tried to kill you. Well, now you've heard it—and if you continue to plague me, I shall find a way to do it again!"

Fury blazed in Rayne's eyes. He strode toward her, his body rigid with contempt, yet Jocelyn held her ground. She was beyond fear of retribution, beyond caring what he did to her or how he intended to make her pay.

"Leave you alone?" he taunted. "Is that really what you want? I don't think so. Not when you look at me the way you do. Your mind may wish me dead, but your body burns for me. That has always been the part of your deadly scheme you couldn't control, hasn't it?"

His laughter rang bitter and harsh. "You want me to leave you alone? I think you want me inside you. I think you ache for me from morning till night, just the way I ache for you." He gripped her arms and hauled her against him.

"You're a fool if you believe I still desire you. I hate you —that is all I feel!"

"Is that so?" He tried to kiss her, but Jocelyn struggled and finally broke free. Furious, she drew back and slapped him, the echo resounding in the silence of the room.

Jo's heart slammed equally hard against her ribs. As angry as he was, surely he would beat her.

"I'm glad they didn't break your spirit," he said instead, his hand coming up to rub his cheek. "It was a part of you I always admired."

Even couched in bitterness, the small admission stunned her. When Rayne dragged her back into his arms, she barely noticed. She felt the muscles of his chest beneath her fingers, then he was tilting her head back, kissing her fiercely, his mouth coming down over hers with ruthless force. She expected him to hurt her, to grind her soft lips against his teeth, to be brutal and cruel, to punish her for the way she had slapped him and her terrible, angry words.

Instead his mouth claimed hers in a kiss of blazing passion. His intent seemed not to take, but to prove he could make her give. There was fire in his touch, demand and unyielding strength, and Jocelyn felt the pull of it with every beat of her heart.

Rayne's hold tightened relentlessly. She could feel his powerful body pressing against her belly, breasts, and thighs. His hands slid into her hair, forcing her head back as he deepened the kiss. He coaxed her lips apart with subtle pressure, teased her bottom lip with his tongue, then eased it into her mouth to tangle with her own.

There was force and command in his kiss, yet his lips felt astonishingly gentle as they moved over hers. He crushed her against him, yet his hands stroked with infinite care down her back to her hips, cupping her bottom, kneading and caressing as he fitted her more solidly against him.

She felt his rigid shaft, knew what it would feel like thrusting inside her, and liquid heat slid through her body.

He was fire and ice, gentleness and fury, scorching abandon and frosty control. He was using every skill he knew, touching all of her pent-up emotions, firing the ache for him he had taunted her with and she could no longer resist. A wave of heat washed over her, scorchingly hot, incredibly delicious. Tendrils unfurled in her stomach; sparks leaped wild and fast into her blood.

She felt dizzy and confused, caught up in the spell he was weaving, her senses disoriented, her body entwined in the passion and fury even as her mind fought the beckoning drug of desire. She found herself leaning against him, moaning low in her throat, lacing her fingers in his hair. She shouldn't let him win his hateful game, but somehow it no longer mattered. It was over between them; whatever they had shared was dead and gone. There was only this raging heat that swept both of them into a passion they could not control.

She felt Rayne's hands at the back of her dress, felt the buttons popping open. Then he was sliding it off her shoulders, filling his hands with her breasts.

"Tell me you want me," he said, teasing her nipples, making them ache and grow distended, making her desire him with a force that left her trembling. "Say it. Tell me this is what you need."

She swallowed and pressed herself against him, her mouth parting softly for a fresh onslaught of kisses, her body strung taut with desire, damp and aching for release.

"Say it, Jo. Tell me that I've got what you want and I'll see that you get it."

He tasted faintly of brandy and tobacco, smelled of dust and leather and man. "Dear God," she moaned, feeling his hands at her breasts, then the wet heat of his mouth as he drew in a tautly puckered nipple. He bent her back over his arm to suckle more freely, the incredible heat tugging low in her belly, the damp fire burning between her legs.

"Say it, Jo." He returned to her mouth, capturing her bottom lip and tugging it gently. "I've got what you need and we both know it."

He teased her breast with his finger, circling the pink areola, spreading the glossy wetness left from his mouth, making the fire race through her. He squeezed gently, then his hand moved lower, his fingers splaying over the feminine heat that burned at the juncture of her legs.

"You want me, Jo. Say it."

She swallowed and pressed herself against his hand. "I —I want you."

"Yes . . . just the way I want you." He drew back a moment and his eyes locked on her face. "Even when I hate you, I want you. Sometimes I think I'll want you with my last living breath."

Jocelyn whimpered in her throat as he took her mouth again. She was burning with need, on fire and out of control. There was so much heat, so much aching that she barely noticed when he turned her away from him and eased her down until her elbows came to rest on the workbench. All she noticed were the arms that cradled her from behind, the hands that caressed her breasts, his mouth nibbling the nape of her neck, his tongue delving into her ear.

She hardly noticed when he lifted her lavender skirt, bunching it around her waist, lifted the hem of her chemise, then unbuttoned the front of his breeches.

But she noticed the rock-hard feel of him pressed against the cheeks of her bottom, couldn't mistake the velvety thickness of his shaft. Taking her this way was his punishment, she realized, but her need swept away the scalding wave of humiliation.

"Spread your legs for me, Jo."

She did it blindly, unthinkingly, longing for his touch, desperate for it. She felt his hand move over the curve of her bottom, testing the smoothness of her skin. His fingers slid between the rounded globes, parting the petals of her sex and slipping deep inside her.

Fire seemed to rain from the rafters. Tendrils flamed in her breasts, moved low into her belly, and fiery biting waves burned the flesh that he caressed. His fingers moved out and then in, along the silky channel, first just one and another. Jocelyn arched her hips for him, urging him onward, needing the release that only he could give.

"Easy, love," he whispered, the tender words surprising her, gentling her since they had never made love this way before. "Just take it easy. I'm not going to hurt you." Then he was sliding his rigid length inside, stretching her with his thickness, filling her with a single long powerful thrust.

Jocelyn moaned with the feel of it, gripping the workbench, trembling all over, her legs unsteady beneath her. Release came on the fourth powerful stroke, hurling her into a chasm of blinding pleasure before she could grasp what had happened. As Rayne drove out and then in with his long measured strokes, wave after wave of pleasure washed over her. He was riding her hard and deep, one pounding thrust after another, until a second spasm shook her.

God in heaven. In all of the times they had made love, he had always been gentle. In time, he had said, he would initiate her into the arts of love. Never in her wildest dreams would she have expected it to be like this.

"Once more, Jo. Let it come."

She couldn't believe it when the third wave shook her. Rayne's hold on her hips as he drove into her seemed the only thing holding her up. She felt him go rigid, felt his seed spilling hotly inside her, and still he drove on.

Finally his thrusting movements ceased and his arm went around her waist to hold her body against him. Jocelyn leaned back, her head coming to rest on his shoulder. Their flesh was no longer joined, but still he held her, his touch somehow protective, almost tender.

She felt his hands on her hips, carefully pulling her dress back down, smoothing the fabric. Then he refastened the buttons. There was a tremor in his touch and something uncertain in the way he moved, something hesitant, almost regretful. Jocelyn kept her eyes pinned on the wall, terrified to face him, afraid of the mocking expression she would see.

Just thinking about it made her eyes fill with tears, and as hard as she tried, she could not will them away. Still, it wasn't until she heard the door closing softly behind her that the wetness began to trickle down her cheeks.

She closed her eyes, but the hot tears slipped from beneath her lashes. She wiped them away with the backs of her hands, her heart nearly breaking in two as she turned to face the silence in the shed. He was giving her time to compose herself, leaving so that she might return to the house alone, allowing her this last shred of dignity. The single small gesture when she had expected vicious taunting was her final undoing.

Jocelyn sank down on the low wooden bench and began to weep. There was no holding back, no way she could control it. Her body shook with the force of her tears, denied for so long, tempered always before with a thin ray of hope that had finally been erased.

The truth she now faced was far more bitter than the devastating lie she had told. The simple fact tore into her heart and hammered like a death knell at her temples.

Rayne would never believe her, and she would never be free.

But one truth was even more bitter. As surely as Rayne despised her, Jocelyn loved him still.

Rayne strode straight from the shed into his study, moved to the cabinet behind his desk, opened it and poured himself a heavy shot of brandy.

He was burning inside with guilt and pain, and taking Jocelyn tonight had only made things worse. He had thought to put an end to his suffering; instead, he had only increased it. How could she hate him and respond to him with so much passion? How could he take her with so much anger yet try so hard to be gentle? How could she make him loathe himself as much as he did her?

He took the glass stopper out of the short-necked crystal decanter a second time and poured another goodly portion of liquor into the snifter. With a grip that was a little unsteady, he lifted it, intending to down the fiery contents, but his eyes locked on the way the liquor slopped over the rim, filled nearly to overflowing, and his hand froze midway to his lips.

Bloody Christ! What in the name of God did he think he was doing? He wasn't some East End derelict dependent on a bottle! He wasn't some sodden gin-swiller down on his luck, his future tied to the corner grog shop!

He had pain, yes, a searing, soul-crushing ache that would not leave him alone. But he also had duties, responsibilities, people who depended on him. He had a plantation to run, crops to get in, people to feed and clothe. He had set himself a monumental task, and he couldn't afford to indulge himself like some delinquent schoolboy.

Had Jocelyn laid him this low?

In truth, he couldn't place the blame entirely on her. He had started on this self-destructive course when he'd been forced to leave the army. With little to do, he drank out of boredom. After the shooting, he had done it to try and forget.

He glanced out the window toward the rich earth fields he had helped till, thought of the long hard hours they had all put in to make Mahogany Vale grow and prosper. He felt good about the work he had done, good about what they'd accomplished. He didn't need liquor. Not even to banish thoughts of Jo.

Rayne glanced at the snifter he still held in his hand, lifted it into the light, then hurled it across the room, where it shattered against the wall. The decanter followed, with a second heavy crash that brought the servants running. He dismissed them with a wave of his hand and they quickly ducked back out the door.

He had never been controlled by liquor the way some

men were, but he had surely abused it. It would not happen again.

Rayne released a long ragged breath and crossed the room to the window. If Jocelyn didn't return to the house very soon, he would have to go get her. He was worried about her, and yet he didn't want to see her. He didn't want her to know that what had happened between them in the potting shed had been just as devastating for him as for her.

He knew he had left her crying. He had stood in the darkness outside the door listening to the terrible sobs that wracked her body. It had been all he could do not to go back inside and comfort her, to hold her and kiss away her tears.

How could he? Jocelyn had finally admitted her betrayal. Or had she? In the very way she said the words, it had been a bitter denial. It only made him more uncertain, more confused.

It would be suicide to trust her again, and yet he wanted to with a power that staggered him.

God's breath, the woman had become an obsession! He had to get her out of his blood, out of his life, and he had to do it soon.

Standing at the window, Rayne caught a flash of lavender moving through the moonlit darkness outside. Jocelyn crossed the lawn and opened the back door leading into the hallway. Rayne sighed with relief to know that she was all right. He listened to her footfalls as she walked down the hall and wearily climbed the stairs. He gave her time to reach her room, then headed upstairs to his own.

He was exhausted—and ashamed of what he had done. He had never taken her like that before, though he often imagined how sweet it might be. Then again, Jocelyn couldn't deny she had enjoyed it. He had never seen her so fiery, so abandoned. Just thinking of it made his blood heat up and his shaft grow hard once more. He found himself wishing he could cross the hall to her room, join her in her soft feather bed, and take her again, this time with tender caring.

Instead he would lie in his bed alone, tossing and turning, unable to sleep no matter how tired he was, staring up at the canopy, burning with his need for Jo.

It was hotter the following day. Unusually warm and humid, and there was an uncommon stillness in the air. They were all feeling the effects of the blistering rays, and Jocelyn was no different. Along with being mired in defeat and despair, she felt sticky and out of sorts, praying for a mild ocean breeze to sweep in and help lighten her mood.

Across the way Chita rested against her hoe, mopping the dampness from her face with the hem of her blouse. Her morning sickness had ended just after her arrival. Her health had returned and the pallor had left her cheeks. Standing at the edge of the garden, she looked as hot and tired as everyone else, yet she had worked unfailingly, hoeing the stubborn weeds and checking the squash and melons for insects.

Jocelyn wondered if perhaps Chita hoped the virile Portuguese man not far away would notice her hardworking efforts.

Chita glanced in the handsome dark-eyed man's direction, only to find him deep in conversation with a pretty cocoa-skinned girl named Hattie. Hattie giggled at something Paulo said, smiled at him sweetly, set aside the hoe she had been wielding and carelessly sauntered away.

At the sight of Paulo staring like a lustful fool at the sway of Hattie's hips, Chita climbed to her feet and stormed toward the edge of the vegetable patch.

"You are letting her quit?" she raged at him in Spanish. "She has only been working for the last two hours. It is I who have been slaving away—I who have been sweating in all of this dirt and heat. It is I, if any, who deserves to quit!"

"All of us work hard, *nina*. It is hotter today. Hattie was a little bit under the weather."

"Under the weather, hah! You men are all fools for a pretty face and a pair of shapely hips. If a woman's behind is all it takes to sway you, why do you not look at mine!"

She whirled around and presented him with a view of her backside, then looked over her shoulder to see his eyes fixed exactly there and a smile of amusement on his face.

She turned back to him, angrier than ever. "I hope you enjoyed the view, because now I, too, am quitting." She tried to brush past him, but Paulo caught her arm.

"You have a very lovely bottom, *nina*. How would you like to find it over my knee?"

She gasped in outrage. "You do not threaten Hattie!"

"Hattie is not behaving like a spoiled little girl."

"What! I will not stay here and let you call me names." She tried to wrench free, but his hold on her arm only tightened.

"It is my job to see to the lawns and gardens. There are others I must be concerned with besides you. If you had but asked, I would have let you sit for a while in the shade. As it is, the others have seen your uncalled-for display, and even now they watch to see what I will do."

For the first time, Chita felt uneasy. Paulo Baptiste had treated her more than fairly, but she had learned he was a strong man, not easily pushed around. "And just what . . . what will you do?"

He grinned then, enjoying her discomfort. "Personally see that you work well past the time the others have finished. If that is not enough to teach you to mind your manners, I am certain I can think of something else that will."

Chita swallowed the angry retort that filled her throat. She stared at him with contempt, black eyes flashing, matched by a pair of equally black ones that told her he meant what he said.

"You are a heartless beast."

"And you, my fiery little *tigre*, had better get your lovely behind back to work."

Calling him every vile Spanish name she could think of, Chita stomped back to the place where she had been working. From beneath her flat-brimmed straw hat, she saw Paulo staring in the opposite direction.

What did it matter if he was enamored of Hattie? What did she care? He was only a man—and that was the last thing she wanted. Still, she watched him as he crossed the lawn to the long-dead rose garden Jo had begun to clear and replant.

"What was that all about?" Jo asked.

Paulo glanced toward the feisty black-haired girl who had intrigued him since the moment of her arrival. "Your friend Chita, she seemed to think I was playing favorites."

"Oh?" Jo used her pointed metal trowel to dig around the base of a withered rose.

"Hattie wasn't feeling good. I told her she could quit for the day."

"Hattie is very pretty. Maybe Chita is right."

"You think I would—"

"No, I don't."

Paulo shrugged his shoulders. "Hattie means nothing to me. She is not a woman I would take to wife."

"A man isn't necessarily thinking of marriage when he finds himself attracted to a pretty young girl."

Paulo grinned. "In that you are right, but I am not a man to let his loins rule his head. Hattie will be back to work in the morning, or I will have the curing woman examine her. If I discover she is lying, I will see she is punished for her deceit."

"If Hattie isn't to your liking, what about Chita? She's pretty enough to suit just about any man, I should think."

"Chita is a child."

"A child? I know in some ways she's naive, but her heart is good, and she's certainly got plenty of spirit."

"I need a woman not a child."

"Children grow into women, Paulo. They marry and have babies. If they're lucky enough to find a good husband, it doesn't take them long to discover what life is about."

Paulo eyed her thoughtfully. He hadn't really considered it quite that way. The truth was, he was mightily attracted to the little Spanish vixen. That he could handle her, he did not doubt. He had only wondered if the trouble would be worth it.

"She's a good girl, Paulo. She'll make the right man a very fine wife."

Paulo smiled down at her. *"Si, menina belo.* Maybe you are right. I will give the matter some thought."

"Sunday isn't far off. Maybe the two of you could spend the day together."

He shook his head. "She will still be angry. She would refuse my invitation."

Jo glanced over to where Chita hoed with such vigor on some poor defenseless weed. "Oh, I don't know. I think you might be surprised."

Paulo grinned. "On second thought, I will give her no choice. I think I will find out if you are right. I will see if I can coax a woman from the fury of a little girl." Touching the brim of his straw hat in farewell, Paulo walked away smiling.

Jocelyn wished she could smile. Instead she sat there brooding, working among the ancient rosebushes as she had all day, trying to forget what had happened between her and Rayne.

Trying to decide what to do.

She still couldn't face him. She was embarrassed by her wantonness, and tortured that he had aroused her so easily. She could imagine what he must think of her, though she vowed he would not touch her again.

Perhaps she should leave. It hadn't crossed her mind until last night. Before those final desperate moments in the potting shed, she had hoped Rayne might one day come to believe her. If not, she had been resolved to serve out her sentence at Mahogany Vale.

Already she had grown fond of the old plantation. She

had started to make new friends here. She had Chita and Paulo and Dulcet and Gwen. She loved the children and they loved her. The island was lush and beautiful, and the warm weather suited her. She loved her work in the gardens.

Now her hopes for freedom were dashed, and staying here with the way things stood between her and Rayne was a torture she could no longer bear. The thought of leaving her friends again, of giving up the small sweet pleasures she had found on Mahogany Vale, made an ache well up in her heart, yet she really had no other choice.

She would have to leave. But where would she go? How would she live? How could she escape the island?

What would happen if she got caught?

As difficult as those questions were, Jocelyn made her mind up to face them. She could make it, she vowed, if she planned well and waited till the time was right.

She wouldn't rush it, no matter how much she wanted to get away. She would bide her time, think things through, wait for the perfect opportunity. When it came, she would see it and she would be ready.

Until then, she would stay far away from Rayne.

Chapter Nineteen

DRIVEN BY UNWANTED THOUGHTS of Jo, Rayne worked extra-long hours in the fields. They were digging a channel along the eastern section where the seedlings were planted, hoping it would help with a drainage problem.

Craving the exertion, he had stripped to the waist and taken up a shovel, much to the awe of his workers. Sweat drenched his body, seeping from every pore, and his thick dark hair clung wetly to his neck and temples. Rayne didn't care. Tonight he intended to get some sleep, and this was the only sure way he knew to accomplish the task.

He rode back from the fields just before midnight, bone-weary but satisfied with what they had accomplished, and headed straight up to his bedchamber. He ordered a bath from his sleepy servants, soaked awhile, then went to bed. He slept after a time, a long deep slumber that overcame his tension, pulling at his tired aching body till he gave himself over to it completely.

With sleep came the dream.

Hazy and elusive at first, it beckoned like a beautiful woman, drawing him back into the past, forcing him to remember. Just as it had each time before, the image re-played the day Jocelyn had shot him.

As had happened a dozen times, he found himself sitting in his carriage on the long ride into the City, feeling all of the old anticipation, the incredible rush of desire that just thinking of Jo always brought him. Just as before, he arrived at the town house, spoke with the butler, strode down the hall into the study, and softly called her name.

He could see her clearly, turning away from the desk at the sound of his voice, looking toward him with a smile, her hand coming up, pointing the gun in his direction. The muzzle of the pistol flashed, and the ball slammed with blazing force into his chest. Then Jocelyn was screaming his name, racing toward him, terror and agony etched on her lovely face.

It was always the same, and yet tonight it was not. This time he saw her welcoming smile, saw her hand come up, saw the flash of silver, but the shape was not long and round like the barrel of a pistol, but flat like a tray, and there was something lying on top of it.

Rayne awoke with a start, his mind hearing Jocelyn's terrified screams, his heart hammering hard inside his chest. Covered with a sheen of perspiration, he sat up in bed, trying to hold on to the last fleeting images, but they were gone in an instant, as elusive as his memory of those long days after the shooting.

Yet unlike before, something about the dream nagged him. He tried to recall, but it only slipped further away.

He wished to God he could remember what it was.

Though it was Sunday, a day of rest on Mahogany Vale, Jocelyn worked among the roses. She'd attended a brief church service in the tiny makeshift chapel, just rough wooden benches beneath an open-air, thatched-roof shed.

She had seen Chita and Paulo off on their Sunday outing, then played ball with Tooney and Mike and several other children, but her thoughts soon strayed, and when she saw Rayne riding off on his big black stallion, they became bleak and morose. She had loved him for so long, and after the lies she had told, he was lost to her completely.

Jocelyn became so engrossed in her dismal mood, she didn't notice when the sun disappeared or that the temperature had begun to drop. But when she tilted her head to look past the brim of her bonnet, she saw how dark the sky had grown. In minutes the first scattered droplets of rain began to fall. Gusts of wind tugged at her skirts, and dense gray clouds appeared on the horizon.

"Get into the house," Rayne commanded, riding the big black horse up beside her. They were the first words he had spoken to her in the past two days. "There's a storm coming in. It may be a bad one. See that the shutters are closed, the larders restocked, and the house and kitchens well battened down. Get Dulcet to help you."

She nodded as Rayne rode away, and tried not to think how tired he looked. Instead she thought of the moments they had spent in the potting shed, recalling the ruthless yet somehow tender way he had made love to her.

She didn't understand exactly what had happened. She only knew that the more time she spent with him, the more her feelings became confused.

She had to get away from him, and as she walked toward the house, it occurred to her that the storm might provide the very opportunity she had been seeking. In the wind and rain it would be easy to slip away unnoticed, and though traveling would be hard, the roads would be empty, and she could get a goodly distance from Mahogany Vale before anyone noticed she was gone.

With that thought in mind, Jocelyn did as Rayne commanded, securing the house, closing the windows and locking the shutters, making sure there were enough supplies inside so they wouldn't need to venture out of doors.

It was the perfect opportunity to gather supplies of her own: an extra blanket, a hollowed-out gourd with a leather shoulder strap she could fill with fresh water, a small cache of candles, a change of clothing, and plenty of extra food.

It was dark by the time she had finished. Gwen sent a cold supper into the house: mutton, cheese, bread, sliced pineapple, sweet sop, and mangoes. Jocelyn set the tray on a table in Rayne's study, took her portion and went up to eat in her room. All she needed now was for Rayne to come in from the fields and go to sleep. Though Dulcet had reported he was no longer drinking himself into a nightly stupor, as tired as he looked, he was certain to slumber soundly. And even if he did not, the sounds of the storm would muffle her escape.

Outside the house a harsh wind howled and shook the tightly closed shutters; lightning flashed around the edges of the wood, and thunder cracked loudly. It was a miserable night to be out, but at least it wasn't cold. And everyone would be inside, out of the weather.

Growing more nervous by the minute, Jocelyn paced the floor in front of her high tester bed, straining into the darkness for the sound of Rayne's footfalls on the stairs. She heard them sometime later, dull, weary steps that betrayed his exhaustion and made something squeeze inside her heart.

He hadn't tarried in his study. She wondered if he had even taken the time to eat. She worried for him, even as she wished he would hurry and fall asleep.

An hour passed and then another, the minutes agonizing in their slowness. No sounds came from Rayne's chamber. She was certain it was safe to leave. Taking a deep breath for courage, she reached beneath her bed and pulled out her satchel.

She peeked out into the hall. The wind still raged in low moans and made the shutters creak, but no one was there. Easing past Rayne's room on slightly unsteady legs, she crept down the stairs, craning her neck right and left, straining to hear the slightest noise. She had reached the downstairs hall and started past the study when she saw yellow rays of light beneath the door.

Sweet Jesu! What if Rayne had returned downstairs? She forced herself not to panic. He had probably just forgotten to douse a burning lamp. Ignoring her wildly pounding heart, Jocelyn started forward. She had taken only a few short steps when the door flew open and Rayne stood framed in the opening.

She froze where she stood, the breath caught in her lungs. The weight of the bag seemed to swell to enormous proportions. The handle seemed to blister her fingers.

"Jocelyn," Rayne said matter-of-factly. "I thought you had gone to bed. I thought—" He broke off at the horrified expression on her face. In an instant his eyes took in the evidence of her departure: the bag itself, the simple dove-gray dress she wore with her sturdy brown shoes, her bonnet, and the shawl tied tightly around her shoulders.

God in heaven—was there nothing she could say? Nothing she could do?

Rayne's cold dark eyes raked her. He knew exactly what she had intended. Something flickered in the hard brown depths, a mixture of fury and something else she could not name.

"The evening is late, Jocelyn. I believe you should return to your chamber."

She would have moved if she could have. She was lucky she could stay on her feet.

"I said you should go to your room," he said with an effort at control. "I'm going to pretend that none of this happened. That I haven't the slightest notion what you are about this eve."

She couldn't seem to grasp what he was saying. Surely he would see her punished or report her to the authorities. At the very least, her sentence would be extended.

"W-What did you say?"

"This never happened, do you hear me?"

Jocelyn wet her lips as his words began to sink in. God, oh God, she wasn't going to be punished! She felt such an overwhelming wave of relief, her knees nearly buckled beneath her.

"Thank you," was all she could manage before she turned and hurried away.

Rayne watched her go, his anger nearly blinding him.

Damn her! Damn her to hell for the vixen she was! If he
hadn't been unable to sleep, if he hadn't come downstairs
for a bite to eat, he might not have caught her trying to
leave. Even now she might be outside in the storm. She
might have been lost or injured—maybe even killed!

It made his insides churn and his chest feel so tight he
could barely breathe. He waited till he heard the door to
her room close upstairs, then began to pace the carpet.

He thought of her creeping past his study, ready to face
the fury of the pounding storm. Was she so upset she had
tried to run away—heedless of her safety, knowing full
well the terrible consequences of her actions? That he had
played the rogue, he did not deny, but Jocelyn could have
stopped him, and both of them knew it.

Rayne slammed a muscled forearm down on his desk
and violently swept away the objects sitting on top of it. A
heavy leather-bound ledger crashed onto the floor, along
with several thin sheets of paper and a cut crystal paper-
weight. Thunder muffled the noisy landing.

He glanced at the mess he had made, wishing the explo-
sive act had made him feel better. He had let her go upstairs so his temper might cool, but it had only grown
hotter. Damn her to bloody hell—didn't she know there
were villains on the road? Men who would love nothing
better than to ravish a tempting young girl. There was
lightning and falling branches and mud slides—

Rayne crossed the room to the door, jerked it open so
hard he nearly tore off the handle, and headed for the
stairs.

Jocelyn stood facing the window, though the shutters
were closed and she couldn't see outside. She had heard
the noise in the study downstairs. She could only imagine
the cause.

Rayne was more angry than she had ever seen him. Just
one more step in the escalating fury between them. It
terrified her to think what might happen if things contin-

ued as they were. *Oh, Rayne, if only I could make you see.*

Her chest constricted when she heard his footfalls on the stairs. He was coming to her room—she was sure of it. His control had been slipping with each of their bitter confrontations. God in heaven, what should she do?

As the door jerked open, she turned and saw him framed in the entry. Long angry strides carried him into the room, the lamplight distorting his shadow and making him look larger and more fearsome than ever. In the flickering yellow glow, she saw the fury etched in his features, the way his hands clenched into fists, and the blood drained weakly from her face.

He crossed the room like a raging bear, stopping only after he had reached her, towering above her, glaring down with fiery contempt. Reaching out, he gripped her arms and dragged her up on her toes.

"Do you have any idea what might have happened out there? Dammit, you could have been killed!"

There was anger in his voice, but there was also fear. Fear for her safety? Concern that she might have been hurt or injured? How could that be when all he felt for her was loathing?

"For God's sake, Jo, you've no place to run on this island. The authorities would find you. There's no way for you to leave."

He released his hold, but still she said nothing. There was nothing left to say.

"I won't have it, do you hear me! I won't let you do that to yourself!"

This last he said with such conviction that she lifted her eyes to his face. "I won't let you use me like that again."

"Use you? Is that what happened? I used you?"

"Didn't you?"

He glanced away. "Perhaps I did, but what of you? You wanted it just as much as I. Never once have you refused me and meant it. Don't lie to yourself, Jo."

Inside she didn't. It was her pride that tried to pretend.

"Perhaps you're right about what happened. It really doesn't matter."

"Doesn't it? I think it does. I think you needed me, just as you did before. Why won't you just admit it?"

She *had* needed him. Once. Desperately, hopelessly, completely. And he had failed her. "There was a time that was so . . . in the past."

He stared at her long and hard, seeing the difference in her, the lengths to which he had pushed her. "You're my responsibility. I don't want you to get hurt."

I hurt now, Rayne. I hurt every time I look at you. "I can't stand this any longer. I can't stand the fighting. I can't stand feeling this way. I'm begging you, Rayne—haven't you punished me enough?"

He gripped her arm, fury sweeping once more into his features. "Can't you see it's the other way around? It's you who punishes me!" He bent his head to kiss her, but Jocelyn turned away.

"No, Rayne, not this time." She tried to wrench free, but he wouldn't let go. She twisted and finally jerked loose, but the buttons up the front of her dress tore free, the soft cloth ripping beneath his hands.

"I'm sorry," he said with regret. "I didn't mean to do that." Her chemise had been caught, too, the strap torn loose, the garment falling away from her shoulders, sliding to the curve of her breast.

His eyes swept down to the pale swell of flesh, and she heard his intake of breath. Then something caught his eye and he stepped closer. Jocelyn realized what it was the instant before his hand came up to touch it.

"What is this?" he asked, moving so that he might better see. The small gold circle flickered and danced in the lamplight, a beautiful scene of serenity resting against a troubled breast, an aching reminder of what could never be.

When he realized it was the tiny hand-painted locket he had given her, the locket he had torn from around her throat and hurled into the corner, his eyes came up to search her face.

"Surely it can't mean this much to you." Beneath his hand, Jocelyn trembled. "Why have you sewn it here . . . above your heart?"

How could she tell him? What could she say? And yet her very silence said it all.

He glanced down at the locket and his hand shook as he traced the shiny surface, still warm with the heat of her skin. His gaze sought hers once more, urging her to speak, yet uncertain of what she might say.

"It means that much to you, then?"

She had steeled herself against his anger, but she was unprepared for this. She wasn't sure how she should answer, but there was only one truth. "It was given to me by the man I loved." It came out on a whisper, and confusion darkened his eyes.

"But I was the one."

"Yes . . ." Her throat closed up, the hot ache swelling, becoming nearly unbearable.

"If you loved me, then why would you . . . why would you . . . ?" His breathing went shallow and the blood drained from his face. He swallowed as the unmistakable truth crashed in, the unspoken words louder than the thunder that roared out in the storm. *If she had loved him, she would not have shot him.*

And surely she had loved him. She loved him still. The proof rested over her heart. It had always been there in her eyes if he had but looked.

Agony distorted his features. His eyes turned dark and cloudy. He looked so desolate that something tightened around her heart.

"You didn't do it, did you? You didn't shoot me." The words sounded raw and tortured, as if they'd been torn from his throat.

Tears blurred her vision and began to slip down her cheeks. "I loved you. How could you believe for an instant that I would hurt you? H-How could you let them—"

"Oh, God." He hauled her into his arms, his anguish swelling with the minutes and the terrible implications of her words. "Oh, God."

She told herself to turn away, to let him suffer as she had. But the torment he couldn't disguise said that he had been suffering, too.

"Rayne," she whispered, her heart aching, her throat so tight she could barely speak.

His hold on her grew tighter and he buried his face in her hair. The arms that held her, always so solid and sure, now shook with agony and despair. She felt his cheek against her own, the heat of his body, the brush of his lips on her skin. She had dreamed of this moment, imagined it a thousand times, yet the dream had never been as sweet as this. He was holding her so fiercely, but the tenderness was there. She felt the tension in his body, as if by his strength alone he could push back the hands of time and undo all that had happened. Then she felt the wetness of his tears against her cheek.

"Jo . . ."

He was so masculine, so strong. It moved her as nothing else could have, told her that his anger had been his weapon, the way he had hidden his pain.

"Don't . . ." Her hand touched his face, brushing away the wetness. "It doesn't matter . . . not anymore. Not as long as you believe me."

Rayne clutched her harder, stroking her hair, whispering her name over and over. "I believe you," he said. "In my heart I knew the truth all along. I was just afraid to listen."

Jocelyn pulled back to look at him, tears blinding her, her throat aching. "I'm the one who's frightened, Rayne. I'm afraid to believe this is real." Jocelyn leaned against him, and his heart thundered madly beneath her hand.

"Don't be afraid, Jo. You never have to be afraid again." Rayne kissed her eyes, her nose, her mouth. Jocelyn cried harder, the sobs tearing into him, taking a piece of his soul. And all he could do was hold her.

His mind screamed with the agony of what he had done. His heart hurt, his throat burned, his chest ached as if he'd been struck by a blade. He thought of the suffering she had endured, the banishment, the weeks of deprivation. He thought how alone she must have felt, how desolate and afraid.

"Why didn't you tell me?" he asked as her tears faded to soft little heartbreaking sobs. He pulled a handkerchief from his pocket. Jocelyn dabbed her eyes and blew her nose.

"Was there a t-time you would have believed me?"

His eyes slid closed against a fresh shot of pain. "No."

"You were that certain?"

"I saw you . . . or at least I thought I did. What were you holding in your hand?"

"Y-Your sister had sent you a note. It was resting on a small silver tray."

Rayne thought he might be sick.

"I didn't know what was in the message. I—I wanted you to see it right away."

He drew in a ragged breath. Alex begging him to let her accompany them to the Campden soiree. It had rested on the flashing silver tray he had seen in his dream and only now remembered. Other pieces of the puzzle fell together. The little things Jocelyn had said that didn't seem quite right. *This time I will put a lead ball in your chest.* The angry way she had described the shooting, which didn't quite fit with the way it had happened.

"Please, Rayne. I just want you to hold me."

"I'll hold you, Jo. I'll hold you and I'll never let you go." Lifting her into his arms, Rayne carried her over to the bed. He could still feel the tremors that racked her slender body, and with each of them, his resolve to make things right grew stronger.

"You'll never have to worry about anything again," he said softly as he stood her on her feet beside the bed. With hands that shook, he started to strip off the gown he had torn, but Jocelyn's hands came up to stop him.

"It's all right," he said softly. "I'm not going to hurt you." At his words, she seemed to relax. Rayne tossed the dress on the floor, then removed her shoes and stockings. Wearing just her chemise, he lifted her up and settled her gently on the bed.

Wordlessly, he climbed up beside her, heedless of the fact he still wore his clothes. He rested his back against the carved wooden headboard, ignoring the ache that had sprung up there, nestling her against his chest, his hands sifting gently through her hair.

He kissed the top of her head, the jet-black strands like silk beneath his lips. "Your hair is getting long. I wondered that you didn't cut it short again when it would have been easier to manage."

"I wanted you to see it long," she said. "I told you once I would grow it just for you."

A sharp stab of pain tore through his chest, though he had guessed the truth even before she said the words. Why hadn't he listened to the doubts that had nagged him for so long? His heart had recognized the truth even when logic said it could not be so. His heart had brought him to Jamaica. His heart had forced him to discover the truth.

Thank God he had finally been able to see it.

"No one's ever going to hurt you again," he repeated, leaning down to place a kiss on her forehead. "I promise you that, Jo. Not me, or anyone else." But she was already sleeping. Exhaustion had taken its toll.

Or perhaps she knew that in his arms, at last she was safe.

Chapter Twenty

JOCELYN AWOKE WITH A START. Her mind was spinning, her thoughts racing, remembering the night before. She glanced around, saw she was in her room, in her bed, and that she was alone.

God, oh God, it was only a dream.

Her chest constricted as the terrible knowledge rushed in. Rayne's arms around her through the long hours of the night had seemed so real an ache rose in her throat to realize she had only imagined it.

Then her eyes caught something on the pillow beside her. She turned to discover a single white orchid. The crisply ruffled petals were still laden with moisture from last night's storm, the dark purple throat damp with tiny shimmering beads of dew.

Jocelyn lifted the flower with trembling fingers. *Not a dream—Rayne was here!* He had held her and believed her. She had awakened not from a dream that wasn't real, but from a nightmare that was.

She threw back the covers and climbed out of bed, still a little uncertain. Where was Rayne? What was he thinking? What would happen to them now?

She drew on her heavy cotton wrapper, then turned at the sound of the latch being lifted on the door. It swung open slowly and Hattie poked her head inside. The small

black girl squeaked in surprise when she saw Jo standing
in the room.

"Massa say not to wake you. He say you need to rest,
then you should eat." She beamed. "He say you no more
servant girl. You plenty big English lady. I take care."

"I see."

"You want food now?"

"Where's Rayne? I mean, where is his lordship?"

"Storm go away. Mr. Spruit, he come bock to fix fields.
Massa leave, go into city." She grinned. "I help you
dress?"

She hadn't had someone help her since she had left Elsa
in London. Still, the good-natured, shapely-hipped girl
looked so excited about her new position that Jocelyn
didn't have the heart to deny her.

"All right, Hattie, you may help." With hair cropped
close and a short button nose, Hattie's saucy looks were
feminine and appealing, though too often she tried to use
them to wheedle her way out of an unpleasant task.

She laid out a pink muslin gown Jocelyn had fashioned
from the fabric Rayne had bought, placed shoes and stockings by the bed, then busied herself straightening up the
room.

"Thank you, Hattie," Jocelyn said when she had finished dressing. "Why don't you see if Dulcet needs some
help?"

Jocelyn arrived downstairs a few minutes later, surprised to find Chita pacing the floor in the drawing room.
She whirled when she saw Jo, broke into a childlike grin
and let loose a torrent of Spanish.

Jocelyn laughed. "You'll have to speak English, Chita.
Paulo hasn't even started teaching me Spanish."

"Oh, *si, si, perdóname.*" She took a calming breath.
"Something exciting has happened—I know it! You must
tell Chita what it is."

Jocelyn hugged her. "Oh Chita, it's Rayne. He knows I
didn't shoot him."

"Aiee! That is good news. The viscount, he came to me

this morning. He tell me I am no longer to work in the garden. I am to be your com-com—how do you say?''

"Companion?"

"*Sí,* that is it—companion. He says I should move into the house.''

A feeling of warmth crept into Jo's breast. "That's wonderful. Now we won't have to worry about the baby, and I'll have a friend close by to talk to." Jocelyn said a silent prayer of thanks and flashed her friend a smile. "Oh, Chita, I can hardly believe it.''

"Everything is going to work out. You will see.''

"I hope so, Chita." Things were far from settled, yet excitement and hope filled her heart.

Chita smiled, too, but something flickered for a moment in her eyes.

"What is it? What's wrong? Did Rayne say something else? Chita, please, if there is something I should know—''

"The viscount, he say nothing.''

Jocelyn fixed her with a long, probing stare. "It's Paulo, isn't it? Something's happened between you two?''

"Nothing has happened. Do not worry for me. It is time for you to be happy.''

"Tell me, Chita. That's what friends are for.''

Chita's brave smile faded and she blinked at a sudden well of tears.

"Why don't we sit down?" Jocelyn led her over to the sofa. It took a while to gather the pieces of the story, but it seemed Jocelyn had been right about the attraction between her two friends.

"Paulo and me, we spend the day together and most of the evening. *Madre de Dios,* he is so handsome it makes my heart pound just to think of it. He is gentle and kind . . . and his kiss—it is like sweet fire. It is nothing like Antonio's.''

"Antonio? Is he the man who . . . is he the father of your baby?''

Chita's pretty face fell. "*Sí.* Anthony Fieldhurst cared only for his pleasure. I let him touch me because I believed he loved me, but inside I feel nothing. When Paulo kiss me—it is as if the heavens have just opened up." She smiled shyly and twisted the folds of her skirt. "I think I am falling in love with him."

"But that's wonderful, Chita."

"It is not so wonderful at all."

"Why not? Don't you think Paulo feels the same?"

"Oh no. I believe he cares for me, too."

"Then what is it?"

"Paulo believes I am a virgin. What will he say when he discovers the truth?"

"If Paulo truly cares for you, that you carry a babe will not matter."

Chita's bottom lip quivered. "Paulo will want a woman who is fresh and untouched. He will not want me."

"Why don't you tell him and find out?"

Chita shook her head, tossing her thick black hair. "I could never do that. I am too ashamed." Tears threatened once more, and Jo took Chita's hand.

"Give it some time. If Paulo really loves you, he'll want you and your baby. If not, you don't want him."

"When I think of Antonio, I could kill him."

"Don't say that, Chita. Believe me, vengeance doesn't pay. It's better left in the hands of God."

Chita smiled wanly. "You are always so wise. In my heart I know Tonio wasn't the only one to blame for what happened. I was a fool to believe him. I did not think things through, and I let him take advantage."

"Whatever the reasons, it's all in the past. A child grows in your womb, and if Paulo truly cares for you, he'll accept the child along with its mother."

Chita glanced down at the slight round swell beneath her hands. "In this you are mistaken. A man will not marry a woman who has been used. Not even if he is the man who did it."

Jocelyn fell silent, finding it difficult to argue. A fallen woman was not someone a man took to wife. It was a fact she had accepted long ago. A fact she had acknowledged before she had welcomed the viscount into her bed. At the time, survival had left her little choice in the matter of her position as Rayne's mistress. She wondered if he would offer her that same position again.

She wondered if she would accept it.

She was upstairs in her chamber when he returned late that eve. The storm had abated, leaving the night sky black and clear and sparkling with tiny jewel-bright stars. From what she had learned, the newly planted year-old seedlings had suffered a good bit of damage, but the slips had survived, and the portion of the fields that had been seeded had gone unharmed.

Jocelyn had been restless all day and into the evening, wondering when Rayne would arrive, knowing the trek to Kingston and back was a grueling one. She'd been reading for the past two hours, though she found it hard to concentrate with one ear cocked toward the door.

At last she heard noises in the entry. Her heart began racing the minute she heard Rayne's deep voice barking out orders and his footsteps rapidly climbing the stairs. His knock at the door was unexpected, since he usually barged right in. When she bade him enter, he shoved open the door with a booted foot and strode in carrying a huge bouquet of roses.

"Where shall I put them?" he asked, as if bringing her a bushel of flowers was an everyday occurrence.

"O-On the dresser, I should think. Thank you. They're lovely." Lush red roses—at least several dozen.

A second knock sounded and Rayne walked back to the door. "Just set those boxes on the bed," he said to a small army of servants. "Put the rest of them down on the floor."

"What in the world is all this?"

Rayne smiled as if she hadn't seen him in weeks. There was a buoyancy about him, as if some terrible weight had been lifted from his shoulders. And yet there was a flicker of some other dark emotion in his eyes.

"Most of the plantings weathered the storm. Since Ber-

trand is back to oversee any repairs, I spent the day in the
city. There were things I wanted to buy you."

"Buy me? I—I don't understand."

"Don't you?" He clamped his hands on her shoulders,
and she had to tilt her head back to see into his face.
"Then let me make things perfectly clear. You are no
longer a prisoner. As soon as I can arrange things, your
sentence will be dismissed and the blot on your record
erased. As Sir Henry's daughter, you will resume your
rightful place as a gently reared lady. From now on you
will be treated as a guest in this house—a very special
guest, with all of the courtesies that implies. I've brought
a seamstress here from Kingston. She is hardly a French
modiste, but with your instruction, I believe she will do
for the present."

"A seamstress?"

"Exactly so. You have done an admirable job of turning
fabric into simple unassuming gowns, but I would see you
dressed in the wardrobe of a lady. You will find slippers in
at least a dozen colors, yards of lace and feathers and
baubles to serve as trim—hopefully everything you'll need
and then some. If not, I shall see that you get more."

Jocelyn searched his face, but his expression remained
inscrutable. She crossed to the bed and tipped the lid off
one of the boxes. Frothy white undergarments spilled out
over the edge. There were stockings, garters, and fine
lawn chemises. Another box contained velvet and satin
ribbons of every color and size. One contained an ornate
ivory and silver hairbrush, comb, and mirror, which sat
atop a matching silver tray.

"Rayne, you didn't have to do this."

"I most certainly did," he said a little too lightly. He
picked up a small flowered box tied with a pale pink ribbon. "I especially liked this. I hoped you might like it,
too."

Jocelyn untied the bow, and her hands shook as she
removed a beautiful porcelain music box. It was covered

entirely in delicate pastel flowers. When she lifted the lid, the gentle strains of a harpsichord emanated from the box.

"It's beautiful." Tears stung her eyes and she had to glance away. Except for the locket he had given her, she had never owned anything quite so lovely. "Thank you."

Rayne cleared his throat, but his voice still sounded husky. "I'm glad you like it."

She unwrapped bags, parcels, and boxes until the room was piled high with bonnets, parasols, velvets and laces, gold and silver embroidery, a mother-of-pearl inlaid rosewood jewelry box—anything and everything that might strike a woman's fancy.

"This is only the start, Jo. I have months to make up for. I want you to have everything your heart desires."

The only thing my heart desires is you. She wanted to tell him, to let him know that he didn't have to buy her forgiveness. After last night she understood why he had believed her guilty. It was a dreadful, horrible mistake that had caused them both to suffer. If he hadn't met her at the point of a gun, if they had known each other better, had trusted each other more, it might not have happened.

Still, it had, and Rayne obviously felt guilty. She wondered where all of this was leading.

"You've been very thoughtful, but this really wasn't necessary."

The muscles tensed across his shoulders, and the darkness she had seen behind his eyes seemed to sweep full-blown across his face.

"Wasn't it?" He gripped her arms once more. "Do you have any idea what it does to me to think of you in that god-awful prison? To know that I was the cause?"

"It wasn't your fault. You had reason to believe I was guilty."

"That is so, and if it were not, I don't think I could live with myself. Still, for much of it I am to blame. Certainly I'm to blame for what has happened between us here."

Her hand came up to his cheek. "Even that blame is not

wholly yours. It's true, you were angry much of the time, but never once did you raise your hand against me."

"And what of the other, Jo? What of the times I forced myself on you? I took you without an ounce of tenderness, without a thought for your feelings. All I considered were my own selfish needs."

"Would you have me believe I couldn't have stopped you—even that night in the potting shed?"

Rayne shook his head, but the pain didn't leave his face. "No. I would have stopped had you but asked."

"It was just as you once said: We took from each other. We both had needs."

He glanced away from her, forcing himself back under control. "The gifts are merely a token of my affection for you. All the presents, all the money in the world, couldn't assuage the guilt I feel for what has happened." He raked a hand through his wavy dark hair. "They are also of a practical nature. You're in need of something decent to wear."

"There is far too much here for my simple needs." *I just need to know where I stand.* "We're miles away from the city. Surely a few new gowns would be more than enough."

"We're four thousand miles from the City. In London you'll need all of these things and more."

Jocelyn's chest went taut. "London! But surely you can't mean to leave! You've just got the crops in. A-Anything could happen. You've got to stay here and see things through."

"There is the matter of your sentence and clearing the blot from your name. I intend that we shall leave just as soon as we are ready."

"W-What about Mahogany Vale? What about all of your efforts, all your hard work?"

He smiled at her indulgently. "Those coffee shrubs won't yield their first crop for at least five more years. For now, the hard part is over. With Bertrand and Paulo look-

ing after things while we're gone, there is every reason to
believe our efforts will succeed."

"But I don't want to go back to England. I want to stay
here."

Rayne's dark brows drew together. "What about
Brownie and Tucker? I thought you missed them."

"I—I do. I miss them terribly." *What if Tuck is the one
who shot you?*

"Then why don't you want to go home?"

Jocelyn felt panic rising inside her. She thought of the
days she had spent in Newgate prison, of the rotting de-
cay and the filth. "What if something went wrong? What if
they didn't believe you? What if they put me back in
prison?" A sob escaped her throat. "I couldn't survive it,
Rayne—not a second time."

Rayne pulled her fiercely into his arms. "I won't let that
happen. The Lords of Appeal will believe me. Why
shouldn't they? I'm the one who accused you. I'm the one
who can tell them you're innocent."

She sucked in a ragged breath, working to keep her
tenuous grasp on control. "You can't be certain they'll
listen. You haven't an ounce of proof. You can't even be
sure yourself that I didn't do it."

She turned her face up to his. "Any day you might wake
up with all your old doubts and suspicions. They might
nag you until you're convinced that somehow I tricked
you into believing me."

"That is never going to happen."

But it could, and she knew it. She couldn't afford to
believe him. *Dear God, be can't think to make me return.*

"As long as we're here, it doesn't matter," she said. "I
can be happy here, even if I have to work in the fields. In
England anything might happen—even my return to
prison. I can't do it, Rayne. I'd rather be dead!"

"Stop it, Jo! I know you don't trust me. Why in God's
name should you? But I swear to you, I'll make things
right."

"I won't go. You said I wasn't a prisoner. You said I was a guest. A guest doesn't have to obey your commands."

"I've got to go back, don't you see? I never came here intending to stay. I've got duties, responsibilities. I've got my sister to think of. I've got to go home, Jo." *And I want you with me.*

"No."

"Please, Jo. Don't make me play the villain again."

"I won't do it, Rayne."

Rayne stepped away from her, his jaw set firmly, his features growing hard once more. "Until your case is reviewed, your custody remains in my hands. You and I are returning to London. That is the end of it."

"It's always the same, isn't it? You command. I obey."

"Dammit, Jo, this is your life we're talking about. You've never been a coward. Don't let your courage fail you now."

Jocelyn said nothing. Put that way, Rayne was right. She wasn't guilty of the crime she'd been convicted of, and though it terrified her to imagine the awful things that might happen, she had to return.

"What of you?" she asked softly, staring into his handsome face. It was tanned even darker by the hours he'd spent in the sun, and his eyes were like rich brown velvet. "If you go back, your life may again be in danger." What if something happened? What if he were hurt again? What if he were killed?

"I'm well aware of the problem. I've spent half the day trying to figure who the culprit might be."

"And did you?"

"You may be certain I will. It's just one more reason I must return."

A chill went down her spine just to think of him once more in danger. Perhaps if she were there, she could make a difference. Perhaps she could somehow keep him safe.

She lifted her chin. "All right. I'll do as you wish."

Rayne swept her into his arms, crushing her against

him. Beneath her fingers she could feel his even, steady
heartbeat. It felt so good to be held like this. Sweet saints,
it felt like heaven. And in his solid embrace, her fears
began to fade.

"You won't be sorry, Jo." He buried his face in the
hollow between her neck and shoulder. "I'll take care of
you. I'll take care of everything. I promise you."

But there had been other promises, and they had all
been broken. This time her very life might depend on
Rayne and the vows he'd just made.

She prayed she was doing the right thing.

"Good evening, Mr. Spruitenberg. Your lordship."

Dressed in an autumn-brown tailcoat, amber waistcoat,
and light beige breeches, Rayne took Jocelyn's arm before
Bert had the chance and led her into the dining room.

His mouth had gone dry at the sight of her, deliciously
feminine and sweetly appealing in her newly fashioned
rose silk gown.

"You look lovely," he said, and wondered if she noticed
the husky timbre of his voice.

"A vision," said Bert as they rounded the table.

They were supping tonight on cream of banana soup,
oysters harvested from underwater mango roots, baked
crab, sweet potatoes, and a fruit mélange made of papaws,
sweet sop, and star apples. Not exactly Continental fare,
and yet Rayne had come to enjoy the delicacies of the
island.

He seated Jocelyn on his right while Bert took a seat on
his left.

"Mrs. Pedigru seems to be working out," Rayne said to
Jo. "The gown suits your figure quite well." He swept the
soft mounds of her breasts with a long hungry glance that
left no doubt as to what he was thinking. He wouldn't
take her. But he would let her know with certainty that
was exactly what he wanted.

"Mrs. Pedigru is very talented," she said softly, her
cheeks pink with a thoroughly charming blush. "She

brought several fairly current fashion plates along with her, and we've been working from there."

"I suppose you're eager to be returning home," Bert said, and Jocelyn's cheeks went from rosy to pale.

"Actually, I've grown quite fond of it here. If I had my choice—"

"Unfortunately, neither of us has a choice," Rayne cut in with warning. "We'll be sailing in less than a fortnight. Unlike Miss Asbury, and though I've grown fond of this old place myself, I find I'm chafing at the bit to return."

Jocelyn's gaze swung to his face. "You've missed your life of leisure so much, then?" Her eyes looked bluer than ever, and suddenly uncertain.

"I've missed my life of leisure not at all. In truth, it's done me considerable good to get away from the City. I've discovered I've no more taste for endless rounds of drinking and night after night of debauchery."

Jocelyn's cheeks flamed scarlet and her eyes flashed with hurt. Bloody hell, did she really believe he was speaking of her?

Bert lifted his goblet and took a hefty swig of wine. "If such a life holds no appeal, what is it you intend to do?"

Rayne hadn't mentioned their problems in England to Bertrand or anyone else; he didn't intend to now. "I've some business to conduct in the City. Once I'm finished, I'm off to Marden."

Jo's head came up. "Marden? What will you do there?" Winged black brows drew together in a worried frown, and her face looked more troubled than before.

They had yet to discuss plans for the future. He had wanted to give her time to accept her return to London and the problems she would face once she got there.

"Marden Manor is one of the largest land holdings in England. It has provided well for the Garrick family for the past hundred years, but little has been done in the way of progress. Here at Mahogany Vale I've learned a good deal about farming techniques, crops, and planting. Once I'm back in Britain, I intend to learn a great deal more. I hope to implement a number of changes at Marden which will increase its production and ensure its future. In short—I intend to make it my home.''

"I see." Jocelyn glanced down at her plate. She pretended to eat, but merely moved the food around with her fork.

Watching her, Rayne suddenly wished he had handled things differently. Tomorrow, he vowed, he would put her fears to rest.

"What news from Kingston, Bert?" he asked, searching for a safer topic. He took a bite of baked crab, found it delicious, and was relieved to see Jocelyn had begun to eat, too.

"Actually, I ran into an old friend from Java. A coffee grower I knew in Haiti. He says he expects a good crop for most of the island. They'll soon be starting to harvest."

"Are the coffee beans picked directly off the tree?" Jo asked, and it occurred to Rayne he had never taken time to explain.

"They come from what's called coffee cherries," Rayne said. "It's an eight-month cycle from bloom to ripened fruit."

"Ah, the loveliest little white blossoms," Bert said expansively. "Like jasmine, they are, and the fragrance just as sweet. When the coffee's in bloom, it drifts over the whole blessed valley."

"That sounds wonderful," Jo said. "I should love to have seen it."

Rayne ignored the slight barb in her words. "There are two beans inside each coffee cherry. They ripen from green to yellow to red. That's when they're ready to harvest."

"Unfortunately, they don't all ripen at once," Bert put in, taking another sip of wine. "Sometimes it takes three or four pickings."

Rayne swallowed a bite of sweet potato he had been eating. "After they're harvested, the cherries are dried and the hulls removed. Then the inside protective covering called the silver skin is stripped off. All in all, it's quite a job."

"It certainly sounds that way," Jo said.

"Ah, but it's worth it." Bertrand leaned back in his chair. "Just imagine—a rich delicious beverage with the ability to expand one's thinking. Why, a cup or two can make even the most difficult problem seem simple. Coffee enlivens, invigorates, practically dispels the paralysis of fatigue."

Rayne chuckled softly. "Whatever it does, there is definitely a market for it, and Mahogany Vale can certainly use the profits it will garner. I appreciate all you've done, Bert."

"You've a grand future here, my lord. You may count on me to contribute in any way I can."

When the meal was finished, Rayne leaned close so that only Jo could hear. "I've a special day planned for us tomorrow. A place I'd like you to see. I thought we might have Gwen prepare a basket of food."

Jocelyn's smile looked forced. "All right."

"Everything's going to work out, Jo."

But she still looked uncertain, an expression that remained with her even as he walked her to her room.

Chapter Twenty-one

JOCELYN HELD THE WICKER-BASKET on her lap as she sat sideways across Rayne's thighs on his big black stallion.

"It isn't far, but the trail's pretty steep." His arm tightened protectively around her. "I promise the trip will be worth it."

In most ways, it already was. She was here with Rayne, the breeze kept the heat of the sun at bay, and the sky formed a crystal-blue dome above their heads. Jocelyn peered over Rayne's shoulder to watch the valley fall away below them, the fields forming quilted patterns, the blue-green ocean tinting the horizon.

Only thoughts of the future clouded the brightness of the day.

"There's a pool up ahead. We'll luncheon there." Rayne turned the horse toward an overgrown gully lined with dense green foliage, and the sound of tumbling water filled the air.

Jocelyn shifted against him, trying to ignore the feel of his work-hardened thighs beneath her own long legs, the solid wall of muscle that was Rayne's chest. She blushed at the thick ridge of desire that had risen against her bottom, the husky tone that roughened the last words he had said.

In minutes he had reined up in front of a high cascading waterfall, the air around it glistening with misty rainbows.

"Oh, Rayne, it's beautiful."

"Paulo told me about it sometime back. I thought you might like it."

"I love it."

He dismounted and helped her down, then turned his attention to the horse. "I won't be long."

Jocelyn busied herself spreading out the patchwork quilt Rayne had brought, and was smoothing out the folds when she stepped backward, stumbling over something she mistook for an odd-shaped log. At a second quick glance, her eyes flew wide and her loud scream rent the hillside.

"What is it?" Rayne came on the run, dragging her into his arms and searching for possible danger.

"O-Over there! It's—It's some kind of monster!"

Rayne stepped away from her and into the thick green foliage.

"Be careful," she warned.

To her relief, he didn't stay long. Picking his way back through the lush growth of palm fronds and ferns, he walked toward her, chuckling.

"Come on. We won't go too near, just close enough for you to have a look." He took her hand and tugged her back through the foliage, Jocelyn peeking around his shoulder.

"W-What is it?"

He was laughing again, and this time she knew why. When she stared into the grass, she saw the biggest green lizard she had ever seen.

"I don't believe it."

"I told you you wouldn't."

" 'You won't believe the size of the lizards,' " they both said in unison. Rayne's thick chest rumbled with mirth, and Jocelyn started laughing, too.

The lizard must have heard them, for he opened his mouth, bunching thick folds of ugly green skin beneath his jaw, and made a sort of hissing sound in his throat. Then he was scurrying away on his bent stubby legs, dragging his long pointed tail. He dove for cover and disappeared into the foliage—all six feet of him.

"You weren't kidding," Jo said, wiping away tears of laughter as Rayne led her back to the blanket.

"It's called an iguana. You don't see them often, but once you do, you never forget."

Jocelyn laughed again, then turned serious. "I'll never forget anything about this place, Rayne."

His expression changed. He trailed his knuckles along her jaw. "After the way I treated you, some of your memories must surely be unpleasant."

She shook her head. "A little sad, maybe. I wish we could have shared the happy times." She smiled forlornly. "I've made new friends here. I've loved being with the children. The island is beautiful." *And you were here.*

"We'll come back, Jo. As often as you like." He sat on the blanket and pulled her down beside him.

Jocelyn searched his face, seeking a clue to his thoughts. *We'll come back, Jo. As often as you like.* What was he saying? Last night he had said he would be leaving London, making his home at Marden. Did he mean to keep her as his mistress, but stay so far away he would rarely see her?

She didn't doubt he still desired her—it was there in every heated look, every brush of his fingers across her skin. She felt that same desire for him, stronger than ever. Each time he touched her, her heartbeat quickened and soft heat slid into her stomach.

But so much had happened. She had so many doubts, so many fears.

"Gwen sent cold mutton and jerked chicken," she said, determined to keep the moment light. "There's cheese and fresh-baked bread, pineapple and jack fruit and coconut. I hope you're hungry."

"Sounds like quite a feast." His dark eyes swept over her, saying he was hungry but it wasn't for food. Instead he reached into the basket to help her set their makeshift table and lifted out a bottle of wine.

Jocelyn's gaze swung to his. "I—I didn't know she had put that in. I know you've stopped drinking."

Rayne set the bottle in the center of the blanket. "I'm not like your father, Jo. I never will be. I'll admit I indulged myself far more than I should have and it wasn't the first time. But it isn't going to happen again."

He smiled warmly. "When I set my mind to it, I assure you, I'm a man of extreme self-discipline. If you doubt that, know that at this very moment there is nothing I would rather do more than pull you down on this blanket and ravish your lovely little body. That I'm not going to do it is a testament to the grueling regimen of the British army."

She laughed at that, but the hot devouring look in his eyes made a ripple of heat slide through her body.

"Surely you wouldn't want to miss out on Gwen's jerked chicken?"

"I'd be willing to give up food for a fortnight to have you installed once more in my bed."

The thought sobered her, and yet it filled her with longing. The laughter slipped from her expression.

"I wish I understood what is happening. What are you saying, Rayne?"

It was all so confusing. He had just said he wanted her, yet since he had discovered the truth of the shooting, he had made no move to touch her. He hadn't even kissed her. Maybe he didn't intend to.

Rayne took her hand. "I brought you here so that we might discuss the future. You know as well as I, returning to London won't be easy."

A trickle of fear crept down her spine. "Are you telling me there is a chance you will fail? That I might be forced to return to prison or transported somewhere else?"

"Good God, no!" He pulled her into his arms and kissed her cheek. Feeling the tension in her body, he began to stroke her hair. "What I'm saying is that there are other problems we'll be forced to overcome."

Jocelyn drew back to look at him. "Such as?"

"The scandal, for one thing. Everyone in London knows the truth of your identity. They know you were never married, never a widow. They know you were my mistress, Jo."

Jocelyn's chin came up. "It was bound to happen, sooner or later. We both knew that. It was kind of you to shield me as long as you did. Now that the truth is out, I shall just have to live with it."

"The bloody hell you will!"

Jocelyn bristled. "What are you talking about?"

"I'm talking about stilling their vicious wagging tongues. I'm talking about ensuring your safety and your future. I'm talking about making you my wife."

The breath she'd just taken seemed to wedge tight in her lungs. "You can't be serious."

"I'm deadly serious."

"Why? Because you feel sorry for me? Because you feel guilty? Don't you think you're carrying your penance a little too far?"

"You can say that after what you've been through? As far as I'm concerned, the next forty years won't be enough to make things up to you."

"You're a viscount, for bloody sakes. I'm a penniless street urchin with a criminal record."

"You're Sir Henry Asbury's daughter."

"You can't just ignore what has happened. You've got your sister to consider, your family holdings and name. You can't think to take me to wife."

"I don't intend to think it, I intend to see it done."

Jocelyn just stared at him. In all the times they had been together, the thought of marriage had never occurred to her. The roads they traveled were too different. Their worlds were too far apart.

From the beginning, the best she had ever dared to hope was that he might come to care for her enough to keep her with him through the years. She had gone so far as to imagine raising his children, but never had she considered they would have a legitimate name.

Now the shooting and the scandal and her long months of torment lay between them. She loved him—she had never really stopped. But no longer did she trust him. She did not dare.

"No."

"What did you say?"

"I said no, Rayne. You asked me to marry you—or at least you assumed I would agree, just as you always do. In truth, I'm not about to."

"You're refusing my suit?"

I'm refusing to marry a man who would have me only out of guilt. What of love? she thought. Lust he had felt for her almost from the start. But love? It had never been mentioned. It wasn't mentioned here.

"If you wish to call it that, yes."

Rayne looked over her head to a point somewhere in the dense green forest. "Your care of me then is gone completely?"

I love you. It seems I've always loved you. But I don't trust you. "A lot has happened these long months past. Now, in only a few short days, I'm supposed to wipe away the weeks of pain and uncertainty. I can't do it, Rayne."

A flicker of something crossed his features, then it was gone. "You've always been practical, Jo. You've always been a survivor. Surely you can see this is the only possible solution to your problems."

She simply shook her head. "I don't want to be practical. Not this time." *I want to be loved.*

Tension seemed to vibrate through his body. "Surely you realize that even now you might be carrying my babe."

Jocelyn's hand flew to her stomach. She had known it was possible, and yet she had never allowed the notion to settle in her head. Hearing Rayne say the words in his gruff masculine way made her insides grow soft and fluttery.

"Even if that were true, it wouldn't change the way I feel. All my life I've been a victim of circumstance. My father's drinking ruined us and forced me into the streets. Poverty and my miserable existence forced me into your bed. A terrible mistake forced me into prison. But nothing in this world can force me to marry you."

Rayne watched her for a long, solitary moment. "What is your wish? What would you have me do?"

"I don't want your money, if that is what you are thinking. But I would like your help in rebuilding my future."

"Go on."

"I'm educated. I love children. I've often believed I would make a very good governess. If you would help me secure such a job, I could make my own way. You would not be obliged to marry me and—"

"I'm not obliged to do anything, dammit!" He took a steadying breath, running his hands over his face. "I've handled this poorly. I should have waited, courted you properly. I only thought to ease your fears."

He leaned closer, brushing her lips with a feather-soft kiss. "You deserve far better than the life you would lead as someone else's servant. You're going to marry me, Jo. We've plenty of time for you to get used to the idea. All that matters is that the deed be accomplished before we arrive back in England."

Jocelyn's fist slammed down on the blanket and her eyes burned with hot angry tears.

"Why is it everyone has choices but me?" She climbed to her feet and started running. Rayne caught her before she had gone more than a few lengths down the mountain.

"I'm sorry," he said, keeping a tight hold on her arm. "Damn, but I've made a mess of this. I'm so used to giving orders that I do it without thinking. I only want what's best for you, Jo. Please believe that. I won't force you to do anything you don't want to. I give you my word." He brushed away her tears with a knuckle on one big hand.

"Do you mean it?"

Rayne nodded. "I'll do whatever it takes to make you

happy. I meant what I said, Jo. You'll never have to worry about anything again."

She relaxed a little and leaned into him, burying her face in his chest.

His hand stroked down her hair, pulled back from her face and tied with a bright yellow ribbon. "We'll just take our time, all right?"

Six weeks, more or less. That's how much time he had. Six weeks to convince her to accept his proposal of marriage. He regretted the way he had pushed her. But he was determined to protect her. As his viscountess, whatever happened, she would be safe.

"I'm still hungry," he said after a time. "What about you?"

She nodded.

It didn't take much to coax Jo out of her tears, just a little light banter and a few teasing smiles. She was always ready to find joy in the moment, always seeking life's simplest pleasures. Once she was his viscountess, he would shower her with earthly delights, to say nothing of those more sensual in nature. And in every smile she gave him, he would find his own moment of pleasure.

Relaxed at last, they shared the luncheon Gwen had sent, eating until all that remained were crumbs and they couldn't stuff in one more bite. When they had finished, they dangled their feet in the pool and frolicked like children, then once again Jocelyn sat on his lap as they rode back down the hill.

By the time they reached the house, darkness had begun to fall. Rayne lifted Jo down from the horse, left the stallion in the care of a small dark stable boy, and walked beside her toward the soft yellow glow beckoning through the open windows.

"Jo! Thank God I have found you." That from Paulo, who raced out of the darkness in their direction.

"What is it?" Rayne asked. "What's happened?"

"I am not sure. I am afraid for Chita. I have searched everywhere but I cannot find her."

"She's probably just visiting in one of the cottages," Jo said.

"I do not think so." Tension marred the lines of his face.

Jocelyn gripped his shoulder. "Tell me what's happened, Paulo. Did you two argue?"

"*Sim,* I have done something stupid. *Deus,* if only I could call back the words."

"She told you, didn't she? That's what this is about."

"Told him what?" Rayne asked. "You two had better explain what's going on."

Jocelyn looked up at him, her blue eyes clouded with concern. "Chita is going to have a baby."

Rayne digested the knowledge then slanted a hard look in Paulo's direction. "If you're the child's father, I'll expect you to do right by the girl."

"If I were the father, none of this would have happened."

"I think you had better start at the beginning," Rayne said to the younger man.

"From the first," Paulo said, beginning the tale, "there was something between us. We spent Sunday at the pool in the mountains. It was a wonderful day, but afterward Chita refused to see me. She said it would never work out between us, but I believed she was just afraid of what she was feeling. It felt so right when we were together, and it was just as Jo said. Chita is a child, but she is also a woman. I wanted to take her to wife. . . ."

"Go on, Paulo," Jocelyn softly urged when he remained silent.

"I convinced her to give us some time. We have been together every moment . . . until today. This afternoon she came to me crying. She said she could not stand by any longer and let me believe in a lie. She told me of the man she had known in England. She told me of the baby."

Paulo shook his head, worry forming creases in his brow. "I was so angry. I called her a *puta.*" At Jo's blank expression, he looked even more miserable. "It means whore."

"Oh, God."

"I didn't mean it. The moment I saw her face, I knew what I had done. I knew also that I did not care about the man before me. I only cared for her."

"But you didn't tell her," Jo said sharply.

"There wasn't time. There was an accident in the fields. One of the workers was injured and I was called away. When I returned, Chita was gone."

"We'll find her, Paulo," Rayne said. "She can't have gotten far."

Jocelyn turned toward the kitchen at the rear of the house. "I'll speak to Dulcet and Gwen. If anyone knows where she's gone, one of them will." She picked up her skirts and raced in that direction.

Rayne looked down at the dark, well-built man beside him. "If we don't find her in the next couple of hours, I'll send men out to search for her."

"This is all my fault. I was the one who was afraid of my feelings. If I hadn't been, this would not have happened."

Rayne laid a hand on the shorter man's shoulder. "It seems to be man's lot in life to cause a woman pain."

Paulo only nodded and set off once more into the darkness.

"Hurry, Rayne! I know where Chita has gone." Jocelyn raced up to him and his arm went around her waist.

"Where is she?"

"She asked Gwen for the name of a medicine woman. Gwen sent her to someone at Tamarind." A neighboring sugar plantation just down the hill. "She had a little money, coins she'd managed to hide from Barz Hopkins."

Jocelyn gripped the front of his shirt. "She's going to get rid of the baby, Rayne. She's too far along. It could kill her."

"Come on." Together they ran toward the stables. Paulo

caught up with them halfway there, and Jocelyn hurriedly told him what had happened.

"*Deus,* I cannot believe she would do such a thing."

"Chita loves children," Jo said. "I know she wants this baby. I can't believe it, either."

"People often do things in anger they later regret." Rayne's look said he was speaking of himself.

"*Sim.* We must stop her."

"Can you ride?" Rayne asked Paulo as the three of them reached the stable.

"Well enough for this."

Rayne pulled Knight from his stall, saddled and bridled him while a stable boy saddled a horse for Paulo. In minutes Jocelyn felt Rayne's hands at her waist, then he was lifting her into the saddle and swinging himself up behind her.

"There is a shortcut through the mountains," Paulo said. "It is the path she would have taken."

With Paulo in the lead, they made their way down the mountainside to nearby Tamarind.

"According to Gwen," Jo said, "there's a cabin at the rear of the slave quarters. A woman there named Penna is the medicine woman. Gwen says she can give Chita a potion that will cause her to expel the babe."

She felt Rayne's chest expand as he sucked in a harsh breath of air. "Let's hope it isn't too late."

They reached the cabin not long after. It was just where Gwen had said. A candle rested on a table in the window, casting a flickering glow into the darkness. Rayne hurriedly dismounted and helped Jo down, then the three of them raced to the door. Rayne's hammering ensured it would open. A tall black woman, thin to the point of flesh over bone, stepped into the doorway.

"We're looking for a woman," Rayne said. "Conchita Vasquez. Have you seen her?"

When the woman hesitated, Rayne pulled a bag of coins from the waistband of his breeches and poured several into her hand.

"I asked if you have seen her."

The woman glanced down at the money, saw that it was a goodly sum, and motioned them into the house. "In there."

Paulo shot past them, shoving aside the tattered woolen curtain dividing a small back room, stepping into the dimly lit space where a narrow cot rested against one wall.

Chita sat on top of it, her knees drawn up to her chin, her smooth dark cheeks wet with tears. Her black hair hung damp and tangled around her face, and her clothes were torn and dirty. Her small hands grasped a mug of murky dark liquid.

Paulo approached her cautiously, as if she were a cornered, frightened animal. "I have been looking for you," he said softly.

"What . . . what for?"

"To tell you I was sorry." He eased a little closer. "I did not mean it, *querida*. If I had known it would bring you to this, I would rather have cut out my tongue."

"How . . . how did you find me?"

"I have been looking all day, but it was Jo who spoke to Gwen. She told us where you had gone."

Chita's hands shook, spilling drops of the dark brew over the rim, but she didn't set it down.

"You do not wish to hurt your baby."

Fresh tears slipped down her cheeks. "No."

Paulo slowly reached for the cup. "Give it to me."

She started shaking harder. Paulo's hands brushed hers ever so lightly. He eased the cup from her brittle fingers and set it on the table beside the cot.

"I could not do it," she whispered. "I have come to love the baby too much." More tears seeped down her cheeks as Paulo eased her into his arms.

"Hush, *namorado*. There is nothing more to cry about. Your babe is safe, and I am here to take you home."

"I'm sorry, Paulo. If I had known I would meet a man like you, I never would have let him touch me."

Paulo rested his cheek on the top of her head. "He has not touched you as I will. He has not shown you love. He has left that for me."

Chita lifted her head and looked at him through tear-filled eyes. "I love you, Paulo."

"I love you, too, *meu amor.*"

Standing in the doorway, Rayne cleared his throat. "I think it's time we went home."

Paulo nodded, bent over the cot and lifted Chita into his arms. Outside the cabin, he settled her in front of him on the horse and they started back toward Mahogany Vale.

Watching them ride off, Jocelyn's fears for Chita suddenly slipped away. *I love you,* Paulo had said, and with those three words, Jocelyn knew Chita's future was secure.

She wondered morosely if she would ever hear those words from Rayne.

Chapter Twenty-two

THE VOYAGE BACK TO ENGLAND was nothing like the one that had carried her to Jamaica.

Rayne had chosen carefully, a beautiful full-rigged sailing vessel just a year out of the Liverpool shipyard. It carried hogsheads of sugar mostly, but it also carried passengers—in fairly grand style. The cabins weren't numerous, but each had been luxuriously appointed, and the salon and dining room, with their ornate carved wood paneling and red velvet upholstery, were extravagant in the extreme.

Jocelyn had been surprised to find Rayne had reserved separated state rooms—hers complete with a traveling companion. Grace Kenwood, an older gray-haired woman Rayne had discovered in Kingston, also traveled to London. With his persuasion, and the lure of a paid-for ticket, she'd agreed to share a cabin, lending a note of propriety to the voyage ahead.

Jocelyn's sigh held a note of disgruntlement. She knew she should have been grateful Rayne was treating her with such respect, but each night after supper when she retired to her room and curled up on the berth across from Mrs. Kenwood's, she felt wretched.

Rayne seemed to mind far less. He was excruciatingly polite and always the gentleman. Yet when they were alone, his eyes seemed to smolder, a carefully banked fire that spoke more honestly than his words.

He said no more of marriage, which should have made her happy, but the relief Jocelyn expected to feel surfaced instead as bitter resentment. How easily he had salved his conscience. How rapidly his good intentions had faded away.

Surely this is best, she told herself. *You don't want a man who would marry you out of guilt.* Not to mention the matter of trust and betrayal, the difference in their stations, the sentence she still faced—and the unsolved attempt on Rayne's life.

But those weren't the thoughts Chita expressed when Jocelyn had told her the news. "What! He asked you to marry him and you said no!"

"Rayne didn't really want to marry me. He just felt sorry for me."

"He is not a man who would marry unless it was his wish. I think he is in love with you."

"Rayne doesn't believe in love." Jocelyn didn't bother to tell her that even if he did love her, it wouldn't solve all of the problems that lay between them.

Still, she couldn't deny he was good to her. The gifts he bought seemed endless, exceeded only by the attention he lavished upon her. When Chita had learned they were leaving, and burst into tears, terrified of having the baby all by herself, Rayne acquiesced to Jocelyn's pleas and agreed to discover where Dolly Whitehead had been sent. In less than a week arrangements were made for Dolly to serve out her sentence at Mahogany Vale.

"Can you not see that he does these things to please you?" Chita said. "Can you not see that he loves you?"

"He wants me. He always has. That and guilt for what has happened is all he feels."

Not like Paulo. Two days after the incident at Tamarind, Paulo had asked Chita to marry him. She accepted with a burst of happy tears, and the couple was married the following Sunday. One look at the pride and love shining in

Paulo's black eyes, and the blindest fool could see how much Chita meant to him.

But Rayne? Sitting across from him now in the dining salon, Jocelyn was no longer certain what Rayne felt. After her weeks at sea, she would have done nearly anything to exchange his polite formality, his ever so charming gallantry, for one of his very ungentlemanly, deliciously searing kisses. Oh, to be dragged into his bed, to be held and caressed until she was senseless, to be swept up once more in a wild burst of passion.

"Enjoying your supper?" Rayne took a sip of his rich red wine. True to his word, he merely savored now, never overdrank. Unfortunately, like everything else of late, his bland moderation only fueled her dismal mood.

"The bass is overcooked," she said tartly, "and the potatoes taste old. Other than that, I suppose it's fine."

She could have sworn his lips twitched. "I'm sorry you are not better pleased. Then again, I've noticed you've been a bit out of sorts of late. I sincerely hope it isn't something I've done."

Don't say it. She couldn't resist. "Quite the contrary, my lord, it is something you have not done." Jocelyn shoved back her carved rosewood chair. "I believe I shall forego our evening stroll. I find I've come down with the headache. I'm afraid you'll have to excuse me."

Rayne quickly came to his feet. "Of course."

He extended his arm and Jocelyn took it. Thick bands of muscle bunched beneath her hand, stirring an unwelcome warmth in her stomach. As they made their way between the tables of elegantly garbed passengers, several of them smiled, but Jocelyn barely acknowledged them.

There were fourteen other travelers aboard the ship, but Rayne had avoided their attentions from the start, making it clear by his subtle withdrawal that he wasn't interested in shipboard companionship—except, apparently, hers. One dark look had most of the male passengers running, and even the women who continually fawned and fluttered around him could see his interest lay elsewhere.

"Ah, Lord Stoneleigh . . . and Miss Asbury. Surely the two of you aren't leaving the company so early?" Most stayed away, but not Fletch Martell, the wealthy shipping magnate who owned the line on which they were sailing.

He was a handsome man a year or two older than Rayne, with light brown hair and sea-green eyes. He was a man of poise and confidence, who obviously appreciated the charms of the opposite sex.

"Miss Asbury has the headache. It is my good fortune to see her safely to her cabin. If you'll excuse us . . ."

There was warning in Rayne's cool words, but when he started to lead her away, Fletcher Martell merely placed himself more solidly in front of them.

"Perhaps Miss Asbury will feel better in the morning." He smiled pleasantly, but his green eyes danced with challenge. "I should love the chance to show her around the ship."

Don't do it, the little voice warned. "I would enjoy that very much," Jocelyn replied.

Martell took her hand and brought it to his lips. "I shall call for you at ten."

From the corner of her eye, she caught Rayne's furious expression. *Go to bloody hell,* she thought. *You want to be gallant and proper. You want me, but you won't touch me. Let's see what Fletcher Martell wants.*

By the time they reached her cabin, Rayne's face looked thunderous. When she stepped into her room, he surprised her by following her in and, seeing Mrs. Kenwood nowhere near, firmly closing the door.

"Just exactly what was that all about?" He pinned her with an unflinching glare.

With quick little tugs, Jocelyn pulled off her gloves and tossed them onto the table. "It was about getting a reaction out of you." She jerked the ribbon beneath her chin, pulled off her bonnet, and set it down next to the gloves. "For the past few weeks, you've been the height of civility, and though I suppose I should be grateful, in truth I am not. I liked you far better when you were ranting and raving, baiting me and—and—''

"Kissing you? That's what you were thinking, wasn't it?"

Jocelyn swallowed and glanced away. "You want me—at least I think you do. But you won't . . . we haven't . . . I don't understand what has changed."

He caught her arm and turned her to face him. The harshness had left his features, replaced by a look she couldn't quite fathom.

"What has changed, my dear Jo, is that I now know you are innocent of all the crimes I once believed you guilty. You are exactly the person I thought you were when we were together in London. You are warm and kind and giving. You are sweet and feminine, and you always find the joy in life, no matter how simple it is. What has changed, my lovely Jocelyn, is that I want you for my wife."

Jocelyn stared at him in amazement. Tears touched her eyes and she had to glance away. "Y-You haven't mentioned it, not once since that day at the pool. I thought you had changed your mind."

He turned her chin with his hand, forcing her eyes to his face. "Changed my mind? It's all I've thought about for weeks."

"Y-You've hardly touched me. You haven't even kissed me."

"I haven't kissed you because I knew if I started I would not stop. It was my insane belief that you deserved better than to be taken like some waterfront doxy every time I got the urge."

Jocelyn's head came up. "Is that the way it was? Is that the way you thought of me?"

"Good God, no! It's my own bloody behavior I fault." He cradled her cheek against his palm. "I believe a man's future wife deserves gentler treatment. And I wanted you to want me—wildly, desperately, without a hint of re-

serve. I thought if I gave you some time . . . if I worked
to make things up to you . . ."

"I want you, Rayne. Every time I look at you I want
you." *I always have.*

"Enough to marry me?"

She chewed her bottom lip. If he cared as much as it
seemed, perhaps one day he would love her. "Yes," she
said, knowing she shouldn't, battling the doubts that assailed her.

Rayne swept her into his arms. "Thank God."

She hugged him tightly, hoping she had done the right
thing. "There is one condition," she said.

He looked down at her sternly, but couldn't keep the
smile from his voice. "And just what is that?"

"That I needn't be a lady all the time—certainly not in
our bedchamber. I should find it extremely boring. You
must promise to continue making love to me as wildly and
passionately as you always have."

Rayne's handsome face broke into a grin. "Never has a
man been more fortunate—a lady in his drawing room and
a vixen in his bed." He tilted her face up and kissed her. It
was a loving, searing, promising kiss that left her totally
breathless. "You don't know how happy you've made
me."

But Jocelyn said nothing. Once more she was giving
him her heart, giving back some of her trust. The last time
it had led to disaster. She prayed this time it would not.

In the end it was Jocelyn who refused to join Rayne in his
bed.

"You say we are to be married. If that is so, then I
would wait until the vows are spoken."

Rayne just smiled. "You may believe, my love, that it
will be so. And since you wish to wait, then you may also
believe that the vows will be spoken as soon as I can
arrange it. With any luck at all, by tomorrow's eve you will
once more be ensconced in my bed, and there you will
remain."

Jocelyn's flashed a mischievous grin. "For just how long, my lord?"

He chuckled softly. "At the very least you may count on every spare moment until we reach port. We've months to make up for, my darling Jo. I intend to ride your sleek little body until you cry for mercy."

Jocelyn laughed. "We shall see, my lord, exactly who will cry out first."

Fletcher Martell was the first to receive news of their betrothal—at ten o'clock the following morning. When Martell arrived at Jocelyn's door right on schedule, Rayne stood out front to greet him and pointedly relay the news.

"Well, old boy," Fletcher said, "I suppose felicitations are in order."

"Yes, I believe they are."

"You certainly wasted no time in capturing the lady's attentions—not that I blame you. She is lovely in the extreme, a woman of intelligence and warmth. Had I the good fortune to have met the lady first, I would have acted in all haste myself."

Rayne chuckled good-naturedly, the happiness lodged in his chest making his mood expansive. The men shook hands, Rayne clapped Martell on the back, and they walked into the main salon to search out the captain. By the time the sun formed a glittering half dome on the bright blue horizon, Jocelyn stood beside Rayne at the stern, the entire ship's company clustered around them.

In a watered blue silk gown the exact shade as her eyes, Jocelyn nervously clutched a small bouquet of dried flowers, a hastily fashioned gift from Mrs. Kenwood, who stood a few feet away, dabbing a hankie against her eyes.

Fidgeting nervously, Jocelyn toyed with the tiny seed pearls dotting the bodice of her high-necked gown. She should have been happy—and part of her was. But the other part had spent the day pacing the floor of her cabin, painfully aware of all that had happened since she had first met Rayne, fearful of the step she was about to make.

What if he were merely easing his conscience? What if he left her at Marden and returned to Stoneleigh without her? What if he took another mistress? Worse yet, what if another attempt was made on his life? What if he were wounded again or this time maybe even killed? As his wife, and considering that she had once been found guilty of just such a crime, Jocelyn would surely be suspect. Who would save her this time?

What if Rayne betrayed her as he had before?

And yet she loved him. More every day.

In the beginning, when he had whisked her from the filthy London streets, she had loved him the way an innocent young girl loves a hero. Now that she knew the man he was inside, the man who had run Mahogany Vale with steely determination, endless grit, and unfailing concern for his people, she had come to admire him, to feel the deep residing love of a woman for her man.

Jocelyn straightened as the gentle breeze across the deck fluttered the blue satin ribbon on her hastily fashioned tulle veil. Captain Owens had been speaking for some time, she realized, his voice growing hoarse as he droned on. Jocelyn forced her eyes to the graying man's face, realized the words he read were being spoken to her, and started to tremble.

"Do you, Jocelyn, take this man, Rayne, to be your lawful wedded husband? Do you promise to love him, comfort him, honor and keep him in sickness and in health and forsaking all others for as long as you both shall live?"

She wet her lips. "I do."

Standing at her side, Rayne smiled down at her warmly. He looked so handsome in his dark russet tailcoat and snug buff breeches. The reddish highlights in his hair glinted beneath the sun, and his face looked uncommonly tan against the brilliant white stock at his throat. She could feel his powerful presence, his strength and comfort, almost as if he touched her.

Jocelyn forced a smile in his direction, but it came out tenuous at best. She hadn't thought taking these vows would be so hard, hadn't considered the impact of the words. But as she repeated her promise to become Rayne's lawful wedded wife for better or worse, her pledge to love and cherish him until death, she realized how much she meant them.

She wondered what the words meant to Rayne and if he would hold to them, especially the part where he agreed to forsake all others.

His voice rang strong and clear when he said his part, and his eyes caressed her face. She wanted to believe. She wanted it so badly. And yet she could not.

"By the power vested in me as captain of this ship, I pronounce that you are man and wife. You may kiss your bride."

She heard the words numbly, unsure how they would affect her future, then Rayne was pulling her into his arms, lifting her veil and taking her mouth in a kiss that surely belonged in the bedroom.

He was grinning when he broke away, and Jocelyn's knees felt weak.

"Champagne all 'round!" shouted Fletch Martell, and it was obvious from the smiles he and Rayne exchanged that the two were well on the way to becoming fast friends.

The wedding feast was sumptuous, given the fact they were miles at sea. A champagne reception in the main salon, then an elegant supper of lobster, sea bass in caper sauce served over rice, a variety of vegetables taken on board in Jamaica, and a rich plum pudding for dessert.

They sat at the captain's table, enduring endless toasts, then Rayne cut short the evening and they made their polite farewells.

"Thank God all of that is behind us," he said with a soft warm smile as they reached the door.

Jocelyn merely nodded and let him guide her out of the salon and down the passage to the cabin he had arranged for them. Rayne caught her up in his arms before they reached the door, worked the latch, then shoved it open with his foot. He carried her inside and let go of her legs, forcing her to slide the length of his body.

"How does it feel, my love, to be a viscountess?"

Jocelyn flashed a teasing smile. "I don't know yet. Why don't you show me?"

He made a sound low in his throat and his mouth came down hard over hers. It was a blazing kiss, the kind she had been craving for the past long weeks, yet it was infinitely tender. Jocelyn wove her arms around his neck and gave herself up to it, lacing her fingers in his hair. Rayne deepened the kiss, his possession fierce yet gentle, his tongue sliding into her mouth to tease and coax.

In minutes she was trembling, pressing herself shamelessly against him, wishing they were free of their too-confining clothes.

As if he read her thoughts, Rayne turned her away from him and worked the buttons at the back of her gown.

"I've been wanting to do this for weeks."

It didn't take him long to strip away the blue silk dress while she took off his shirt. Her fingers touched the wound on his shoulder.

"Does it still pain you?"

"Only a little."

She pressed a soft sweet kiss on the puckered skin, then reached up and kissed him. Rayne pulled off her chemise, then removed her stockings and garters. A peach-colored sheer silk nightgown awaited her on the bed, but when she reached for it, Rayne caught her hand.

"I would see you as you are, as I haven't these long months past. I ask this gift of you on the day of our wedding."

Jocelyn felt the heat creeping into her cheeks. "Then I ask the same gift of you," she said, ignoring her embarrassment. "You are beautiful, my lord. I would see you as I have long remembered."

Something shifted in Rayne's eyes, but he merely nodded. In minutes he had stripped off his shoes, coat, waistcoat, and trousers. Striding the distance between them, he came naked and unashamed to where Jocelyn stood at the foot of the wide berth serving as their bed. Already his shaft had grown hard. It rose up boldly against his flat stomach, promising delights she could only imagine.

Rayne's eyes caressed her in that same bold manner. "I've missed seeing you like this." He trailed a finger between her bare breasts, making gooseflesh rise across her skin. "I had almost forgotten how exquisite you are."

Jocelyn's cheeks burned brighter. "Thank you, my lord."

"Turn around . . . very slowly. I would see all of you."

She did it without reserve, wanting only to please him, to give him the gift he had asked for, prepared to become the wife she had pledged to be. Until she heard his quick intake of breath.

"Good God, your back." Rayne moved closer as she spun toward him. The pleasure on his face just moments ago had been replaced by a look as hard as steel.

She wet her lips. For the most part, the marks of the whip had faded. She hadn't thought it looked that bad.

"I—I'm sorry. I had forgotten they were there. I—I don't think the scars will be permanent." She reached for the nightgown to cover herself.

"Don't," he said in a voice gone husky. "I would know how this happened."

Jocelyn glanced away, then replied with a shrug of her shoulders. "Chita was sick. Dolly took food from the larder on board the ship, and the captain ordered her flogged. She was too old and Chita was too ill. So I—"

"So you took Dolly's place."

"That was my intention. Fortunately, I received only the first blow. I had made a friend in the second mate. He very bravely took the rest."

Rayne said nothing, but his eyes looked dark and forbidding.

"I should have remembered they were there. I'm sorry you had to see them. I wanted only to please you."

"You're sorry I had to see them?" Rayne's hands shook

as he settled them on her shoulders. "I'm the one who should have been horsewhipped. Do you have any idea how this makes me feel? I should have protected you—that's what you came to me for—that's what you expected in exchange for your beautiful body. I should have kept you safe—but I failed."

"It doesn't matter. All of that is behind us."

Rayne only shook his head. "What else am I responsible for? I've got to know, Jocelyn. I'll ask you just this once, but I've got to know."

She touched his handsome face and smiled up at him softly. "You are responsible, my lord, for teaching me the beauty that can exist between a man and woman. For giving me infinite joy, for hours and hours of mindless pleasure. If you are concerned that another man might have taken from me what I have given to you, you may ease your mind. The money you paid was protection enough for that."

Rayne's eyes slid closed and his breath came out on a harsh sigh of relief. "Thank God," he whispered, pulling her into a fierce embrace.

He smelled of soap and fine cologne mixed with a hint of tobacco. Jocelyn kissed his throat, then began to trail small wet kisses along his shoulders and down his chest. "If you wish to make amends, my lord, you may do so by keeping your promise to make passionate love to me."

Rayne pulled back to look at her. "If I believed for an instant that a single night of loving was enough, my conscience would be clear by morning. A thousand such nights would be closer." One corner of his mouth curved up in a roguish half smile. "Of course, we've got to start someplace."

Rayne kissed her then, crushing her soft breasts against his chest, a hard-muscled leg pressing intimately between her thighs.

She gasped at the erotic feel of it, the steel-honed ridges of sinew flexing as he nudged her legs a little farther apart, forcing her to straddle him. Pleasure swept through

her; wild damp heat slid into the place between her legs.
Rayne's mouth and tongue teased her lips; one hand lifted
and caressed a breast, while his palm curved over her
bottom to hold her against him.

Sweet saints in heaven. Each time they made love
seemed more erotic than the last. This time she was his
wife; there was no holding back. Whatever barriers still
lay between them had nothing to do with this.

Jocelyn trembled at the thought. Beneath her feminine
heat, Rayne's thick-muscled thigh continued to rock, lifting her nearly off the ground, sending shivers along her
skin and tendrils of heat into the flesh pressing against
him.

She felt his lips on her shoulder, kissing a thin line of
scar, then his hands at her waist, lifting her up and settling
her on the edge of the bed, yet keeping her legs wide-
spread as he stood between them.

"Rayne?" She tried to sit up, but he pressed her back
down on the bed.

"Easy, love. I know we've never done this, but I've
imagined giving you this kind of pleasure at least a thousand times. Surely you won't deny me."

She wasn't exactly sure of his intentions, but his look
said her protests would do little good. Whatever he
planned, he meant to see it done. Jocelyn relaxed in the
knowledge that she had trusted him to guide her in the
ways of passion before and she had never been sorry.

He must have felt her tension ease, for he leaned over
and kissed her. More kisses followed in a line that traveled
from her mouth to her breasts, down to her navel, where
his tongue dipped in and the fire within her spiraled
higher. Then he was kissing her thighs, kneeling at the
foot of the bed, settling his mouth over her most private
place, kissing and teasing, then sliding his tongue inside.

God, oh, God. Jocelyn arched her back as her fists
curled into the smooth satin counterpane. Flames engulfed her, racing through her blood, roaring in her ears.
Instinctively she slid her hands into Rayne's hair, uncer-

tain whether to shove him away or pull him closer. He seemed heedless of her halfhearted protests, just laved and suckled, teased and tasted, his hands sliding under her buttocks to bring her closer to his mouth.

"Sweet God, Rayne!" Then she was cresting the silvery peak of pleasure, plummeting over the edge of the chasm, floating to the bottom, then soaring back up on bright shiny currents of air. Sweetness washed over her; her tongue traced her lips as if she might capture it. She drew in a great ragged breath and waited for the moment to end.

It didn't.

Rayne rose up in its wake, his big hard body towering above her. He settled himself at the entrance to her core, eased himself in, then drove himself inside her; one deep, powerful thrust, one potent male stroke that filled her and claimed her as his.

When he kissed her, she tasted her own musky scent on his tongue, but the strange sensation only stoked the fires raging through her and turned her body to flame. He was riding her hot and hard now, driving deep, probing the depths of her, and she was meeting each of his demanding thrusts. Beneath her fingers the muscles across his chest grew taut. She felt the springy texture of his dark mat of hair, then moved her hands to his back and down to grip his buttocks. They were tight and round, as solid and smooth as satin over steel, hard and flexing with each of his pounding strokes.

Heat washed over her, hotter than before, coming from a deeper, more primal place, as if his soul had called and hers was about to answer. A small sound came from her throat, followed by the flashing heat of a second, all-consuming climax.

"Rayne!" she cried out as she made the leap of pleasure.

She felt his muscles tense, saw his head fall back, felt the hot wet pumping of his seed. Instinctively her body tightened around it, as if she could somehow hold onto the life-giving force and it would take root in her belly. Never before had she felt such a need to keep something of him inside her.

They spiraled back down slowly. She felt Rayne's fingers in her hair, brushing damp black tendrils from her cheeks.

"All right?" he asked, easing his heavy weight off her and settling her in the curve of his arm.

"It was perfect."

He kissed her temple. "All of it?"

"Every beautiful moment."

He chuckled softly. "I hoped you would enjoy it. Some women don't."

More fools they, she thought but didn't say it. Instead she felt a slow burning heat rise in her cheeks as she remembered what Rayne had done.

"What of you?" she asked with some hesitation. "Surely most men would find such a notion offensive."

He grinned wickedly, bent down and brushed her mouth with his lips. "Not this man." And then he was kissing her again, tugging her beneath him and sliding himself inside.

"I warned you, milady wife, I should ride you until you cried for mercy."

Jocelyn grinned, too, and arched her body into his. "And I warned you, my lord, that we shall see who cries out first."

Chapter Twenty-three

PEACEFUL DAYS FOLLOWED. Jocelyn had never felt so cared for, so protected. What Rayne felt for her might not be love, but certainly he felt great affection. There was always the chance it would fade, that he would grow bored with his role as perfect husband, yet there wasn't a woman aboard the ship who wasn't envious of her position.

Jocelyn reveled in Rayne's attentions, his charm, his concern. She refused to heed the voice that warned her he had treated her this way before.

How can you forget the bitter end to which he led you? How can you forget how it felt behind those thick gray walls?

This is different, she argued, *this time I am his wife.* But all the arguing in the world couldn't completely silence the voice.

The following week, Jocelyn's worry took a turn in another direction. She awoke to a pounding headache and a terrible bout of seasickness. At least that was what she thought until she realized the ocean was calm. She had missed her monthly flux for the second month in a row, but until now believed it to be the strain she had been under.

What would Rayne say, she worried, if she truly carried his child? She still wasn't certain how he felt about this marriage. Would he see the babe as one more chain to bind him?

The second morning confirmed her suspicions, and with that knowledge came a fierce, sweet yearning like nothing she had known. She wanted this baby, loved it already, though it was yet little more than a merging of their seeds. She found herself praying she was not mistaken. She had always wanted children; she would especially love his.

God in heaven, let him want this babe as much as I do.

When Rayne discovered her bent over the chamber pot for the third morning in a row, his loud whoop sent a shimmer of surprise down her spine.

"For heaven sakes, Rayne, what was that all about?" She wiped her face with a cool damp cloth as he strode toward her, grinning. The unmistakable look of pleasure on his dear, handsome face made her heart turn over.

He slid his arms beneath her bottom and lifted her up to face him. "Tell me that what I am thinking is the truth."

Jocelyn propped her arms on his shoulders, giddy with relief at the happiness dancing in his eyes.

"The truth is if you don't put me down, you are very likely to suffer some very unpleasant consequences."

"I don't care."

Her smile grew wider. "I believe there is every chance I carry your babe."

He whooped again, louder than ever, and his hold on her grew tighter.

"Don't you dare spin me around!"

Deep laughter rumbled from his chest. Rayne set her gently on her feet. "I wouldn't dream of it. In fact I wouldn't dream of doing anything that might upset our babe."

Jocelyn's fingers nervously smoothed the lapels on his coat. "You're pleased, then, truly? I wasn't sure what you would say. I thought to wait a while, make certain before I told you."

His smile slipped a little. "You never have to be afraid to tell me anything. I'm your husband, Jo. Your problems are mine—but your joys are mine, too."

She reached up to touch his face, but another wave of nausea hit her. Turning away from his concern, she raced behind the screen to the chamber pot in the corner.

"I wish my morning sickness was yours as well," she said tartly from behind the screen, and heard Rayne's bark of laughter.

The sickness eased after the first two weeks, plaguing her only occasionally, or if she had eaten unwisely during the day. She and Rayne returned to their arduous bouts of lovemaking—once Jocelyn assured him the babe would be safe—and because of that part of him she carried, she had never felt closer to him. She prayed he felt some of those feelings for her.

The day before they were set to reach England, Rayne stood beside her at the rail. Wind-tossed clouds drifted by in the late afternoon breeze, blocking the sun and making her shiver. Gulls had begun to follow in the ship's wake. They screeched and cawed and set her nerves on edge.

"I wish we never had to reach the shore," she said. Rayne cradled her back against his chest, his arms protectively around her.

"In some ways, so do I."

She turned in his arms, her eyes searching his. "We've spoken little of the problems that lie ahead. What of our return, Rayne? What will people say? What will they do? The thought of you and Alexandra being shunned because of me is enough to make me sick all over again."

Rayne kissed her forehead. "Whatever happens, it isn't because of you. I'm the one who stole an innocent young woman's virtue. I'm the one who accused you of a crime you didn't commit."

He was also the one with an enemy who wanted him

dead. Her stomach clenched to think of it. "We'll be outcasts, won't we?"

Rayne sighed and glanced out at the water. "We've power and wealth on our side. We've mended our immoral ways. A good deal worse has been overlooked by members of the *ton*."

"I can hardly credit that."

"Have you ever heard of Canis, Racky, and the Rat?"

Jocelyn laughed. "No, I don't believe I have."

"How about the fifth Duke of Devonshire, his duchess Georgina, and Lady Elizabeth Foster? They were quite a threesome at one time."

"A threesome? You don't mean . . ."

He grinned. "Exactly so."

"They were . . . the three of them were . . . involved?"

"Ménage à trois, the French say."

"But surely their relationship was a well-guarded secret."

"Lady Elizabeth moved in with the duke and duchess. Eventually both women bore him children. It was all rather seedy, yet through it all, the three of them remained fast friends."

"And respected members of the *ton*?"

"If not respected, certainly tolerated. The duchess was considered one of the most celebrated hostesses in London."

Jocelyn relaxed against him, letting her head fall back against his shoulder. His finger entwined a flyaway ringlet of her hair. "If that is the case, then perhaps there is some hope for us."

"You just leave everything to me, love. If the feat can be managed, I shall see it done."

He made it sound easy, yet she knew it would take a minor miracle. And now she had the babe to consider. Jocelyn sighed and glanced out at the dull, gray-blue sea.

* * *

Rayne hadn't anticipated the joy he would feel at his homecoming. He was eager to see his sister, his good friends Dominic and Catherine, eager to settle his wife and the child she carried safely in their new home.

He had posted a letter to Dominic on an earlier ship, giving the week of their arrival and informing them with all confidence of his upcoming marriage, though at that early date Jocelyn had not yet agreed. He had wanted to give them time to accept his decision, had explained the mistake he had made and how he intended to set things aright. He prayed they would understand and welcome Jocelyn as his wife.

As the ship approached the harbor, Rayne stood beside her at the rail. The London docks were just as he had left them, flags of every country streaming from the masts of the endless ships crowding the busy wharf. Merchants plied their wares along the quay and doxies strutted their stuff, their pox-scarred faces hidden behind a thick screen of powder. Broad-backed stevedores offloading cargo strode beside sailors dressed in duck pants and wide-striped shirts, or the uniform of His Majesty's Navy.

The signs of the ongoing war were there, cannon amidships, excessive men and supplies headed for ports unknown, officers striding briskly, their heads filled with thoughts of battles not yet won. The sight stirred Rayne's blood as it always did, making him remember a time when he had felt more a man than he ever had before or since.

He amended that. Working the land, rebuilding Mahogany Vale, had made him feel that way. Making a baby with the woman who stood beside him. Something swelled in his chest as he looked down at the top of his young wife's head, and he had to clear his throat to ease a sudden lump there.

"They'll be waiting for us at Stoneleigh," he said. "They know we'll be docking sometime this week."

She slid her arm through his, and he felt her tremble.

"You've nothing to be afraid of," he said softly, wishing he knew a way to ease her fears. "They know you didn't shoot me. They know we're married. Everything is going to be fine."

"Just because you believe me doesn't mean they will."

They were words he had said to himself. "They trust my judgment. For now that will have to be enough." Until he discovered the man responsible for the shooting.

His fist clenched unconsciously. After what both of them had suffered, he would make the bastard pay. He had already posted a letter to Harvey Malcom, an investigator Dominic had used in the past and heartily recommended. Hopefully, the man had already begun the tasks Rayne had set him.

The ship reached the dock with all good speed. Their trunks were carried from the cabin and loaded onto a hackney coach. Jocelyn said good-bye to Mrs. Kenwood, thanking her for her company on the voyage, though in truth they had spent little time together. Then Rayne saw the older woman to a hackney which would carry her to a reunion with her son.

Soon Rayne and Jocelyn had set off themselves, rumbling along the crowded London streets, listening to the familiar cant of beggars, the shouts and jeers of merchants —bakers, weavers, rubbish sellers, rag pickers—passing wagons piled high with building supplies or vegetables headed for market, hearing the raucous laughter and occasional tears that drifted in through the window of the carriage.

Jolting and swaying, the coach passed ale houses and gin shops, shoemakers, milliners, and restaurants crammed to overflowing. The smell of roasting meat tinged the air, then the dank unpleasant odor of rotting garbage.

On the seat beside him, Jocelyn seemed to notice none of those things.

"I should like to visit the children," she said softly, drawing his attention from the bustling throng outside. "I can't imagine how much they must have grown."

He had seen to the orphanage long before the shooting,

working with Ezra Perkins, the chief officer, to resettle the children and see to their proper care. Jocelyn had accompanied him, first to their temporary home in Bell Yard, then to the newly fashioned structure once the children had moved in.

Rayne squeezed Jo's slender white-gloved hand. "We'll visit just as soon as we're settled in." He smiled gently. "I promise."

She tried to smile back but her bottom lip trembled. She was uncommonly nervous; he could read it in her troubled blue eyes. He wished he knew how to make things easier.

He prayed his sister and his friends would not make things worse.

An army of servants met them on the front steps of Stoneleigh, welcoming smiles all round. Farthington actually grinned, a feat he hadn't accomplished since the day Rayne returned from the war. Rayne helped Jocelyn down from the carriage and led her up the wide stone stairs.

"It's good to see you, milord," said the butler.

"Thank you, Farthington. I trust you've kept things well in hand during my absence."

"Of course, milord."

Rayne slid an arm around Jo's waist. "I should like you to meet your new mistress, Lady Stoneleigh."

The small, gray-haired butler inclined his head in a very proper greeting, pretending, just as Rayne did, that this was the first time they had met. "Welcome to your new home, milady."

"Thank you." She faced the little man with her head held high, but a hint of color tinged her cheeks.

"I'll let your sister and the others know you've arrived." But of course he didn't have to. They had heard the commotion out front and now raced into the foyer.

"Rayne!" Alexandra was the first to arrive, hurling herself into his arms and clutching his neck as he lifted her several feet off the ground.

"How are you, brat?"

"Fine—now that you're home." She hugged him again, grinning in a way that made her look even younger than her just-turned seventeen years.

"I've a birthday gift for you someplace. I'm sorry I missed the occasion, but I promise I'll make it up to you." He eased himself away. "I believe you and Jocelyn have met. Jo, you remember Alex." Jocelyn smiled, but Alexandra stiffened.

"Yes, I believe we met right here," she said with a tight little smile. "How do you do?"

"Hello, Alexandra."

"All right, what's all the commotion out here?" That came from Dominic, who stepped in front of the women. "Surely all this fuss isn't because this old war horse has finally had the sense to come home?" The men shook hands, then warmly embraced, and Catherine stepped in for a hug.

"Welcome back, Rayne." She smiled at him with affection, then turned to his slender, slightly pale wife. "And this must be Jocelyn. I'm so glad I finally get to meet you."

There was so much warmth in Catherine's voice, Jocelyn finally smiled as if she meant it. "Rayne has written all about you. I've been looking forward to this for a very long time."

Dominic turned onyx eyes in Jo's direction. "I believe I owe you an apology, Lady Stoneleigh. For Rayne's sake I hope you'll put our disagreement in the past."

"Y-You owe me nothing. It was all a dreadful mistake. I'm sorry any of it had to happen."

Dominic smiled, his dark skin brightened by a flash of blinding white that could charm the most jaded female in London. "Spoken like a true lady." He brought her fingers to his lips. "Welcome home, Viscountess."

From there things moved forward rather well; at least that was what Rayne thought until the women retired upstairs to ready themselves for supper, leaving Rayne alone with Dominic in the drawing room downstairs.

"Well?" Lounging like a panther against a wall in the

Red Salon, Dominic's piercing black eyes followed Rayne as he crossed the crimson Oriental carpet.

"Well, what?" he said, bending down to withdraw a cigar from the crystal humidor on the carved rosewood table.

"Well, are you going to tell me how this blinding revelation came about? How you happened to discover Miss Asbury was innocent?"

Rayne worked to keep his expression bland. "How I know is unimportant. The fact is, I do."

"You've proof of some sort, then?"

"I'm telling you that Jocelyn is not guilty. I am asking you, as my closest friend, to put your faith in my judgment. I am asking you to accept the woman I have chosen as my wife, just as I have accepted yours."

Dominic said nothing for the longest time. Then, "We've been together far too long for me to refuse anything you might ask. If you're willing to bet your life on this woman, then I know how strong your feelings for her must be. As you said, she is your wife. That is good enough for me."

"And Catherine?"

"Catherine is a romantic. She's always looking for the good in people. I believe she wanted to find that good in Jocelyn from the moment she discovered your feelings for her. She will champion your wife in any way she can."

Rayne nodded, pleased with Dominic's words. He clipped the end off his cigar, clamped it between his teeth, fired the end and took a long slow pull that made the tip glow crimson.

"Unfortunately," Dominic added, "I can't say the same for your sister."

Rayne arched a brow. "What do you mean?"

"Alexandra is convinced Jocelyn is guilty. She thinks you've somehow been duped into believing her innocent of the shooting. Where your sister is concerned, Jocelyn is in for a tough go, I'm afraid."

Rayne sighed. "That girl needs a husband."

"She's had more than her fair share of offers. Peter Melford of late, but of course she turned him down. The poor fool actually believed he had a chance. From what I hear, he took the news pretty hard."

Rayne grunted. "I should imagine. Remind me to pursue the matter of a betrothal as soon as we've put all of this behind us."

Dominic moved away from the wall, his long lean strides carrying him gracefully in Rayne's direction. "Which brings us to the problem at hand, does it not?"

Rayne took a draw on his cigar. "Which is?"

"Which is, who the hell shot you?"

Rayne blew a smoke ring into the room and leaned back in his brocade chair. "I'm afraid I haven't the faintest idea. I've a bloody long list of suspects, as you might imagine, but none upon whom I can squarely place the blame."

"You said in your letter you intended to hire Harvey Malcom."

"That I have. I've also given him a list of persons who might wish me dead and instructions to discover the whereabouts of each of them at the time of the shooting."

"He's a good man, Rayne. If anyone can discover the culprit, Malcom can. In the meantime, I hope you've arranged for some sort of protection."

"Not yet, but I will."

"Don't wait. Even now your life could be in danger."

It galled him to be cosseted like a child, and yet he knew he should heed his friend's words. He'd see to it, he vowed, then he'd nail the bloody bastard who had caused them all such pain.

The longer he stayed in London, the more frustrated Rayne became. Instead of the quick rescinding of Jocelyn's sentence he had expected, the magistrate questioned him over and over. Then he faced the Lords of Appeal, who were certain his infatuation for his lovely young wife was blinding him to the truth.

"I should like to see her," said one of the four men

presiding, a gaunt man who looked at Rayne down his hawklike nose and scratched his curly gray wig. "I've a few unanswered questions. We'll have to be satisfied we've got the truth before the matter can be laid to rest."

Rayne thought of how terrified Jo would be. He had promised her she would be safe. Perspiration gathered on his forehead.

"I assure you, my lord, there is no need for that kind of trouble. My wife is the innocent victim of a terrible injustice. I'm the one who should pay, not her." He forced himself to smile. "If you would allow me, I would gladly make restitution. There's been talk of a badly needed wing here at the Inns of Court. I would be honored to contribute, say, ten thousand pounds? I'm certain your lordships would see the money put to good use."

"Well . . ." The man's weasellike eyes fairly gleamed. He glanced at the others, who nodded in agreement, and Rayne breathed a sigh of relief. The deed was done; Jocelyn would be free. Though he wouldn't feel at ease until he held the papers in his hand, he was making steady progress.

His meetings with Harvey Malcom had gone far worse. Though the stocky balding man was as keen as Dominic said, so far he had turned up little in the way of clues.

"Lady Campden's whereabouts have been accounted for," he reported one afternoon at his office. "She spent the day of the shooting at her modiste. Of course, she could have paid someone to do it. I'm working on that possibility now..

"What about Bartlett?" Rayne asked.

"He's still the most likely suspect. No one seems to know where he was at the time of the shooting. He was drunk the night before. It appears he made several rash statements about your villainy. One of the members of your box club"—he checked his notes—"a Lord Schofield, claims Lord Harcourt said someone ought to shoot you for what you'd done. No one seems to know precisely what he meant, but apparently that is what he said."

"Bartlett." Rage welled up inside him just at the sound of the name. "I wouldn't have thought he'd go that far, but if he has—"

"If he has, you will turn him over to the authorities."

Rayne said nothing. He nodded, but inside he wasn't sure exactly what he would do. He remembered the days he had lain near death, of the pain he had suffered, and the heartbreak. He thought of Jocelyn, alone and frightened, surviving in the filth of Newgate prison, of her long, stifling journey, of the cat-o'-nine-tails marking her lovely white back.

He thought of what might have happened if he hadn't gone to Jamaica, and each day the anger he felt toward the man who had shot him festered and grew.

Only at night did his anger wane. Lying in bed, sated and content in a way he had never been, Rayne thought of his growing feelings for Jo. In Jamaica he had wrongly believed that taking her to wife would be enough. It would ease his conscience, solve the matter of her future —and his own—and accommodate the incredible desire he always felt for her.

But as he had suspected all along, there was far more than practicality involved in his feelings for Jo.

What of her? he now wondered. What was she thinking, feeling? Had he touched her as she had touched him? On the ship he had thought the fact she carried his child would bind her to him. And of course in a way it did. But was it enough? He couldn't help recalling the love she had felt for him at his town house. *It was given to me by the man I loved . . . man I loved . . . man I loved.*

Could she love him again? Could she trust him completely as she had once before? Did she feel more than the rioting desire that crackled between them every time they were together?

Why it meant so much was unimportant. He only knew he wanted her to love him. She wouldn't until she trusted him, and he knew in many ways she still did not. Not even now that he had settled things with the courts and would soon have the papers ensuring her freedom. She had accepted the news with relief and gratitude, crying as she hugged him, thanking him though he told her it was nothing less than her due.

But her trust remained elusive. And without it, so did her love.

Jocelyn spent her first week at Stoneleigh coming to know her new home. Or at least the home she would share with Rayne whenever they weren't in residence at Marden.

It was as grand as she remembered, and it amazed her to think she was now mistress of such a vast and beautiful estate. Already she was coming to love it, though the idea of living much of the time in Marden's wide open spaces also held great appeal.

And at Marden, Rayne would be farther away from the City, farther from any possible danger. It was one of the reasons she hadn't pressed him to find Brownie or Tucker.

Jocelyn knew Rayne had hired a man to look into the shooting. Brownie and Tucker were bound to be suspects. She was certain Brownie had not been involved, but what of Tuck? Even if he had been responsible, he was only a boy, and she was sure it could only have happened out of some misguided sense of justice. She couldn't stand the thought of him hanging, or spending his life in prison.

On top of that, there was the problem of Rayne's sister. It was obvious Alexandra still believed her to be guilty. She was wary, elusive, and unfriendly. Not in Rayne's presence, of course, even Alex wouldn't risk that. Jo wished there was something she could do.

She sighed as she climbed the stairs to her room. Rayne should have been home some time ago, yet she hadn't heard him come in. On the chance that he might have, she opened the door to his chamber and was surprised to see him standing in front of the cheval glass mirror, tying a fresh white stock around his throat.

"I didn't think you were here," Jo said, taking in the evening clothes laid out on his bed.

"I've decided to go out for the evening. I may be late. You won't need to wait up." He grabbed his black broadcloth tailcoat and shrugged it on.

"But where are you going? It isn't safe for you out there, especially at night." There was something in his manner, something a little elusive. Jocelyn wet suddenly dry lips.

"I can't stay in this house forever. Besides, Finch will be driving me. He's a capable man with a gun."

"Where? Where are you going?"

"There's a house party at Schofield's. I thought I'd test the waters, see how fares the wind."

"I don't like it, Rayne. Something might happen."

"Nothing's going to happen."

"If you're going to face the gossips, why can't I?"

He bent down and kissed her. "Because I want to soften them up first. Sort of like feeding the lions a sacrificial lamb before confronting them in their den."

Why didn't she believe him? "Are you certain I can't go with you?"

"No, love, not this time."

Bloody damn, what wasn't he telling her? She opened her mouth to ask, but he only kissed her again, turned and strode through the door.

Jocelyn stared after him, her stomach balled into a knot. Was he seeing another woman? She had known from the start his affections might wander, yet her instincts told her this was something different.

Was it something to do with the shooting? She knew it preyed on his mind night and day. God only knew what would happen to the man when Rayne found out.

If the man didn't find Rayne first.

"Elsa!" Jocelyn called into her adjoining chamber, suddenly convinced of what she must do and bringing the little blond maid on the run. "Ready my blue and silver gown. And ask Farthington to have another carriage brought round. I'll be spending the evening out."

Jocelyn dressed hurriedly, thinking about what lay ahead. Lord Schofield lived on Berkeley Square. She had followed Rayne there back in the days when she'd been roaming the streets with Brownie. If the Stoneleigh carriage was parked somewhere out front, she'd go in. If she found him, she could see what he was up to and keep a protective eye out for him.

If Society didn't approve, they could go hang.

Chapter Twenty-four

Rayne arrived at the Schofield town house at quarter past eleven. House lights beckoned and guests spilled out into the street. It was drizzling, the Little Season on its way to an end. Rayne turned up the beaver collar on his great coat and strode on in.

"Good evening, my lord," said Lady Schofield, an overly delicate yet somehow attractive woman in her forties. "We heard of your return to the City."

He'd been relatively certain he could count on Emma and Max to accept him, no matter what he had done. At least they were speaking to him. "Yes. My wife and I are finally getting settled."

"So I gathered," Max said. "Congratulations." He didn't miss the gleam of speculation in Schofield's shrewd eyes.

"Thank you. I believe when you meet my wife you'll discover I'm a very lucky man." They made polite conversation, Rayne making Jocelyn's apologies, all the while scanning the room for the Earl of Harcourt.

He spotted him near the doors leading out onto the terrace.

"If you'll excuse me, Max, I believe I see a friend." A room full of them, actually . . . if he used the term loosely. By the time he got halfway through the crowd, he realized the buzz in the air was directed at him.

"Scandalous, I tell you." The spoon-faced dowager hid

behind her quizzing glass, but didn't bother to lower her voice. "I knew the man was a scoundrel, but this is absurd."

Rayne's jaw tightened.

"They say he picked her up right off the streets! A filthy, ragged urchin. Why, she's probably diseased!"

It took every ounce of his will to keep on walking. Only his determination to reach Harcourt kept him from unleashing his wrath on the scandalmongers wagging their vicious tongues.

Instead he ignored the knowing smirks and speculative glances, the fans being fluttered as if his presence alone might make them swoon, and kept on walking toward the terrace. Harcourt had been conspicuously absent of late. Rayne was determined to find out why.

Even in the darkness, Jocelyn easily spotted the Stoneleigh bear and serpent on the door of Rayne's carriage. She released a small sigh of relief. He was here, just as he'd said. But what exactly was he doing?

A footman helped her down from the landau to the street. She pulled her ermine-lined cloak more closely around her and started toward the gray stone building leaking light from every window. At the front door she paused, uncertain yet determined, hoping she was doing the right thing.

A servant took her cloak, and she grudgingly gave it over, missing the security of the voluminous folds but knowing she could pass unnoticed more easily without it.

"Good evening, madam. I don't believe we've met." That from a stately man with a dash of silver in his hair who appeared to be the host.

Jocelyn nervously wet her lips. "I'm Lady Stoneleigh. I'm looking for my husband. I believe he's here."

One silver-tinted brow shot up. "Last I saw, he was headed toward the terrace. I'm Lord Schofield. I'm glad you're feeling better."

"What? Yes . . . well, I thought it might do me good

to get out for a while." The Stoneleigh mansion wasn't exactly next door, but his lordship had the good grace not to make a point of it. "It's a pleasure meeting you, my lord."

He opened his mouth to say something more, but Jocelyn hurriedly started walking. Behind her the woman at Schofield's elbow leaned forward to ask him who she was. Jocelyn heard his response and the woman's quick intake of breath.

Her head went up a notch but she kept going, passing through a gilt and emerald drawing room surging with excitement. The cream of the *haute ton* had arrived in force, decked out in their shimmering finery. Liveried servants hustled to obey their every command, and even though the doors stood open and the air outside was chill, the room felt overly warm.

"Excuse me, please. I should like to pass." Jocelyn pushed her way through the thong, catching curious glances along the way. She had almost reached the doors leading out to the patio when she realized how much quieter the room had grown.

". . . certainly no ragged urchin," someone said, a sandy-haired man dandied up in mustard breeches and a forest-green coat. "I can see why Stoneleigh was so eager to take her in."

Jocelyn's head went higher.

"Why, she's the woman I saw at Vauxhall Gardens," another man said. "It never occurred to me *that* lovely bit of fluff could possibly be the same notorious creature half the City's been gossiping about."

Her bottom lip trembled. It shouldn't hurt, but it did.

"It's scandalous, I tell you." A woman in velvet stepped out of the way as if to avoid her touch.

Jocelyn just kept walking. She could see the terrace now. Rayne was standing just outside the leaded glass doors. Her heart started pounding at the sight of him, so tall and completely composed.

Then she saw the woman. She was ravishing, all supple

curves and silver-blond hair. She was laughing at something Rayne said, flirting outrageously. Jocelyn's footsteps faltered. She had known this might happen. She had known, and yet she wasn't prepared for the angry heat suffusing her, the heavy weight crushing her chest.

Then she saw Rayne's face. His eyes weren't focused on the woman, but over the top of her silver-blond head. He was nodding in the woman's direction, but his attention lay elsewhere. Halfway through one of her fawning sentences, he excused himself and walked away.

Jocelyn could have sagged in relief. The indignant whispers around her faded away and a tiny smile curved her lips.

Unconsciously squaring her shoulders, she walked through the doors to the terrace, stopping for a moment as her eyes searched for Rayne. He was striding away from her, crossing the terrace toward a tall blond man, his expression suddenly thunderous. When the blond man turned, Jocelyn recognized Stephen Bartlett, Lord Harcourt—and her heart started pounding against her chest.

"Good evening, Stephen."

"Stoneleigh." An icy smile curved Harcourt's lips. "So you've finally come out of hiding. You're braver than I thought."

"Why, because someone might shoot me?"

"Because you've lost your throng of admirers—at least all but a few—or hadn't you noticed?"

"I noticed. It hardly comes as a surprise."

"I hear you married the girl. Where is she?"

"Home. I'd scarcely subject her to this."

"Why not? You've subjected her to just about everything else."

Rayne clamped his jaw, and his hand balled into a fist. "I came because I heard you'd be here."

Harcourt eyed him coldly. "What do you want with me?"

"I want to know if you're the bastard who shot me."

Stephen took a sip of champagne. "There've been times I've wanted to. I don't deny it."

"So you sneaked into my house, pulled the trigger, and let Jocelyn take the blame."

"Even you can't be fool enough to believe I'd do that."

"Why shouldn't I? No one seems to know where you were. Unless, of course, you'd care to enlighten me."

"It's none of your business."

"And is it none of my business that you were drunk the night before, threatening to kill me?"

"I believe my exact words were, 'Someone ought to shoot you for what you've done.' "

"And that someone was you."

"Hardly."

Rayne watched his eyes. There was nothing furtive in his manner. His gaze was cold and pitiless, almost mocking, but he seemed to be telling the truth.

"If I'd known Rosalee meant that much, I wouldn't have interfered."

Harcourt scoffed. "I made a fool of myself over that one. Actually, you did me a favor. No, it wasn't what you'd done to me I was discussing that eve. It was what you were doing to the obvious innocent you were squiring about as your mistress. The girl was clearly out of her league. There's a limit to good taste, my friend."

Rayne absorbed that piece of news, knowing he deserved every harsh, condemning word. "You're saying you had nothing to do with the shooting."

"If I wanted to kill you, I'd simply call you out."

"Where were you?"

"I told you before, it's none of your business."

Rayne reached out and gripped the front of Harcourt's shirt, spilling the drink from his fingers.

"You had better get your bloody hands off me."

"Rayne!" Jocelyn ran out of the shadows. Slender, frantic fingers tightened around his arm. "Please, Rayne. You mustn't do this. Not here."

Damned but she was right. It took all his control, but he

released his hold on Harcourt's shirt. Stephen smoothed the wrinkles, anger still flashing in his ice-blue eyes, but now there was something more.

"Lady Stoneleigh," he said, bowing over Jocelyn's hand. "A pleasure to see you again. You have my heartiest best wishes." He might have said condolences for the tone he had used.

"Thank you." Jocelyn glanced from Stephen to Rayne, silently pleading with him to desist.

"Stephen?" A petite blond woman stepped through the doorway. "I hoped you might be out—I'm sorry, I didn't realize you were busy." Color rising in her cheeks, she smoothed her white organdy gown and tried to turn away, but Harcourt gently caught her arm. She was delicate and lovely, almost fragile. Scarcely Harcourt's cup of tea.

"It's all right, love," he said, the tightness suddenly gone from his face. Rayne had never seen him look at a woman with such longing. He slid the girl's arm possessively through his, glanced from her to Jo, and with only a moment's hesitation, began to introduce them.

"Lady Stoneleigh, this is my fiancée, Lady Ann. She's just in from the country." He turned to Rayne. "I believe you know her father, his grace, the Duke of Burlington."

Already the women had begun to smile and make conversation, the lovely Lady Ann sweet and shy, Jocelyn accepting her friendly overtures with gratitude and warmth.

Rayne looked at Stephen. "Thank you," Rayne said, knowing exactly what the man had just done by his forthright introduction. "I believe I know where you were the day in question, and I owe you an apology."

Stephen made a slight nod of his head. "Accepted."

"Why did you do it?" His acknowledgment and that of the duke's daughter almost certainly assured their return to the fold, as Harcourt had known it would.

"You did me a favor ridding me of Rosalee; now we're even. Besides, I rather enjoy our rivalry. If you weren't around, whom would I have to lock horns with?"

Rayne nodded. He extended a hand and Harcourt shook

it, then Rayne urged Jocelyn toward the terrace door. As they passed through the milling throng of people, already he noticed a shift in the air.

"She's certainly not what I'd been led to believe," an older, graying woman said.

"An innocent to be sure," said another. "Her father was knighted for his outstanding contributions to English literature, you know. Stoneleigh ought to be ashamed of himself."

"Come now, Sarah, the viscount's made amends. He's married the girl, hasn't he?" She sighed wistfully as the two of them passed. "Besides, it's obviously a love match. I can't imagine anything more romantic than having a man like Stoneleigh cross an ocean to rescue me."

Rayne smiled to himself, brushed a kissed on Jocelyn's lips, and hurried her out the door.

Jocelyn peeked out the window at the shroud of gray fog clinging to the grounds around the house. At Rayne's insistence, she had napped in the afternoon and they had taken an early supper. The baby had been making its presence known. She felt sluggish this evening, and a little bit out of sorts.

Rayne was working in his study, making plans for upcoming changes at Marden. He had told her he would be tied up all evening. Jocelyn sighed, feeling listless and uncertain. Maybe she should settle in with a book. She had just reached the door when she heard light footfalls behind her.

"Good evening, Alexandra." Jocelyn smiled at the green-eyed girl, trying, as she did each day, to bridge the gap between them.

Alex's pretty lips thinned. "Is it? I thought it rather dreadful."

"Why is that?"

"This weather, for one thing. And of course there's all the gossip. I heard about last night—how did you have the nerve to face them?"

"I've done nothing I'm ashamed of, Alex."

"Nothing you're ashamed of! You may fool my brother with all that nonsense, but you can't fool me. I know you're the one who shot him, and every moment you spend in our house puts his life once more in danger!"

"Alex, please—" But the girl brushed past her, angry tears glistening on her cheeks. She left a few minutes later to join Lady Townsend and her daughter.

Jocelyn sighed. Give it time, she told herself. Rayne would eventually discover the culprit, and Alexandra would finally see the truth.

Jocelyn started again for the library, but her nerves were even more on edge. Though it was foggy out of doors, the quiet of the garden beckoned. Maybe she could find a little peace. Returning to her room, she cloaked herself warmly, headed back downstairs, and slipped outside to stroll the gravel paths.

At Stoneleigh, the gardens were immense and manicured to perfection. Jocelyn found herself walking between the neatly trimmed rows of box hedges, her shadow drifting in the dim light of the torches. With thoughts of Alex still near, her hand slid down to her belly. Her stomach was well-rounded now, and occasionally she felt the babe move.

She wondered if the child would love the out of doors as she and Rayne did, and whether it would be a boy or a girl. Alexandra never spoke of it, but the only softness she had ever seen in the girl's green eyes came when she glanced at the feminine swell that was Rayne's child.

Jocelyn plucked a pink camellia bloom and held the fragrant blossom beneath her nose. Calm at last, she had just turned back toward the house when the loud crack of gunfire shattered the quiet night air.

Sweet God! Rayne! Picking up her skirts, she raced toward the back of the house, her heart thudding wildly. Jerking open the door, she rushed inside and down the hall, her legs shaking so hard she could barely make them move. *Don't let him be hurt. Please God, don't let him be hurt.*

He was nowhere in sight when she ran in, but the window stood open and the curtains billowed softly. She ran toward the spot and frantically leaned outside. "Rayne! Where are you?" *Please be all right.* As he walked back to the window, she could hear his labored breathing.

"What happened?" she asked. "You aren't hurt, are you?"

He shook his head, but his eyes searched the darkness. "Someone took a shot at me. I thought I might be able to catch him, but it's too bloody dark and foggy."

"You didn't see anyone?"

"Not a soul."

"Neither did I," she said. "I was out in the garden. I heard the shot, but I didn't see a thing."

By now a dozen servants stood in the study. "I'll be right in," Rayne said, opting for the door this time.

"Is everything all right, milady?" Farthington stepped forward, his gray brows drawn together in a worried frown.

"I—I'm not sure."

Rayne returned just then, and Jocelyn rushed into his arms. "Thank God you're all right." Seeing him whole and unharmed, she nearly collapsed in relief. Rayne held her tightly, tension still rippling through his body.

"What's happened? What the devil's going on?" Both of them turned at the unfamiliar voice, though Rayne's arm remained protectively around her. "Your footman says there's been some sort of trouble." A stocky, balding, sandy-haired man with cool gray eyes stood in the doorway.

"Someone took a shot at me," Rayne said to him. He turned to Jo. "This is Harvey Malcom. The Bow Street man I told you about."

"Yes."

"Good evening, my lady." Though he'd answered her, the stocky man appeared distracted.

"A pleasure, Mr. Malcom," Jocelyn said, "I'm so glad you're here."

"I only wish I'd arrived a few moments earlier." Malcom was already roaming the room, assessing the billowing curtains, fingering the small round hole embedded in the wall behind Rayne's desk. He followed the line of fire to the still-open window.

"I tried to run him down." Rayne shrugged his powerful shoulders. "Not a trace of him."

"My guess is he was somewhere out in the garden," Malcom said with authority, and Jocelyn felt the blood drain from her face.

Out in the garden? Dear God, *she* had been out in the garden. Rayne knew it. She had admitted as much when he had stood beside her at the window.

"Have all of your servants been accounted for?"

"Not yet, but they soon will be. Alexandra left to visit some friends."

"Was anyone you know of outside?"

Jocelyn's eyes swung to Rayne's face. *God, oh God, this couldn't be happening—not again!* She wet her lips and tried to speak but couldn't force out the words. Rayne's arm around her waist grew tighter.

"Jocelyn had just walked into the room," he said matter-of-factly. "I'm only grateful she wasn't in the bastard's line of fire."

She made a little sound in her throat. She couldn't help it. Sweet God in heaven, Rayne had lied for her! He knew she could have done it. He knew! After all that had happened, how could he not believe her guilty? Believe he had been wrong in trusting her? In marrying her?

Even his sister believed it.

Jocelyn studied her hands, careful to keep them from trembling. Her heart ached at the doubts she was certain to see in Rayne's face. Still, she forced herself to look at him. The lines around his mouth were set, and hard lines streaked his forehead. But in his eyes there was only the fierce, possessive light of his determination to protect her.

She could have wept at the sight of it. When she saw the suspicion in Harvey Malcom's gaze, she nearly did.

"I'd like a word with Mr. Malcom," Rayne said to her gently. "I know this has been upsetting. Why don't you go upstairs and wait for me there?"

She swallowed past the lump in her throat. "All right."

"We'll have to report this to the authorities," Malcom was saying as she passed him on her way out of the room.

"I don't think so," Rayne said and firmly closed the door.

Chapter Twenty-five

SHE WAS STANDING in front of the huge, ornately carved cheval glass mirror when he walked into the room. She was staring at her reflection but not really seeing it, wondering what he would say, what she should say to him.

Jocelyn turned at his approach, but his determined strides didn't slow until he reached her. He said her name on a soft breath of air, carefully gathered her into his arms and cradled her head against his chest.

"It's all right, love. Everything's going to be fine."

She didn't mean to cry, but the tears welled up and spilled over onto her cheeks. Jocelyn clung to him, terrified of what had almost happened, of what he must be thinking, praying she would say the right thing.

She brushed at the wetness, trying to hold back the scalding torrent, but all she could think of was Rayne, fiercely protective, lying to keep her safe, defying anyone who might put her in danger. She felt his fingers in her hair, his hands stroking down her back, his voice repeating her name, soothing her, telling her everything would be all right.

"You don't have to be afraid," he said, his voice rough with emotion, "I won't let anyone hurt you."

But she only clutched him tighter, clinging to his neck as if, in the way she held him, he would know how much he meant to her, how much she loved him for what he had done.

"W-Why did you do it?" she asked with a sob, pulling away to look at him. "Why?"

She felt a tremor in the fingers that gently smoothed the damp black hair from her cheeks. "You have to ask that? Don't you know?"

"I know I was out in the garden. I c-could have been the one. I could have—"

"No you couldn't," he countered, his hold unconsciously tighter. "You couldn't hurt anyone. I've known that since the night of the storm. I've known it without doubt, without reservation. I know it in my heart and in my soul."

He meant it—fiercely—she could see it in his eyes. With the knowledge came hope, and the tightness in her chest began to ease. It was a pain she had buried, but it had never really left her. The pain of uncertainty and re-membered betrayal.

"I'll never doubt you again, Jo. I promise you that. No matter what happens, I'll never doubt you. I love you. Tonight I realized just how much."

Time seemed to still, each tick of the clock slowing to fill the missing beats of her heart. She wanted to believe him—more than anything else in the world, and yet . . .

"You hated me once."

A flicker of pain crossed his features. "I know it must have seemed so. I even fooled myself for a while, but it wasn't the truth."

"You followed me, you despised me that much."

He ran his knuckles along her cheek. "Do you really believe I would travel four thousand miles to find a woman I hated?"

Jocelyn's eyes searched his face. "You're a man of con-science, Rayne. You married me out of duty, not love."

"Duty?" he repeated, pulling a little away. "Is that what you think?"

"You felt responsible. You still do."

"I married you because I love you. It took a while for me to see it—I can be damned stubborn at times."

She smiled at that, and Rayne sighed.

"I know it's hard to believe." He pressed a hard possessive kiss on her mouth. "In time I'll make you believe."

"Rayne," she said softly, sliding her arms around his neck. *I love you so.*

Rayne kissed her again, his mouth like sweet fire, his tongue invading, thrusting deep, staking his claim. She could feel the rapid thudding of his heart, feel his caring and concern in the tender way he held her.

She kissed him back with all the love she felt, but couldn't yet speak, and he groaned low in his throat. Lifting her into his arms, he carried her over to the huge four-poster bed. In minutes he had stripped off her clothes and his own, then he kissed her, long and deep. There was passion in his touch, but also a tenderness more poignant than ever before.

It was the sweetest of moments, steeped in love, alight with hope for the future. Jocelyn prayed it would last forever.

Then she recalled the deadly shot fired in his study. *Dear God don't take him from me again.*

Rayne felt slim fingers drifting through the mat of hair on his chest. The sun was barely up, but already they had made passionate love. Rayne felt languid and sated and undeniably content. He had finally admitted his love for the sleek little beauty beside him, and though she'd said nothing in return, her passion and care of him spoke more than words.

One day, my sweet waif, you will come to me as you did before. You will trust me and be unafraid to love.

At least he prayed that it would be so.

Wishing he could spend the day in bed with her, but recalling all too clearly the events of the evening and knowing he had too much to do, Rayne swung his long legs to the side of the bed and reached for his dressing gown, tossed over a nearby chair.

"What did Mr. Malcom say after I left?" Jocelyn asked softly, propped upon an elbow behind him.

Rayne sighed with resignation. No matter how sweet the moment, their still-unsettled problems always seemed to intrude.

"He says he's investigated most of the names on our list. Lady Campden is heavily involved in an affair with the Duke of Haverland. Lord Campden apparently knows nothing of my liaison with his wife and is becoming too addled to care, even if he did. Rosalee Shellgrave has taken a lover. She never was a serious threat, as far as I was concerned. I'm satisfied that Harcourt was not involved. He merely wanted to protect the reputation of his lady. I can hardly blame him for that."

"What about all of the others?"

Rayne arched a brow in annoyance. "I'll grant the number of suspects is lengthy, but it hardly includes every chap in England."

Jocelyn laughed. He loved the sound of it, like bell chimes peeling in a faraway church. "That's not what I meant and you know it."

He smiled, though his answer would hardly be a comfort. "To put it simply, Malcom is still without a clue."

"But surely he must have found something." Jocelyn sat up in bed, shiny black hair falling softly around her shoulders. He loved the feel of it, like rich jet silk in his hands.

"Not much, I'm afraid. I've had him looking for Brownie and Tucker. I know you're worried about them. Malcom's put the word out on the streets, but so far he hasn't made contact." Rayne didn't mention that although the older man had been seen in the stable at the time of the shooting, no one seemed to know the whereabouts of the boy. For Jocelyn's sake as well as Tucker's, he prayed the lad wasn't involved.

"I wish I could see them before we leave for Marden."

"I know you do. If Malcom can find them, we'll have them brought round straightaway."

She pressed a soft kiss on his shoulder. "Did Malcom say anything else?"

"Nothing of importance, though he did make one rather curious statement."

"What was that?"

"He said perhaps we were looking in the wrong direction."

"Meaning?"

Rayne hesitated only a moment. "Though you've been cleared of the attempted murder charges"—*damn, where were those papers?*—"Malcom found out you tried to shoot me in front of Lord Dorring's. He asked me why."

"What did you tell him?"

"That you had mistaken me for my father. I explained about the fire on Meacham Lane, about your cousins, and how you wound up on the streets."

"And?"

"That was the curious part. He asked me if there was anyone else who might want me dead for the same reason you did. I told him there was no one I could think of. Only your father, and Sir Henry was deceased."

Rayne leaned over and kissed her cheek, then climbed out of bed. Behind him Jocelyn sat immobile. Brownie and Tucker had once meant to see Rayne dead for the same reasons she did. She knew Brownie hadn't done it. Which pointed the finger of guilt once more at Tuck.

Sweet God in heaven. She had made things clear to him, hadn't she? She had explained that Rayne wasn't to blame, that he hadn't even been in the country during the time of her bitter misfortunes. Surely he had understood —or had he?

"I want you to spend the day packing," Rayne said as he pulled on his breeches and buttoned them up the front. "Tomorrow we're leaving for Marden."

"Thank heavens for that," Jo said, wanting him as far from danger as possible.

"In the meantime, I've got to go into the City. We'll be needing a few extra men. I don't want this bastard getting another chance to kill me." He strode over and kissed her hard on the mouth. "I've got too damned much to live for."

In the end Jocelyn convinced Rayne to let her accompany him to London.

"There are a few things I need before we leave for the country." It seemed certain that she was in no danger. Rayne was the target. Only Rayne.

"You'll take Elsa, of course."

She forced herself to smile. "Of course." The truth was, she had to find Tucker. She wasn't sure exactly where to look, but if she could find Brownie, there was a good chance the boy would be with him.

Wearing a simple brown serge gown and carrying a plain hooded cloak, she started down the hallway on her way to join Rayne in the dining room for chocolate and toast before heading into town. She was just passing Alexandra's room when the door swung open and the auburn-haired girl stepped out into the hall, nearly colliding with Jo head-on.

"Good morning, Alexandra."

"I—I was just on my way to see you." She fiddled with the ties on her soft peach jaconet gown. "Do you think we might speak for a moment?"

"Of course." They stepped into the younger girl's room, a frothy pink and white confection of ruffles and more ruffles that seemed a little young for Alexandra's seventeen years. Jocelyn made a mental note to speak to Rayne about letting his sister redecorate.

They faced each other across the Aubusson carpet. "What is it, Alex?"

Alexandra wet her pretty pink lips, and for the first time Jocelyn realized how nervous the young girl was. As Jocelyn eyed her with growing speculation, Alex's chin came up and she stiffened her shoulders, a gesture that reminded Jo a little of herself.

"It appears I owe you an apology," Alexandra said. "I heard what happened last night . . . Rayne told me about the attempt on his life. He also told me you were in his study at the time. It seems I was wrong about you. I'm sorry for what I said. I hope you can forgive me."

"Alex—"

"I was just so worried. I jumped to conclusions when I should have known better. My brother would never have married you unless he was certain of your innocence. I should have had more faith in him."

For a moment Jocelyn said nothing. She wanted this young woman's friendship, wanted to be an accepted part of Rayne's family.

But to do it on a lie?

"Rayne means everything to me," Alexandra finished. "I was just so afraid I would lose him."

Jo took a steadying breath. "I know how much you love your brother. I know how close he came to dying. I know as terrified as I was for him, that is how you must have felt."

Unconsciously, Jocelyn moved closer. "You and Rayne are the only real family I've had in years. I want you to trust me, Alexandra. I want us to be friends more than anything in this world."

"I want that, too," Alex said softly.

For an instant Jocelyn wavered. It would be so easy to let Alexandra believe . . . She took a second deep breath. "Friends don't lie to each other, Alex. So I'm going to take the same sort of risk your brother has taken. I'm going to tell you the truth."

"Truth? What truth? I don't understand."

"I wasn't in Rayne's study last night when the shot was fired; I was out in the garden. Rayne lied for me. He loves me, so he lied." Alexandra's face went pale. "But I am telling you that I didn't try to kill him." She stepped closer, reaching out to her, praying the young girl would understand.

"I love your brother, Alex. I carry his babe, and I love him more than anyone on this earth. You're a woman, Alexandra, surely when you look at me you can see the love I feel for Rayne."

Alexandra searched her face then glanced down at the hands she clutched in front of her. When she looked up, her troubled green eyes glistened with tears.

"I can see it, Jo. I saw it the very first time I met you. I knew you loved him even then."

Jocelyn's own eyes suddenly misted.

Alexandra brushed at the wetness trickling down her cheeks. "It took a great deal of courage for you to say what you just did. You may be certain that you will not regret it. My brother loves you. I know that I will come to love you, too."

When Jocelyn reached out for her, the younger girl went into her arms. "Thank you. You'll never know how great a gift you've just given me."

Alexandra only nodded. Jocelyn pulled away with a last warm smile, turned and started for the door.

"Jocelyn?"

"Yes, Alex?"

"Do you think you would mind calling me Alexa? All of my friends do. Everyone but Rayne."

"Alexa." Jo looked thoughtful. "Yes . . . it's a lovely name, and I believe it suits you better. From now on, Alexa it shall be." The younger girl smiled and Jo smiled back.

Closing the door behind her, Jocelyn walked down the hall and descended the stairs. She had risked a good deal in trusting Alexandra. Somehow she felt certain that trust had not been misplaced.

She was smiling to herself when she reached the dining room. Rayne glanced up and smiled, too.

"You're certainly in good spirits this morning."

"Considering all that's happened, I suppose I am."

"Mind telling me why?"

"You'll have to ask Alexandra. Which reminds me, I think she should redecorate her room. She's practically a grown woman now and—"

"Alex—grown? That will be the day."

"It isn't far off, my lord, I assure you."

But Rayne only grumbled an answer she didn't catch. They finished their light repast and set off for the City. On Bond Street the driver pulled the horses to a halt in front of Grossman's Millinery Shop.

"You're certain you won't need the carriage?" Rayne said.

The Stoneleigh coach and four was the last thing she needed where she would be traveling. "No. I'll just be shopping these few blocks while you're gone."

"All right, then, I'll meet you back here in two hours." He kissed her lightly on the lips, and a faint blush rose in her cheeks.

"You'll be careful, won't you?" she asked.

"By the time I return, I'll be surrounded by guards. I'm sure I shall feel a bit like Sir Walter on his way to the tower."

Jocelyn laughed. "Just as long as you're safe." This time it was she who did the kissing. "Take care," she repeated as he climbed back into the carriage. She watched until it disappeared round the corner.

"I've got something I need to do," Jocelyn told Elsa, who waited patiently for her on the boardwalk. "I shouldn't be gone long."

"But milady, surely you'll be wantin' me to come with you."

She considered it only an instant. It would be comforting to have the girl along, but the odds of finding Brownie and Tucker would go down considerably at the sight of a lady accompanied by her maid. Besides, she'd be traveling back alleys, looking for familiar faces, asking questions of the kind of people who scurried into hiding at the slightest hint of alarm.

"It would be best if you stayed right here. Why don't you see if there's anything we'll be needing for our trip into the country? Just tell the merchants it's for Stoneleigh and they'll put it on his account."

Elsa's face lit up at the prospect of spending the viscount's blunt. "As you wish, milady, whatever you say."

"I'll meet you back here in less than two hours."

Elsa nodded and started to walk away.

"Oh, and Elsa . . . if Rayne should happen to arrive before I do, tell him I spotted an old friend and we went off for a moment to visit. Tell him I'll be right back."

"What old friend, mum?"

"Just tell him, Elsa." Jocelyn opened the hooded cloak she carried over her arm, swung it around her and started for the corner.

In minutes she had hailed a hackney carriage and climbed in. She had no idea where Brownie might be living or if Tucker would be with him, but she knew a number of his cronies, some of the places where he passed time. Someone, somewhere would know where her friends had gone.

Rayne's meeting with Harvey Malcom took far less time than he had imagined. Malcom had even taken care of the matter of hiring competent guards. On top of that, the man had discovered where Brownie was living.

Rayne smiled. The old reprobate was the dearest present he could give his little wife, and he intended to see it done. He had plenty of time before their appointed meeting. If luck rode with him, Brownie might be somewhere near the address Malcom had given him, a basement room beneath a gin shop in a court off Holburn and Gray's Inn Lane.

It didn't take long to get there. He knew he'd arrived by the smell of rotting fish and human excrement. A sign on the gin shop read, DRUNK FOR A PENNY, DEAD DRUNK FOR TWO-PENCE, STRAW PROVIDED FREE.

Decent of them. A place for the poor sots to sleep off a

drunken stupor, only to wake up and start all over again.
He felt a twinge of guilt that he had once acted nearly that
bad, then wondered if the basement where Brownie lived
was such a place. He shivered to think of his wife fighting
for survival in those sordid conditions.

Since the entrance to the basement was supposed to be
in the alley, Rayne walked in that direction. He passed a
pair of ragged mumpers, sidestepped an aging doxy, saw
the open doorway, and started down the rickety wooden
stairs. He'd gone only two or three steps when he heard a
woman's muffled curses. A doxy he was certain, playing
hard-to-get in hopes of collecting a few shillings more for
her favors. He could hear the pair scuffling, but the basement was dim and he still couldn't see them.

At the bottom of the stairs, he caught sight of the man,
a thick-muscled, flat-bellied sailor, grinning as he fondled
the smaller figure mostly hidden by her cloak. Rayne
searched the otherwise empty room, looking for Brownie,
but there was no sign of him. He had started to walk
away, disappointed that his trip had been in vain, when
he heard the woman scream. She was fighting in earnest,
he realized, a small, hooded female pressed up against the
wall.

"You'd best be behavin' yerself," the sailor warned
with a slap that resounded off the low ceiling rafters.

Calling himself ten kinds of fool, Rayne turned in the
woman's direction just as the sailor shoved her down on
the dirty straw, followed her down and began to unbutton
his breeches.

"You bloody sod! Let me go!"

Rayne sucked in a breath, stunned to near disbelief by
the voice of the woman hissing and cursing the man
who'd attacked her. He knew that voice, knew only too
well the pretty face framed by a cloud of glossy black hair.

Fury swept over him. "A little early for our appoint-
ment, aren't you, my love?"

"Rayne!"

Gripping the sailor by the neck, he jerked the man to

his feet like a puppet on a string and smashed a hard right fist into his face.

Jocelyn scrambled off the floor, her heart hammering wildly. *Rayne!* She had never been more terrified—and never more grateful to see her tall, powerfully built husband.

The sailor swung; Rayne ducked the blow and landed another solid punch, sending his huge opponent staggering. Rayne threw two quick lefts and a right, bobbing and weaving now, relaxing into his fighting stance. The sailor feigned a right and landed a left, a solid blow to Rayne's jaw. Rayne took a step back and surprised her by grinning.

Bloody hell! The blackguard was enjoying himself! Yet she didn't miss the undisguised fury in his eyes. She winced to think how much of that fury was bound to be directed at her.

Rayne dodged three more hard-thrown blows, seemed to tire of the sport, and threw two long-reaching punches that brought the sailor to his knees. The man groaned as a last solid right knocked him over on his back and into the black void of unconsciousness.

Jocelyn glanced from the big man on the dirty straw floor to the equally big man who strode toward her. There was fury in every line of his face.

"Would you mind overly, madam," he said softly—far too softly, "telling me exactly what it is you are doing in a place like this?"

Jocelyn lifted her chin, though it felt a little wobbly. "I —I came to find Brownie. I asked some old friends. I discovered that this was where he was living. I wanted to see him, so I came."

"I ought to put you over my knee."

She smiled at him weakly. "I admit I probably deserve it. But I should much rather leave this dismal place if you don't mind."

One corner of his mouth twitched. "You frightened the

bloody daylights out of me. Are you certain you're all right?"

"I dare say I've been better."

Rayne just grunted. Then he was lifting her up and carrying her off toward the stairs. She wrapped her arms around his neck to steady herself as he made his ascent, and thought how fortunate she was that he had come when he did.

As he set her on her feet in the alley outside the basement, Jocelyn glanced at her surroundings, taking in the stagnant pools of water, the stacks of rotting garbage, the scraggly yellow-striped cat making a meal of a dead rat lying near the top of the stairs.

"I'd forgotten how dreadful all of this was."

Rayne turned her face with his hand to survey the darkening bruise along her jaw. "If you ever even think of coming to a place like this again, my love, there's going to be bloody hell to pay."

"I'm sorry."

"I mean it, Jo. I'm your husband. I mean to see you safe."

Funny, she thought, how wonderful it felt to know someone cared enough to make such a threat. "You're right, of course. I shouldn't have come, but I've got to find Brownie."

Someone chuckled gruffly from behind them. "Brownie, is it? If it's Brownie ye be lookin' for, gel, then I'd say ye've found 'im."

"Brownie!" Jocelyn turned toward the gruff sound of the voice and rushed into the beefy older man's arms. He hugged her so tight she thought her ribs might pop.

"Are you all right?" she asked. "Have you been getting enough to eat? Where's Tucker? Is he here with you? I've been so worried."

"And ye think I 'aven't been?" Brownie noticed the bruise on her cheek, bristled, and tossed a hard look at Rayne.

"He didn't do it." Jo smiled softly. "He's my husband."

Brownie relaxed his stance. "'Usband, is it? It appears ye've a bit o' explainin' to do, gel."

It didn't take long to relay the story, and the relief on the graying man's face made Jocelyn's heart swell with love for her friend.

"What about Tucker, Brownie? Is he still with you?"

"Boy's 'ere, all right. Showed up not long after they sent ye off. 'E just went 'round the corner. Ought to be back any minute."

"Jolie!" The thin blond boy spotted her and came on the run.

"Tucker!" Jocelyn rushed into his outstretched arms and hugged him hard.

"I can 'ardly believe me eyes."

"It's good to see you, Tuck," she said. The boy eyed Rayne warily, but his smile remained in place.

"'Ow'd you get back 'ome?" Tuck asked. "And what the bloody 'ell are ye doin' with 'im?"

"Rayne and I are married." Jocelyn's eyes searched Tuck's face, trying to read his thoughts. "It's a long story. I was hoping to find you. I—I was hoping—"

"It's all right, gel," Brownie said gently, laying a hand on her arm. "The lad didn't shoot 'im. Ain't that the right o' it, son?"

"I was scared that's what you'd think," Tuck said. "That's why I run." He glanced at Rayne, then turned back. "God's truth, Jo, I ain't never shot no one. I mighta got meself a bit arse backwards fer a while—what with me best friend turnin' into a bleedin' lady an' all, but ye can be sure I ain't about to do murder—leastwise not without good cause."

"Thank heavens." Jocelyn reached out and hugged him. "I didn't really think you would, but things have been so mixed up . . . I was worried is all."

"It's all right, Jo. I've 'ad a bit o' a time tryin' to sort things out meself."

Rayne slid an arm around Jocelyn's shoulders. "Now that we've cleared things up, why don't you and Brownie get your things? My carriage is just around the corner. Your old jobs are still open, if you want them."

Brownie clapped the boy on the back. "Think o' it, laddie! A full belly again." He turned to Rayne. "Ye don't 'ave to ask me twice, gov'nor."

Tucker hesitated only a moment, then he was nodding in agreement, running off toward the basement to get his meager possessions.

"So ye ain't found the bloke what shot ye," Brownie said to Rayne.

"Unfortunately, we haven't."

"Good thing we're 'ere then, ain't it?" Brownie said with a grin. "Somebody's gotta be protectin' ye. Me and Tuck, we'll keep an eye out. Ye can bet a prime piece o' scut on that."

Rayne chuckled and Jocelyn tried not to blush. Brownie would never change and she didn't really want him to. "Thank you," she said. "Knowing that makes me feel a good deal better."

Jocelyn felt as if a weight had been lifted from her shoulders. Rayne was still in danger, but her friends were not involved. Tomorrow they'd be leaving for Marden. She prayed fervently that at last Rayne would be safe.

Chapter Twenty-six

JOCELYN FIDGETED NERVOUSLY ALL EVENING. She was eager to leave for Marden, could hardly wait until morning, though Alexandra wasn't too happy about it.

Alex was once more "all the crack" among her friends, the scandal of the viscount's marriage to a former Newgate inmate already beginning to fade. In fact, the Grand Injustice, as the affair became known, only enhanced Alexandra's status. After all, hadn't her handsome, wealthy brother righted a terrible wrong? In the end hadn't love conquered all?

If women had found Stoneleigh attractive before, they now considered him a hero of epic proportions. Like a knight in shining armor, he had battled the odds to save his damsel in distress. The viscount and viscountess were the talk of the *ton*. There was little doubt that when the Season came around in the spring, their names would grace the top of the most-sought-after guest lists in London—a fact about which Rayne reminded his sister as she stoically made ready to leave.

"The Little Season is almost at an end," he said gently. "The fashionable elite will be retiring to the country very soon. You'll just be a bit ahead of the vogue."

"I don't mind, really." Alexandra's smile held an air of noble sacrifice. "I'd rather see you safe."

On that opinion no one disagreed.

If only Harvey Malcom could discover the man posing the threat to Rayne's life, Jocelyn thought, then things could return to normal.

She amended that.

When had life with Rayne ever been normal? Still, she fearfully awaited the day her husband would finally be out of danger.

It wasn't until they reached Marden that she began to feel better. The vast land holding was much as she remembered from her childhood: rolling hills, timbered forests, rich dark earth, and well-tended fields. Though she had never visited the huge estate, having lived in Marden Village not far away, she recalled the way it sat on the distant knoll, surveying its surroundings like a powerful aging king.

William Dorset, Rayne's estate man, cared for it well, she could see even from a distance. Rising against the horizon, the massive white house was twice as large as she remembered, and far more sprawling. There was a main facade with a columned exterior as well as two additional wings, forming a U-shaped main compound, which was entered by twin flights of stairs leading from the ground up to the main-floor level.

There were towers and turrets and outbuildings. Capability Brown had done the gardens, designing them to blend with the open, rolling, natural surroundings. A funny little moat hidden beneath the tall grass kept sheep from grazing too near.

Surveying it all, Jocelyn smiled then frowned, suddenly uneasy to think how accessible it was, how many places it offered an assailant to hide.

"Tomorrow I'll show you around," her husband said, once he had presented her to the servants and shown her to their huge suite of rooms.

Jocelyn smiled. With its vast marble entry and towering rotunda, its endless array of drawing rooms, withdrawing room, dining rooms, and salons, the house was even more extravagant than Stoneleigh. And yet she felt welcome here. The servants seemed pleased their lord and lady would be in residence, and of course Rayne had brought along his personal retainers to see to their needs as well.

Nevertheless, the move was a strain. Jocelyn had dropped into bed like a stone that first eve, exhausted from the long hours of travel, and Rayne had left her to sleep alone—much to her chagrin. Tonight she felt better. If he didn't seek her out, she intended to go to him.

She thought of him now as she walked down the sconce-lit hall toward her bedchamber. When she stepped into the room, she felt his babe move inside her and her hand came up to cradle the spot.

"I take it my son is making himself known." Rayne stood just a few feet away.

Jocelyn smiled, more than a little pleased to see him. "Yes." She walked to his side, reached for his hand and settled it on her thickening stomach. "He's going to be strong like his father."

"Or courageous like his mother," Rayne said softly.

Just then the babe kicked out, nudging Rayne's hand, and his face lit up with pride.

"Your child may be a girl," Jo warned.

"I won't be disappointed." He bent and kissed her cheek. "Besides, I intend to see a houseful of the noisy little beggars before we're through."

When Jocelyn laughed, Rayne's mouth moved warmly along her throat, absorbing the gentle vibration. Then he was lifting her up, carrying her through the door that adjoined their chambers, letting her go but holding her close, forcing her to slide the length of his long hard body.

"I missed you last night." He pressed a warm kiss on the nape of her neck. "It occurred to me how much I hate sleeping without you." He nipped an earlobe, then his mouth moved over hers, nibbling softly, making her limbs feel suddenly weak.

"Rayne," she whispered, a little breathless ·as he stripped off her clothes. She wondered if she would ever get enough of him.

"How do you like your new home?" he asked between small, soft kisses.

"I like any place you are."

The answer pleased him mightily. Or so it would seem by the ardor of his touch. They made love with fiery abandon, then once more with tenderness. Jocelyn brushed strands of damp brown hair from his forehead as he drifted off to sleep, but for her, sleep remained elusive. *If only I could be sure he was safe.*

It was a thought that lingered even as she nestled against him.

Rayne had been back in his country home almost two weeks when Harvey Malcom arrived. Engrossed in the changes he had long ago decided to make, Rayne had spent the day working to enclose the fields with hawthorn hedges and planting clumps of trees. He intended mixed sheep and cattle grazing and the planned rotation of crops. The second Lord Townsend had championed the use of root crops to cleanse the soil in a new four-stage rotation. From what Rayne had read, it was exactly what Marden needed, and he intended to see it done.

It meant long days in the fields just like this one, but it gave him a feeling of accomplishment and that same sense of purpose he had felt at Mahogany Vale.

As tired as he was, his steps didn't falter as he strode into his study and extended a hand to Malcom. The danger he faced daily was a thorn in his side he wanted to see removed.

"What news, Malcom? You've come a good long ways. Surely you've run across something."

"Indeed I have, my lord." The stocky man walked toward the chair Rayne indicated in front of the hearth. For once there was something besides frustration in the man's cool gray eyes. "I believe I may have come up with exactly what we have been searching for."

"You've discovered the man who shot me?" Rayne leaned forward in his chair.

"Very likely, sir. It was just as I feared. We had been going at the matter entirely backward. It wasn't an enemy of yours, my lord, but of your father's. I believe the man who shot you is Sir Henry Asbury."

"Asbury! But it can't be. The man is quite dead."

"I'm afraid he isn't. After our last conversation, I decided to speak to her ladyship's cousin in Cornwall, Barclay Peters. There was slim chance of turning up a lead, of course, but that is exactly what happened. You see, when I inquired of the fire on Meacham Lane, Peters seemed overly uncomfortable. I pressed him on the matter, and he finally admitted Sir Henry hadn't died that night. The old man was badly burned, but somehow he managed to escape the flames even after the roof caved in. Unfortunately, his mind faired even worse than his terribly ravaged body."

"What happened to him?"

"Peters and his wife believed it was in her ladyship's best interest not to tell her about her father. He was, after all, badly disfigured and mentally deranged. Once his injuries healed, he was taken off to Bethlehem Hospital, his mind completely gone."

Bedlam. Rayne thought of how Jocelyn would take the news and his stomach knotted. "I gather Sir Henry escaped."

"Quite so, my lord. The man's been at large since two months prior to the shooting. Undoubtedly he holds you responsible for everything that happened—in your father's stead, of course."

"Have you any idea where Sir Henry might be?"

"As a matter of fact, I'm on my way this very eve to Kingsbury. One of my runners heard tell of a badly disfigured man in residence at the Knight and Garter Tavern."

"Kingsbury is less than a half day's ride. You don't suppose he's hunting me again, do you?"

"I'm afraid so, my lord."

Rayne pulled his watch fob from the pocket of his waistcoat. "The hour grows late for travel. Since I intend to go with you, I suggest we wait until morning. We'll get an early start and put an end to this matter once and for all."

"What about her ladyship, my lord?"

"What about her indeed?" Rayne sighed wearily, his eyes fixed on Harvey Malcom's face. "Not a word of this to Jocelyn. Not until it is over. I don't want her overset, and she is bound to be when she discovers her father's condition."

"You needn't be concerned, my lord. I have always been the height of discretion."

"So Gravenwold has said." Rayne came to his feet and Malcom did the same. "I'll have the butler show you and your man to a chamber upstairs. We'll be on our way at dawn."

"As you wish, my lord."

Rayne indicated the door, and the two of them walked in that direction. After Malcom had been led upstairs, Rayne went up to his own suite of rooms. He was worried for Jocelyn. He knew how terrible she would feel when she discovered the truth of her father. He intended to delay that knowledge for as long as he could.

At the door to her chamber, he paused. She was damned perceptive, and he didn't want her to read his concern. Still, he needed her this night, just as he always did.

He would wait until her lamp went out before he approached her. Then he would take her with so much passion, she could think of nothing but the pleasure he stirred in her body.

Tomorrow, Rayne vowed, would be soon enough to face the problems to come.

Jocelyn emerged lethargically from a deep, satisfying slumber. Rayne had been an arduous lover last eve. So much so, she had slept late and he was already up and gone. Color throbbed in her cheeks just to think of it. He had taken her hard and fast, then started all over and made slow languid love to her for hours.

After such a wild night of passion, she should be grateful he had business in Kingsbury that would keep him away this eve. During the day, she could begin preparations for the gala Rayne planned, an affair designed to celebrate their marriage, reacquaint the Garrick family with the local gentry, and present Jocelyn as his viscountess.

With her husband gone, she could spend the evening with Alexandra, fast becoming a very good friend, then catch up on her reading. She would be grateful for a night of peace and quiet.

But by the time supper with Alex—Alexa, Jo corrected with the faintest of smiles—had ended and she herself had retired to her room to read, Jocelyn was entirely of a different mind.

She sighed with a bit of frustration. She missed Rayne already, and he had been gone less than one full day. It only pointed out how much she had come to love him.

A wave of guilt washed over her. Last night Rayne had spoken his love a dozen times in the course of the evening. He had whispered the words against her lips, said them as he teased her nipple, breathed them between small kisses he trailed along her belly to her secret woman's place.

But she had not said those same words to him.

Why? she pondered, ashamed of herself since she knew without doubt it was the truth. She was in love with Rayne. Had been almost from the start. Why hadn't she said so, when she knew how much he wanted to hear it?

Trust, she told herself firmly. After what had happened between them, she had to be certain she could trust him. She scoffed at the lie she told herself. There was no man on earth she trusted more than Rayne.

A crimson flush rose as the bitter truth dawned. *Penance.* She was making him pay for the weeks and months she had suffered. It was selfish and unkind, yet she hadn't been able to stop herself. Every time Rayne spoke his love and she said nothing, she was paying him back for what she'd been forced to endure.

Hasn't Rayne suffered, too? her inner voice argued. *Do you still play at vengeance, or are you ready to set aside the past and be a warm, willing wife to the man you love?*

Sweet God above, surely with his kindness and care of her, his tenderness and loving, he had paid far greater penance than he deserved.

Like clouds lifting after a storm, Jocelyn's turmoil faded and her thoughts grew crystal clear. The past lay behind them. She loved Rayne and he loved her. It was high time she told him.

Jo crossed the room smiling, happiness bubbling in her breast. She couldn't wait to see Rayne. Sweet saints, she wished he was coming home this eve. He wouldn't, but this night she would sleep soundly. Her decision had been made. At last her heart would be unburdened.

The hour of three chimed dully, barely breaching the haze of her dreams. It was difficult to emerge from the pleasure of Rayne's hands, the softness of his lips, though deep inside she knew it was just an illusion.

It was the vague sense of wrongness that wriggled its way into her senses, the certainty that something was strangely amiss.

Jocelyn's eyes slid open with more difficulty than they should have. Her lids felt heavy and sluggish and an instant later began to sting. That was the moment her lungs dragged in a great gulp of air, only to discover it was thick with soot and nearly unbreathable. Great coughing spasms shook her fully awake, and with them came the certain knowledge the room was ablaze.

Fire! God, oh God, oh no! The room billowed with thick black smoke, and tendrils of orange and yellow sucked up the curtains and ate at the fringe at the edge of the carpet. *Fire!* It was her greatest terror, had been since that night at the cottage. Panic surged through her, and for a moment her mind went blank. She sat frozen on the bed, staring at the growing wall of heat, knowing with dawning horror that if she didn't do something, and quickly, she would be overcome by the smoke before anyone could guess what had happened.

She tried to make her lips move, tried to force out a scream, but the sound remained locked in her throat, as frozen as her trembling arms and legs.

You can't just sit here—do something! But her body refused the simplist commands and the fire crept closer. Where were the servants? Why had no one come for her? Remotely, it occurred to her the fire must have started in this wing of the house and the others had not yet been alerted.

She was the only one aware of the terrible danger.

In the back of her mind another set of flames burst into fiery balls of heat. The vicious blaze engulfed her small parlor, licked the rafters, and devoured the walls, consuming every trace of the world she had known. The roar of the flames filled her senses but they couldn't blot out the screams. Her father's agonized voice pierced even the shotlike crackle of the falling, splintering wood.

She might just have sat there, recalling the horrors of that long ago moment, staring at the encroaching barrier of fire, if the babe had not moved. But his will to live seemed to far outreach her own, and in the silence of her mind his small voice cried out to her.

God, oh God, not my child. With the instinct born of a thousand generations, Jocelyn overcame her terrible fear and moved to save the babe she carried. The curtains blazed with flame, blocking escape out the windows, but even if they hadn't, it was nearly three stories to the ground. What would happen to the babe?

Slipping to the floor, a trembling hand cradling her swollen belly, she crawled under the bed toward the door. Fire wreathed the frame, but even the crackle of the blaze and the thickness of the heavy wood couldn't muffle the shouts of the terrified servants coming from beyond the enclosure.

Jocelyn pulled her nightgown out of the way and grabbed the handle, but let it go with a shriek when the hot iron seared her fingers. Bending low for a quick breath of air, she made her way to the dresser, snatched a small linen towel from beside the basin, wrapped the cloth around her trembling hand, crawled back, and jerked open the door.

"Jocelyn!"

"Merciful God, my lady!" That from Alexandra and a crowd of hysterical servants who battled the blaze from across a gaping ten-foot hole in the floor of the hall.

The west wing of the house was a scene from hell, the walls aflame, orange flames roaring along the edges of the thick Persian carpets, the ceiling alive with fiery heat, and of course there was always the menacing, unbreathable thick black soot.

"You mustn't try to come this way!" Farthington shouted, as if there was the least possibility. "You've got to go back!"

Jocelyn's stomach twisted. "But I—I can't go back in there!" By now the room would be engulfed in flames.

"Make your way down the hall!" Alexandra shouted. "Try to find a bedchamber that isn't on fire." Flames scorched the corridor behind her, but the floor remained intact—what she could see of it before it disappeared into a mass of thick black smoke.

"I can't! I can't do it!" But there was more to consider than her fears. She had Rayne's child to think of. She couldn't let him die.

"You've got to, Jo!" Alexandra pleaded. "We'll try to reach you from the servants' stairs. You've got to make it at least to the end of the corridor!" Her heavy auburn braid flying out behind her, Alex turned and raced down the main staircase followed by half a dozen teary-eyed servants.

"Hurry, milady!" Farthington shouted. He and the others still fought the blaze, trying to confine it to the wing she was trapped in. But there was no way they could reach her. "Hurry!"

Coughing against the smoke in her lungs, crouching in an effort to breathe, Jocelyn said a prayer for strength, raised the hem of her nightgown over her mouth and moved barefoot down the hall into the smoke and heat. The first three doors revealed rooms swept up in the inferno, and Jocelyn's heart sank with every failed effort.

Her eyes watered, and it wasn't just the swirling black smoke. If she didn't find a way out soon, she wasn't going to make it. Ending her life in the flesh-melting flames was a horrible way to die—she knew that firsthand—yet mostly she was thinking of Rayne. He would never see his child, never know how much she loved him.

The tears were falling freely now, a floodtide she couldn't control, but it didn't really matter. The smoke was so thick she couldn't see even an inch ahead. She felt the paneling of another door behind her as she scooted along the wall, but flames curled up from the crack beneath it. Where was the narrow servants' stairway leading down? Why hadn't the others come to get her?

When she rounded the corner, she saw the answer. A wall of fiery flames blocked the path in front of her while a second blazing barrier encroached from behind.

There was nowhere to go, nowhere to hide, no way to escape. It was the ultimate nightmare—and it was real.

Jocelyn's heart pounded with a thousand painful drumbeats, then it began to slow. A terrifying but welcome numbness began to set in. It would be over soon, and yet not nearly soon enough. Would she deal with it bravely? She didn't want to die screaming, the way her father had.

She prayed she wouldn't disgrace herself.

Trembling all over, her stomach sick with fear, she summoned a last bit of courage and cried out toward the stairs somewhere behind the towering flames.

"I-If anyone can hear me, tell Rayne I love him! Tell him I never stopped. Tell him I'll love him forever!"

"You can tell him yourself," came a deep male voice through the thick hot smoke and fire.

"Rayne!" She couldn't see his face beneath the soggy blanket covering his head, but she couldn't mistake the tall frame striding toward her, enveloping her in the folds of a huge wet cloth that matched his own. He didn't wait for her answer, couldn't know the leap of hope that mixed with the greatest terror she had ever known—the awful fear that Rayne might die here, too.

Certain that at any moment both of them would be lost, she felt Rayne's arm around her, forcing her into the tide of flame, then he was lifting her, carrying her through it, descending the narrow blazing staircase.

Heat seared her lungs and singed the hair on her arms. The wet blanket smoldered and hissed, and still he kept going. Coughing and gasping for air, he stepped on a flaming stair, and the fire-ravaged wood gave way beneath his boot. Jocelyn screamed; Rayne swore a savage oath, got his footing beneath him, jumped that stair and yet another.

The next floor wasn't much better, just a mass of flaming tapestry and blazing carpet. Rayne never slowed, his powerful legs carrying them unerringly. Then the black smoke lifted and they were through, descending the last flight of stairs amid the cheers of the servants and the sound of Alexa's tears.

Brownie and Tucker were there, faces smoke-blackened from fighting the fire, shouting with joy and relief at the sight of them.

"Ye did it, gov'nor. Ye save me lit'le gel." Brownie wiped a tear from his cheek, and Tucker sent up a cheer.

"She's my girl now," Rayne said with fierce possession, urging them all out to safety. He didn't stop walking until they could breathe fresh air. The servants went back to fighting the fire, which had begun to slow as it reached an older, thick-stoned section of the mansion.

Jocelyn watched the dying flames over Rayne's broad shoulder. When they had reached safety some distance away, he stopped beneath an overhanging sycamore and set her carefully on her feet.

"Are you all right?"

"You came for me," she said softly. "Just when I'd lost the last bit of hope, you came."

Rayne kissed her eyes, her nose, her mouth. "I came for you, just as I did before. Just as I always will. I'd give my life to protect you, Jo."

"I love you, Rayne. I love you so much." She rested her palm against his cheek and felt the roughness of his day's growth of beard. "I meant what I said up there. I never stopped loving you. Even when I wanted to, I couldn't. I'll always love you, Rayne."

Rayne's arms around her grew tighter and he kissed her softly on the mouth. "I thought I'd lost you." A shiver ran through his body. "I've never been more afraid." Rayne sat down beneath the tree and pulled her onto his lap.

He kissed the top of her head. "Say it again, will you?"

Jo smiled at him softly. "I love you. I should have told you sooner. I wanted to tell you when we were in the town house."

Rayne kissed her gently, then eased himself away. "I've something to tell you, too. I'd give anything in this world if I didn't have to."

Her eyes swung to his face.

"It was your father, Jo. He's the man who shot me."

"My father? But—"

"He didn't die that night in the fire. At least his body survived the ordeal—unfortunately, his mind did not."

"M-My father tried to kill you?"

Rayne nodded. "Malcom was right. We'd been looking in the wrong direction. When he interviewed Barclay Peters, he discovered the truth of what had happened, and that Peters had been keeping the secret of your father's insanity."

He told her as gently as he could that her father had been locked away but that he had escaped.

"In Sir Henry's state of mind, my father and I were the

same, equally guilty of whatever crimes he imagined. He set the fire, Jo."

"What?"

"Your father set the fire. Malcom and I went to Kingsbury in hopes of finding him. When we got there we learned he had already gone. We guessed he was headed this way, but we weren't completely sure. By the time we discovered his circuitous route, he was several hours ahead of us. I foolishly believed my being gone from the house would keep you safe. It never occurred to me he might do something like this."

He looked back at the crumbling remains of the west wing, aglow with hot red embers where the ceiling and several floors had caved in. "I just thank God I wasn't too late."

Jocelyn pressed trembling fingers against her throbbing temples. Her chest felt leaden and her heart ached unbearably.

"Where is he?"

Rayne's hold tightened protectively. "He didn't get out, Jo. Malcom saw him go in. He was very badly scarred, there was no mistaking who it was."

She left out a soft little whimper. "Dear God in heaven."

"Malcom tried to reach him, but I don't think he meant to get out. A beam fell on him. Harvey thinks he was dead before the fire ever reached him."

Jocelyn's fingers curled into the front of Rayne's jacket. She buried her face in his shirtfront and tears streaked down her cheeks.

"Go ahead, love. Let it all out. The past is behind us now. Once you've let go of it, we can go on."

Jocelyn raised her eyes to her husband's handsome face. Weary as it appeared, black with soot and smudged with cinders, the dear worried lines reflected the love he felt for her. She knew that same love shone in her own.

"I love you, Rayne."

He kissed her softly. "I'll never tire of hearing you say it."

"I love you," she said, and Rayne kissed her, content that it was the truth.

Epilogue

Jamaica 1809

A NOTHER TERRIBLE SCREAM rent the air, then another and another, each one louder than the last.

"It's almost over," Jocelyn soothed, wiping the perspiration from Chita's damp forehead. "Just keep pushing. You're doing fine."

"The head's nearly clear," said Dolly. "The worst is pret near over, lamby. One more good strong push and ya'll be through."

Chita did as she was told, breathing hard and fighting back waves of pain. Though this was her second delivery, this birthing had been far more difficult than the last. Her baby girl had come with relative ease. This strapping child of Paulo's appeared to be far more stubborn.

"Push!" Jo said.

"I am pushing." Exhausted and discouraged, Chita unleashed a torrent of Spanish curses, but the next great heave brought results. The tiny body slid wetly into Dolly's waiting hands.

"Ya've done it, lamby!"

While Jocelyn cut the cord and worked to remove the afterbirth, Dolly slapped the child on the bottom. The moment it issued a lusty roar, the door slammed open and Paulo crashed in.

"What is it? What has happened?"

Jocelyn laughed. "Exactly what's supposed to happen. You're the father of a fine baby boy."

"And Chita? She is all right?"

"She's fine, Paulo." Jocelyn held up the blanket-wrapped babe. "Black-haired and dark-eyed just like his father."

Paulo's already broad chest swelled even more. He examined his child, hurried to Chita's beside, bent down and kissed her. *Obrigado*—thank you, my lovely wife." He grinned foolishly at the women. "And you, my dear friends."

Just then Rayne strode in through the open door. "So you've a son now, have you?" He crossed the room and clapped his friend on the back. "A playmate for Andrew Augustus. Congratulations."

He turned a radiant smile in Jocelyn's direction. "I suppose, my love, that means we had better get busy and have a girl for little Serena to play with."

Serena was Chita's first child, Paulo's unabashed delight —next to his wife, of course.

"I think all 'a yas best be goin'. Let my poor little lamb get some rest."

Jocelyn squeezed Chita's hand, and Dolly settled the babe in the curve of her arm. Though Paulo remained by his sleepy wife's side, everyone else left the room, Dolly setting off for the nursery to check on baby Andrew. Rayne quietly closed the door.

"Would you like a little girl?" he asked Jo once they were alone.

"You know I would."

"Then why don't we go see if we can make one?"

Jocelyn smiled. Sweet God, how much she loved him. Since the night of the fire, her love had grown tenfold.

She had mourned her father, of course, but the healing took less time than she had thought it would. She had dealt with his death four years earlier and finally accepted his loss. This other man was a stranger. She grieved for what he had suffered, but in time she was able to put it in the past.

The fire had been stopped before it consumed the house, leaving only the west wing in ruins. It had been rebuilt on an even grander scale—with several extra sets of stairs.

Jocelyn felt Rayne's arms around her waist, urging her toward their chamber. "What about Alexandra? She's due back home any moment." Alexa was visiting a neighbor at Tamarind. They had sent her away from the house, away from Chita's terrifying screams. Alexandra had been through enough, poor dear.

"She'll be fine," Rayne said. He kissed Jo soundly. "Come on."

Alexa had finally recovered from a tragedy of her own— the death of her friend Peter Melford—but it had taken her nearly two years. Lord Peter's death had changed her, since she blamed herself for the shooting, though the young man's suicide was hardly her fault. He'd been in love with her, yes, but so had half the young swains in London.

It spoke well of her character that she had taken the matter so hard.

"Come on, love," Rayne coaxed. "Last night you ravaged my body, today it's my turn."

He nibbled her ear and softly bit her neck, raising goose bumps along her arm.

"All right, all right, you win." She turned into his arms and kissed him.

"I win? What do I win?"

"Vengeance for last night. A little *sweet* vengeance."

He looked at her and smiled. "I thought you believed the sweetest vengeance of all is just being happy."

Jocelyn smiled, too. "That is so, my love. There is no one on this earth who knows it better." To show him just how wise she was, Jocelyn led him toward their room.

KAT MARTIN

Award-winning author of *Creole Fires*

GYPSY LORD
_____ 92878-5 $5.99 U.S./$6.99 Can.

SWEET VENGEANCE
_____ 95095-0 $4.99 U.S./$5.99 Can.

BOLD ANGEL
_____ 95303-8 $5.99 U.S./$6.99 Can.

DEVIL'S PRIZE
_____ 95478-6 $5.99 U.S./$6.99 Can.

MIDNIGHT RIDER
_____ 95774-2 $5.99 U.S./$6.99 Can.

ANITA MILLS
ARNETTE LAMB
ROSANNE BITTNER

*Join three of your favorite storytellers
on a tender journey of the heart...*

Cherished Moments is an extraordinary collection of
breathtaking novellas woven around the theme of mother-
hood. Before you turn the last page you will have been swept
from the storm-tossed coast of a Scottish isle to the fury of
the American frontier, and you will have lived the lives and
loves of three indomitable women, as they experience their
most passionate moments.

THE NATIONAL BESTSELLER

CHERISHED MOMENTS
Anita Mills, Arnette Lamb, Rosanne Bittner
_____ 95473-5 $4.99 U.S./$5.99 Can.

Only in his dreams has Burke Grisham, the once-dissolute Earl of Thornwald, seen a lady as exquisite as Catherine Snow. Now, standing before him at last is the mysterious beauty whose life he has glimpsed in strange visions—whose voice called him back from death, and the shimmering radiance beyond, on the bloody field of Waterloo. But she is also the widow of the friend he destroyed: the one woman who scorns him; the one woman he must possess...

A Glimpse of Heaven

Barbara Dawson Smith

"An excellent reading experience from a master writer. A triumphant and extraordinary success!"
—*Affaire de Coeur*

A GLIMPSE OF HEAVEN
Barbara Dawson Smith
_____ 95714-9 $5.50 U.S./$6.50 CAN.

For years John Logan had searched for the infant
daughter his wife had taken from him. The trail leads
to Autumn Welles, an artist who paints tinware for a
living and who is posing as the mother of his child.
John knows that Autumn's world is built on the shifting sands of deceit and he plans to use all means necessary to reclaim his child.

Luring her into a tangled web, John leads them across
three states, from Connecticut to Ohio, bound to each
other by a marriage that is supposed to be a charade.
But as the awakening fires begin to touch their souls,
they find in each other a love born in secrets and
deception, and a love that may not survive the chang-
ing seasons of their hearts.

The Fire in

❧ Autumn ❧

Delia Parr

It only takes a second filled with the scream of twisting metal and shattering glass—and Chris Copestakes' young life is ending before it really began.

Then, against all odds, Chris wakes up in the hospital and discovers she's been given a second chance. But there's a catch. She's been returned to earth in the body of another woman—Hallie DiBarto, the selfish and beautiful socialite wife of a wealthy California resort-owner.

Suddenly, Chris is thrust into a world of prestige and secrets. As she struggles to hide her identity and make a new life for herself, she learns the terrible truth about Hallie DiBarto. And when she finds herself falling for Jamie DiBarto—a man both husband and stranger—she discovers that miracles really *can* happen.

ON THE WAY TO HEAVEN

TINA WAINSCOTT

ON THE WAY TO HEAVEN
Tina Wainscott
_____ 95417-4 $4.99 U.S./$5.99 CAN.

Against the backdrop of an elegant Cornwall mansion before World War II and a vast continent-spanning canvas during the turbulent war years, Rosamunde Pilcher's most eagerly-awaited novel is the story of an extraordinary young woman's coming of age, coming to grips with love and sadness, and in every sense of the term, coming home...

Rosamunde Pilcher

The #1 *New York Times* Bestselling Author of *The Shell Seekers* and *September*

COMING HOME

"Rosamunde Pilcher's most satisfying story since *The Shell Seekers*."

—*Chicago Tribune*

"Captivating...The best sort of book to come home to...Readers will undoubtedly hope Pilcher comes home to the typewriter again soon."

—*New York Daily News*

COMING HOME
Rosamunde Pilcher
_____ 95812-9 $7.99 U.S./$9.99 CAN.